an Angel Academy novel

Prophecy Girl

cecily white

Entangled Publishing, LLC
2614 South Timberline Road
Suite 109
Fort Collins, CO 80525

Visit our website at www.entangledpublishing.com.

Edited by Liz Pelletier
Cover design by Liz Pelletier

Ebook ISBN   978-1-62061-293-4
Print ISBN   978-1-62061-294-1

Manufactured in the United States of America

First Edition April 2013

To Avery and Evan:
I love you forever, around the universe and keep going…

Prologue:
The End

Death is a lot like prom—loud, overdone, and although the guy you came with was cool, you never know who'll end up taking you home.

Jack's soul unwound itself from mine in hesitant, twitchy movements. The space it left behind felt cold and damp, how a cloud might feel before a snowfall.

"You couldn't have stopped it, Amelie. He had to die. They all did. The prophecy says—"

I quit listening.

This wasn't fair, not one bit of it. For five days Jack and I had been chased through hell and told to be heavenly. We'd been buried alive and ordered not to scream. And for what? A stupid, semi-apocalyptic prophecy?

I brushed a kiss across his forehead where my tears had fallen. I didn't care about fairness, or prophecies, or wars. This war wasn't mine anymore.

Jack was mine.

With a violent tremor, my fingers coaxed the sword out of his lifeless grip. Yeah…things were about to get ugly.

Chapter One:
The Beginning

(. . . five days earlier)

"I'm not going to the dance, so quit asking," I announced, extending a hand to my best friend Lisa Anselmo. "Binoculars, please."

Lisa yanked a pair of black, dual-tube goggles out of her backpack and handed them over with a calculated pout. Enough to tug the heartstrings, not enough to wreck the mascara.

"Amelie, it's our senior year. We've been planning this forever."

"You've been planning this—"

"*We've* been planning this," she insisted. "Katie and I have our dresses and everything. Don't you remember? We swore never to go to these things without each other."

"That was second grade, Lisa."

"Like that makes it *okay* to ditch a pinkie swear?"

Groaning, I stared through my goggles into the dimly lit, fish-scented night.

The evening had begun pretty normally. Well, normal for me,

anyway. Out the window by midnight, encamped at New Orleans' Commercial Street wharf by twelve thirty, scoping the area for demons by twelve thirty-three. Not that there were any demons to be found. Apart from an Irish setter who tried to hump Lisa's leg, the only activity we'd seen was a drunken sorority girl stumbling along the water's edge. She looked young. Nineteen, maybe twenty. Her green sequined minidress hung off one shoulder, dyed-blond hair in rumpled disarray. Obviously trashed.

Hmm. Why would a girl like that *be wandering around* here?

"Seriously, Amelie, a pinkie swear is a pinkie swear. It's like BFF code. You of all people should know that." Lisa glared at me, her frosted plum lips curled down at the corners. "And don't give me any garbage about how you can't get a date."

"I didn't say I couldn't get a date," I muttered, distracted. "I said I didn't *want* a date. Now, can you zip it? We're on a stakeout here."

"What about Paul? He'd go with you."

"Waterfall Paul? After the Jell-O shot incident? No, thanks." I flipped the visor down to increase the power on my new night vision binoculars. (Okay, not *mine*, exactly. Borrowed. Certainly not stolen.)

"How about Zeke?"

"Beer-breath. And he wears skinny pants."

"There's always Matt," she suggested hopefully. "He doesn't drink."

"Matt's awesome. He's also in love with *you*," I reminded her.

Lisa flicked a handful of thick chestnut curls over her shoulder and gave a tolerant sigh. "I don't understand why this is so hard. We're *Guardians*."

"We're trainees."

"Same diff. *Every* Guardian Channeler needs a Watcher. We're *supposed* to bond with them, Ami. It's like *destiny* or something. If our friendship means anything to you, you'll do this for me."

Uh, yeah. Like I would dignify *that* with a response. At this point, Lisa's friendship was less of a choice than a fact of life. It worked out well—kind of symbiotic, actually. I beat up anyone who messed with her, and she made sure my homework got done. Fair trade, right? Honestly, if not for Lisa's constant nagging, I'd probably still be crouched in our kindergarten sandbox eating glue and playing with Neferet demons.

"Are you even listening to me?" She prodded me annoyingly in the shoulder.

I swatted her away. "Look, if it means that much to you, I can ask Keller Eastman. I'll probably get herpes from holding hands with him and die a miserable, humiliating death...but for you, Lisa, it's worth it."

"Amelie Lane Bennett." She gave me that look—the one she reserves for small children and people who wear white after Labor Day. "You need to take this seriously. Guardian bond assignments go up at the end of the year. It doesn't matter how pretty you are, or how well you fight, or even how perky your boobs have gotten since last summer."

I frowned and shifted my ladies so they tucked benignly against the concrete wharf ledge. "Can we leave my boobs out of this?"

"I don't know, can we? I mean, look at you! Stained sweats, holey T-shirt, no makeup. And...*this*." She flicked a clump of sweaty red hair poking out the rubber band at my neck. "You have so much potential, Ami. Must you waste it?"

"Lisa!" I grumbled. "Focus! This is life and death we're dealing with."

"I *know* it's life and death," she insisted. "There's *nothing* more crucial than this dance."

"Oh, for the love of—"

"I'm just saying, your mom had a great bloodline, but there's no guarantee you'll carry it. And with your parents' history…" She trailed off, too polite to finish the sentence. "You're lucky they let you stay at St. Michael's after your mom died. I mean, you could easily have wound up in residential. Or worse, the human sector. Would it kill you to play by the rules occasionally?"

"Would it kill you to mind your own beeswax?"

"Probably," she admitted.

I tried to concentrate on the sorority girl, but Lisa's accusation drilled into me. Loathsome though it was, she had a point.

When my parents, Bud and Charlotte Bennett, abandoned the Guardian Community seventeen years ago, they'd tried to pretend things were normal. Not easy, since my dad had been labeled a defector and my mom a traitor to our mission. I suspect they planned to lie to me indefinitely—you know, *ignore* the fact that our family was about as human as the Loch Ness Monster's. They'd put me in a human preschool, hid the broadswords and spellbooks, let me have human friends…right up until the day I channeled our kindergarten class turtle into the demon realm.

Thus began my career at St. Michael's Guardian Training Academy.

My parents enrolled me mid-year with the understanding that I would be properly trained, sheltered from harm, and, most importantly, they would never hear another word about "the war on demonkind." That denial lasted two years—the exact amount of time it took Mom to get shredded by a demon at a holiday PTA event. Merry Christmas, right?

I suspect Bud still awakens each morning with the faint hope I'll transform into some tree-hugging, dirt-loving hippie daughter he can be proud of. I, by contrast, awaken each morning with a nasty urge to kill things.

Demonic things.

Big black flappy things, little green squirmy things…We don't talk about it. It's one of many topics we don't talk about.

I lowered the extra binocular lens and tipped up my night goggles.

"Lisa, this is the third night in a row we've staked out this location. And the third night you've spent driveling about Watchers and bonds and dances. I know it's important to you but I need you to respect that *this* mission, sanctioned or not, is important to me. We're technically at war here. Professor D'Arcy's body was discovered not thirty feet from where we sit, and I, for one, am interested in finding out who killed him. Now, are you going to help me or not?"

She squinted her eyes, contemplative. I could practically see the thoughts processing in her head, the gravity of the situation weighing in. Finally, she spoke.

"What about Lyle? He still likes you. *And* he was at the top of class rankings last year. Any girl would be lucky to land him as a bondmate."

"You're not going to let this go, are you?"

"Nope."

I gave a weary sigh. Seriously, the girl was like a dog with a giant wad of beef jerky. "Lis, I'd rather die a cat lady than go out with Lyle Purcell again."

"There's an idea. You could borrow Brutus for the gala," she mused. "You might get a hairball off the goodnight kiss, but his kitty carrier would make a nice accessory."

"You're hilarious. Now shut up."

I flipped the goggles back down and kept scanning the horizon. A good thing, too. Sorority Sally had collapsed, giggling, against a wrought iron bench, head lolled back and throat bared like the cover of a Gothic romance novel. I guess the greasy homeless dude napping two benches down must've had a thing for Gothic romances. As soon as he heard the giggle, he pried open a bloodshot eye, emptied his rum bottle, and hauled himself vertical. Streaks of dirt clung to his coat and his shoulder-length hair dripped with sweat as he staggered toward the girl.

"Hey, Lis, we've got a situation."

"Vamp, were, or demon?"

"Vamp, I think."

She pulled a wooden arrow out of the quiver and watched as I threaded it into my bow.

"Remember," she cautioned, "you have to wait until human blood is spilled. Any unprovoked attack on a Crossworlder violates the Peace Tenets. Do you need thermal imaging for vamp confirmation?"

"Do we have thermal imaging?"

She rummaged in the backpack. "No."

"Add it to the shopping list."

Thermals or no, I was ninety-eight percent sure this was a

vamp attack. Maybe ninety-seven. My hand drew back the bow as the dude crouched over Sorority Sally, a predatory look in his eye. His fingers tapped her cheek, tenderly at first, then harder. I could see his lips forming the words, *Hey, baby. Want to party?*

Yeesh. After a hundred thousand years of verbal evolution, could a guy not produce a better pick up line than that? I barely had time to stifle a groan before the girl's eyes fluttered open. Faster than thought, her hands gripped his collar, her mouth in a vicious twist.

That's when I released the arrow. The shaft wasn't as tight or familiar as the weapons at school, but it flew straight enough.

"Bull's-eye," I said as it entered her shoulder.

I'm not even sure if the poor schmuck noticed, he was so wasted. *She* definitely noticed. Her eyes narrowed to angry slits as she turned in our direction, fangs bared. Served her right. Maybe next time she'd remember to flick some water on her face before she went hunting. Only vamps and zombies wouldn't sweat in this humidity.

"Duh, why didn't you just kill her?" Lisa asked, annoyed. "Two more seconds and it would have been justifiable vampicide."

"Lis, for all we know, she volunteers weekends at the soup kitchen. Besides, it wasn't a vampire who killed D'Arcy."

"Yeah, well," she sniffed, "it wasn't a demon, either."

I was about to ask what she meant when I noticed a stirring in the distance.

The blond girl had shooed her would-be snack on his way and was in the process of working the arrow out of her shoulder when something dropped from a tree about fifty feet away. It scuttled toward her, razor sharp talons scraping the pavement, a bubbling snarl at its lips.

"Oh, crud. New target. UV arrow."

It took me less than two seconds to reload and take aim but by the time I did, the demon had already launched itself at the girl. Its skin was black and mottled, with coarse, oily hair along its shoulders—one part beetle, one part gorilla, three parts Sicilian mafioso.

"Uh, Lis? I need an ID."

Lisa slipped on a second pair of night goggles and started paging through the ginormous Encyclopedia O' Demons she'd brought along. Headmistress Smalley *seriously* needed to get that thing in an e-book format.

"Got it! Rangor demon, third level. Head shot only, everything else is armored. Left eye for the kill," she summarized aloud. "I hope you know what you're doing."

"Me, too."

The Rangor slashed at Sorority Sally with manic glee. For a second, it looked like they might topple down the embankment into the Mississippi where I couldn't get a clear shot, but the girl recovered enough to get her arms up. She rolled to the ground, tossing the beast over her head. Not as fast as some of the vamp videos we'd seen in training class, but way faster than *I* could have moved in that dress. Impressive.

"Hey, Guido," I called.

Startled, the demon jumped to its feet *(um, claws?)* and ran toward us, gathering momentum. Arms raised, it let out a howl of fury. Its whole face seemed to fold open, rows upon rows of teeth bared in serrated ridges.

That's when I sent off the second arrow.

The shaft pierced the beast's left eye, spilling bright UV liquid down its face in a trickle of purple acid. A cry ripped through its throat. Inhuman. Screechy. Like the emergency brakes of a railway car. Lisa clamped her hands on her ears.

"Wow, this is super subtle," she yelled over the ruckus. "Maybe next time you could take out an ad in the *Times Picayune*?"

In hard lurches, the demon writhed and twisted on the ground. Rangors weren't known for their passive deaths, but really, it seemed to be taking longer than necessary. In the distance, horns honked and garbage trucks clanged, sure signs of human approach.

"We're so gonna get busted."

I sighed. Lisa was right. If a Guardian caught us, that would be one thing. But involving humans was a whole other enchilada.

"All right, give me a knife," I ordered.

She handed me a hooked blade about the size of a banana and stood back.

It took less than twenty seconds to separate the crucial parts, at least enough to stop the twitching. By the time I finished, my arms were scratched, my hair was clumped with mucus, and the vampire had fled into the night.

"You're welcome," Lisa yelled after her. She humphed and turned back to me. "Omigod, did you see that? Ungrateful toads, every last one of them."

"Tell me about it," I said, wiping the demon goo off my arms. "You want to get the body or the weapons?"

"I'll get the body. You'll probably end up summoning a demon horde if you try to dismiss it. Remember Veronica's sweet sixteen?" She smirked. "Priceless. I thought she'd never get her hair back to its normal color."

I frowned. "It's not my fault I have allergies."

"Oh, is that what we're calling it?" Lisa gestured to the boardwalk where the drunk human lay, passed out in a pool of vomit, not twenty yards from my pile o' demon. "Amelie, how many times do I have to say this? Birthday parties are one thing, but it's *illegal* for unbonded Channelers to mess around with Crossworld beings. Not without a Watcher present, and *certainly* not around humankind. Our handbook specifically says, *The fist of eternal damnation shall fall heavily upon he who knowingly reveals the existence of the Guardians.* Didn't you read it?"

I had read it, actually. That handbook was where I got my best ideas.

"Well, technically, we didn't channel anything. And *that*," I said, pointing at the Rangor pieces, "is not a 'fist of damnation.' That's just an obese demon. There's no law against killing obese demons."

"There is, actually," Lisa noted, "for trainees. Which we aren't going to be anymore, unless we get this mess cleaned up and get to class."

I grudgingly gathered the weapons and spread some fallen leaves over the sticky, tar-like substance that had oozed out of the Rangor demon. Gulls flew in slow, lazy circles overhead, pastel light glinting off their wings.

Lisa called open the Crossworld channel. "*Inergio.*"

As soon as the word was spoken, yellow flickers appeared and a narrow gash of light tore through the air. Chill winds swirled around the rift, spits of black fire lapping at the demon body.

Lisa sank to her knees, out of breath. "I'm done. You're up."

"*Exitus!*"

Instantly, the flow of power shifted to me, a hard fist in the middle of my chest. Fingers of Crossworld poison trailed over my skin, reaching into me with claw-like insistence. Without a Watcher to drain it, my defenses were weak. Lisa had done most of the work, as usual, but I still couldn't shake the unsettling sensation of drowning in darkness.

When there was nothing left but a few gloppy demon chunks, I collapsed next to her. "That sucked."

"My thoughts exactly."

"Maybe we should take tonight off."

She rolled to her side just enough to shoot me a nasty look. "Maybe you should get a boyfriend."

Chapter Two:
Play With Fire

The eastern sky had begun to lighten as we stumbled back through the French Quarter toward Lisa's Prius. That was good news, at least. Third level subterraneans tended to dissolve in sunlight.

Cars were pouring into the Quarter now, the usual rustles and clangs echoing over the cobblestone streets. I tried not to think what would happen if someone had seen us disposing of the demon. Much as I joked, the secret nature of the Guardians' existence was nothing to laugh at. Guardians and demons and Crossworlders had been around for thousands of years with only minimal security breaches *(thank you, Anne Rice)*. It clenched my stomach imagining *I* might be the one to upset the delicate balance we'd struck with humanity.

"If you had a boyfriend," Lisa said, shimmying around in the front seat until her white button-down and tartan plaid uniform skirt slid into place, "you wouldn't need me for all your insane schemes."

"I thought you liked my insane schemes."

"I see value in them," she qualified. "Doesn't mean I don't worry about you getting killed or expelled. I mean, for crying out loud, Amelie. This is our senior year. You can't keep breaking rules and expect it to be okay. You're an *angel*. You should act like it."

Okay. I know what you're thinking.

Angels don't exist.

Flawless skin, perfect hair, flowing white robes, all topped off with an adorable set of fluffy pink wings. Yeah. If you see *that* wandering around, you've probably stumbled onto the set of a Victoria's Secret catalog shoot. Prepare to get your butt kicked by security.

I'm a Guardian.

You know, the secret race of mortal warriors, fashioned from the flesh of the archangels and charged with protecting humankind from the Crossworld, blah, blah, blah. It may sound romantic and glorious, but I'll let you in on a secret—being a Guardian sucks. It's dangerous. It's lonely. The retirement plan is for crap. And the worst part is, nobody appreciates us. I've been trounced by demons plenty of times in combat class, but do you think I've ever gotten a thank you note?

Nope. Nada. Zilch.

"Hey, Lis." I fastened the hook on my skirt and plucked one last piece of Rangor out of my hair. "What did you mean D'Arcy wasn't killed by demons?"

Lisa frowned, her face blank.

"Before, when you said—"

"Oh, right." She nodded. "It's just a rumor, but you know how my mom's on the PTA? Well, she says Templeman and Lutz got hit this month, too. No one's confirmed it, but they think it was one of the Gray Ones."

I squinted, thoughtful. "Right. The Gray Ones. Obviously."

"You have no idea who that is, do you?"

"Not a clue."

She glared at me. "Seriously, Ami. Graymasons? Wraithmakers? *None* of this rings a bell? Were you even conscious for Meeks' lecture series last spring?" She stomped the brake and hit the ignition…rather violently, I thought. "Fasten your seat belt."

I snapped the belt over my waist and slurped my lukewarm coffee. "Are you talking about Lucifer's bloodline? I thought they were extinct."

"The bloodline's recessive. It must have been dormant."

"But what would a Graymason want with Templeman and Lutz? What would he want with *any* Guardian? They only take human souls, right?"

"How should I know?" she said, annoyed. "And quit dripping on my upholstery. God made beverage containers for a reason, hello?"

"Sorry." I righted my coffee cup.

To be fair, a Guardian getting killed wasn't so unusual. I mean, every other day we heard reports of ultra-badass Enforcers getting eaten by subterraneans. But *Professor Lutz*? The man had been on faculty since bell-bottoms hit the fashion scene. Taunts about his comb-over hairdo and getting hit with spitballs at lunch should have been the worst he'd had to endure.

"Gray Ones, huh?" I asked, skeptical.

"That's a secret, by the way, so don't go asking around about it. Mom told me not to say anything. Especially not to you."

"Why? I don't gossip."

She shrugged. "Maybe she didn't want Bud to freak. I'm only telling you so when you hear it at school, you'll know the Elders have it under control and you'll *stay out of it*. Now, can we talk about something else?"

In silence, I slipped off my loafers and drew my knees up to my chest.

According to the ancient texts, Gray Ones were the soul-swallowing giants born of Lucifer's Fallen, aka, the Anakim. We'd started calling them Graymasons a few thousand years ago because of the empty, pale husks they left of their victims. Not exactly people you'd want to mess with in a dark alley.

Dr. Gunderman once said they were the ones who'd originally cracked the mortal barriers and let the Inferni out—vampires and werecreatures and other unholy demon-hybrids. When Gabriel realized what Lucifer had created, he called the remaining archangels together to make a new race—the Guardians—a species forged of the same stuff as Lucifer's children. Only *we* didn't have to steal souls. We had souls of our own.

It took us generations to hunt down and kill them all. After a few thousand years, we'd assumed Lucifer's line was extinct. There'd been no "giant" sightings, no deaths by soul-suckage, no seers forecasting the rise of a Gray army. The only thing left for *us* to do was keep the demons down, the cracks sealed, and the Inferni in check.

I did my best to listen as Lisa launched into the ever-so-fascinating rundown of her classes. Within sixty seconds, my attention had shifted to the street outside.

Depressing isn't normally a word I'd apply to my beloved home town but this morning, with the Crossworld taint still working its way through me, I couldn't help feeling gloomy. Brittle oak and cypress trees lined the streetcar tracks. Old New Orleans houses, which any other day might have been quaint, seemed hunched in neglect. Humans scrambled around, totally oblivious to the hell that burned beneath them. They were like children, so addicted to their toys they'd probably never notice the mortal world collapsing.

"...just need to *focus*, Amelie, or you'll screw things up for both of us. This year is too important and I, for one, do *not* want to be left behind. Got it?" Lisa's concerned voice broke through my thoughts. She'd obviously been talking for a while, though I hadn't heard a word of it.

"Totally," I agreed. "You're one hundred percent right."

"You weren't listening, were you?"

"Not really."

With an indignant sniff, she pulled into a parking spot in front of our school and killed the engine.

Just as it had for over a hundred years, the main building of St. Michael's rose like a monolithic wedding cake out of the intricate uptown landscape. Imperious white trim hung over the gray stone exterior, a line of Corinthian columns standing sentry along the front porch. The sun had begun to peek over a cluster of magnolias on the front lawn, and its reflection in the second story windows made the main building look like it was lit from the inside with orange fire.

Unstable as my student career had been, I dearly loved my school. It even *smelled* like magic...that faint aroma of gunpowder and leaves burning in the distance. It always confused me how Smalley managed to keep enrollment limited only to Guardian bloodlines. I don't know, maybe she put some charm up that made people think about dead puppies every time they stepped on campus. That's what I would have done, anyway, if I were headmistress.

"Do you want to go scope the new Watcher prospects before assembly? I heard we got a senior transfer," Lisa said as we stepped out of the air-conditioned confines of her car.

"Tempting, but no," I replied. "I think I'll shove bamboo shoots up my toenails instead."

"Suit yourself. I'll give you the lowdown later."

"Can't wait."

As we walked together through the wrought iron main gate, a crackling sensation broke over us, the school's protective wards flexing to allow us entry. Without a backward glance, Lisa skipped off toward a crew of smartly dressed boys.

I hurried into the main building, eager to get out of the heat and away from the throng of "date prospects." Lisa wasn't usually so aggressive about the hook-ups. It made me wonder if I was being a bad friend, refusing to go to the formal with her. I mean, if she was willing to get dirty for me every night the past week, the least I could do was clean up one night for her, right?

Maybe.

The smell of old paint and new textbooks wrapped me in a welcoming hug as I stepped into the hall where the senior locker block stood. I'd nearly made it to my locker when a *squeak-squeak* of loafers sounded behind me. "Amelie!"

I quickened my pace. *Please, not today.*

"Hey, Bennett, wait up!"

In a choking cloud of Drakkar Noir, Lyle Purcell descended on me. His dark hair was slicked off his forehead in meticulous waves, khaki pants perfectly pressed, and shoes polished to a shine. Gag.

"Where were you last week?" He panted, out of breath. "Didn't you get my messages?"

"Um, messages?" I opened my locker with a clang and began briskly shoving books into it.

"Yeah. Like, six of them. And two emails."

"Nope, no messages. See ya later." The locker door slammed behind me as I made a beeline for the exit.

That was a lie. I did get his messages. The truth was, I'd deleted them.

Let me say for the record, I *hate* lying, even to someone like Lyle. Rule bending? Petty theft? The occasional forced entry? Yes… yes…and if-they-didn't-want-me-in-there-they-should-have-put-up-better-wards. *Lying*, however, is totally pointless unless you're trying to get away with something…or if you have a darned good reason.

I, unfortunately, had a darned good reason.

Last May, at Lisa's insistence, I'd agreed to go to dinner with Lyle. Huge mistake. What was supposed to be a fun, simple evening ended as a nightmare of Freddy Kruger proportions. He showed up late to get me, bought me Burger Barn take-out on the way back to his place, then spent three hours slobbering in my ear and trying to feel me up while I watched *Top Chef* reruns. For a solid week after, all I heard was rumors of how I couldn't get enough of him. It was epic.

"Hold up. Is this because I hooked up with Veronica Manning over the summer?" He scuttled to the side, blocking my path. "I swear it was totally casual. She means nothing to me."

"Lyle, I don't care who you date."

"Good, because I want you to know that thing with Skye was

also a mistake. We both knew it as soon as it happened."

I nodded. "Again with the not caring."

"Right, so anyway, I thought if you didn't have a date to the dance on Friday, you might want to go. With me."

I poked at the warped binding of my Demonology text, avoiding his eyes. "Friday's not good."

"You sure? I rented a tux," he said. "I can order a corsage if you want."

"That's not it. I have, uh, plans." Lie number two.

"What kind of plans?"

"Family stuff." Three. *Crap.* At this rate I'd reach my daily quota of venal sin by lunchtime. "All right, let's just assume I have big, huge, personal, top-secret family plans I can't discuss with anyone. Now quit asking about it."

He squinted at me. "You're lying, aren't you? Your lips twitch when you lie."

I frowned and tried not to look twitchy. "Okay, Lyle, listen. You're a really nice guy " Four. "—and I appreciate the offer—" Five. *Dang it.* "—but I don't think it's going to work out between us. We're very different, you and I. There's no...zing."

His cocky smile faltered. "No *zing?*"

"That's girl-code for 'not interested,'" I said. "Now, if you don't mind, you're kind of in my personal bubble."

Enough light filtered through the transom windows that I could see annoyance flare in Lyle's eyes. Firm but gentle, he pushed me against the locker bank and leaned forward, arms flexed in hard barriers around me.

"Amelie, what's your problem?" he whispered. "With your family's track record, you'll be lucky to get a Watcher assignment at all. I've got great placement scores. I've logged more demon kills than anyone else in our class. You should be begging me to bond with you."

"And yet, I'm not. It's a mystery," I said. "Now get off me."

He didn't move. "You're making a mistake."

"I'll survive."

"Maybe. But I doubt your career will."

Instantly, my skin prickled, and *not* in a good way.

It might have bugged me less if what he'd said weren't true. My future as a Guardian depended on me bonding with a Watcher. If I couldn't manage that by graduation, well, I might as well sign up for janitorial duty.

I'd lifted my fingers, ready to summon something small, dark, and vengeful that could make Lyle bleed in interesting ways, when Headmistress Smalley's voice shrieked out of the PA system. "Amelie Bennett, report to my office, immediately."

"What? Why?" I shouted at the air, indignant.

"*Immediately.*"

"But I didn't do anything!"

A chorus of giggles rose from the cluster of students and my face flushed pink. "I'll see you later, Bennett. Maybe Friday?" Lyle said.

"Dream on," I snapped.

But he just backed away, one hand flipped up in an insufferable little salute.

I paused to kick the doorjamb and swear a little, then took the stairs to the main office two at a time. *How could I possibly be in trouble so soon?* There was no way Smalley could have found out about the wharf, was there? Vamp-girl didn't know Lisa and

I were trainees and we'd gotten the demon cleaned up before human authorities showed. So what was it? Had I triggered some campus alarm system when I started to channel against Lyle? Was I getting expelled?

Smalley's door had just creaked open when I arrived at the main hallway. With tottering steps, the pudgy, orange-haired woman backed into the hallway, her arms filled with cardboard boxes. I grabbed the door to help her.

"Thank you, hon." She blinked absently. "I'm afraid I forgot to deliver these to the attic last week. Would you be a dear and take them up for me?"

"Um." Not that I minded doing tasks for Smalley—I probably had more experience with it than any other student given the amount of time I spent in detention—but she usually made an effort to *legitimately* bust me before she put me to work.

"Ma'am, may I ask—"

"We had sensors installed in the senior hall last week," she explained. "Incidentally, if you *had* channeled against Mr. Purcell, I would have had to suspend you."

"Ah," I said, and took the boxes from her. No sense pushing my luck. "You want these some place specific?"

"The bottom four go to Mr. D'Arcy's substitute, the top two to supply storage."

"Yes, ma'am."

As she waved me in the direction of D'Arcy's old attic office, I began to understand why she hadn't just brought them herself. It took me a good five minutes to get up the eighty or so steps to the fourth floor, then another two to locate the supply closet, all while balancing the boxes in a precarious tower. Normally, I wouldn't have minded. But the morning's adrenaline spike coupled with three nights of sleep deprivation had left me with an unholy urge to curl up in a corner and nap.

As I wrestled with the door, a heavy scent of mildew settled in my nasal passages. Yesterday's thunderstorm had left a dull coating of mold and dust over the windowpanes and my allergies were going berserk. I lifted a knuckle to swipe at my nose.

"Ahh-choo!" Before I could stop it, a high-pitched sneeze erupted out of my mouth, along with about thirty rohms of raw Crossworld power.

My cargo clattered to the floor in a flurry of sparks. Narrow shoots of flame seared through the cardboard like bullets through bread as I sneezed again and again, streaks of light in an otherwise dim cave.

"Oh, shiitake mushrooms," I muttered.

Scarlet fires sparked up everywhere, funnels of smoke curling into the air like mini tornadoes. I dug through my backpack for something to smother the fire, but came up empty. Dang, why didn't I bring a flame-retardant sweater?

"Crud!" I swore. "Monkeycrud!"

"I'm no expert," an amused voice said from behind me, "but 'monkeycrud' doesn't sound like an official Guardian command."

I whirled, heart hammering.

A guy, maybe three years older than me, lounged in the doorway, arms laced across his chest in an easy slouch. He was tall, at least six-three, and dressed in the typical staff uniform—pressed black button-down, black slacks, and tough-soled boots. A leather weapons belt draped in a double loop across his hips, with two glyph-carved swords and a few slim daggers tucked at the sides. Despite his school garb, the guy looked way too young to be a trainer. And *waaaay* too hot. His tousled blond hair glinted in a soft halo around his face, and with the flames reflected in his charcoal eyes, I'd swear I was staring at the downtown sky at sunset.

Zing. *Major* zing.

"Looks like you could use a hand," he observed. "Or maybe a bucket."

"A bucket?"

"Of water. I hear that's what they use on fire." The guy smirked. "Unless you've got a better idea."

I blinked at him, momentarily speechless. He hadn't said anything insulting, but I couldn't shake the feeling I was being mocked. I managed to snap myself out of the hormonal trance long enough to glare at him. "Look, can you go get a fire extinguisher? Or do something…useful?"

"Sure." He kept lounging in the doorway. "Take a deep breath."

Okay, not to be rude but what kind of idiot, when faced with a room full of paper and flames, instructs the arsonist to *take a deep breath*? "Are you insane?"

"Never diagnosed," the guy said. "How's that deep breath going?"

My cheeks flushed with heat as I huffed in and out. "Satisfied? Now go get me a fire extinguisher."

"Not yet," he said. "I want you to try the '*sine lucé*' command. It's a forty-rohm energy draw. Hefty for a newbie, but you should be able to manage it without a bonded Watcher." He flicked a glance at the growing fires. "Quickly, if you don't mind."

My eyes narrowed. "You want me to channel."

"Yes."

"A mid-level command."

"Correct."

"In an un-warded room with no Watcher."

He smiled again, and I had a nasty flash-forward to the ten o'clock newscast—scenes of carnage as the New Orleans Fire Department broke down Smalley's door, drenching the school in foam.

I shrugged. "It's your funeral." With another deep breath, I held up my palms, faced the fire, and gave the command. "*Sine lucé.*"

I was fully prepared for it to fail. Anything over twenty rohms usually did with me, unless I could time it to a mold spore outbreak, in which case it succeeded in surprisingly destructive ways. So when I felt a firm yet controlled tug at the back of my chest, the zip of Crossworld power bouncing between the guy and me, I nearly fell over with shock.

It was like the stars had aligned just for this moment. A swirl of energy shot out of my fingertips, engulfing the flames in a soft white fog. Instantly, the fires went black...along with the hall lights, the office lights, and the torchiére lamps at the edge of the stairway. Before I knew it, we were plunged into utter darkness.

"O-kay," I said, trying to recover the use of my toes. "That was new."

"I'll say," he agreed, equally stunned. "You sure you haven't done that before?"

"Pretty sure."

"Huh." He paused. "Sit tight for a sec."

I heard him fumble at the wall, then the shallow clang of metal on metal sounded as he opened a circuit panel. After another click, the lights came back on and I stood.

The damage wasn't nearly as bad as it'd looked when everything was aflame. In fact, apart from a few singed box tops and a ream of charred paper, there wasn't anything that couldn't be fixed with five minutes and a roll of wet paper towels.

"What did I tell you?" Mr. Fantastic reappeared in the doorway, dark eyes alight with amusement. "Much cleaner than a fire extinguisher, and no need for an incident report."

My jaw dropped. *No incident report?* Well, that settled it. If I wasn't in love with him before, I *definitely* was now. The knots of panic in my belly slowly unwound themselves.

"I don't know what to say. Thanks, I guess."

"You guess?"

"No, I'm sure. *Thank you*," I said. "I'm already on probation. If this got back to Smalley…"

He raised an eyebrow. "Probation? On the first day of school? What'd you do?"

"Nothing worth mentioning." I waved his question away. "I'll clean this up, I promise. Just let me know what was damaged. I can pay for it out of my allowance."

The guy's lips curved into a grin that sent tingles down my legs. "How about we call this a training session. On the house, so long as you keep it contained next time. Deal?"

"Deal," I breathed, and stuck out my hand. "Wow. Thank you. Seriously, I owe you one."

"Don't worry about it."

Then he took my hand. And quit smiling.

I should have known right then I was in trouble. As soon as

our fingers touched, an electric shock zipped through me, ice and fire and everything in between. I couldn't let go. I didn't want to. Every nerve ending ignited as he tightened his grip but all I could think was, *Yes. More. Closer.* Like if he didn't kiss me in the next six seconds I might shatter into pieces.

I shuddered when he finally broke contact. Faint threads of yellow light swirled near his chest like a glittery swarm of fireflies. As I stared at them, my heart began to thud.

"What's *that*?"

He glanced down and, for a second, I swear he looked as rattled as I felt. His fingers fumbled as he drew a pair of wire-rimmed glasses out of his pocket and slipped them on. It was like watching the light come on in a dark room. As soon as he looked at me his eyes sparked, first with recognition, then with something else.

"You." He frowned. "Please tell me you're not Amelie Bennett."

"I'm not Amelie Bennett," I repeated after an uncomfortable silence.

His breath came out in a *whoosh* of relieved laughter. "Thank goodness. That could have been really awkward."

"Yeah, totally." I tried to mimic his laughter but only succeeded in sounding like a choked goat.

This was just weird. My brain clamored to make sense of the past few minutes. The light strands. That burst of power. The only times I'd seen anything similar was in bonding ceremonies or battle footage, and neither of those seemed applicable. You had to have *serious* experience to draw that kind of residual. I'd never even met this guy before. *No way* could it be bond-related.

Before I could think of anything that wouldn't add to my sin tally, the light-strings curled into a tight fist, their tails whipping like a nest of wild snakes. They twitched angrily for a second, then dissipated in a puff, as if they'd never existed at all.

Around me, the world seemed to clarify, and I was suddenly aware of warmth on my skin where he'd touched me. But it wasn't the kind of warmth that came after a channel. It was different. More ordinary. The kind of effortless human magic I'd always wanted but never thought myself capable of.

"Okay, not that I'm admitting to anything," I said, poking at my arm where the light had vanished, "but if I *was* Amelie Bennett and happened to be lying to you about it right now, would I be looking at expulsion, suspension, or just some friendly detention time? Hypothetically, of course."

The guy stared at me for a long second before he sighed, carefully removing his glasses. "Well," he said. "Monkeycrud."

Chapter Three:
Any Other Monday

"Miss Bennett, stop following me." The office door whooshed shut in his wake. I managed to wedge my foot in just in time to get it smushed.

"Ow! I'm not *following* you. Smalley ordered me to deliver these to D'Arcy's old office. That's what I'm doing." I trailed after him, still lugging my tower o' boxes.

He snatched them out of my hands. "Okay, you've delivered them. Thank you. Good job."

"No problem." I wiped my palms on my skirt. "So how do you know me, anyway? And what was that weirdness before?"

His lips tightened as he shifted his weight. "Just a normal side effect of the channel. And no offense, but everyone in the Guardian educational system knows you. You don't exactly keep a low profile."

I caught one of the boxes from his stack as he scurried to add them to another pile. "Is that a bad thing?"

"Let me think. Overturned locker banks, doors ripped off their hinges, Headmistress Smalley's desk on the front lawn covered in ectoplasm?"

"None of that was my fault."

He gave me a meaningful look. "Every violin in the orchestra hall re-tuned to a minor key, every book in the library shelved binding side in? Reanimated *eels* in the cafeteria Kool-Aid dispenser?"

Okay, maybe a *few* things had been my fault.

"At least you read my record," I noted. "That's flattering."

"I read the summary sheet of your record," he corrected, "and it was *terrifying*. You should be in juvenile lock-up. By the way, when I said, 'Thank you' and 'Good job' before, what I meant was *good-bye*."

"I gathered. Can I call you Jack?"

Two more boxes clattered against the back wall as he muttered something un-angelic. "How did you know—"

I pointed at the gold nameplate sticking sideways out of his garbage can. *Jackson Smith-Hailey, Resident Guardian.* "I'm guessing you're D'Arcy's sub. Unless you've knocked the poor guy out and stashed his body under the couch. I wouldn't narc if you did."

Jack flushed but said nothing.

While he continued to brutalize box piles in the name of organization, I took the opportunity to glance around his office. The place looked more like the sub-basement of a Quickie-Mart than an actual workspace. Cardboard boxes lined every wall. The couch was draped with a sheet and shoved in a corner. Even D'Arcy's cool ninja books were gone, replaced by texts so boring they made my dad's DVR owner's manual look like J. K. Rowling.

All that remained of our former R.G.'s Chuck Norris obsession was a squashed *Texas Ranger* hat and a few pale wall outlines where Chinese throwing stars used to hang.

"Hey, Jack," I said. "Have you heard of Ikea?"

He gave me a decidedly dark look and set the last box down in the corner. "It's *Mr. Smith-Hailey*. And my office decor"—his frown deepened—"is none of your business. Now, if you'll excuse me, I have to get to—"

"Assembly, I know. I'll walk with you."

"That wasn't what—"

"It's okay, I'm going that way."

I held the door open and gestured to the hallway. He still looked vaguely anxious, like the slightest breeze might make him reach for his broadsword, but at least he wasn't glaring at me anymore.

After an impossibly awkward pause, he sighed. "All right, but hurry up. I don't want to be late."

• • •

One of the things I love about St. Michael's is that it doesn't look like a regular school. Wooden wainscoting and sage-colored silk paper lined the main hallway. Tasteful settees snuggled against the walls. Scrolled metal sconces cast warm strips of illumination toward the ceiling, where puddles of light collected like rainwater. If not for the distant clang of lockers, I could almost believe we were strolling through an antebellum mansion. Jack kept his head low and mumbled a lot as we walked. It reminded me of my last visit to see Aunt Verna at the mental hospital only Jack smelled more like marshmallows than liniment oil.

"So," I said, hoping to normalize things, "what's someone so green doing filling in for an old guy like D'Arcy? Shouldn't you be off killing demons with your bondmate, or something?"

He gave me a strange look and mumbled something unintelligible.

"I'm sorry, what?"

"I said, I graduated from Monroe two years ago," he repeated, annoyed. "I'm not green."

"Ah, residential. I almost got sent there after my mom died. It was really…" I grappled for an adjective that wasn't a synonym for "craphole" but nothing surfaced. Like every other memory surrounding Mom's death, my recollection of St. Michael's north Louisiana campus was fuzzy at best. Still, I'd be hard pressed to find any word beyond "dismal" to describe it. Rows upon rows of isolated concrete blocks, broken only by the occasional chain link fence. The place was like Danté's ninth circle…with a playground.

"It looked sturdy," I finished. "Y'all probably watched a lot of television."

"We didn't have TV."

"Nintendo, then?"

He shook his head.

"Fantasy football? Xbox?" I frowned. "Please tell me you had *Angry Birds*."

"We had a library," he said, "and a few educational magazines."

"Huh. Well, that's just tragic."

Jack ushered me into the Hall of Angels and tugged the heavy door shut behind us. Technically, it was a shortcut to the assembly hall though students rarely used it. Too intimidating, I suppose. Antique furniture lined the walkway, the deep mahogany stain

perfectly matched to the vaulted eight-foot doorways on either
end. Tulip-shaped torchières hung on the walls and Italianate
crystal chandeliers dangled above, framed at the ceiling by hand-
carved medallions. Gorgeous, in a chilly, you-break-it-you-buy-it
kind of way. But what separated this room from any of St. Michael's
dozen other breathtaking halls wasn't the decor.

It was the art.

Along one wall, seven alcoves had been hollowed out, each
holding a statue more glorious than any piece of rock had a right
to be. They were the founders of our race: Michael, Raphael,
Gabriel, Uriel, Raguel, Remiel, and Lucifer. They were carved
of stone, each holding a forged metal weapon—bow and arrows,
staff, trident, dagger, pollaxe, and, at the center, the golden sword
of Gabriel. The only angel not holding a weapon was Lucifer. He
held a silver serpent, coiled around his fingers and glittering like
poison.

"My mom was a child of Raphael." I pointed at the archangel's
statue. Its cold, white eyes seemed to follow us down the hall. "I
guess they've told you your bloodline already. I mean, they'd have
to, right? For bonding?"

The first assembly bell wailed in the distance, but Jack didn't
look at me. I wasn't sure if he'd specifically chosen *not* to look at
me, or whether it was just his way of demonstrating what a small,
insignificant part of his day I was. Either way, it didn't bode well.

"So, I've heard bloodlines don't always carry to the next
generation," I continued. "I'm kind of hoping Mom's will.
Gunderman told us in lecture last year the Enforcement Guild
recruits heavily from Michael and Raphael's bloodlines. Gabriel's,
too, though his children are more often teachers or politicals."

Jack's gaze flickered to the side. "You know about bloodlines?"

"A little. Because of all the drama with my parents. My mom—"

"Of course," he said. "I'm sorry for your loss."

I shrugged, trying to look casual. "It's okay. I barely knew her. I mean, I *feel* like I knew her but the memories are so cloudy. Maybe Dad's right that I was just too young. No big deal, right?"

When I looked up, he was studying the floor again.

No surprise there. That tended to happen whenever I mentioned my parents. Mom especially.

When Charlotte Lane first graduated St. Michael's, she was a total rock star in Enforcement—like Lara Croft and Wonder Woman rolled into one. Record levels of demon slaughter, seven zombies in a single bound. Seriously, the woman walked on water. Then, about a year after graduation, she married my dad instead of her assigned bondmate.

Insta-melodrama.

It was huge. Ugly. A scandal unlike anything you've read in *People* magazine. I mean, *every* Guardian married his or her bondmate. The Elders practically did somersaults to make sure our bloodlines combined in favorable ways. Marrying outside recommendation was like a steel-toed boot to their collective face.

To make matters worse, Dad chose to defect to the human sector in protest over the whole thing, which made him about as respectable as a garden gnome. The longer it went on, the harder he pushed her to quit the Guardians. Likewise, Mom's bondmate, Bobby something-or-other, kept pushing her to ditch Dad and hook up with him. By the time Dad knocked her up she must have been an overinflated balloon of hormones. It's a miracle the accident with Bobby didn't happen sooner.

"Enforcement might take me even if I'm not Raphael's bloodline," I filled in the silence, "but every edge helps. Especially with field exams coming up. I should do okay…as long as the new examiner's not a jerk."

"Did someone say he's a jerk?" Jack opened the door to the external corridor, holding it wide for me.

"No," I said, "but faculty always are. Not to speak ill of the dead, but even Lutz could have used a personality overhaul. I still think it's weird that a Graymason would target—"

About the same moment I remembered I wasn't supposed to mention the Graymason, Jack let go of the door abruptly. So abruptly, in fact, I stumbled right into him to keep from getting hit by it. It wouldn't have been such a big deal if the full-body contact hadn't sent zippy yellow tingles down every inch of my skin. Swear on my life, I actually lit up—like *glowed*—for half a second.

"Sorry." He steadied me awkwardly, then yanked his hands back and stuffed them deep into his pockets.

Beyond the hallway, a warm puff of breeze drifted in, chilling the sweat at my neck. The corridor had reached a forking point and, for a moment, I worried Jack might take the north fork to the faculty lounge, where I couldn't follow.

After a pause, he veered south.

• • •

By the time Jack left me at the door to the assembly hall, the senior class's assigned rows had already started to fill up.

There was a vague sense of dread attached to being at school again. Don't get me wrong, I was as excited as the next girl to get back to the supernatural grind. Still, the sight of my classmates dallying with each other—showing off their new cars or comparing tans or swapping stories of lake demons—left me a smidge depressed. I had no tan. I had no car. And Dad had been working all summer, so the closest I'd gotten to a lake demon was when I volunteered to help Mrs. Terwilliger clean her fish pond. And I use the term "volunteer" very loosely.

At least our assembly hall looked the same. Heavy blue curtains cloaked the stage, curved stairs cascading down either side. Gently arched, floor-to-ceiling windows lined one wall, while the opposite wall shrieked with the myriad of colors of our class banners. Somehow, it managed to be both bright and depressing, as well as ten degrees too cold. Like a cheerful mausoleum.

Underclassmen eagerly filed into the youngling section at the back while the seniors took our places up front. I barely noticed the squeals of excitement. My brain was so blissed-out reviewing every second I'd spent with Jack, a hellgate could have opened and I wouldn't have blinked. I didn't even see Matt Marino's messenger bag sticking out from under his chair until my feet were hopelessly tangled in its straps.

With the speed of a seasoned Guardian, Matt caught me mid-plummet. "Yo, Ami! Falling for me already?"

I snatched my backpack from where it had landed and ruffled his untidy brown hair. "Nice moves, my delusional friend. If only you were as quick at combat practice."

"Blasphemy," Matt said, a dramatic hand at his chest. "Are you implying I'm not the fastest, most skilled Watcher on the planet?"

"I would never *imply* that, Matthew." I winked at him. "See you at lunch?"

"Maybe. Depends on Lisa."

"Ah, right. She broke up with you again, didn't she?"

He flopped back in his chair, lanky legs hooked at the ankles. "She also reserved a tuxedo for me with a cummerbund matched to her formal dress. I sense ambivalence."

"Very perceptive."

Matt's grin widened as I pushed my way past him into the social fray of our class.

About halfway down the row, Veronica Manning, queen bee, sat with her entourage, obsessively fluffing her shoulder-length curls. Keller Eastman, the only Watcher in history ever to fail study hall, sopped up adoration from a row of misguided sophomores in the back. A few senior boys clustered in groups to trade stories of their summer conquests, Lyle included. I did my best to ignore their sidelong glances as I scooted across the aisle to where the other Channelers sat.

"Hey, you." I nudged my friend Katie Shaw on the shoulder. "Where were you yesterday?"

She looked at me blankly for a moment, then something registered in her eyes. "We were supposed to go jogging, weren't we?"

"I circled the park like twenty times!"

"Sorry, I got distracted." Her stubby, nail-bitten fingers clutched the smudged true-crime update she'd printed off the Guardian database. "Half of these unsolved mysteries sound like Inferni attacks. It's ridiculous. I mean, do they think we can't tell the difference between a demon kill and a vampire attack? Ugh! Tell me again why we have to protect them."

"Because it is written, K." I winked and patted her head. "Anything with a soul, right?"

"Yeah, *if* you believe they have souls." She grunted. "Look, don't let me off the hook with the jogging thing again. I'm sick of being at the bottom of the fitness rankings. It's humiliating."

With a sigh, I slumped into the seat next to her and extracted a well-worn copy of last month's *Guardian Times* magazine from my bag.

There was a reason Katie didn't get invited along on Lisa's and my little hunts. Much as I loved her, I had to admit that, when it came to battle, the girl lacked. Seriously. She'd been chasing the dream of physical fitness since the day she got her braces off. But no matter how hard she tried, "satisfactory" always seemed to loom a good ten pounds away. Ditto with combat skills. And weapons. And ward drawing… Okay, let's just say, if I ever had to go up against a demon horde, I'd want Lisa by my side and Katie back home baking me a batch of après-kill cookies.

I'd barely made it past the Guardian monthly feature, *Ten Ways to Romance Your Watcher*, when I spotted Lisa hurrying down the aisle with a giant smirk on her face. It made me nervous.

"Hey, Lis," I said carefully as she plopped down in the chair next to me. "What's up?"

"What's up? *WHAT'S UP?*" she faux-whispered. "Skye told Kelsey, who ran into Taylor, who happened to mention to Shane that you got busted by Smalley for snogging Lyle outside homeroom this morning. And you're asking *me* what's up? Honestly, Ami, *how could you not tell me?*"

I stared at her blankly, trying to figure out how to answer. For half a second, I toyed with the idea of letting her think Lyle and I had rekindled our *(ick!)* "romance." With a Graymason on the scene, professors dying, field exams around the corner, and the commencement gala fast approaching, the last thing I needed was Lisa micromanaging my nonexistent love-life.

"I'm your best friend, right?" She pouted. "So, I have to hear all the good gossip from Skye Benedict?"

I sighed. Forget it.

"Lyle's an ass," I said out loud. "I'd rather get groped by Creepy Daniel."

On the off-chance I wasn't kidding, Lisa scanned the room for our psychotic former trainer. After a moment, she gave up. "Fine, but if you didn't kiss Lyle, then why are you so happy?"

I frowned. "Am I not allowed to be happy?"

"Not *that* happy. And don't change the subject. We're talking about you and Lyle."

"Speaking of ex-boyfriends," I changed the subject again, "Matt asked about you. I think you should get back with him."

She cast a measured glance at our longtime friend. "I can't. You saw his class rank last year, and he almost failed his practicals. Plus, I can't look at him the same since I ran into Mrs. Marino at our family reunion. It's not comforting to learn you've made out with your cousin."

"Third cousin once removed," I argued. "It's hardly incest."

"Life is like a box of chocolates, Lisa," Katie noted around a half-chewed carrot stick. "You never know what you're going to get."

Lisa narrowed her eyes, confused. "Did she just quote *Forrest Gump* at me?"

"It's Matt's fault," I said. "She lost a bet and now anytime his name gets mentioned, she has sixty seconds to drop a relevant movie quote."

"That's insane."

"Yup," Katie piped in, "insanity runs in my family. It practically gallops."

"Classic." I high-fived her.

Lisa glared at us for a second then shook her head. "You're both nuts. My point is, dating one's cousin can't be good for the bloodlines. Besides, I've already picked out the next Mr. Anselmo."

With a flick of her finger, she directed our attention to the end of the row where a good-looking boy had just entered. He stood about six feet tall, with silky black hair and murky aqua-green eyes that glittered like the country club kiddie pool. Even the drab white button-down of our school uniform looked good on him.

"His name is Alec Charbonnet," Lisa said. "He's a senior, just transferred in. I heard his dad's a political, or something. He totally wants me."

"Charbonnet?" Katie pursed her lips. "Do you mean the guy with the pretty eyes?"

"Yeah, why?"

"That's Chancellor Thibault's son." Katie dropped her voice to an octave reserved for hot guys and medical conditions, then snatched the *Guardian Times* magazine out of my hands. "They did a spot on him last month. Check this out."

Lisa and I craned to see as she flipped to the society pages.

"There." She pointed to a small photo of Alec and his father on the front steps of the Atlanta Guardian Consulate. The picture was blurry, but apparently you don't need focus to convey sex-appeal.

"*'At the Guardian embassy banquet in New York last month'*," she read, "'*angelblood wunderkind Alexander Charbonnet, adopted son of Chancellor Robert Thibault, made a splash when he drowned a mid-level Oaxachta demon in the champagne fountain.'* He's supposed to be some kind of Watcher prodigy. Unbonded, as far as I know."

"That's so hot." Lisa gave the boy a coy wave. "Do you think Matt'll mind if I go out with him?"

Katie pulled out her iPod. "I'm going to pretend I didn't hear that."

"You need to get out more," Lisa muttered, but Katie had already stuffed in the ear buds.

Despite my Jack-addled brain, I had trouble taking my eyes off Alec. He was cute, definitely, but that wasn't why I stared. Something about him seemed to radiate energy, like a thin coating of light over his skin. It bugged me.

"Hey, Alec," Lisa called, ignoring Matt's sullen glare. "Sit with us at lunch, okay?"

Alec opened his mouth to respond but the microphone cut him off with a piercing squeal. "Later," he mouthed to her.

I managed to drag my attention off him as all heads turned to the front for the faculty procession. To say that our faculty was "a force to be reckoned with" wasn't exactly accurate. They were more like "a force to be tolerated and sometimes mocked."

Dr. Gunderman, tall and lanky, his nose hooked like an over-educated hawk, led the procession with long, important strides. I'd always liked Gunderman, and not just because he reminded me of Gumby. He often seemed to sense when I was about to get in trouble, and he usually let me do it anyway. I respected that. Professor Meeks waddled close behind, his balding head and ruddy complexion barely visible behind the enormous potted houseplant he hugged to his chest. I had no idea what the plant was all about, but he seemed rather fond of it.

A few feet behind Meeks, Ms. Hansen glided down the aisle, perfectly balanced in her platform heels, like a petite *Sports Illustrated* model. I hated her. Granted, she was easy to hate. Early twenties, maybe. Barbie doll body. Exotic, heart-shaped face. Sheets of flowing raven-black hair…all wrapped up in that saccharin sweetness you only find in church-ladies and Girl Scout moms. It was enough to make a girl sprint to the nearest shopping mall for a free makeover.

I let my eyes trail after their black polyester robes, half expecting to see a cadre of guards on their tails. If Graymasons were as unstoppable as the stories said, we'd need an army to fight even one of them, right?

But I didn't see an army. All I saw was the usual staff.

A massive, platinum-haired trainer named Marcus strode after Hansen, heavily armed with two curved swords at his hips, runes and glyphs etched along each blade. Like one of those Viking dudes with the horned helmets and women named Brunhilda on each arm.

The most ghoulish of the crew, Creepy Daniel, followed with his customary scowl, equally bedecked in gleaming weaponry. Knowing Daniel, he probably had a slew of concealed daggers and a spare set of nunchucks in there, too. He used to be normal, I swear. But since his bondmate died a few years ago protecting a nest of vampires from some rogue bloodhunters (long story, don't ask), he'd gotten progressively weirder. Sometimes, we'd see him crouched in the middle of the quad, swinging his sword at the air and cursing the angels for no apparent reason. Creepy, right?

I watched a few other trainers file in, most of them so rickety they could barely take down a stray hedgehog, let alone a Graymason. It made no sense. Even if Lisa's rumor was false and this was just a series of fatal demon attacks, I still would have expected some show of strength. After all, three faculty members were *dead*. Hardly business as usual for the start of the school year.

Jack was the last to enter and the easiest to spot. Amidst the gray-haired instructors and middle-aged trainers, he stood out like a Greek god in an Eskimo village.

"You're getting all glowy again," Lisa whispered, her hand against my forehead. "Do you feel okay?"

Without lifting my gaze, I asked, "What do you know about D'Arcy's replacement?"

"Who?" Her eyes followed mine and she let out a short breath. "Oh, for pity's sake, Amelie. That's *Lutz's* replacement."

"No, I'm talking about the young guy. The super hot one—"

"With all the scars and the Guild tattoos, who looks like an ad for bad boy college soccer? Yeah, that's our interim examiner." She scowled. "That's the jerk who'll make or break our careers this year."

With the grace of an athlete, Jack took the steps two at a time, sliding into a seat in the front row of the dais. My heart launched its resonant *thump-thump-thump* as Lisa's words sank in.

Jerk.

Did I accidentally call the finest male specimen on the planet a *jerk?* To his face? On the eve of his rendering judgment that could kill my career?

"But…I thought he was the R.G."

"He's both. Mom says he's also covering for Fiori as senior

trainer until they can get somebody else."

"Fiori's dead?"

"Retired, as of last week," Lisa explained. "*I* would retire, too, if it were me. Working in this place is like being the drummer in *Spinal Tap.*" She mimed an explosion. "Seriously, Ami. I know you've got an issue with rules, but I'm begging you. *Don't.* That guy is a disaster. I heard he blew off the Elders' bond assignment at graduation even though it meant a year on probation. He's total bad news." Lisa began digging around the bottom of her purse for a breath mint.

Bad news. I couldn't argue that. From forty feet away, I felt the heat of his glare ripping into me, sparklers igniting on my skin.

"Hey, Lisa," I whispered. "I think I've got a problem."

"Uh-huh. What else is new?"

"No, I mean, I think I'm supposed to—" I stopped. Supposed to what? *Bond with him?* There was no way I could explain the magnetic draw I felt, not without sounding like a total idiot.

I watched Jack slump back in his chair, his fingertips forming a prayer-shaped cage in front of him. His eyes narrowed as he surveyed the room, like he was making notes. It was artful, how he took everything in. Filed it. Cataloged it. Along one arm, a curved tangle of black lines peeked out from under his shirt cuff. It twined along the fleshy part of his wrist in a circular pattern, like vines growing up the path of his veins. I couldn't see details, but I recognized them instantly.

Enforcement Guild glyphs.

My mom had those same tattoos. Technically, they'd been removed when she left the Guardians, but puffy, pale scars had remained. A distant memory sparked in my head of Mom singing me lullabies at bedtime. I used to trace those marks out on her forearms—memorize them—so I could copy them onto my own arms later with the black Sharpie I'd stashed under my pillow. They'd swirled and curved like bracelets around her wrists, intricate and beautiful, each one matched to a glyph on the skin of her Watcher.

In almost meditative silence, my finger rose to my wrist, etching out the marks I saw on Jack's arm. A gentle slope like a tilted S and a sideways V with a tiny eye in the middle—the glyphs for fortitude and insight. My flesh hummed beneath them.

When I looked up, Lisa was staring at me in frozen-eyed disapproval.

"Ami," she warned.

I gave an innocent shrug, but didn't say anything.

Rain had started to fall outside. Trees and azalea bushes smeared into a complex watercolor beyond the glass. I sank a little deeper into the cushions. If the Elders had sent an Enforcement agent to St. Michael's, even a newbie like Jack, then maybe this Graymason rumor wasn't total crap. At the very least, it made me curious.

When the flock of faculty was finally seated, the double doors squeaked open again and we all rose in a show of respect.

Headmistress Smalley shuffled in, too-tight sandals *clip-clopping* across the floorboards to the podium. Her amber eyes glimmered under the spotlight and her smile seemed to take up half of her face. Even the black academic robes, which should have flowed in soft waves, clung to her rounded form. She looked like a friendly sausage.

"Good morning," she greeted us warmly. "I am Headmistress

Judy Smalley, and it is my great pleasure to welcome you all back to St. Michael's Guardian Training Academy."

Polite applause swept through the hall, punctuated by the soft hiss of students settling into their chairs.

I was tempted to tune her out since I'd heard this welcome speech a zillion times before. It was always the same. Watchers and Channelers: two halves of a whole. We couldn't tap the Crossworld without them to drain us and they couldn't survive the mortal world without us to heal them. It was a neat reciprocal setup. Of course, it came with a price.

Once, my mom's bondmate visited our house. It happened late one night, long after she'd left the Guardians. He was nothing remarkable. (Although I can't imagine what a seven-year-old would find remarkable about *any* grown-up who wasn't Big Bird.) What I did remember was the effect he'd had on my mom. As soon as she saw him her whole body exhaled—not like what happened when she looked at my dad. More desperate. As if some part of her had been locked in a dark cell, holding its breath for years.

I didn't pretend to understand it. All I knew was that the bond was intense, it tied us to each other forever, and, if focused properly, could enable us to take out a small city block.

I looked at our headmistress. A thin yet tangible light curled out from her chest as she gazed across the dais at Henry McFarland, our bookish campus Archivist. Henry wasn't much to look at, with grayish hair, brown eyes, and the telltale wrinkles of pre-retirement. The best I could say about him was if you ever needed something translated or defined he could do it. He beamed back at Smalley like she was the most beautiful thing he'd ever seen. At first glance, it certainly looked like they were bonded—the crackle of power, their glow of connection—but I knew better.

They'd been assigned as bondmates at their own graduation eons ago. Before they could complete the ritual, Henry was infected by a demon virus and deemed unfit for battle by the Elders. He hadn't gone vampiric. In fact, he'd made a full recovery. But because there was demon DNA somewhere in him, he and Smalley were forbidden from finishing their bond. Or marrying. Or starting a family. Of course, the Elders couldn't stop them from getting jobs at the same school, taking up residence on the same street, and spending every waking moment together.

I might have been sad for them if they weren't so disgustingly happy.

"Once you pass your field exams," Smalley addressed the seniors, "you will be told the origin of your bloodline. That information is yours alone until you submit your request for a bond assignment at the end of the year. Each of you will submit your top three choices, rank ordered, drawn from the unbonded Guardian Community. With input from our faculty, final assignments are made according to your ranks at graduation, and bond rituals shall commence at the summer solstice."

I saw a lot of students nodding, the tension in the room palpable. Most of them were so jazzed they'd already started making out their pref lists.

"We are also very fortunate to welcome a valuable new recruit," Smalley said, her gaze skittering over the crowd to rest on me. "Mr. Jackson Smith-Hailey is a former valedictorian at our Monroe campus and liaison to the Institute of Paranormal Convergence. He has agreed to take a leave of absence from his position at the Enforcement Guild to fill in as Examiner and Resident Guardian until we can find suitable long-term replacements. You will each get to know him well over the next week as he conducts your field exams and determines your initial class rankings."

Jack stood to accept the applause and I groaned. Valedictorian? Paranormal Convergence? The Enforcement Guild? Jeez, the guy's résumé read like someone running for public office. And now he was in charge of our field exams?

Oh, I was so screwed.

If I bombed my exam, then for the next six months I'd be stuck in paranormal preschool learning how to clip my fingernails without decapitating myself. I'd be denied my bloodline and instantly demoted to the bottom of every decent Watcher pref list. Alternately, if I rocked my exam, I'd probably be suited up, *paired* up, and taking down rogue demons before Mardi Gras.

My resolve thickened. Come hell or high water, I *would* ace that test.

I dragged my attention back to the stage. Jack's gaze had riveted to a spot in the middle of the hall, about ten feet above the center aisle, where a slight ripple twitched like fumes off a desert highway. It wasn't a big deal, but, for some reason, the sight made my chest constrict.

With crisp, sudden hand motions, Jack signaled to the middle school guards at the rear of the hall and the back rows started emptying out, elementary first. At the same time, a handful of trainers broke from their posts at the front, taking up a defensive formation along the exits.

Katie and Lisa looked clueless, so I prodded Veronica in the back. "What's happening?"

"Like I'd tell you if I knew." She flicked a haughty glare over her shoulder.

"Maybe it's a training exercise," Skye suggested, ignoring her friend's rudeness. "I wouldn't mind a little training with him. The *personal* kind, know what I mean?"

It would be hard *not* to know what she meant.

After a few more hand gestures, Jack strode to the edge of the stage and leaped off. He ambled down the aisle to a spot not twenty feet away and waited, his gaze fixed on the air.

The younger grades had already evacuated. The only Guardians left were our class, the faculty, and a smattering of trainers and staff who'd formed a loose perimeter around the outside of the room.

"Eyes front," Smalley called from the podium. "If everyone could please proceed as calmly as possible to the rear of the assembly hall, we have trainers posted at each door—"

A rough sound, like cardboard tearing, interrupted Smalley as spits of black fire sparked overhead. Despite the thickness in the air, I kept my eyes glued to Jack. He had extracted something from under his robes, and I could just make out the silver glint of a short sword clenched behind his back.

"There's no need to panic," Smalley insisted from the stage. "If you'll find the nearest exit, your trainers will be happy to—"

That's when the chandelier began to vibrate.

Without understanding why, I stood and edged down the row toward Jack. If something big was going down, I wanted to be next to him. I *needed* to be next to him. As the space between us closed, his eyes locked with mine.

"Go," he mouthed silently.

I shook my head in refusal. As if I could just…*go*. The thought of leaving him here alone paralyzed me.

"Amelie, what are you doing?" Lisa snapped. "Smalley told us to evacuate."

"I know. Just give me a sec—"

"Hey, y'all," Katie's voice trembled behind us. "I think something's coming."

All at once, a sharp scraping of wings and claws tore through the air, clouds of black smoke billowing out of the narrow rift. It poured like blood across the floor, stung my skin, and made my eyes water. As the terrified screams of my classmates rose up around me, realization crystallized in my head.

Katie had it wrong. Something wasn't coming.

Something was here.

Chapter Four:
Hellgate

"We've got to get out of here!" Lisa gripped my arm in a panic and pulled me toward the back of the hall.

Above us, misshapen creatures squirreled to get through the rift, their hooked claws and talons gleaming in the smoky haze. Obsidian holes glared from the sockets where their eyes should have been, dark and hollow like inky wells with no bottom. Something inside me froze as I watched them, and my blood chilled to ice water.

Then all hell broke loose.

Literally.

Bolts of lightning shot out of nowhere. More demons flooded from the rift. A jolt of horror seized me as flames blanched the ceiling, with singed demon hair leaving odd puffs of smoke around the light fixtures as if the air itself had been set on fire.

Frantic, I scanned the room. The smoke hung so thick I could barely make out Jack's outline. His body blurred in the half darkness as he twisted and lunged at the demon onslaught.

Matt had snapped the leg off his chair and swung it at the air, Alec Charbonnet's head seemed to be bent in prayer, and Lyle, in an unlikely show of heroism, held up his Theories textbook to shield a whimpering Channeler behind him. In the distance, I could hear Marcus shouting evacuation orders, but, for the most part, it was just screams. High-pitched, horrible screams.

"Lisa!" I yelled. "Get Katie and get out!"

"But—"

"I'm right behind you, I swear. Go!" I wrenched my arm out of Lisa's grip, desperate to find some foothold in the madness.

So far, only lesser demons had come through—small creatures that scratched and bit with nasty precision but rarely killed. Under normal circumstances, they were about as threatening as a swarm of winged ferrets.

Except *this* was far from normal.

Through the haze, I watched Jack raise his sword in a defensive arc. His face held no fear as he parried the demon attack, deflecting blow after blow. Bright streaks of crimson appeared on his cheeks, his shirt shredded to bloodstained ribbons. He swung his blade with the force of a battle-axe, sheets of black ichor spreading down his hands. Yet as fiercely as he fought and as much damage as he inflicted, I knew it wouldn't be enough. Until that gate was closed, the demons would keep coming.

And they'd get bigger.

We'd been warned to expect hand-to-hand combat challenges, the occasional loose fiend, trainers lurking behind corners to pounce on us for "training purposes." But untamed demon hordes and blasts of *hellfire*?

No way.

Somebody had to do something.

I squinted against the heat and lifted up my hands. "*Exitus,*" I yelled weakly. The swirl of heat and fire tightened in my fingers for a second, then went slack.

"What are you doing?" Like a shot, Jack's head snapped in my direction.

"I'm helping," I shouted from my hiding spot behind the chair.

"You're irritating them. Go away!"

"*I'm* irritating them?" I mumbled as he sliced through another demon wing.

Much as I ached to argue, I had to give him snaps for honesty. It was true, I sucked at the channeling thing. Once, I had tried linking power with Lyle during Fundamentals class last year. Total disaster. It had taken a solid month for his eyebrows to grow back.

Still, did Jack really expect me to sit and do nothing? He was getting slaughtered. Alone. Smalley and the rest of the faculty huddled near the exits. Even the trainers, who were allegedly hired for stuff like this, bustled safely toward the back.

I watched as another charcoal-skinned demon slid through the opening, its serrated teeth snapping at the air.

"Jack! Behind you!"

He turned in time to see the thing flying at his back. With inhuman speed, his sword came up in a glittering sweep to slice through its neck. Black blood spilled across his chest as the monster crashed to the floor in a stringy heap…just as two more like it hurtled through.

It was insane. Why was no one fighting?

Marcus and Daniel had funneled the last Channelers through the exits and were circling back to collect the Watchers and senior faculty. I recognized what they were doing. It was standard protocol for a rift-kill. First, they would clear the room and ward all the vulnerable points of exit. Only a small contingent would be left inside, one or two bonded pairs. When the demon flow had cleared, the Watcher would launch a charmed explosive device, etched with glyphs powerful enough to collapse the gate from the other side. We'd seen it a hundred times in training videos.

But *this* made no sense.

If I left the room now there would be *no* Channelers. No one to shield him when the gate collapsed.

Terrified, I stood and pushed through the demon horde to where Jack fought, his sword slicing the air like a whip. My chest was taut, and, with every step, heat seemed to billow up inside me.

"Give me a weapon," I yelled.

"Bennett, I told you to get out of here. That's an order!"

"I'm not leaving you. Give me a sword and let me fight, or give me your hand and help me channel."

His eyes were dark with fury as he whirled. "It's not your fight."

"You're going to die."

"Bennett, for the last time," he said, thrashing at the black-skinned horde. "*Get! Out!*"

With a final hacking swipe, he flipped his sword to the opposite hand and made a grab at my arm. I'm not sure what he intended— to push me back, or maybe march me to Smalley's office for a quick disciplinary lecture. Whatever his intention, it vanished the instant his hand touched me.

It was as if I'd been electrified, like a toaster oven suddenly plugged into the wall. All the power from the rift hurtled toward us, raw and hot and terrifying. I lifted my free hand again, black flames lapping at my outstretched fingers.

"*Exitus! Concedia! Incendia!*"

Every command I could dredge up from last year's Defensive Fundamentals class sprang to my lips. White and gold sparks flew out of my fingers and a hot wind blew, whipping the curtains into tight little circles. It felt like someone had injected liquid flames into my veins, as if the building and everyone in it were suddenly bleeding fire. Crossworld energy swelled inside me, blackening my heart and everything around it.

"Holy hell!"

Jack ripped his hand off my arm but it was too late. Energy hung between us, thick and ropey ribbons of light. I could feel my power reverberating off his. My eyes slammed shut as a whip of heat cracked across my face, the darkness intensifying. Every instinct told me to duck, to run, to hide. But I didn't. If I let go of the channel, the gate would open again, and I couldn't let that happen. I couldn't let him die.

With an ungodly grunt, Jack launched himself at me, his weapon clattering to the floor beneath an acidic wave of black flame. The dull ache of impact ripped through my shoulder as we hit the ground and began to roll. Maybe it was instinct, maybe cowardice, I don't know. But as soon as I felt him on top of me, I melted. My body sealed itself to his, every part of us fitting together like pieces of an ancient puzzle. Every hard plane of his chest, every inch of his warmth against me…even the smell of him, all sweat and soap and salty blood.

He felt like home.

Crossworld energy stretched across my soul as he tucked me

beneath him. Somewhere in my ribcage I could feel my spirit suffocating, helpless and weak. I wanted to will the flames into submission but my control was gone.

I was drowning.

"No! No, not again." Jack's voice broke through the darkness. "Ami? Listen to me. You have to let it go. Try to remember, it's like breathing."

The Crossworld shadow roiled inside my chest, snarling and angry and relentless. I shook my head.

"You can do this, I know you can," he promised. "Breathe, Ami. Just breathe for me."

My fingernails scraped against the hard tile, my whole body brittle and hot. He sounded so sure...but how? How could *he* know something that I didn't understand myself? I leaned my head against his shoulder and drew a ragged breath.

"Yes." He rewarded me with a smile, hands stroking frantic lines over my forehead. "Yes, like that. Keep going."

I took another breath.

Inch by inch, the Crossworld taint drained out of me, replaced by his warmth. Above us, the flow of air reversed itself to pull the demon horde back into the rift. It whooshed past us like a giant industrial vacuum cleaner. Through cracked eyelids, I saw tiny threads of light knitting up the rip in space, perfectly synchronized to Jack's and my collective heartbeat. The scrabbling sounds of demons slowed, then ground into silence.

Clouds of smoke had left a dim haze over the hall, with light scorch marks where demons had combusted against the walls. Dark smears spattered the aisle with a few bits of black carcass, and giant fingers of soot streaked the ceiling. A twinge of dread curled in my belly as I looked at the chandelier, now a dangling black skeleton of twisted metal.

Oh, yeah. *This* would go down on my permanent record.

Somehow, Jack had ended up on top of me, his body curved around mine in a protective cocoon. If the situation had been different, I might have felt self-conscious about how tightly I held him. I didn't think he minded. He held me just as tightly. When he finally pulled back enough for me to see his face, I almost laughed. It held the same look my dad always got when I did something exceptionally reckless, that odd mixture of fear, fondness, and anger.

"What were you thinking?" he whispered. "You could have been killed."

I tried to speak, but nothing came out. My cheeks were damp, and I felt dizzy and shaken, like I'd been stuck on an amusement park ride with no brakes. But it was worth it. Jack was safe, the demons were gone. Everything else was gravy.

"I think I'm going to throw up," I managed softly into his ear.

Chunks of dust drifted to the floor as Jack shifted his weight back, fingers poised at my waist. A few threads of light still quivered where he touched me, but, for the most part, they'd dissipated with the rift. He'd just opened his mouth, I assume to launch into a lecture, when Daniel and Marcus emerged from the smoke, swords drawn.

"Stay," he ordered gruffly. "I'm not kidding. Don't move. Don't speak."

"Don't worry," I croaked, trying not to hurl. My head swam in sickly circles, and, much as I longed to lay into Creepy Daniel about his lackluster performance during the battle, I doubted I could manage it without spewing on Jack.

"Sir?" Marcus took a step forward, blade still raised.

Jack winced at the effort it took to push himself up. His shirt was torn and sticky with blood. Bright red scratches ran in angry lines down his cheeks.

"Stand down," he said. "Marcus, make sure there's no collateral damage among the students. Daniel, check the perimeter and confirm nothing got through. Then both of you report to Headmistress Smalley for debriefing. I'll finish up here."

From a few feet away, Daniel dropped a look of suspicion at me. "Sir, shouldn't we—"

"You have your orders," Jack cut him off.

The trainers exchanged cautious glances. For a second, I thought they might argue. Daniel's ears were bright red and his eyes had that crazy look they got sometimes. I didn't even realize I was holding my breath until Marcus lowered his weapon and backed away. Daniel reluctantly followed suit.

As soon as they were gone, Jack sank onto the ground beside me. His hands were shaking, but the rest of his body seemed calm. I lifted myself up beside him, fingers laced across my forehead. Never in my life had I experienced such a raging need for chamomile tea.

The smoke had begun to dissipate, rustling sounds of life filling the room. Little flutters of ash drifted like snowflakes to settle in his messy golden waves. It took me a moment to realize the smoke used to be demons and the ashes used to be curtains.

"Wow." I pointed to the air. "That's kind of pretty. Did we do that?"

"*You* did that." Jack frowned, looking faintly greenish. "*Exitus* is the rift closure command. *Concedia* is the demon dismissal. You can't close a rift before you dismiss the demons. And you *definitely* can't set them aflame after you've closed and dismissed. Were you trying to blow up the school?"

I wasn't. Not lately, anyway.

I lowered my head to my knees, waiting for the room to stop spinning. We were sitting so close our shoulders practically touched. If I moved my hand even a few inches, it would've been on top of his. "Jack, what happened back there? Why wasn't anyone helping you? Is this about the Graymason?"

He eyed me carefully. "What do you know about the Graymason?"

"I know three of our profs are dead." I demonstrated my handle on the obvious. "I know whoever called open that rift was probably inside the school wards. And I know the Elders think this is a big enough deal to send an agent in. So, either we're dealing with a massive conspiracy—"

"Uh, *we?*"

"Or it's something new. Like a Graymason," I finished with a narrow glare. "And yes, *we*. You can't deny we work well together. I could be your sidekick, if you want. Like Superman and Lois Lane. Or Peter Pan and Tinker Bell."

"Tinker Bell isn't menacing."

"Which proves how much you need me," I insisted. "Fairies are terrifying."

He sat up straighter and dusted off his pants. "Fairies don't exist. Neither do Graymasons."

"That's what humans say about vampires and werewolves," I argued. "So we're agreed. You pass me on my field exams and I'll help you bust the Graymason?"

Jack grunted at that, but didn't argue.

His glasses had been knocked off during the fight, and this close, I could see details I hadn't noticed before. Little worry lines edged his mouth and tiny scars streaked his left cheek and forehead. It made me wonder what kind of battle he'd gotten himself into, or if maybe he'd ridden his tricycle into a thorn bush when he was a kid. Either way, he wasn't as perfect as I'd first thought, but I didn't care. It made him more interesting to look at.

I was so hypnotized by those gorgeous eyes I barely noticed him getting closer until his face was only a few inches away. In a heartbeat, all thoughts of Tinker Bell vanished. As inappropriate as it was, I couldn't help wondering what the school policies were on students hooking up with substitute teachers. Especially hot, young, unbonded ones. Did we even have policies on that?

"How do you feel?" His hand cupped my face and he hit me with an intense I-can-see-your-soul stare. "Any dizziness? Disorientation?"

I tried not to panic as he gazed into my eyes. "I was thinking about school policy. So, yeah, a little disoriented."

"Your pupils are dilated," he said. "I think—"

"Yes?" I breathed.

"I think you have a concussion."

I blinked. *A concussion*? That's *so* not where I thought he was going.

"You do," he decided, jerking his hand away. "Report to Dr. Gunderman for eval."

"But…but he'll tell me to go home."

"Then you should go home. In fact, I think you should stay

home this week to recuperate. I'll mention it in your incident report."

"*Incident report?*" I frowned at him as he yanked a yellow notepad from his back pocket and started scribbling. It wasn't that I hadn't gotten incident reports before. Or that I hadn't deserved them. But this was such a clear case of wrongful persecution I had a hard time not screaming "objection."

Narrow rivulets of blood trickled from his temple down one side of his face. I noticed with a jolt that one of his shoulders must have been dislocated, the muscles forming ropey knots at his neck. Even his eyes looked haunted from the power drain.

"Okay, no offense, but you just downed like two hundred rohms of Crossworld power. And your face looks like you made out with a lawn mower. You're telling *me* to go see Gunderman?"

"I'm *ordering* you," he corrected, still scrawling on the paper.

"Uh-huh. Because that worked so well last time?"

He glanced up, annoyed. "Miss Bennett—"

"Oh, for pity's sake, hold still." Before he could stop me, I lifted my hands to his face and squeezed my eyes shut. "*Salve!*"

It began almost instantly. Heat sparked on his skin and I felt something gnaw at my chest. Although healing channels draw on Crossworld power, they're a much milder brand of poison to Channelers. Vodka instead of hemlock. When I opened my eyes, shadows slithered across my skin. But instead of seeping in, they left only a tiny sting, then dripped away like rain before it turns into hail. With the tenderness of an artist's brush, my fingertips stroked along Jack's forehead, the cut on his jaw, then over his eyelids and lips. Everywhere I touched, his injuries knitted together.

Healing was the first thing we learned in school, around the same time we started writing our names, so it was one of the few things I did well. But in all the times I'd done it before, it had never resonated quite like this.

Each touch was a sigh through my body, the soft rush of eagles in flight. Colors flashed through my head. Then, before I could consciously register what was happening, my mind flipped channels and Jack and I were dancing. I didn't recognize the place—some huge hall filled with golden light—but the "me" in the vision seemed comfortable there. Near us, people whirled and swirled around a giant ice sculpture of an angel, its wings outstretched in flight. Jack wore a tuxedo and I was in a fitted white dress with pearls embroidered down the bodice. And even though I kept stepping on his toes with my stupid high heels he didn't seem to mind. He just smiled and held me tighter.

It couldn't have been more than a few seconds before my eyes fluttered open, the vision melting away. For a moment, I thought I might faint. My brain hummed lightly. His forehead was pressed against mine, eyes shut and breath shallow. A wash of dizziness hit me, but it couldn't eclipse the warm, wonderful feeling of being right where I was supposed to be.

"Jack?" I whispered.

He swallowed, Adam's apple working nervously. "Yeah?"

I didn't know what to say. All the questions I had—What just happened? Who are you? Is this normal?—died before they reached my lips. His breath was so sweet, his fingertips digging into my ribcage. The world spun in little circles and for a second, I felt a need to kiss him so fierce I wasn't sure I'd be able to resist.

"Jackson," I whispered again, because I couldn't think of anything else.

The sound of his name seemed to shake him out of whatever trance he was in. With a muffled grunt, he sprang to his feet, nearly tripping over one of the fallen chairs in the aisle. I reached out to help him, but he jerked away like I was made of acid.

"I-I have to go."

"Wait!" I scrambled after him, the barest hint of a golden sheen beneath my skin. My head vibrated from the power draw and I struggled not to wobble as I stood. "Let me come with you. I can help. Don't you see that?"

But he didn't see it. The way he blew all the air out of his lungs, fists balled at his forehead, he was definitely angry. I hated to admit it, but the guy's reaction made sense. Even for an R.G., this kind of boundary violation was *so* far from the borders of "helpful," it might well have been declared its own country.

For a moment, he stood still, staring down at me in bewilderment.

"Say something," I begged.

But he didn't. It was like he was afraid to speak.

Thin trails of light draped between us, cobwebbed and delicate, but I barely noticed. I couldn't stop looking at the unhappy shape of his lips, thinking about how badly I wanted to kiss him and how ludicrous it was to want that.

"Go to the infirmary," he said quietly, "then go home. If I see you again, I'm filing an incident report."

I watched in silence as he walked away. Every bit of me screamed to go after him, to get away from the burned stench of demon death that filled the hall. It didn't matter whether he wanted my help or not. Without him, I had no reason to stay.

Chapter Five:
Shaking the Tree

For the record, infirmaries suck. Fluorescent lights. Strange smells. People in lab coats peeking at your orifices. Pretty unrelaxing, if you ask me.

Most of the beds were empty when I reported for my exam, though a few curtains had been drawn. Probably survivors from the demon attack in Slidell last weekend. Smalley tried to keep us shielded from the front lines until after graduation, but with the Elders carting in fallen warriors all the time it was hard not to notice. Too many wounded, too few facilities to treat them, I guess. The patients' low moans and ragged breathing made for a weird soundtrack to my physical exam.

"Are you seeing spots?" Dr. Gunderman flashed a penlight in my eyes, making it impossible not to see spots.

"No," I said. Lie number six. Or was it seven? Crud, I'd lost count.

"Dizziness?"

"No."

"Nausea? Vomiting? Diarrhea?"

"No, no, and yuck," I said. "Dr. G, can I please be excused?"

"Not yet. How many fingers am I holding up?"

"Eleven."

"Amelie."

I scowled, ignoring the way my body still tingled where Jack had touched me. "Sir, I'm fine. Just let me go to class. Please?"

Gunderman unhooked the blood pressure cuff from my arm and looked at me like I'd asked to borrow his credit card. "Young lady, the fact that you *want* to go to class gives me definite pause for concern. I will, however, grant you a pass—"

"Thank you." I started to rise, but he pushed me back down.

"On one condition. You go straight back to the assembly hall and wait for dismissal. If you feel dizzy or need a healing charm for *any* reason, you are to see Ms. Hansen immediately. Understood?"

"Consider it done."

"And I'd feel better if you'd agree to talk to Dr. Evans. You channeled a lot of energy today, Amelie. Most girls your age would be in the hospital after that kind of power draw."

"And yet," I said, gesturing to myself, "I am fine. No need for a healer or a shrink."

"So you say." He frowned. "Stay here. I'll get your paperwork."

I sat for a minute while Gunderman retrieved my pass slip. As soon as I had it in hand, I bolted. No sense giving him a chance to change his mind. Besides, being in the sick ward was starting to give me the willies.

On the way out, I noticed most of the patients had gone quiet, either too drugged or traumatized to moan. There was one, though, who left me with a softball-sized knot in my belly. A cute

Watcher—curly hair, about twenty-five—tucked in an alcove near the door. His curtain wasn't fully drawn, and, through the opening, I could see him curled in a fetal position on the bed.

Normally, I'm pretty good with people in pain. Comes with the healer territory, I guess. But this guy's pain was so palpable, so intense, it radiated through the curtain. It filled up the room in such a bleak, dark way I had no choice but to stop.

"These things happen." A resigned murmur jolted me out of my trance and I turned. Henry, the Archivist, stood behind me, a grim look in his eye. "More than they should, these days. We're lucky, you and I."

"We sure are," I agreed. Then I asked, "How are we lucky, exactly?"

With a sad smile, he nodded to the man behind the curtain. "His bondmate was killed. That's the fourth Channeler they've taken this month."

"They?" Did he mean Graymasons?

Henry lowered his head. "You witnessed this morning how dependent we are on our Channelers for Crossworld riftwork. Well, the demons have noticed it, too. And with our forces spread so thin—"

"Wait a sec, they're *targeting* us? I didn't think demons were smart enough to mount an offense like that. Don't they usually go after their own? Vamps and weres?"

"They used to." He shrugged. "Not as much since the Peace Tenets passed. Now there are too many souls, not enough Guardians."

I was about to ask what he meant when the squeal of a curtain pulling shut cut me off.

"Miss Bennett," Gunderman warned, "I thought I told you to return to assembly."

"Yes, sir. Sorry." I whirled back to where Henry was but he'd already wandered off to browse the latest *International Classification of Demon Diseases*. Yeesh, no wonder the man knew everything.

I glanced at the door, fully prepared to follow Gunderman's order. I didn't want to think about the unnatural hunch of that Watcher's body, the wracking sobs of silent pain. But I couldn't block it out.

Gunderman had already drifted into another patient's alcove. As soundlessly as possible, I slid behind the curtain and laid one hand across the wounded Watcher's sweaty forehead. I didn't know him, didn't know anything about him. But if I were hurting like that, I'd want someone to help me.

"*Salve pacem*," I whispered. "*Salve.*"

A soft burn passed through my palm into his skin as the Crossworld energy coursed between us. His face took on a look of drowsy peace. I knew unauthorized healing was prohibited in the student handbook, but I figured Smalley would understand. I'd done far worse for less noble reasons, right? And it wasn't exactly a sin. I waited until his breath settled into the soft rhythm of sleep then, quietly as I'd come, I eased out of the infirmary and returned to assembly.

• • •

Which may have been a mistake.

As soon as I set foot in the room, Jack started glowering at me from the now-splintered dais. Like, *serious* evil-eye. I barely had time to obsess about it before Lisa hit me with a full-body tackle-hug so energetic you'd think we'd just survived Armageddon.

"Oh, thank heavens you're okay!"

"Oof! Lis! Oxygen!"

"Sorry." She released me. "Wow, you look awful."

I scowled at her. "Thanks."

Lisa sat beside Katie and me, clutching my hand, while Smalley gave some lame speech about what a brilliant job our new examiner had done with the "simulated emergency situation." What crock! *That* nightmare was no more a planned exercise than I am an international supermodel. Don't get me wrong, I understood why she had to spin it. *And* why they believed her.

Our families were promised St. Michael's was safe; the wards around the school's perimeter kept the villains out and the heroes in, no exceptions. That was one of the main reasons why, in spite of the constant demon threat, Guardian parents still let their kids come here. If they admitted for even one second that someone *inside* the wards had summoned a swarm of homicidal subterraneans, the world as they knew it might just disintegrate. They *needed* to believe her.

By the time Smalley wrapped up, the vibe for most folks had returned to a tense little corner of normal. For me, however, normal was at least three buses and a cab ride away. My skin still had a faint glow to it, and, every time I caught Jack's eye, electric shivers shot through my nerves.

"Quit that." Lisa jabbed an elbow at my ribs.

"Quit what?"

"Quit looking at him like that," she warned in a hushed tone. "I'm not kidding, Amelie. He's dangerous. He boils kittens in ritual sacrifice."

Katie wrinkled her nose. "He does not, Lisa."

"You don't know that. Look what he did to this place!"

"He didn't do this," I said. "You know as well as I do a rift that big was no exercise. And the perimeter wards are still active. That means it had to be an inside job."

"Oh, here we go." Lisa rolled her eyes in exasperation.

"Has anybody checked Creepy Daniel's bloodline lately? What about Veronica Manning? Anyone who spends fifty grand on a Mardi Gras dress *has* to be the spawn of Satan, right?"

Lisa's smile faded as she laced her arms across her chest. "You sound really paranoid, you know that?"

"Just because you're paranoid doesn't mean they're not after you." We both turned to where Katie stood, absently stacking her books in a neat pile organized by color, size, and topic of study. "Sorry," she said, when she noticed us staring. "Habit."

Around us, everyone stood to pack their things. It would have resembled a normal dismissal but for the charred walls, splintered furniture, and light fixtures dangling like bones. While I didn't believe for a second Jack had orchestrated this catastrophe, I had to admit Lisa wasn't completely off-base. There *was* something dark about the guy. Even when we'd had our special moment before, I could feel it lurking beneath the surface. He lacked that certain "bunnies and rainbows" vibe I'd always imagined my boyfriend would have. Not that I like bunnies. Or rainbows. Demon dismemberment, on the other hand...

"I thought he seemed nice. I liked his glasses and he has a nice smile." Katie blew her limp blond bangs out of her eyes.

"Katiebear, grow up. Just because a guy wears glasses and

smiles at you doesn't mean he's *nice*." Lisa dug around in her purse for a tube of lip-gloss. "Maybe he's a visually impaired cannibal. Did you ever think of that? Like one of those serial killers you love so much."

"I don't love serial killers," Katie argued, defensive. "Not romantically, at least."

"He probably *is* a serial killer," Lisa prattled on. "Smalley said he's with Paranormal Convergence, right?"

"So?"

"So, those Convergence freaks hang around with Inferni. It's all bloodlust and bondage with guys like that. I'll bet he snacks on entrails and bathes in the blood of his victims."

"Lisa, I don't think you're supposed to say stuff like that anymore," Katie noted. "It's not PC...even if it's true."

Over the sea of students' heads, I watched as the visually impaired cannibal wrapped up a heated argument with Smalley, punctuated by angry gestures in my direction. His glasses hung from his pocket like twisted sculpture art, his shirt ripped and stained scarlet. I'd healed all the scrapes on his face as well as the dislocated shoulder, but he still had streaks of blood, dirt, and demon slime all over him. He cast a withering look in my direction and stalked toward the exit.

"You guys, I've gotta go," I mumbled to Lisa and Katie. "I'll see you in class."

"Whatever. Don't do anything I wouldn't do," Lisa called, annoyed.

I picked up my pace as the door swung closed behind him. If I could just catch him, maybe I could make him understand I wasn't the child he thought I was. Maybe he'd see that I could help him.

I'd barely made it past the front row of chairs when Headmistress Smalley's hand caught my arm.

"Not so fast, young lady," she said. "Some things can be fixed with words. This isn't one of them."

"But—"

She gave my shoulder a hard squeeze. "Go back to class. Whatever you have to say will keep 'til tomorrow."

Grr. Did I look like I needed advice? Hokey as it sounded, Jack's departure was like a magnet to my heart, complete with gut-wrenching ache. I didn't know if it *could* keep 'til tomorrow.

"Amelie," she said, obviously using some mind-reading mojo, "whatever problems exist between you two are as much your responsibility as his. If you insist on making him hold your end of the burden, it will only lead to suffering for you both."

"But ma'am, I just want to talk to him."

"And tell him what?"

I opened my mouth to answer, then shut it. What *did* I want to tell him? That I had feelings for him? That he made me jittery and happy all at once and, by the way, I believed we were meant to be together forever?

I scanned myself in quiet appraisal. My uniform was ruined, torn and stained with smears of Jack's blood. My feet were covered in demon splooge, a chunk of mottled black skin caught in the laces of one shoe. I shuddered to think what might've been nesting in my hair. Even if I could convince him to talk to me, I doubted my appearance would move him toward anything beyond a barf bag.

"I'll think of something," I mumbled, self-conscious.

Smalley's eyes softened. "I'm sorry, Amelie. I know this isn't easy. Please remember, everything we do at St. Michael's is with your best interests in mind. Which is why it pains me to give you this."

It took me a moment to focus on the familiar yellow slip she held, though heavens knew I'd seen my share of them.

STUDENT INCIDENT REPORT:

NAME– *Amelie Lane Bennett*

VIOLATION– *Unauthorized channeling within school grounds; assault of a faculty member; non-consensual healing.*

DISCIPLINARY ACTION– *Official warning; restricted contact with aforementioned faculty. If behavior re-occurs, student will be suspended indefinitely.*

– J. Smith-Hailey

I took it from her with a robotic motion. "But…I was protecting him. He knows that."

"Amelie," Smalley sighed. "There is no limit to what a man can know and disregard in the service of his ego. He'll see you tomorrow morning for your field test, then I'm afraid the rest is up to fate."

I listened as if her words made sense, but they didn't. I had tried to *help*. I was the *only* one who tried to help. Everyone else had just sat back, content to watch Jack get shredded. How was that fair?

"This sucks," I said.

"Indeed. Just remember, dear, life is suffering." She patted my shoulder. "Love, even more so."

And that was how she left me—with guts in my hair, goo on my shoes, and that infernal yellow note in my hand. Jack's cramped lines swam together like worms in a rain puddle as I reread them, again and again. Love, huh? This wasn't love. It was betrayal, pure and simple. Why would he do this to me? We were on the same side…weren't we?

Lisa's voice startled me when it sounded a few feet away. "There you are! Everything okay?"

I quickly refolded the yellow slip and stuffed it into my shirt pocket. "Yeah, everything's fine," I said. But it wasn't fine. I had a feeling it wouldn't be fine for a while.

Chapter Six:
Good Intentions

We made it to Demonology class in plenty of time. Not that it mattered. I couldn't concentrate on a single word Gunderman uttered. Anatomical vulnerabilities of demons, the boiling point of fiend's blood, a hundred and one ways to shield your Watcher against demonic energies… It went in one ear and out the other.

All I could think about was Jack. The silk of his hair, the lingering scent of him, like soft rain and warm sugar. About midway through class, I looked down to discover that the margins of my notebook were littered with vines and flower doodles.

So, so lame.

I closed the notebook and shoved it away. A thousand questions still pressed their way into my brain, the same questions that had been lurking since Lisa first mentioned the Graymason. Who could orchestrate something like this? Who would want to? Did it have something to do with the war? If so, why kill *instructors*? They were nobodies—a few class lecturers and a glorified hall monitor. Lutz was the only one with any real influence, and that was tenuous at best. If someone truly meant to disable the Academy, the ideal person to kill would be Headmistress Smalley. It's not like she was a hard target—a middle-aged Channeler who lived alone with a bunch of cats and a semi-retired half-bondmate next door. No, it had to be something else.

The demon attack must have been orchestrated by someone *inside* St. Michael's walls. Someone with power. Someone nearby when the rift opened. I'd watched enough *C.S.I.* with Katie to know that every serial killer chooses his victims according to a pattern. The Graymason had to have a pattern, too, and I was willing to bet today's attack was part of it. So if I wanted to figure out who was doing this, I needed to access the victim files. That meant breaking into…

"The Archives," I muttered under my breath, pen tapping against my lip.

"Excuse me?" Lisa paused her obsessive note-taking. "Did you say something?"

"Hard drives," I said, louder this time. "Dad needs a new hard drive. For his laptop."

"Okay, whatever." She gave me a funny look then returned to her notes.

Gunderman had lapsed into some tangent about the Crossworld aristocracy and how if made-vamps didn't watch their step they'd end up serving tea and bloody crumpets to the new Immortal Sovereign for the next six billion years. Personally, I thought the *Borgias* were more interesting.

I returned to my plotting.

The wards on the Archive room would be comparatively light. Henry stayed in there most of the time, which could make things complicated, but even he had to take lunch, right?

I glanced at my watch. 11:05.

If Henry kept to the patterns we'd noted on last year's stakeout, he would go to lunch early with Smalley. Which meant I had about thirty minutes to get to the Archives, find what I needed, and get out without being seen.

My hand shot into the air. "Dr. Gunderman?"

"Yes, Miss Bennett? Would you care to enlighten the class on the proper technique of cutting through a Nero demon's hind plate?"

"Uh, no, sir." I let a slight waver enter my voice. "I-I think I need to see the guidance counselor. I feel a little blue from the training exercise this morning and I can't concentrate. Would you mind terribly if I left class?"

Gunderman set down his scalpel to give me a long, hard look. I could hardly blame him, after our discussion only a few hours ago. He was probably remembering the last time I'd left class, when all the campus livestock went missing. Not my fault, by the way. How was I supposed to know Virox demons aren't vegetarian?

"To the guidance office and back," he warned. "That's it."

I thanked him and took the hall pass.

The sun had inched higher, so I tried to keep to the shadows as I crossed the front lawn to the main building. I gave up halfway. Everyone who mattered was still in class anyway.

When I entered the hall to the faculty offices, beads of sweat immediately chilled into goosebumps along my spine. The windows at both ends of the hallway were open and swaths of gauzy curtains rippled in the breeze like restless spirits. Most of the office doors were shut, locked up tight while professors held class.

I could feel their wards pulsing under the hardwood thresholds. Far down the hall, one door remained ajar, light stretching across the floorboards in a long, yellow beam.

The Archives.

If I'd been thinking clearly, I would have gone back the way I came. I could already see shadows moving inside the room, and quickly recognized the hushed echo of Smalley's voice.

"Henry, have faith. It's pointless to get upset over something so beyond your control—"

"I'm not talking about faith, Judy. I'm talking about *you*. The more you involve yourself in this, the more likely you are to get killed."

"She's not a killer, Henry."

"That doesn't matter. Whether it's her or someone else, I don't like you putting yourself in danger. The boy is here now. Let him handle it."

"It's not that easy."

"It *is* that easy!" Henry insisted as a deafening crack of ceramic against drywall rang out across the hall. "This is not your responsibility."

"Henry..." Smalley sighed in her world-weary, here-we-go-again voice.

"Have you ever stopped to consider what will happen if you're wrong? If the Elders are mistaken? If the killing doesn't end with the prophecy?" he ranted. "Are you willing to die for something so uncertain?"

A tense silence fell across the room like a muted blanket of snow. Henry was usually so calm that it weirded me out a little to hear him yell like that. Smalley must have been surprised, too, because the silence lasted forever.

Finally, Henry let out a deep breath. "I'm telling you, Judy, there's more to this than the Elders know."

I barely had time to flatten myself against a doorway before Henry emerged, hair wild and eyes dark. The tips of his knuckles were raw and bloodied, like maybe he'd spent the morning slamming them against a brick wall. He barreled toward the main foyer with methodical steps, thankfully at the opposite end of the corridor.

"Henry, wait." Within seconds, the *clomp* of Smalley's high heels followed, and a heavy door slammed behind her.

Once they were gone, I peeked out.

The Archives were still open.

My dad has this theory that you can tell everything about someone by how they keep their office space. Vacation photos, bonsai trees, ceramic knicknacks. If Bud's theory was correct, then Smalley's beloved Archivist was in serious need of a spa day.

Sheaths of paper lay scattered across the long rectangular room, and most of Henry's *Precious Moments* figurine collection lay in decapitated disarray. The walls were marred with spits of white dust where ceramic angels had exploded on impact, and the framed prints of soothing beachscapes had either tipped chaotically or fallen to the floor. Even Henry's frog-shaped doorstop looked like it'd attempted suicide once or twice.

I didn't wait to find out if they were coming back. I had files to pilfer, and the gods of opportunity did not knock twice.

Whenever a faculty member retired or left the school system for any reason, his or her records went into a special locked cabinet known as "the dead file." I'd only accessed the dead file twice before—freshman year, when Katie needed the old choirmaster's address so we could summon a small demon to his house, and again sophomore year, so we could send a note of apology to his new house after the old one was demolished by the larger-than-anticipated demon.

It took a few seconds to find the right cabinet, then another minute to unmake the wards on the locks. When I finally got the right drawer opened, I was already dizzy from the Crossworld energy draw.

If you had a boyfriend to drain it on, this wouldn't be an issue, an irritatingly familiar voice whispered from the back of my brain.

Inner voices are rarely helpful.

My fingers tripped over the manila folders—dog-eared personnel files, archaic disciplinary reports. Finally, near the back, I hit paydirt. Templeman, D'Arcy, and Lutz. All in a row.

I tugged the files out and set them on Henry's desk. It helped that I knew what I was looking for; I didn't have to waste time riffling through unnecessary documents. Their lives weren't important, only their deaths.

I tried to keep things in order as I pulled out the stack of crime scene photos, starting with Templeman's.

At first glance, it looked more like a tea party than a massacre. He sat alone at a table in the courtyard of his French Quarter house, bushes and ferns lush behind him. White linen napkins lay neatly folded beside a tray of half-eaten cookies, with two bone china teacups perched at opposite ends of the wrought iron bistro table. Even the centerpiece bloomed with fresh white flowers.

I scanned the photos quickly, muscling through the gag reflex when I got to the close-ups. His throat was slit from ear to ear in a single stroke. Fountains of wet, painful red doused the pristine white of his shirt, all the way to where it tucked into his trousers. His hands were carefully folded in his lap, head bent forward. For a moment, I wondered if he'd been praying...then I noticed something even stranger.

Apart from the mortal wound to his neck, there were no injuries, no defensive scuffs of any kind. Even his hands looked freshly washed. With the Quarter as busy as it was on Saturday afternoon, I found it hard to believe no one would have heard him if he'd screamed.

D'Arcy's crime scene, by contrast, looked like a Bruce Lee fight scene gone wrong. Every part of him was raw and bloodied, sword slashes and defensive marks all along the outside of his forearms. His clothes had been torn, buttons ripped off his shirt. One sleeve of his jacket dangled by a thread, and his cheek had begun to swell purple from the broken capillaries of impact. It didn't surprise me that D'Arcy had fought. He'd never taken crap from anyone in life, so why would his death be any different?

My fingers trailed over the final, blurry photo of Lutz.

It confused me. His jaw was slack, the corners of his mouth turned up in the slightest smile, as if he'd fallen asleep on a sunny beach instead of in the clutches of a madman. He sat in his rocking chair, hair slicked over his head in the usual careful combover, a framed photo of his dead wife clutched tightly to his chest. Nothing broken, nothing out of place. I might have believed he'd died in his sleep, except for the eyes. The blue of his irises had faded to a muted gray that covered his pupils, like a demon's, only burned from ice instead of fire.

"Why didn't you fight?" I asked the photo. "Why did you give up?"

"Let me know if he answers you," a voice interrupted from the hallway. "I have a few ideas, myself."

My head snapped up to see Jack leaning against the doorframe. He hadn't cleaned up from earlier, his hair still matted with dried blood and sweat, black streaks of demon goo staining his shirt. I wondered how long he'd been watching me.

"At the risk of sounding redundant," he said, "you don't belong here."

"So I've heard. But first things first." I forged ahead, ignoring the zip of power between us. "Why did Templeman fix tea for the guy who murdered him? And why does D'Arcy look like he body-surfed a cheese grater, while Lutz went down without so much as a broken fingernail?"

"You tell me."

"I don't know. None of this makes sense," I continued. "I've seen what demons can do. These weren't demon deaths. You know that, right?"

"I know you need to leave. Now."

Okay, it wasn't like I expected him to stand there and let me poke around in the school's secret files. But did he have to be so harsh about it? I tried not to flinch as he walked around the desk and began gathering the photos back into their file folders. Every brush of his arm littered my skin with golden sparks.

"That's so cool," I murmured, unconsciously reaching for the flutters of light. They melted on my fingers like snowflakes on water. "Is that why you hate me? Because I healed you?"

"I don't—" He pulled away with a brittle exhale. "Miss Bennett, I gave you an order. Several orders. You ignored them.

If this is the extent of your regard for authority, then I question whether you're cut out for Guardian duty at all. Maybe you'd be better off serving in the human sector like your parents."

A ripple of annoyance ran through me at the mention of my parents. That was a low blow. "I'm not like my parents," I said.

"Doesn't mean you can't be realistic," he argued. "There are plenty of things a girl like you could do. You could try a cooking class, or get a desk job, or something."

"A *desk* job?"

"It happens. People *do* leave the Guardians. You know that better than anyone."

Jack spoke calmly, but I couldn't ignore the flood of fury in my throat. He *had* to know how idiotic he was being. If Henry was telling the truth, then the female Guardian population had already been decimated by demon attacks. So here I was, a Channeler, desperate to train and willing to fight. Why would Jack encourage me to *quit*? It was insane, especially when he knew what kind of power we could generate together.

"You're not being fair," I said.

"Life isn't fair."

"Yeah, and no man is an island. Any other clichés you'd like to share?"

He held my gaze for a split second before glancing away.

"Look," I said, "I don't understand what's going on here. But nothing I did this morning gives you the right to treat me like a criminal."

"I'm not—"

"You are," I insisted. "You talk to me like I'm six years old and give me orders that make no sense. You're not even old enough to order a beer, so get over it."

"I'm trying to protect you."

"I don't need to be protected. I'm a grown woman who can do whatever—"

Before I could finish, he swiped at my wrist and spun me toward the exit. "You're not a woman. You're a child—"

"I'm a Channeler!"

"A *child* who should be with your father in the human sector. Where you can live. Where you can be happy, with no demon battles or rules about where you can go and who you can be with—"

"I won't be happy—"

"You *will*, just not here." Heat crept up my wrist where he held it, an electric hum vibrating into my bones. "Our world is full of death. You don't belong here—"

"I do."

"No! You belong somewhere safe. You belong—"

"I belong with you!"

Every inch of him froze and, for a second, he stared at me, his face pale with shock.

I don't think either of us expected me to say it. But once I had, there seemed no place big enough to shove it back in. The words still echoed between us when he started toward the door again, pulling me along by the hand.

"Don't say that. Not ever," Jack muttered. "It's dangerous. *You're* dangerous. Not to mention impulsive, immature, and too selfish to understand that people get hurt when you're around."

A hot flush crawled over my face. "Funny. That's what Lisa said about you."

"Well, maybe you'll listen to her next time." Then, as if I were a particularly revolting piece of garbage, he shoved me through the doorway. "We're done talking. Your field test is tomorrow morning. I don't want to see you until then. And when it's over, I don't want to see you again. Ever."

I glanced down the hall but didn't move. I couldn't. Ribbons of heat coalesced in the air, thick and taut, linking me to him with unmistakable clarity. I was still standing there, staring at him, when he slammed the door in my face.

Chapter Seven:
The Ugly Truth

"Does this look poisoned to you?" Lisa poked at the edge of her pizza slice.

I glanced up, distracted, then gave the pizza a dutiful look. "It's probably not organic, if that's what you're asking."

Lisa wrinkled her nose. "Katie said if she wanted to kill a whole bunch of Guardians, she wouldn't mess around with all this demon crap; she'd go for their food supply. Not that I buy your conspiracy theory, I'm just saying…"

I stared across the lunchroom table, mouth paused mid-chew. Suddenly, the melted cheese on my tongue tasted suspiciously metallic. "Smalley must have thought of that."

"I don't know. Smith-Hailey was poking around in the kitchen when we first got here, and I doubt it's because he's hot for Mrs. Bertle."

My gaze tripped to the apron-clad, overweight human, her kinky black hair tucked under a hairnet as she doled out slice after slice of the now decidedly arsenic-flavored pizza. Bright sunlight poured through the glass walls of the cafeteria, morphing the chipped, lime-green tabletops into a glittering sea of Formica, unfortunately making Benita Bertle's chubby, mocha-colored outline glisten with sweat. Despite my foul mood, the image of Jack romancing Bertle the Turtle in the pantry made my mouth curl up at the corners. Who knows, maybe that was exactly what he needed to tame his burning angst into pure, unbridled man-passion.

"I don't know, Lis. Bertle's pretty sexy."

The woman swiped a palm across her sweaty forehead and, without breaking stride, reached down to grab a slice of pizza for the next student in line.

"Yech!" Lisa gagged. "Wouldn't it be great if Smalley could implant some respect for hygiene next time she has the staff's memory modified?"

I set down my lunch, overcome by a sudden queasiness. I'd felt on edge ever since Jack shoved me out of the Archives. The sharp ridges of his crumpled incident report still poked through my shirt pocket and I found myself reaching up to give it another pat.

He'd done an excellent job of avoiding me since our run-in—not easy when I knew he had to keep interrupting class to fetch students for the field tests. It was almost as if he'd memorized my class schedule, then specifically arranged the tests so he never had to intersect with me.

I'd just lapsed into another cozy cloud of self-pity when Lisa sat up tall beside me. Her hand shot into the air.

"Alec! Over here!" she yelled, then whispered to me. "Ami, you have to meet this guy. I told him you didn't have a date to formal yet and, I can't be sure, but he didn't seem too repulsed by the idea."

"I thought you called dibs on him."

"I did, but you can have him first. After he dumps you, imagine how good I'll look in comparison."

"Thanks, that's not insulting at all." Where were Matt and Katie anyway?

Lisa rose beside me, her hand still waving madly as she gestured him over. "Alec, come meet Amelie. She's the one I was telling you about. My dateless friend."

"A pleasure." The boy's brilliant green eyes studied me as he gave my hand a sympathetic squeeze. "Nice work in assembly this morning."

Lisa laughed. "Seriously? She nearly blew up the school."

"I prefer to think of it as an opportunity for renovation. No one got killed—that's a success in my book."

"Too bad the disciplinary gods failed to read your book." I tossed a piece of crust at my plate.

"Disciplinary gods?"

"Smalley cited her for assault of a faculty member," Lisa said.

"And non-consensual healing." I popped a ketchup-covered fry in my mouth. "But that was bogus. He totally needed it."

Alec stared, silent, for half a beat, then exploded into laughter. He actually had to lean against a chair to keep from falling down. Finally he wiped his eyes and said, "This school is so much cooler than my private tutor. Mind if I join you?"

"Hold that thought," Katie broke in from a few feet behind Alec. She held her lunch tray in front of her like a battering ram nudging her way through the crowd toward our table. "Looks like I'm just in time for the show."

"What show?" Lisa glanced up, eyes bright. "Is Matt back from his test yet? He was so nervous—"

"Different kind of show." Katie plopped her tray on the tabletop then cocked her chin toward the table near the window. The popular table.

Veronica Manning unfolded her long, salon-tanned legs and rose from her queenly perch between Keller Eastman and Lyle Purcell (who appeared to be—ugh!—*waving* at me). We watched her adjust her push-up bra and flip a curtain of thick, banana-taffy-colored hair over her shoulder. The primping was nothing new, though I'd never seen her eyes look quite so…predatory.

"Good grief," Alec muttered.

"Be afraid," Katie quoted. "Be very afraid."

Alec squinted at her. "That sounds familiar. Revelations?"

"David Cronenberg. It's a long, scary story."

"I like scary stories."

Katie smiled. "Then you'll love this."

Veronica sauntered over with regal strides, Skye Benedict trailing at a respectful distance. Compared to the rest of us, she looked almost obscenely attractive. Her hair had been smoothed back with pearl and crystal studded combs the exact azure color of her eyes, and her lips glistened a frosty shade of neon. Everything about the girl reeked of money and plastic.

"Why, Alec," she cooed, her Baton Rouge drawl on full throttle. "I couldn't help noticing you have no place to sit for lunch."

Alec cast a glance at his tray, happily nestled between Katie's and mine, then back at her.

"No one decent, I mean." She tossed her hair seductively. "Perhaps you'd be more comfortable at our table? With people of your caliber."

He arched an inquisitive eyebrow at her, then turned back to us. "Is she serious?"

"Serious as a demon pox outbreak," I told him.

"She thinks high school is a reinvention of the caste system," Katie added.

"My Lady Katherine, do you mean it's not?" He frowned, feigning confusion. "Most disturbing news. However shall we oppress the rabble?"

"Ritual floggings?" Katie suggested.

"At least forty lashes," Skye agreed, as Veronica rolled her eyes.

"Omigosh, there's Mattie!" Lisa rose out of her seat, waving, while Katie grumbled something unhappy-sounding.

As usual, Matt looked like he'd recently escaped incarceration by the fashion police. His shirt was covered with soot and clung to his chest in wet patches. At least he was wearing a shirt. Over the summer, we'd gotten so used to seeing him in a swimsuit and flip-flops, the lack of sunburn seemed the most striking thing about him.

"Hey, y'all," he greeted us. "Vee! Slumming it today?"

"Don't call me that." Veronica let out a bored sigh, her lips forming a flawless, heart-shaped pout. "Alec, if you decide to join us, our table's available. So am I, for that matter." She eyed him head to toe then said, "Come on, Skye."

Matt waited until they were gone, then slapped Alec on the shoulder. "Dude, I see you've met our self-appointed royalty. How'd that go?"

"Strangely intriguing," Alec commented, "yet not enjoyable

at all."

"I find people are either charming or tedious," Katie groused out her requisite movie quote. "She manages to be both. FYI, if anyone else says Matt's name I'm leaving. I'm low on movie quotes."

Matt grinned broadly and plopped himself into the seat beside Lisa. He'd foregone the lunch line in favor of vending machine munchies, which he set on the table with a measured thud. "You're still doing that? I thought you'd cave days ago."

"So did I," she said. "Then I remembered my pride."

He laughed and ruffled her hair. "All you have to do is admit the Inferni have souls and it all goes away. Simple as that, kiddo. What do you say?"

"I'd rather kiss a wookie. Or Veronica Manning." She tossed another French fry in her mouth. "Probably a wookie. They're nicer."

Lisa and Katie groaned while Matt made an awful-sounding wookie noise.

The sad thing is, Veronica's crowd actually used to be cool back in middle school, before everyone started obsessing about bloodlines and class rank. Nowadays, it seemed like every decision we made had to be based on social strategy. Take Lisa, for example. She and Matt were perfect for each other. Beyond perfect. They knew each other inside out and still found ways to fall in love every day. Yet here she was, willing to screw it up over a few stupid points on a field exam.

I didn't get it at all. If *I* could fall in love with someone easy like that, I would do it in a heartbeat. For example, if I could care about Lyle the way I cared about —

The thought halted abruptly. It was a ridiculous, painful thought, one that left me with unhappy chills. Clearly, Jackson Smith-Hailey wanted nothing to do with me. Caring about him was like trying to love a tree stump—a cold, mean-spirited, paternalistic tree stump. With fungus.

"Alec," I cut into the conversation beside me, desperate for a distraction. "Your dad works with General Manning on the High Council, right?"

"He does, though I'm not sure how much actual work they do."

"Have you heard anything about these attacks on our instructors? I heard it's not demons this time."

"Amelie!" Lisa snapped. "I told you to leave that alone."

Alec chuckled, his arm hooked around the back of Katie's chair. "The Graymason rumors, you mean? Yeah, I did hear about that, but I can't say I paid attention. The way the war is going, we don't have time for fairy tales."

"See," Lisa snapped. "Now drop it."

I frowned, disappointed. I wasn't sure what I'd hoped for— some sense of outrage or injustice. It just struck me as *wrong* how blasé everyone was.

By the time we finished lunch, Alec and Katie were chatting as if they'd known each other forever. It was hard to miss how his fingertips kept brushing her shoulder, how she giggled and blushed whenever he said something funny. It might have been my imagination, but I could swear Lisa's eyes got the tiniest bit stormy when they stood up to leave. Together.

I'd be lying if I didn't admit to a nugget of jealousy, too. After all, if Alec and Katie hooked up, and Matt and Lisa got back together, where did that leave me? Alone? Or, worse, huddled on

Lyle's rec room couch trying not to hurl?

I was in the midst of another mope-fest when a commotion broke out at the front of the cafeteria — a flood of students coming in early for the second lunch seating. Creepy Daniel's dark head bobbed through the middle of the crowd, a glyph-carved metal coat of arms by his side, as he pushed his way through the swarm of students. What caught my eye more than Daniel's unique approach to crowd control, however, was the broad-shouldered hottie holding the cafeteria door.

Jack had changed out of his blood-stained clothes, opting instead for a tailored, gray-blue oxford that almost matched his eyes. Damp jeans hugged his long muscular legs and uneven clumps of wet hair curled over his ears. Even as I sat there, I had to forcibly push back the urge to go pat him dry with a few spare napkins. It wasn't until Ms. Hansen sidled up beside him that the world came to a screeching halt.

Her hair was brushed and pinned back in a low ponytail, and her smile glittered playfully. A wave of acid swirled in my belly as she slid her hand across his back. Like she owned him, or something.

Okay, granted, I had no right to be jealous. He'd made his feelings toward me clear. But did Hansen have to make it look so *easy*? No fighting, no tension, no threats or insults. Just two shiny, happy people spending time together.

"What's wrong now? You look like you just swallowed a Spivax demon," Lisa whispered, handing me a napkin. "Is this because Alec's into Katie? I know it's disappointing, but he's not the only available Watcher."

"I still say Lyle's your best bet," Matt suggested, wiping his hands on his khakis. "He dresses well and he's super cute."

"Mattie, that's not a very heterosexual thing to say," Lisa pointed out.

He shrugged. "Just trying to help."

I fixed my gaze on the stained green cafeteria table. Touched as I was by their meddling, the notion of bonding with Lyle, or anyone else, made my stomach curdle.

"Alec's not the issue," I said.

"Then what is?"

Unconsciously, my eyes flickered toward the door. Lisa scanned the cafeteria, finding nothing of interest. Then her face twisted in exasperation.

"Oh, for Pete's sake, Amelie. *Him* again?"

"Who again?" Matt asked. "Did I miss something?"

"She's got a thing for Smith-Hailey. Or maybe just an addiction to lost causes. Hey, I heard Stan the janitor is unbonded, by the way. He's human *and* gay. Right up your alley."

I glared at her. "This is not funny."

"It is. You just don't appreciate the humor."

Matt's chair gave a loud squeak as he leaned back. "I don't know. She could do worse than Mr. S. In my field test last period, the task was to quell a water demon in the back fountain—nasty buggers, by the way. I completely panicked. I swear, the thing was about to drown me. So Smith-Hailey whips out a knife and jumps on its back, all the while giving me a pep talk about the 'indomitable spirit of Guardiankind.' He even gave me a second shot at the demon. If I was a girl, I'd be all over that."

"Pookie." Lisa plucked the last potato chip from Matt's hand. "Remember how we talked about those times when your opinion is better kept to yourself?"

"Is this one of those times?"

She smiled.

"Say no more." Matt blew her a kiss and obediently zipped his lips. In silence, he carried her lunch tray to the cafeteria line and began emptying it onto the conveyor belt. So sweet I thought I might vomit.

"You've got to get past this, honey. Trust me. You with him is like the Hindenburg of romantic disasters." Lisa's gaze drifted over my shoulder to where Jack stood. "Look, Hansen's touching his chest. They're leaving together. See? It's hopeless. He's taken. Let it go."

I slunk lower in my chair, trying not to look. Sure, I had no claim on him. And he obviously didn't want me. So why did the thought of him walking off with someone else suddenly make me feel like an abandoned vehicle?

Chapter Eight:
Deadline

At some point after my Advanced Wards class, it started raining. I didn't mind. I liked it when the weather matched my mood. As Lisa drove me home, I couldn't help staring out the window. It was oddly satisfying to see the wind whipping people's hair into little rats' nests, their umbrellas flipped inside out under the force of the storm. Seemed like a lovely first-day-of-school metaphor.

When she pulled into my driveway, I noted with chagrin that our front yard had branches down across the walkway and landscaping. Definitely a task for tomorrow. Or, better yet, never.

Picking my way through the obstacle course of fallen oak leaves and Spanish moss, I barely registered the screech of a very black, very European car with dark, tinted windows pulling up to the curb behind me. It was what Katie and I liked to call "vampire chic"—sexy in a way that let everyone know the driver didn't just have money, he had *lifetimes* of accrued wealth. Technically, there was no law that said a vamp couldn't hang out in my driveway if he wanted to. Heck, he could come right up to the front door and still be in compliance with the Peace Tenets. As long as I didn't accidentally shout, "Please, suck my blood," I stood very little chance of getting attacked.

Nonetheless, vampires being what they are, I decided to set up a quick, warded perimeter. Nothing too complicated—just a simple vamp repellant.

A cool blast of oak and incense hit me as the front door swung open. My mom had decorated this house when she and Dad built it the same year I was born. Parts of it looked like a museum, crowded with weird things: Egyptian urns, grandfather clocks, huge, throne-like chairs with eagles' beaks carved into the arms. Of course, my favorite were the random antique toilets scattered around. They looked like little cabinets, for the most part, but I still smiled when I walked past them.

My school bag made an undignified *thunk* against the lacquered brick floor as I cruised into the kitchen to grab a soda from the fridge. I took the back stairs two at a time, oriental carpet squishing under my feet, and hurried down the hall to my room.

I *loved* my room.

Mahogany wood trim edged the ceilings and doors in an elegant contrast to, well, *everything* else. Mom had let me redo it myself the year before she died and I'd milked the autonomy for all it was worth. Pepto Bismol walls, rainbow stickers everywhere, Hello Kitty curtains. Even a dusty white mosquito net hung from the ceiling. I didn't care that it looked like Toys R Us exploded in there. I couldn't bring myself to get rid of any of it. Walking into that square haven was like stepping into a much needed hug, especially after a day like today.

As I changed into grubby shorts and a holey T-shirt with the dubious slogan, *Licensed to Chill,* I tried hard not to think about Jack. Impossible, since everywhere I went it felt like he should've been there. In fact, the whole time I did my homework, I kept imagining him working next to me, our legs touching...

Psycho, I know.

By the time Bud pulled in the driveway a few minutes before sunset, I had not only finished my classwork for the next three days (mostly correct, I think), I'd also boiled some pasta, baked a pan of chicken parmesan, and chopped up carrots and cucumbers for a salad.

Before I go any further with this, I should probably mention that, despite his overprotective tendencies, Bud's a decent dad. He gives me my vitamins and allergy meds every morning (okay, *most* mornings), he makes me wear a helmet when I ride a bike, and he has never once told me I couldn't watch my reality TV shows. However, according to the Internet, raising a healthy child requires actual *food*. Like, beyond popcorn and Lean Cuisine. So, about six months after my mom died I started cooking—vegetables and lean meats and all that stuff. Not bad for an eight-year-old. And once I stopped counting lime gummy bears as fruit, my mood improved dramatically. Over the last ten years, we'd found such an easy groove; I sometimes wondered if he missed Mom at all.

I definitely did. It still bugged me that I couldn't remember stupid things about her. Like whether she was a good cook, or if she liked rainbow sprinkles with her ice cream, or if she minded when I played dress-up in her evening gown collection. I would have killed for a few memories, even the bad ones. The night she died, for example. All I knew was what other people had told me: that there'd been a demon attack, and I had blacked out somewhere in the middle of it. Dr. Evans, the school shrink, used to promise me those memories would return when I was ready. But after a decade of silence, I wasn't so sure.

"Hey, Daddy," I called as the back door opened and closed with a familiar *click*.

"Hey, yourself." He sniffed the air, tossing his briefcase and jacket over the granite-topped island. "Dinner smells great. Extra garlic?"

"Keeps the vampires out."

Bud grimaced. "That's funny, sweetheart. Did you think that up while fleeing a graveyard?"

I decided not to explain about the vampire still parked across the street. Since my dad is such a liberal about human causes, I figured he'd probably support the Paranormal Convergence movement, in theory at least, if not vamp-snuggling reality. (Think supernatural ACLU with an interspecies truce thrown in.) Unfortunately, I'd never know. The Peace Tenets weren't proposed until after Bud left the Guardians, which meant I wasn't officially allowed to discuss them with him.

The premise was simple. Turns out the Crossworlders (excuse me, *Inferni*) we'd been hunting all these millennia—vampires, werewolves, etc.—weren't as evil as we'd thought. Sure, they might have some demon blood from whatever infection they'd caught in the Crossworld but their origins were human. So were their souls, *if* you believed they had souls. The folks at Convergence did, which meant Guardians were now technically responsible for protecting them. Weird, right?

It wasn't so bad. Werecreatures can be friendly when it's not a full moon, and all the vamps really want is a little blood and a safe place to snack. Once the Peace Tenets recognized those needs, the random violence pretty much ended.

Still, I couldn't get used to it. Vamps creep me out. If Bud found out we had one parked down the street, he'd probably impale himself trying to make a stake out of the kitchen table. Lisa once said Bud reminded her of a young George Clooney with a little extra paunch around the middle. Frankly, if I had to go up against a vampire, I'd rather have George Clooney.

I settled into the chair across from him, plopping my elbows on the antique table we'd salvaged after Katrina. My bare toes slid idly along one of the warped legs carved to resemble a lion's paw, of course, with huge cat knuckles and claws as the feet.

"So, how was your first day at school?" Bud asked. "Any excitement?"

"Not a bit," I lied. That was part of our agreement, by the way. He asked. I lied. "How'd your deposition go?"

"Eh." He shrugged. "I have to deliver another appeal in Baton Rouge tomorrow. You have no idea what kind of monsters show up in the legal system."

"Do any of them have claw-tipped wings and cloven feet?"

"No."

I smiled. "Then I win."

Incidentally, Professor Meeks claims that greater demons take government office all the time, especially here in Louisiana. So Dad might have been wrong about the cloven feet thing. Somehow, it seemed a bad time to point that out.

"Carol Anselmo called this morning," he said after a minute of silence. "Lisa told her to remind me that the commencement formal is coming up. She says I should encourage you to go with someone named Lyle."

"Good to know. Thanks for the vote." *Note to self: Kill Lisa.*

"So, are you going?"

"I don't think so," I said. "I've got a report to write and that Druidic spellbook isn't going to translate itself." I gulped down some water and stuffed another bite of pasta into my mouth. I could tell from the twitch above his left eyelid that he had comments. He set down his fork. Not a good sign.

"You know, sweetie, you're getting to the age where you need to start thinking about the future. I'm not saying you should rush into a blood bond prematurely. I just don't want to see you left behind. Is this 'Lyle' person someone I should know about?"

I shook my head. "Definitely not."

Dad nodded. "Well, you don't have to decide right now. I just worry about you after—" He broke off, hesitant. "I just worry."

"Daddy, I'll be fine. Smalley says some people are late bloomers, that's all."

Actually, what she'd said was, *'Tis a marvelous bud that opens its petals at midnight—not so eager as the weeds of daybreak.* I figured that translated to, *Just because you're not a slut like Veronica, doesn't mean you'll end up alone.*

"If it's any consolation, I did meet someone special," I admitted. "He's super smart, cute in a brutal-yet-bookish way, *and* a kick-ass fighter."

His eyes widened. "Sounds terrifying."

"Exactly." I laughed. "The whole thing's a little weird because he's already graduated and I get the feeling we weren't supposed to hook up. But we did, sort of, and now I'm in trouble."

Dad's face paled to a greenish tint like he'd swallowed expired milk. "I'm sorry, you're *in trouble*?"

"It's not a big deal."

He folded his hands on the table and leaned forward like he was about to take someone's deposition. "Amelie, this is a *very* big deal. This is one of the biggest deals you'll ever encounter. I'm just not sure you're ready to raise a child."

I blinked at him, too stunned to speak. *A child?*

"Not that your mother and I didn't start young," he fumbled on. "I admit we did. Some might say we were *too* young. But you have to understand, times were different. The passion we shared—"

My fork clattered to the table as I clamped both palms over my ears. Close as Bud and I were, this was not a topic we had ever, or would ever, discuss. EVER. "Stop! No visuals!"

"Sweetheart, listen to me. It's natural to be curious. Sex is nothing to be ashamed of."

"La-la-la-la." I screamed louder.

"Every girl your age has urges, I'm just not sure you're ready for the consequences of—"

"Dad, please!" I slammed my hands down on the table, nearly cracking a chunk off the edge. "I'm not having sex, okay? New topic, please."

"You're not?" Bud frowned. "I'm confused."

In an effort to avoid speaking, I snatched the rumpled incident report from my pocket and tossed it across the table at him. *Urges? Seriously?* I would already have to bleach my brain. Did he want to damage me permanently?

I stayed quiet as Bud's eyes scanned over Jack's writing, a vein beginning to throb in his neck. When he was done, he set his elbows on the table and lowered his forehead into his hands.

"*J. Smith-Hailey*? That's your 'special someone'? You're in trouble with *Jackson Smith-Hailey*?"

"Yeah," I said. "He's subbing as the new R.G. at school. The Examiner, too, unfortunately."

Bud stared at me, eyes frozen, face rapidly darkening to an eggplant-like shade. My appetite had evaporated, but I stabbed at a clump of pasta anyway. The red and white swirls my fork made on the plate were easier to look at than him.

"All right." Dad closed his eyes, the heels of his hands digging dents into his eye sockets. "Don't worry, I'll take care of this. You'll stay home from school for the rest of this week and I'll talk to Headmistress Smalley. I think, with a little pressure, I can get Smith-Hailey removed from his duties—"

"*Removed*?"

"It's not meant as a punishment. I just don't want him bothering you until after—" He broke off. "Until next week."

"But he's supposed to administer my field test tomorrow morning. It's the most important test of the whole year."

"Ami, honey, it's just a test," Bud soothed. "Maybe they can give you a different examiner. What about that Archivist guy, MacFarland? He can grade you, can't he?"

"That's not how it works." I stared at him, stunned. "Is this because I said we hooked up? Trust me, it's a non-issue. We didn't even kiss. Besides, he's on the faculty. He'd never be interested in—"

"He's only twenty."

I stopped. "What did you say?"

Bud shook his head. "Look, it's not important. This isn't about him. It's about you being safe. If Smalley gives you any grief over missing class, just tell her to call me. Elder Horowitz from the Council still owes me a favor. I'm sure he'd be willing—"

"That's not the point," I said, thoroughly confused. How did Bud know how old Jack was? For that matter, how did he know Jack's name? And why was he willing to tap one of our family's last Guardian allies just to keep me home from school? "Daddy, I can't miss my field test. Why are you freaking out so bad?"

"Because it's not safe."

"It's a *war*. They are, by definition, *unsafe*."

"That's not what I meant and you know it."

"Actually, Dad, I have no idea what you mean."

The rain had started up again outside, branches scraping against the windows in an uneven rhythm. A crack of lightning sounded in the distance and the lights flickered, but Bud stayed silent. The set of his mouth hardened and I could tell I wasn't going to get anywhere with this line of defense.

"All right," I breathed, a new plan brewing. "Give me tomorrow morning. Just let me take my test, that's all I ask. Then, I'll come straight home and stay put until you tell me I can go back."

"Amelie, it's too—"

"Dangerous, I know," I filled in dismissively. "What if I make chocolate mousse cake? And clean up all the branches from the storm? I'll even wash your car. All I ask in return is to take my test."

Bud glared across the table, stony-faced. "No."

"Daddy, come on. Don't you remember when you were my age? How crucial rankings were?"

He frowned. "It's that important to you?"

"You have no idea," I said. "If I don't take my test, I'll never get ranked, and I'll never bond. Is that what you want? A desperate daughter trolling the streets, hunting demons *alone* because no Watcher is willing to fight by her side?"

He sighed and swore under his breath. "I'm not going to talk you out of this, am I?"

"Not a chance," I said. "Please? I'll do anything."

I met his eyes in silence as he drummed his fingers on the wooden table. I was about to re-initiate the begging when, like a good, loving father, Bud picked up his fork and pointed it at my face.

"*One* day. Against my better judgment, I'll give you *one day*, but that's it. When I get back from Baton Rouge on Wednesday morning, I want you locked in this house until that boy is gone. Do you understand me?"

"Yes! Thank you!"

I planted a kiss on his cheek and hurried out of the room before he could change his mind. Wednesday morning…that gave me thirty-six hours to ace my field exam, figure out what Jack was hiding, and prove I wasn't the useless, selfish brat he thought I was. Not too difficult.

Thank goodness I work well on a deadline.

Chapter Nine:
Lessons and Nightmares

"Do you need to stop by your locker before first period?" Lisa asked as we pulled up to school the next morning. "I don't want to be late for Meeks' Theories class. He's assigning lab partners today, and if I get stuck with Zeke Abbott again I'm going to hurl."

"Would this be the same Zeke Abbott you want me to ask to the dance?"

She rolled her eyes. "Don't start, Amelie. Let's just be on time."

"You go ahead," I told her. "I have to deliver something to Smalley first. Save me a seat?"

"Of course." Lisa blew a kiss as she hurried off to lab, and I hustled toward the main offices.

It looked like a normal weekday morning. Students wandered the halls. Ty Webster bugged the cheerleaders. Zeke and Paul hid behind a bush chugging something out of a paper bag. Keller Eastman pledged undying devotion to some random sophomore whose name he probably couldn't recall.

Despite all the familiar hoopla, I couldn't shake the feeling that something was off. *Way* off. The sun was too bright, the shadows too long. I felt like someone had poured a bottle marked "drink me" in my mouth and shoved me down a rabbit hole.

Last night's little father-daughter bonding session had ended with Dad retreating into his office while I prowled the Internet for "clues." I periodically heard swearwords from behind Bud's door (which I won't repeat) followed by a few angry messages to Smalley's voicemail. Finally, it vanished into a deep, yogic chant that meant he was probably meditating in the shape of a pretzel.

I still had my binoculars trained on the vampmobile across the street when Bud finally went to bed.

As I banged on Smalley's office door, my hand tightened around the note he'd handed me at breakfast. The—wait for it— *twenty page* note stuffed in a manila envelope and sealed with wax, lest anyone wonder where I get my paranoia.

"Yes?" Smalley called.

I pushed open the door and peeked my head in.

Despite the four-zillion disciplinary lectures I'd heard in this room, the sight of it never failed to set me at ease. Giant carved bookshelves were set against two of the walls, the other two framed by ornate vaulted windows with cream-colored silk curtains. Even the painting of archangel Michael (covered in the blood of the infidels, of course) was comforting.

Smalley stood behind her massive desk, hands flattened on the desk blotter, her skin flushed as if she'd run a race. "Amelie, dear, this isn't the best time—"

"Nonsense!" A booming voice cut her off. "Come in, come in."

The owner of the voice stood, a puff of cigarette smoke encircling his head. He couldn't have been more than forty, though something about him seemed to command a respect that usually accompanied an AARP card. He was handsome, with thick brown hair grayed at the temples and liquid-brown eyes. His charcoal suit was tailored and pressed, obviously expensive, and his hands were slim and artistic like a pianist's. But what drew my attention were his legs.

Even under the dress pants, I could see how bent and knobby they were, one knee so hyper-extended I thought it might snap at any moment. He held a wooden cane with a carved ivory handle that he used to hobble forward.

"Amelie, this is Chancellor Thibault," Smalley said briskly. "Robert, you remember Amelie Bennett, Charlotte's daughter."

"Of course." He smiled tightly. "She takes after her father."

"Uh, I guess," I said, unsure how to respond. Bud's reputation was too far down the toilet for it to be a compliment.

The Chancellor looked thinner than he had in the picture with Alec, yet more distinguished. It took a decent amount of effort not to stare at his legs, unstable as they were. Despite his imposing presence, every time he moved I wanted to reach a hand out in case he took a nosedive to the ground.

He flicked the tip of his cigarette against a dish on Smalley's desk, bits of ash scattering onto the smooth wood surface. "Well, my dear, your performance made quite an impression on my son yesterday. I could hardly keep him quiet at dinner last night."

"I'm sorry about that."

"Please." He waved my apology away. "That's why we're here, yes? To end this demon blight on humanity?"

"Uh, yes sir." My eyes flicked to Smalley. Chancellor Thibault obviously hadn't heard the full version of yesterday's little kerfuffle, otherwise he'd have known my "performance" was *far* from appreciated.

"The High Council is always interested to hear of new talent," he continued blithely. "What are your plans after graduation? Teaching? Politics? Perhaps I could recommend you."

"Uh—"

For some unknown reason, I kept looking at Smalley. Something about the man niggled at my brain like pieces of a dream I couldn't recall.

"When the time is right, Amelie will enter the Enforcement Guild with her bondmate. She won't need any help from the Council." The headmistress turned to me with a tense smile. "Now then…did you need something, dear?"

"Yes, ma'am." My fingers tightened around the envelope in my hand. "This is from my father. It's about…the report yesterday. He said it's self-explanatory."

"Then I expect it is." She stuffed the note into a desk drawer. "Anything else?"

"Nope, that's all."

With a mix of fear and relief, I beat a hasty retreat toward the door. I'd almost reached the hallway when Smalley's voice stopped me.

"Amelie, one more thing," she said. "*Fides via vi, in infinitum.*"

"Excuse me?"

She smiled. "Don't forget. And good luck on your test."

I blinked, suddenly nervous. With all the weirdness of meeting the Chancellor, I'd almost forgotten my test. I *wanted* to forget my test, especially now. It may sound like tea-bag superstition but in a school like ours, folks didn't usually mess around with ancient languages unless it involved the Crossworld. I had no idea why Smalley would throw one at me this morning.

"Thank you, ma'am," I said, backing toward the hall. There wasn't time to worry about it now. If I hadn't figured it out by lunchtime, Henry could help me look it up.

. . .

By the time I got to class, my heart had quit doing the pile-driver thing, but my stomach still felt like a toilet stuck on perma-flush.

Lisa wasted no time in pointing out the encrusted cinnamon sugar on my chin and commenting that my hair resembled, and I quote, "a mouse habitat." Alarming, since I'd made a special effort to blow it dry that morning. I wiped off my face and laced my tangled mouse-house into a quick French braid.

At the front of the class, Professor Meeks stood behind a long, black-topped table identical to the ones where we sat. Despite its weird Frankenstein vibe, I liked the Demonology lab. With all the jars of pickled bat wings and formaldehyde-soaked sheep's brains, the place held a delightfully creepy feel that always gave me the urge to cackle.

"Hey," Lisa whispered as I took my seat next to her. "Your test is this period, right?"

"That's the rumor."

"Skye said Smith-Hailey's in a foul mood this morning. Whatever you do, don't mention werewolves."

"Werewolves?"

"Yeah. Or vampires."

Unsure what to say to that, I shifted my attention to the front of the room. Meeks had started waving a dry erase marker and yammering incoherently. Something about time paradoxes, folds in the space continuum, and speculations as to why non-demonic beings had such trouble with inter-dimensional portal travel. According to his math, it required more than four hundred rohms of Crossworld power to successfully shield someone from demonic exposure through a jump—more power than most bonded pairs could manage. The few times it had been tried, most of the Channelers wound up dead, and the Watchers came back acting like grilled-cheese sandwiches. Not great for morale.

"Of course," Meeks said, "there are exceptions to every rule. In a few cases, portal jumps have been made with stunning success, which is why every bonded Channeler must have a portal locus code to a safe exit point." He lifted his marker to where I sat. "In fact, we have with us the daughter of one of the most successful portal jumpers in history. Did you know that, Miss Bennett?"

I hadn't, but it figured.

"It was before your time, of course, before all that nasty business with…" His voice trailed off. "Never mind."

I tried to listen as he progressed through a brief, yet thoroughly confusing lecture on the biomechanics of cross-dimensional energy transfer and the rohm conversion effect of greater demon blood. Snore. Within minutes, I found myself spacing out on a squirmy tank of demon-hybrid gerbils at the front of the room. The wards around the cage were similar to the ones I'd erected on my house last night, except these were designed to keep the monsters *in*.

While we're on the topic, I still hadn't figured out why Inferni were staking out my house. The vamp-mobile had vanished at some point during the wee hours, replaced by a huge pickup truck I could only assume belonged to a werewolf. Or a Republican from north Louisiana—hard to tell the difference. Their presence left me unsettled. Unfortunately, so long as they didn't break the law, there wasn't much I could do about it.

Halfway through his lecture, Meeks ambled to the locked cabinet and drew out a potted plant—the same houseplant he'd been carrying at assembly yesterday morning. He stroked it lovingly.

"I'd like you all to meet Balthazar. You may recognize him as the species *begonia coccinae*, or Angel-Wing Begonia, but I assure you Balthazar is no ordinary plant." Meeks set the plastic pot down on the lab table. "Since the day he was seeded, Balfie has been watered with an increasing concentration of greater demon blood—enough to protect him from the usual degradation of Crossworld travel, but not so much that he'd revert to a demonic existence. Can anybody guess why we would do this?"

The scratch of Lisa's pencil was the only sound over the air conditioner. Most of us were probably too busy wondering where Meeks got the blood of a demon lord to bother taking notes. It's not exactly something you pick up at the local drugstore.

"Does it have to do with portal travel?" Matt asked finally.

"Very good, Mr. Marino. Balthazar is, indeed, the first mortal life form to travel, unshielded, through a Crossworld portal and emerge, still flowering." Meeks went on to explain how, because of the natural shielding effect of greater demon blood, the total power draw of Balfie's jump was low enough for any mortal life form to manage.

"Have you tried it with anything sentient?" Alec followed my gaze to the gerbil tank. "Something simple-minded and morally vacuous? A hamster, perhaps? Maybe Veronica?"

"Excuse me!" Veronica griped from the back table.

"Those are gerbils, Mr. Charbonnet, not hamsters. And I'd thank you to minimize the insulting commentary."

"My apologies, sir." Alec nodded. "The gerbil is a noble beast. I shouldn't have compared it to Veronica."

The class erupted into sniggers as Veronica flushed an attractive shade of pink.

"It's not a bad idea," Katie said. "If greater demon blood works on begonias maybe it could work on something bigger." She paused. "Like one of us."

Immediately, the class exploded into discussion—the ethical implications of a demon-infected Guardian, speculations as to whether it would render them unbondable. I think even Lisa stopped taking notes after a while.

Meeks's cheeks had turned an annoyed shade of red, verging perilously close to eggplant. He slapped his palm down on the table. "People, settle down. We are men and women of high morals. We do not demonize the innocent."

"What if we're not innocent?" Alec winked at Katie.

Lisa smacked him on the head with her notebook.

Katie giggled and Meeks gave a weary sigh. "Mr. Charbonnet, please report to Headmistress Smalley's office."

Laughter rippled through the classroom while Alec, still with his slightly bored smirk, stood and slung his messenger bag over one shoulder. As I watched him go, I couldn't help thinking it had taken *me* a whole month at St. Michael's before I got sent to Smalley's office. Maybe I wasn't the craziest one in our school after all. The thought was oddly comforting.

"Hey, Ami?" Amidst the chaos, Lyle scooted his stool across

the aisle next to me. "Can I talk to you? It's kind of important."

"In a sec. I want to hear the gerbil thing."

He frowned. "Who cares about that? Screw the gerbils."

"Screw them?" I raised an eyebrow. "Lyle, this is not your personal recreation time."

With a sigh, Meeks picked up Balthazar from the lab table, muttered something about scruples, and headed for the back door. He'd made it halfway there when I realized someone else had already come through it.

My heart gave a twitch.

Jack slouched against the doorframe, one hand tucked into his pocket, the other lightly balancing a clipboard. His face held a mixture of exasperation and dismay—not a happy combo, but one I was rapidly becoming familiar with.

Meeks said something to him that made, if possible, his frown deepen. Then Jack nodded at me.

"Amelie Bennett," he said. "You're up."

I tried not to smile. Even after hearing him lecture me like a toddler yesterday, his voice still made me all melty inside. Whatever clichés exist about girls liking guys in power, I tell you, they exist for a reason.

"Jeez," Lisa whispered. "I didn't even hear him come in. Is he like a ninja, or something?"

"Or something," I said. "See you in a few."

"Good luck!"

I tucked my schoolbooks into my backpack and hoisted it onto one shoulder. As soon as the door clicked shut behind us, my body relaxed. I'd missed him.

"You're almost late," I noted.

"I'm on time."

"Same thing." I followed him down the hall, doubling my pace to keep up. "So, my dad hates you, did you know that? He almost didn't let me come to school today."

"What a shame that would have been," he muttered, loping off toward the faculty parking lot at a speed my legs had trouble matching.

Normally, students drove themselves to the test site, but since Katie didn't have her license and Lisa wasn't dumb enough to let me borrow the Prius, Jack would be my chauffeur for the day. Amped as I felt at being in a car with him, my excitement turned to horror when I saw the rust-covered scrap heap he approached. It looked like a lump of white Play-Doh that had been rolled in mud, then fashioned into a car by a three-year-old.

"What is this?" I asked.

"What does it look like?" Jack yanked at the passenger door but it didn't budge. He pulled harder, and the handle came off in his palm.

"It looks like my grandma's old VW Rabbit after the Berlin Wall fell on it. Twice."

I watched him reach through the open window to pop it from the inside. The door gave a screeching howl of pain as it fell open, revealing ripped upholstery and—no kidding—rust holes in the floor so big you could see the pavement below.

"Is it roadworthy?"

"Yes, it's *roadworthy*."

I eyed the thing with uncertainty. "Are you sure?"

"Get in the car, Miss Bennett."

I squinted up at Jack. "So, where are your glasses today? Can you even see enough to drive? How many fingers am I holding up?"

Jack heaved an exasperated sigh. "Just get in the car."

The morning clouds had cleared by the time we pulled up to a pale blue, Empire-style house. Yellow sunbeams stretched lazily above the line of trees, promising a scorcher of a day. My palms still felt sweaty, but I knew it wasn't from the heat. Much as I liked to cop an attitude about school, the truth was some things actually *were* important to me. This test was one of them.

Goosebumps rose along my arms as I studied the place.

It definitely looked like a house that could be haunted, even by the most conservative New Orleans standards. Cobwebs draped in languid strands across the corners of the window frames, and the front staircase shed paint chips like a dog with dandruff. Palm fronds and fleur-de-lis were etched with handmade precision into the ironwork, details rivaling any of the old mansions on St. Charles. Still, something about the sag of the gallery left me with a tight seed of nervousness in my belly. The whole thing looked like it might tumble down at the slightest sneeze. Wrought iron lanterns hung on either side of the front door, one with its bulb blown out and the other dangling at an odd angle. Vines had grown up along the lower half of the hardwood siding, and some of the planks had started to rot under the growth. Whoever was in charge of maintenance and repair had some serious explaining to do.

"Charming," I commented as Jack's engine sputtered to halt. "Is this where you take all your dates?"

He ignored me. Understandably.

"Your task is to locate the demonic manifestation inside the house, open a portal, send the creature back to the Crossworld, and close the portal without incurring any damage to the house. You're permitted to use me as an energy repository, though you will lose points if that energy output exceeds fifty rohms. You have thirty minutes," he said with a glance at his watch. "Starting now."

I took a deep breath as Jack trailed me to the front door, clipboard in hand. "It's locked," I observed, my thumb *thwapping* the handle. "What am I supposed to do?"

He jotted down some notes on his clipboard. "Maybe you should give up and go home. One little homicidal demon wandering the human world won't make a difference."

I glared at him. "Matt said he got a pep talk at his test. I don't rate a pep talk?"

"You want a pep talk?" He made a fist with one hand, then punched it through the air in a victorious motion. "Go get 'em. You've got twenty-eight minutes."

"Dude, do *not* join the pep squad." I crouched by the door and peered at the lock. It looked like a basic security set-up, no visible demonic booby-traps…not that I'd know what those looked like.

It took me a few seconds to blow the dust away and draw an opening glyph on the lock. My finger-strokes hissed as the shape flared and sank into the metal surface. I placed one hand over the symbol and spoke, "*Abertura.*"

With a *click*, the door fell open.

Cool air seeped out from the foyer, carrying with it the inevitable musty odor of last night's rainstorm. Jack must have administered at least ten tests so far, though I was betting none of them had been here. The dank taste of mold collected at the back of my throat as I watched cockroaches scurry for cover.

"Home, disgusting home," I mumbled.

My Guardian spidey-sense tingled as it led me up the stairs toward what looked like a teenager's messy bedroom. It would probably be a Chelax demon. FYI, teenagers and Chelax demons go together like bread and butter, sugar and spice, movies and popcorn, pizza and… What goes with pizza?

Eh, never mind.

I touched the door lightly, the creaky hinge inching open. For all the atmospheric build up of the house, I had to admit I was disappointed. There were no pentagrams, no animal sacrifices, no voodoo talismans. It just looked like a boring, old room. We'd been told to expect the unexpected for our tests, but this wasn't quite what I'd had in mind.

Semi-rumpled piles of dark laundry were folded at the foot of the bed, a couple of teenage romance novels scattered around. Other than that, it was completely empty. No orb, no vortex, no giant mess at the hand of the angry demon. The only disruption I could make out was a quivery black mass in the corner about the size of an overweight Labrador.

I regarded the demon, only vaguely aware of Jack's silent presence behind me. "Why is it acting like a spanked puppy?"

"I don't know. Perhaps you should ask it?"

I frowned at him. "Isn't sarcasm the opiate of the masses?"

"You're thinking of religion," he replied. "Sarcasm is the Xanax of the morally bereft."

With my index finger, I sketched the requisite four binding wards (North, South, East, and West) to make sure nothing snuck through from the other side.

"I have a theory on why you never got bonded," I said. "I think you ridiculed all your potential bondmates until their self-esteem imploded. Then, when it came time to list prefs, no girl could write your name without bursting into tears. Am I close?"

He tucked the clipboard against his chest. "What makes you think I'm not bonded?"

"Are you?" I asked, looking around innocently. "Where was she yesterday? Why isn't she helping you with this Graymason thing? Enforcement *never* breaks up bonded pairs," I pointed out ultra-reasonably. "That would be suicide."

"Maybe she's dead," he said, his face perfectly blank.

I shot him a skeptical look as the glow of the wards intensified. "Nice try, but I don't think so. You've seen those guys. They're like shells, or something. You don't feel like that to me."

Electricity crackled up my arms, and the skin between my fingers began to pink as I called open the Crossworld channel. I had no idea why everything was going so seamlessly. Maybe it was the mold count in the house or the last gasp of summer ragweed. With school starting and the whole business with the incident report last night, this was the second day in a row Bud had forgotten my allergy meds.

I began the portal incantation, "*Caret initio et—*"

"Include translation, please."

"Seriously? Am I five years old?"

He made a few notes but said nothing. Smug bastard.

"Fine." I cracked my knuckles and wiggled my fingers theatrically. "*Caret initio et fine.* There is no beginning and no end. *Ab initio, ad patres.* From birth unto death. *Deficit omne quod nasciture.* Everything that is born returns."

In an icy hot rush, energy shot out of my fingers into a wide arc in front of me. The air between the wards began to ripple as if someone had painted the scene on a bed sheet and given it a rough shake. A sound like ripping silk echoed through the room and, when I glanced up, the portal had opened. Disaster free.

Hah! I felt a nugget of pride bloom in my chest. *Take that, Jackson Smith-Hailey!*

The pride might have lasted more than a nanosecond if I hadn't caught Jack jotting what looked like a frowny-face at the top of his clipboard. Annoyed once more, I turned my attention to the center of the room.

Looking into a Crossworld portal is a little like looking in a mirror, only it's made of thickened energy instead of silvered glass. I managed to hold it open with one hand while the other scrawled an immobilization glyph over the Chelax demon. Not that the poor thing needed it. His eyes were so wide with fear he looked like a harsh word might convince him to hurl *himself* into the portal.

Tendrils of oily dust whipped about the room, then curled back in wild, chaotic arcs. "Something's wrong," I noted. "This doesn't feel right."

Jack gave me a dismissive touch on the shoulder, drawing the last shreds of darkness out of my head. At the same time, little spurts of golden light flashed over my skin. "Try not to think about it," he said. "A job well begun is half done."

"Thank you, Mary Poppins."

I tried to focus on my breath and not on the deafening sirens in my head as the demon tumbled into the portal. I was about to turn toward Jack for approval when the world…shut off.

Seriously.

Whatever platitudes he was about to spout were lost under

a curtain of thick, black silence. And when I say "black" and "silent," I don't mean "kind of dim" and "naptime quiet." It was as if someone had dropped one of those heavy, fireproof blankets the EMTs use in emergencies over the entire building. It shut out *everything*. Light, street noise, air, even the sounds of birds and crickets vanished. The result was something so oppressively empty it felt deafening.

"Okay, what just happened?" I whispered, certain that anything louder than a whisper would shatter my eardrums. I was wrong. Even if I had screamed, the words wouldn't have made it more than a few inches in front of my face. They disappeared as I said them, sucked into oblivion.

Jack's hand still rested at my shoulder. He tightened it now. "Don't move," he said.

The cadence of his voice suggested yelling though I could barely hear him. His arms threaded snugly around me, tugging me against the firm lines of his chest.

"What's going on?" I said louder.

"Don't let go of me."

"Wasn't planning on it."

His lips must have been just a few inches away from my ear, but I swear, it sounded as if he was whispering from the end zone of a football field. All noise seemed to evaporate like an early morning fog. With both hands tight around my waist, he started moving toward the place where I remembered the door having been. Maybe. Frankly, I couldn't tell squat given the sensory deprivation tank the room had become. Jack, thankfully, could. When we'd reached the doorframe, he freed one hand, groping at the wall in search of a doorknob.

With sight and sound gone, the rest of my senses seemed to sharpen into hyper-focus. Jack's touch was velvet on my arms and he smelled amazing—like shampoo and marshmallows and something uniquely musky. Sunshine, if sunshine had a smell. *Sigh, I could die happy now.*

Wait, not literally.

Watcher, you are a traitor to the Guardian line. Surrender now, and the girl won't be harmed.

It was odd how the words seemed to appear in my head, deep and scratchy, like sandpaper. I tiptoed up until my lips brushed Jack's earlobe. "What is that?"

Jack's entire abdominal wall tensed as he shouted back, "*Ant hill.*"

Except he said "ant hill" the way most people said "certain death" or "gushing bloodbath." Which is why it took me a minute to get that he wasn't saying "ant hill" at all.

Anakim. The Gray One?

"Seriously?" I asked, trying not to freak out.

"No escape," he yelled. "It's okay. Tell Smalley…perceptual vortex. Warded perimeter."

It's okay? No, it was definitely not okay! I knew about warded perimeters. We'd studied them junior year so we could understand how the one around our school worked. I'd even drawn a few simple ones myself around my house. But unlike my or St. Michael's wards, this one wasn't letting *anything* through. Not nature or light or sound. Nothing. There would be no call for help, no signal to the outside. If a Graymason was holding it, I probably couldn't even channel an energy burst. The only reason Jack and I could sense one another at all was because we'd been touching when the barriers went up. Now, I understood why he'd said not to let go of him. If we lost physical contact for even a second, I'd never find him again.

The choice is yours, Son of Gabriel. Surrender, and she goes free, the voice repeated. *Fight, and she dies with you.*

"Is this part of the test?" I shouted.

I felt Jack shake his head. "Thought you…Gray One…kill me… Not enough time." He sighed. "Gotta go."

"*Go*? With him? Are you deranged?" I yelled, genuinely curious.

Clumps of hair fell into my eyes but I blinked them away blindly. I was too afraid to loosen my hold for even the second it took to brush them back. If this was the end, I couldn't think of anyplace I'd rather be than in his arms. Lame, I know, but totally true.

My mind flipped through the possibilities for escape. Weapons? None. Emergency beacons? Not likely.

This sucked! I was going to die, and I'd never even been to the beach. Or bowling. Crap, I hadn't done anything cool!

Panic gripped my heart as Jack's arms loosened around me, the tips of his fingers sliding up to cup my face.

I clung to him like a barnacle. Granted, we'd had our issues, but if he thought he could push me away *now* he had another think coming. Not until I felt something brush my lips did I understand.

He wasn't pushing me away.

Last summer, when Lyle tried to kiss me, it was like kissing an impatient guppy. Clumsy, greedy, and so, *so* messy. This was none of those things.

It started as a whisper, no more substantial than butterfly

wings. At first, I didn't know how to answer. Then, I realized it didn't matter. My body knew.

My arms moved up his chest and twined around his neck like vines reaching toward the sun, my lips parting for him. For a second, he froze, and I worried he might pull away. But then his body flexed against mine, his mouth warm and insistent. Suddenly, the kiss stopped being soft and turned hungry. His hands knotted into my hair, pulling me into him like he could consume me. His heart fluttered madly against my chest. Or maybe it was my heart, I couldn't tell. All I could sense was his body next to mine, and all I could think was…*yes*.

By the time he pulled away, I felt like I'd been spun in circles and pushed blindfolded down an elevator shaft. Only it wasn't unpleasant. Because, as empty as the world had become, I found myself seized with irrational fullness. Hope. Faith, even. It would be okay. *We* would be okay.

I had a plan.

Jack was right about one thing: there wasn't enough time for binding wards or rescue attempts. *But there might be enough time to save us.*

Last chance, the voice rasped softly inside my head. *Surrender, or die.*

My hands tightened around Jack's waist. "Don't let go of me."

"Ami, I have to—"

"*Caret initio et fine, ab initio, ad patres.*" I began the incantation. The portal flared its answer, weak and hollow, as if it, too, had been sucked dry by the vortex. "*Deficit omne quod nasciture.*"

As soon as he sensed the channel, Jack lurched away from me. I could feel him trying to pry my grip loose, desperate to stop it.

"*Inergio.*" I pushed harder at the spell.

Although I couldn't see it, I knew the portal was there. It throbbed with silent power. I mumbled one last prayer that I had enough strength to protect him, and said the words that Smalley had given me—the words that would change everything.

"*Fides via vi, in infinitum.*"

With a crack and a whoosh, the world ripped in half, and Jack and I pitched forward. Into nothingness.

Chapter Ten:
While You Were Sleeping

"Miss Bennett, wake up."

Two rough hands hefted my torso and I felt a tug at the base of my spine. At first, I thought I must be having some strange dream, but I couldn't quite hang onto the details. Something about a Graymason, and a boy, and a *totally* epic kiss...

Mmm...kiss. I felt my lips curve into a smile.

Somewhere in the back of my head, a slow, mechanical beep picked up pace. Yes, a kiss. A spine-tingling, toe-curling, life-changing kiss. With Jack.

Images slipped through my mind like water, but the feel of him, all warm and hungry and sweet against my mouth...*that* I recalled vividly. What an awesome dream. I was about to roll over and return to it when something pungent invaded my senses, like acid up my nose.

"Gak!" I screeched.

A hand slapped over my mouth as my eyes flew open. It took a second to realize the reason I couldn't see was because I was blindfolded, and the reason the bed didn't feel like mine was because it wasn't.

"*Whtthfrknghllzzgngnnhrr?*"

"Great, you're awake."

Daggers of purple fluorescent light stabbed into my retinas as Jack yanked the blindfold over my head. One of his hands stayed clamped over my mouth, while the other ripped medical tape and IV needles off my arms.

"Sorry about the smelling salts, but I needed to talk to you. Nod if you understand."

After a few confused blinks, I nodded.

"Good. Do you know who I am?"

I rolled my eyes and nodded again.

"Okay, I need you to be very quiet, stay still, and do exactly as I say. Can you do that?"

"*Ryuukddng? Wtthhlllddyuddttmeh?*"

"I didn't do anything to you," he said defensively. "You're being held prisoner in St. Michael's infirmary. The reason you can't move is because you're in restraints—"

As soon as he said the word "restraints," a current of fury zipped through me. I tried to lift my arms but leather straps tightened against my wrists like baby anacondas.

"*Rruufrkkngnsn?*" I yelled into Jack's hand, which was still glued to my mouth.

He sighed. "What did I just say?"

I flashed him my nastiest look but quit struggling.

"Thank you. Now, I removed the spinal block they had on you, so you should be able to feel your legs again in a minute. It'll take longer for the anesthetic to get out of your system, but I'm not worried about that. What I *am* worried about is the huge dose of Otrava they gave you. It's a poison and I need to get it neutralized before I can take you anywhere. Do you understand?"

I strained silently against the leather straps. Apparently, I was in no position to argue.

Jack reached into the breast pocket of his trench coat that, if we're being honest, looked like a *Spies R Us* clearance rack item, and pulled out a black leather pouch with a zipper. I watched as he unzipped it with one hand and extracted the longest, most sinister looking syringe I'd ever seen.

"I'm going to take my hand off your mouth. If you start to yell again, I *will* sedate you. Got it?"

I hesitated. The dream-that-wasn't-a-dream still hovered in the back of my head with at least a thousand questions clinging to it.

"*Ddyukssmmh*?" I asked, carefully.

He frowned. "I prefer to believe you kissed me. If you'd like to apologize I'm happy to hear you out."

"*Pllogze*? *Whttfrr?*"

"I don't know. Drooling?"

"*Gscrwyrrsllf*," I said into his palm.

Jack gave me a warning look before he lifted his hand away. Unfortunately, my head was in way too much of a whirl to take warnings. Yelling seemed the best option.

"Have you completely lost your mind? What did you put in my mouth? It tastes like," I smacked my lips to get some saliva flowing, "fabric softener. And why am I so hungry? And how *dare* you imply *I* kissed *you*? Now you've tied me up and drugged me? My dad is so gonna *kckyrrrasswhnhehrrs*—"

Jack's hand came down over my face again.

"Obviously, there were aspects of your field test that didn't go as planned," he admitted in a hushed voice. "I'm making an effort to move past it. I suggest you do the same."

"*Unnthkklbstrd!*"

He glared at me. "Once we're out of here, you're welcome to file an ethics grievance with my superiors. Just remember, *I* didn't tie you up, nor did I drug you. Your mouth tastes like fabric softener because the Elders gagged you in case you woke up during the trial. And you're hungry because it's Wednesday. They didn't bother to feed you since they were planning to kill you. Now," Jack paused, his eyes stern as he gazed into mine, "are you finished?"

Planning to kill you. The words stuck in my head like rubber cement.

Suddenly, the walls around me seemed to loom a bit taller, the locks on the doors a bit thicker. When his hand came off my mouth this time, I hesitated. This was bad. Not flat-soda-on-an-airplane bad. I mean, *nuclear winter* bad. Call me a romantic, but whenever I'd imagined myself in a bed with Jack there weren't usually arm restraints and death threats involved.

I shot him a sharp glare, a challenge while wearing Curious George underpants and a puke-colored hospital gown.

"Not that I condone any part of this, but what are you talking about? Who's on trial? And who wants to kill me?" I squinted at him. "Are you in some kind of trouble?"

Jack quit flicking the syringe long enough to give me a dubious look. "You're tied to a bed, half-paralyzed, with deadly poison coursing through your veins…and you're wondering if *I'm* in trouble?"

"You are, aren't you?"

"Well, yes," he conceded. "But not as much as you are. Hold still, this may hurt."

I bit down on my lip as he slid the needle through the tender skin of my forearm, pulling it back until it was securely lodged in the vein. Then, he depressed the plunger.

Instantly, my arm filled with liquid fire. It felt like someone had funneled a gazillion volts of electricity right into my eyeballs via every nerve ending in my body. I swallowed a scream as he pulled the needle out and slapped his hand back over my mouth.

"Shh," he said. "This is called a Queller. It's a metabolic agent for the poison. I know it hurts a little, but you'll be fine."

Hurts a little? I was dying, I had to be. There was no way anything so painful could *not* end in death. I heard muffled screams coming from somewhere in the room, and it took a moment to realize they were mine.

You never really know how you're going to deal with pain until you're in the thick of it. It isn't like the movies where the hero gets trounced then comes back to fight again, pissed off and energized. It was debilitating. Crippling. My body convulsed on the bed, the leather straps around my wrists and ankles rubbing raw welts against my skin.

"Breathe," he repeated as he stroked my hair with his free hand. "Just breathe."

Much as I hated him at that moment, I'd be lying if I said his presence didn't help. Every touch of his fingers filled my mind with texture and color, lifting me out of the pain for a fraction of a second at a time. Sparks skated over my skin, the same golden light that had danced between us Monday morning. Only, this time, it didn't scare me. It floated over me like a transparent armor, absorbing all the darkness as effectively as a sponge in water.

When the torture finally subsided, Jack pushed my sweaty hair back and stared at my eyes. He was trying to look calm, but his trembling hands told me he wasn't.

"That's not so bad, is it?"

I sank back on the pillow, drained but relieved. It *was* bad. Worse than the time I broke my arm falling off Smalley's balcony in second grade, and way worse than the time Matt dared me to eat a worm pie and I spent two hours hurling. I had just opened my mouth to say so when a soft *click* sounded at the infirmary door. The deadbolt slid to the side and Marcus stuck his head through. Normally, when a trainer walks into a room, I might say hello or, if I was busy, I'd ignore him. What I *wouldn't* do is whip a gun out of my Kevlar overcoat and point it at his head.

That's what Jack did.

My breath caught as a soft *shink* rang out and Marcus crumpled to the floor with a thud. The *beep-beep-beep* of my heart monitor went wild.

"Calm down, he's not dead," Jack said. "Just tranquilized."

He set down his gun long enough to unfasten my restraints. Maybe it was the drugs, but his hands seemed to leave shiny streaks on my calves as he swung my legs to the side of the bed and helped me get vertical. At least, I think I was vertical. Hard to tell when the room kept flipping over.

"I don't mean to rush you, but, in a few minutes, this place is going to be crawling with guards, and I'm almost out of tranquilizer darts. Can you walk?"

I wanted to answer him, but my eyes refused to move from the crumpled heap of guy by the door. Marcus looked dead. His body was folded like a napkin, his head lolled forward at an awkward angle. Obviously, I hadn't read the handbook too carefully, but I didn't think murdering the trainers was allowed.

"Miss Bennett!" Jack snapped his fingers in front of my face. "Can you walk or do I need to carry you?"

I stared at him blankly, a hollow ringing in my ears. My muscles felt rigid and uncooperative. Cold antiseptic air still burned my nose and everything in my gut screamed at me to run. But I couldn't. I couldn't move. Somewhere in the back of my head, I knew that if I started running, I would never stop.

"I'll carry you."

"No!" I snapped, glancing past him at the door. "I'm fine. Let's go."

That was all Jack needed. Without further delay, he took my hand and half-dragged, half-carried me toward the main building. It was odd creeping through the halls in such utter silence. The classroom doors hung open. Even the lockers had a ghostly, abandoned feel. Clearly, Jack had done something to the lights, and it troubled me how unfazed he seemed that we kept stepping over the bodies of fallen guards. I stumbled, but he caught me.

"You okay?"

In silence, I looked at the gun in his hand, then down at a guard with blood trickling out of his ear. I wasn't okay. "What did you do to these guys?"

"I did what I had to."

"But why did you have to do anything?" I felt dizzy and oddly light-headed. "You're not going to hurt me, are you?"

"Only if you annoy me. Now stay back."

I let him tug me against the wall, his hand huge and calloused around mine. As scared as I was, I knew I'd be dead without him. I just didn't know why.

"We have to get out of the main hallways. It won't be long before they figure out we're gone."

"Jack, what is this about? Did that vamp girl rat me out for the Rangor?"

He frowned. "The who for what?"

"Okay, so not that," I said. "You want to give me a hint?"

He whipped his head around to peek through the door to a stairwell and, for a moment, I thought he wasn't going to answer. When he did, I wished he hadn't. "Miss Bennett, you've been convicted of multiple murders."

I stared at him, open-mouthed, certain I'd misheard him.

Without looking at me, he extended one arm across my torso, tucking me behind his body. "Don't look so surprised. There was a trial. The Elders heard the evidence. You've been sentenced to die at dawn."

I blinked as the hallway started to swim. Every clever quip faded on my lips. The wave of nausea hit so hard I could barely remember my name, let alone think of anything to say. Pinpricks of darkness flooded my peripheral vision and the floor began to buck.

"I think I'm going to throw up."

Instantly, he holstered his gun, looking both ways down the empty corridor. He caught me as I sank and pulled me across the hall into the girls' bathroom. I let him maneuver me through the dark room to the mirrors, my brain (and stomach) still processing what he'd said. Murder? *Multiple* murder? Was this some kind of sick joke?

"Okay, listen up." Jack set me on the counter like a ragdoll, his hand cool against my neck. "You know I'm with Enforcement, right?"

I nodded.

"And you know I was sent here because of the Graymason... the one who's been killing Watchers."

"I figured. But what does that—"

"Amelie...Miss Bennett." He shook his head. "I've been trying to think of a way to finesse this because I realize you have no idea. And I know it may confuse you but you're going to have to take my word for it."

"Take your word for what?"

He stared at me helplessly. "You're the Graymason."

Chapter Eleven:
Fight, Flight, and Revenge

There are many fabulous ways to kill a romance. For example, you could spend the whole night talking about your ex. Or you could comment repeatedly on your date's ability to utilize the all-you-can-eat feature of a buffet. Maybe you could finish up by detailing, ad nauseum, the price tag of each aspect of the date.

As effective as those tactics are, I have to say, *nothing* kills the snuggle urge quite like accusing your date of serial murder.

"*I'm* the Graymason?" I said.

"Yes."

My eyes narrowed. "Seriously? *That's* the vibe I give off? Bloodthirsty soul-sucker?"

"It's not a vibe," he said evenly. "It's what you are. That's why I've been so weird around you this week. *You're* Lucifer's bloodline. You always have been. If you wanted to kill me right now, you could do it." He took my hand and placed it against his chest. Threads of heat and light pulsed beneath my palm, gripping my arm like an eager child. "Go ahead. All it would take is a tug.

One little tug, and I'd be dead. You feel it, don't you?"

I ripped my hand away. The thought of killing him, even by accident, filled me with such terror I could hardly breathe. "H-How?"

With a sigh, he stepped back, hands still braced on either side of me. "We knew we didn't get them all. When the Gabrielites hunted them the first time, some of Lucifer's offspring survived. We figured the bloodlines went dormant. If they were breeding with humans, we'd have heard about it. Human blood mixed with angel blood is outlawed for good reason. Anyone who's read the Apocrypha knows that."

"The Apocry-what?"

He shook his head. "Never mind. We thought they might be mating with Guardians, we just didn't know who. Until the bloodline resurfaced. With you." He paused to let it sink in.

It didn't sink very far. "There must be some mistake. Does Dad know about this? Because he's going to throw a serious fit—"

"Bud knows. The only reason you aren't manifesting more power is because he's been giving you small doses of Otrava every day since your mother died. Your 'allergy medication.' It was part of the terms of his custody of you."

I blinked at him in uncomprehending silence. My own father had been poisoning me? For ten years?

"You were put under surveillance when Lutz's body turned up last week," Jack continued despite my silent wish that he would shut up. "The Elders wanted you in lock-up, but Smalley wouldn't allow it. She knew it wasn't you doing this. That's why she called me in. She knew you'd never purposely use your abilities to—"

"What *abilities*?" I snapped, trying not to hyperventilate. "I can't even close a damn rift without blowing up half the school. I'm a complete basket case. Smalley knows. Ask her if you don't believe me—"

"I can't."

"Yes, you can. Call her. She'll tell you—"

"I *can't*," he repeated. "Smalley's dead."

And time stopped.

Silence buzzed through my head, louder than any silence should. I don't even think my heart was beating anymore.

"But...I just saw her. She was with Chancellor Thibault. She's—"

"Dead," he said with finality. "Her soul was taken, just like Lutz. It happened right after your test. Don't you remember?"

My test. I slumped against the wall as the details flooded back to me. The portal I had drawn, the vortex, the voice in my head. "*Graymason.*"

Jack nodded. "That locus code you used took us to her office. I drained as much power off you as I could, but I passed out in transit. The Anakim must have come through the portal after us. By the time I woke up, you were having some sort of seizure and she was dead. The Elders think you killed her, too."

"That's insane. I didn't—"

"It doesn't matter." Jack tightened his hands on my shoulders. I couldn't breathe, and my whole body shook in tiny, spastic quivers. "The Council had to convict you. You're their only suspect. As soon as you channeled us out of the test site they knew the Otrava wasn't working anymore. They figured if you channeled enough power to shield me *and* keep yourself alive, then you've become too dangerous to live. When Lisa testified you'd killed a demon—"

A picture of the Rangor demon popped into my head. "But…
we were protecting a vampire!"

"I know. She tried to explain. They wouldn't listen."

"What about you?" I demanded, my voice rising. "You were
there when the Graymason came—the *real* one. At my test.
Wouldn't they listen to you?"

"I didn't testify."

His words hit me like a slap in the face. "What do you mean,
you didn't testify?"

"I mean, High Elder Akira called for my testimony and I said
I had nothing to add." Jack ran a hand over his forehead. "Look,
can we do this later?"

I felt like all the air had been sucked out of my lungs. Jack
knew I was innocent, but he let them convict me anyway? Of
murder? My whole body shook at the betrayal. "This makes no
sense," I said. "Why wouldn't you tell them?"

He sighed. "It's complicated."

"What's complicated? Am I that much of a pain in the ass?
Do you really hate me so much—"

"Hate you? You think I *hate* you?"

"I know you do. You have since the day you got here." A few
angry tears rolled down my cheeks, alongside a trickle of snot.
I sniffed it up loudly. "Why didn't you just let me die Monday
morning? If I'm such a monster why'd you bother to save me?"

"Miss Bennett, please—"

"What, are you going to gag me again?" I dared him. "I *hate*
you. I hate you, I—"

With a sound of frustration, Jack swooped in close and
pressed his mouth to mine. At first, it was like he didn't even want

to kiss me, like some reflex or something. His lips were hard and unyielding, as effective a muzzle as his hand had been earlier. I wanted to struggle, to kick and punch like I'd learned in my defensive combat classes. But I couldn't. I couldn't do anything but cling to him.

A sound like rushing water drifted through my mind as his grip tightened on my shoulders. Around us, the air crystallized, thick and bright and hot, as my power began to merge with his. I forgot about the guards. I forgot about Smalley. I forgot about the guns and the trial and my impending death. All I wanted was him. Which is why I can't explain what happened next.

I wasn't even aware of my hand forming itself into a fist or of the fact that we were still kissing until my knuckles cracked against his jaw. He stumbled backward, clutching his face.

For a long moment he stared at me, silent. In the distance, doors slammed and boot soles pounded, the thud of death's approach. But all I heard was the blood in my ears.

"I'm sorry. That was—" Jack stopped, shaken. His forehead was beaded with sweat and his eyes were wide. "There's no excuse. I'm sorry. You had every right to hit me."

He levered himself away from me, my knuckles still aching from the impact. I'd punched guys before, plenty of times, but it usually happened during sparring drills. This was the first time I'd ever hit someone who was trying to make out with me. Ironic, since he was the only guy I'd ever actually wanted to make out with.

"It won't happen again, I swear." His eyes stayed glued to the floor as he spoke. "Look, for the record, I don't hate you. And I'm sorry things can't be different between us. But we have at least twenty minutes before the Otrava is dissipated enough for you to make a portal jump. In the interest of not dying, do you think we could maybe call a truce?"

My mouth opened and closed a few times. I wanted to say stupid stuff, like how I didn't mind if he wanted to kiss me again. In fact, I'd be up for almost anything he suggested so long as it didn't involve me getting killed. Unfortunately, I couldn't say that since my mouth refused to form complete sentences.

As if on cue, a rumble of footsteps rang out somewhere beyond the bathroom door. Instinctively, Jack spun so that his body was positioned between the threat and me. Before I could shriek or duck, he shoved me into a corner stall and ran out the door. I heard a few dull thuds and cracks, then he was back, a guard I didn't recognize slung over his shoulder. He dumped the man on the tile and returned for another one. By the time the third guard's body hit the ground, I was staring at him with freaked-out eyes.

"You have something to say?" he asked.

I shook my head, mouth clamped shut. The only things I had to say would far exceed my four-letter-word quota and probably wouldn't be very useful.

Lazy beams of moonlight spilled through the bathroom window, casting an incongruously gentle glow across his face. It was weird, like I could see two people inside him at once; one, a violent psychopath and the other, a guy so sweet and cool, I wanted to curl up in his arms and suck on his earlobe. Too bad I had no idea which one was real.

It took us a few minutes to get down the hallway to the middle school campus. I held my breath as he pushed me into the paper supply closet and pressed his ear against the door.

"Wait here. Someone's coming," he whispered, motioning me

back.

I crouched behind a stack of textbooks while Jack drew his sword. In one swift motion, he threw open the door and grabbed another stunned guard by his collar. The guard's head smacked against a box of staplers as he fell, releasing a perfumed cloud of... Drakkar Noir?

"Jack, wait!" I threw out a hand. "It's Lyle."

Jack halted the sword strike midair. "Who?"

The boy on the floor grunted and tried to push himself up. It took Jack a second before recognition registered.

"Mr. Purcell, what are you doing here?"

"What does it look like?" Lyle frowned at Jack, rubbing the knot on his forehead. "I'm rescuing my girlfriend."

"Your *girlfriend*?" Jack's eyes narrowed.

I felt my face flush. "We're not together anymore."

"Actually, that's what I wanted to ask you." Lyle scrambled to his feet and crossed the space between us. "Lisa told me why you dumped me and I wanted you to know, I *wasn't* just trying to have sex with you."

I glared at him, doubtful. "You *didn't* want to have sex with me?"

"No, I did," he admitted. "I'm just saying, I think we could be good together...even if your dad's a defector and your mom's a traitor. If you'll give me another chance, I'd like to make it up to you. We could go out for real this time. I mean, not anywhere public—"

Jack's gun made barely a whisper as he pulled it out and, at point blank range, put a tranquilizer dart into Lyle's jugular. With an ungraceful thump, Lyle fell to the ground, unconscious.

"Sorry." Jack shrugged. "Reflex."

I didn't have time to do more than shoot him a dirty look before another siren started screaming in the distance. Without thinking too hard, I rolled Lyle over and pulled the black T-shirt over his head. Not the most fashionable minidress in the world, but if I was going to be on the run for my life, I would *not* be doing it in synthetic fabrics and Curious George.

"Turn around," I snapped at Jack.

"What are you doing?"

"Duh, what does it look like?" I untied the hospital gown, inching it down over one shoulder. He whirled so fast you'd think I'd fired a bottle rocket at his retina.

We made it across the hall to an empty classroom without further incident. From the look of things, the guards had already tossed this sector. Furniture was overturned, bookcases peeled back from the walls. Even the air had taken on a smoky haze. Jack pulled me to my knees behind a toppled desk in the back of the room, his hand resting possessively on my back.

"Miss Bennett," he whispered. "Can you try a small channel?"

I tried to minimize the sarcasm as I answered, "You know, we've made out twice now. You can call me Amelie."

His eyes narrowed for a second as he considered this. "I don't think I'm comfortable with that."

"No?"

He shook his head. "Sorry."

And, just like that, the topic was closed. As long as I live, I will never understand guys.

"Okay, whatever." I held out a hand, palm up, and tried to clear my mind. It was an impossible task. Everywhere Jack had touched, goosebumps ran up my skin. It took a few seconds, but soon the air began to thicken, a silvery mass collecting over my hand in a tight swirl. "I can do it. I think."

"You think? Or you're sure?"

"I'm sure…ish."

With hesitant motions, my fingers scrawled out the containment wards. No one would follow us through this time, but I didn't want to take the chance of opening a demon rift in the wake of our escape. Maybe I *was* a Graymason like Jack said, but I certainly wasn't a killer. I just hoped I'd have enough power left over to close the portal once we landed.

"So, Smalley knew, huh?" I asked him, finishing the last of the wards. "That's why she gave me that incantation…to portal us back?"

Jack paused, then nodded. "She wouldn't have called me here if she didn't care about you."

I swallowed the prickle behind my eyes. There wasn't time for tears now. This portal would have to be smaller than the one at the test. Even with Jack drawing Crossworld power off me, I wouldn't have the strength to hold a big one. The frantic energy was already seeping out of my limbs, replaced by a deep physical exhaustion. Smalley was dead. I was wanted for murder. And apart from a semi-deranged Watcher with intimacy issues, there was nothing standing between a legion of executioners and me.

"Ready?" he asked.

With a quick nod, I spoke. "*Caret initio et fine. Ab initio—*"

Down the hallway, doors slammed, desks clattered against the floor, and men shouted at each other. I shut my eyes, pulling hard against the rising tornado.

"Ab initio. Ad patres. Deficit omne quod nasciture."

I had just finished the incantation when the door to the classroom exploded, Ms. Hansen's petite form filling the doorway. She looked like an ancient warrior goddess—bosom heaving, arms outstretched, black hair whipping wildly. I ducked as shards of the shattered door hit the wall behind us.

"*Terminé*," she screamed.

In a heartbeat, the gusts slowed, my wards dimming to gray.

"Dammit." Jack stood from behind the desk, his gun leveled at her face. "Lori, back off. This has nothing to do with you."

"Have you lost your mind? She's a murderer!" Hansen yelled at Jack, her doe-eyes wide.

"She didn't do this." Jack's finger tightened around the trigger, but he didn't fire. "You know it. The Elders know it. This isn't justice, Lori."

I crawled under the fallen desk. Even if I could get the portal open again, I wasn't entirely sure where it would send us. Smalley's incantation had been linked to a locus code for her office, so I couldn't use that again. The only exits *I'd* ever established were for school pranks and dares. Odd places. Places you wouldn't want to drop into unannounced.

"Justice?" Hansen gaped at him. "She's *Anakim*, Jackson! A soulless, remorseless *killer*. She should never have been allowed to live. The prophecy says she'll bring death to the Sons of Gabriel—"

"The prophecy says *a* Gray One will. It doesn't say it's her."

"'*Blood of taint and hair of fire?*'" Hansen quoted, furious. "Who else could it be? You're *helping* her bring the end of your own bloodline—"

"Leave it alone, Lori," Jack said, gun still pointed at her head.

"It's none of your business."

"The hell it isn't!" She shook her head, stunned. "You told me it was over between you. You promised—"

"It is," he insisted with an uncomfortable glance in my direction. "That's not what this is about."

I had no idea what they were saying, and, frankly, I didn't care. The more time they wasted, the closer the guards got to us. Jack already looked a little beat-up, and I doubted he could dispatch them so easily with Hansen breathing down his neck.

I edged around the side of the desk to reach for Jack's ankle. Maybe we weren't bonded, but he'd boosted my power before. If I was in contact with him, I might be able to channel enough—

"*Revelo!*"

Hansen's wrathful little voice shrilled through the room as soon as my hand came into her view. Before I could flinch, the desk flew straight up into the air and slammed into the ground a few feet away from me. The legs snapped off it with a hard crack, drawers splintering into a thousand pieces. I ducked as Jack threw his body in front of me, his arms coming up to wrap around my head in a protective hug.

"*Desarmé!*"

The gun ripped out of Jack's hand and smacked against the blackboard at the front of the room. Tight wind tunnels whipped through the air, little tendrils of electricity spiking out of them.

"Lori, stop it," Jack shouted. "You're better than this."

"You're right," she hissed, "I am. *Doloré!*"

Jack grunted at the sound of the curse, his body jerking away from me. It was as if someone had poured gasoline on him and lit a match. His spine arched, fists driving into the ground. Hansen stepped forward, her pretty face twisted with fury. I didn't have to read the handbook to know it was against Guardian law to use a curse like that on one of our own.

"Stop! You're hurting him." I scrabbled over to Jack and ran a hand over his forehead. It was on fire. *"Salve pacem,"* I said, pouring light into him.

"Selfish whore! Look what you've done to him. He could have died a hero! Now he's just another victim." Hansen's lips drew back over her teeth, her perfect nose tugged up like a rabid Chihuahua's. *"Dolore magnum."*

"Silentium!" I frantically painted protective wards onto Jack's chest, but every symbol I drew dissipated.

I needed her to turn her fury onto me. Knock me unconscious, kill me. *Something* to take the focus off of Jack.

The Crossworld taint had already seeped into her, blackening her eyes to a charred and ugly shadow. It was poisoning her. But instead of falling down or passing out like I would have, she just watched, smiling, as Jack descended into madness.

And all I could do was whisper, *"Salve, salve."*

Tears streamed down my face. Jack's body was rigid and tense in my arms, his lips mumbling words I couldn't understand.

Funny how the smallest emotions sometimes hold the most power. I had no idea what this was between Jack and me. Heck, I didn't even know where he came from. Graymasons? Prophecies? It made less than zero sense to me. But when I looked at him, his eyes glazed from the pain, I knew something with absolute certainty.

He could *not* die.

I'd just opened my mouth to summon a demon and hope for

the best when the sweetest sound in the world rang out through the room. It wasn't what you'd expect. It wasn't a choir of angels or anything celestial like that.

No, it was the hard crack of a Precious Moments figurine smacking across the head of my psychotic Advanced Wards instructor. I swear, like music to my ears.

The winds died instantly. Hansen slid to the floor in an unconscious heap. Henry stood motionless in the doorway, staring at the shattered remnants of a porcelain statuette in his hand. He looked horrified.

"Nice work, Mr. M!"

Behind him, Lisa tumbled into the room with Alec, Matt, and Katie on her heels. They were clad head-to-toe in black, with the two boys carrying curved swords I recognized from the school arsenal—the *very off-limits* school arsenal. It occurred to me again what deep trouble I had to be in if Lisa "The Rule Mistress" Anselmo was willing to crack the arsenal for me.

"Darn," Lisa muttered, surveying the room. "Y'all think we'll get detention for this?"

Matt let out a low whistle from behind her. "I thought the guards were tough. What'd you do to piss Hansen off so bad?"

Jack rolled to his side and pressed his forehead into my stomach. A light trickle of foam appeared at the corner of his mouth. He may not have meant that as a sign of devotion, but that's how I took it.

"What are y'all doing here?" I asked.

"Saving the day, of course...with a little help from the establishment." From his post by the door, Matt slapped a grief-stricken Henry on the shoulder. "Dude, are we heroes?"

Alec snorted with an elvish grin. "She's just lucky there was nothing better on TV tonight. Nice outfit, by the way," he said to me.

I glanced at Lyle's T-shirt, hiked in rumpled folds over my thighs, and shot Alec a nasty look. The sounds in the hallway had settled again, though it didn't quite calm me. Whatever my friends had done to subdue the guards probably wouldn't last long. Through the window, the sky glowed a muted purple, streaks of blue and orange smearing across the clouds in a pre-dawn haze.

Katie stuck her head around the doorway. "You can thank Alec for the rescue. It was his idea."

"Babe, I meant it as a joke."

She blew him a kiss.

"What's *he* doing here?" Lisa gestured to Jack, still quivering against my belly. His eyes were pressed shut, hands clenched in tight fists. Under other circumstances, it might have been weird having a teacher curled up in my lap, clinging to me like he was on the *Titanic* and I was the last life-preserver. At the moment, however, it seemed utterly natural.

"He's saving me."

She snorted. "Stellar job."

Jack must have been at least semi-conscious, because as soon as Lisa said that he made a sound like a dying moose and rolled onto his back. "Portal," he grunted. "Now!"

My eyes met Lisa's. Much as I hated it, I knew he was right. We had to get out of here.

Matt and Katie took up defensive positions by the door while Alec fingered Jack's tranquilizer gun. "I knew this would be better than reruns."

Lisa shoved a backpack into my hands. "Here's everything you'll need for a few weeks. Clothes, money, some granola bars… and one of those cute disposable cell phones with the little yellow daisies. I'll call you from a secure line once things die down here. Don't call me, though. And don't call Bud…too much surveillance. I told him to stay in Baton Rouge a little longer but they'll find him eventually. They've probably already tapped our lines."

I grinned at Lisa. Surveillance? Phone taps? I'd trained her well.

"Shut up," she said, smiling back. "Alec's dad has political connections. He's going to do what he can for you, but I wouldn't get my hopes up."

"Hurry up, y'all. More guards are coming," Matt hollered from the door. "Alec, cover Katie. Henry—" Matt looked at the silent, broken man slumped helplessly against the wall. "Never mind. I'll take lead."

Alec whipped his sword around in a sweeping arc as he sauntered over to the door. "See you later, kiddo. Don't do anything I wouldn't do."

"Good luck, Ami," Katie yelled from the doorway. "We'll see you soon."

Lisa threw her arms around me in a hug so tight I thought I might suffocate. "I'm sorry I told them about the Rangor," she whispered. "They wouldn't listen—"

"I know, Lis. It's all right."

"You're my sister, Ami. You know that. Whatever you need—"

I squeezed her tighter. "Just take care of Bud for me, okay? Don't let him do anything stupid."

She nodded. Jack and I hadn't talked about it, but I knew once we left we wouldn't be coming back for a long, long time. Unless I could figure a way out of this, the Elders would do everything possible to erase me…including memory modification on Dad and Lisa if they didn't cooperate.

The knowledge sat in the pit of my stomach, dark and ugly. As optimistic as my friends sounded, there was a very real probability I would never see them again.

I held Lisa for as long as I dared. It couldn't have been more than a minute before Jack put his hand on my shoulder. "It's time."

"Okay." I brushed her wild hair back from her face. "Be careful, Lis. Whoever did this is still out there."

She nodded again, her eyes puffy. The clatter of footsteps spilled down the length of the hall, a stampede across the linoleum. "You ready?"

"Ready," I replied, my voice tight. "*Inergio.*"

I held out a hand to the portal, the old wards sparking to life. Ribbons of energy flew out of my fingers, stronger and thicker than before. Heat pooled in a tight column and I could feel the boundaries of the portal as they stretched like a rubber band around space and time.

"Go," she yelled over the power-sizzle. "Don't worry about sealing it once you're through. I'll close it remotely. They won't track you."

Jack tugged the backpack onto his shoulders and gathered me in his arms, flinching slightly when I wrapped my arms around his waist. I shut my eyes for a moment as a familiar current of electricity zipped between us. It would be okay. As long as I was with him, it would be okay.

The air began to crackle, portal walls shimmering in a vertical column of air.

"Where to?"

"Somewhere safe, but not too far. We've got work to do."

I pressed my face against his chest. He smelled clean, and warm, with just a hint of perspiration. His heart pounded like a bass drum in a hurricane, and I waited until my own heart slowed to match it.

"I think I know a place."

Chapter Twelve:
Accommodation

"Omelets?" Jack complained under his breath for the fifty-millionth time. "A legion of warriors behind us, a killer on the loose, and you take us out for...*omelets*?"

I stuffed another cheesy forkful of heaven in my mouth. He'd been muttering like that since we landed in the men's room over an hour ago. Not that I could blame him. When you drop out of midair into a public toilet, then spend a half hour explaining to the management why there's an unconscious girl having seizures on the floor, your sense of humor is bound to take a hit. At least it gave us time to recover.

"Omelets are delicious," I mumbled around a mouthful of the fluffiest eggs this side of the Mississippi. "Besides, it's crowded here. We totally blend."

We did not blend.

Amidst the sea of gray hair and polyester, Jack stood out worse than a Green Beret at a nerd convention. A purple smudge darkened his jaw, and a few narrow cuts on his eyebrow and lower lip were scabbed with dried blood. In questionable Guardian form, he took a tense yet hunched seat beside me, one hand wrapped around the weapon beneath his jacket, ready to dispatch anything evil that might wander in for a Belgian waffle.

I felt like royalty. Massive feast lain out before me, smokin' hot bodyguard at my side ready and willing to take a bullet.

Too bad I looked like Lady Gaga.

Lyle's T-shirt barely skimmed the top of my thighs and, despite the spandex shorts and skinny belt I'd thrown on from Lisa's backpack, my outfit was way more trailer-trash pajamas than retro-chic minidress. The frayed Converse sneakers didn't help much.

Jack had every right to be edgy. The restaurant was a riot of noise and movement. Heavy scents of coffee and sizzling sausage hung in the air, barely detectable under the fog of floral perfume from the Mah-jongg game raging beside us. An elderly woman with a huge nose and a stiff wig leaned across the aisle.

"So nice to see a girl with a healthy appetite," she cooed, her blue-veined fingers tapping my arm. "I can't stand these young things, eating nothing but salad all day long. It's enough to give me an ulcer."

"Thank you." I happily popped another bite of sausage in my mouth.

Jack groaned from his post beside me.

Yeah, if I'd had tons of options, the *Breakfast Nook* might not have made the top ten. But between this or an Airline Highway strip club called *The Rowdy Beaver*, I think I made the right call.

I finished my smorgasbord while Jack hobbled outside to grab us a cab.

It helped my headspace a bit to watch out the window as we drove through downtown toward the Marigny district. Bright Creole cottages dotted the sidewalk, the occasional shotgun house thrown in for character. Even the warehouses and check-cashing centers looked upbeat and familiar.

I leaned my head against the tempered glass window, trying not to think too hard about what my life had become. The past, the future... It all scared the crap out of me. I could joke about commitment issues 'til next Tuesday, but the sad truth was, Jack was all I had. In a few hours, my father would either be imprisoned or have his memory wiped, my friends would be in custody undergoing interrogations, and every Guardian in the free world would be looking for me. I'd never be safe again. And the only person willing to help me was a guy who seemed to alternate between hating me, wanting me, and barely tolerating me out of some displaced sense of justice. If we couldn't solve this, who knew how long he would stick around?

Heck, who knew how long I'd let him?

Much as I hated to admit it, I had serious feelings for him. No one had ever left me so simultaneously relaxed and knotted-up all at once (except maybe Rhett Butler, which doesn't count since he's not a real person). It didn't matter that all Jack did was order me around and bleed on me. I still liked him. More than "liked" him, if I was being honest with myself.

The problem was, I had nothing to offer. I was a Graymason. A monster. All the things I'd seen when I touched him before... love, marriage, a life together. *He* could have all those things. *He* could be happy. Just not with me.

I closed my eyes, a deep sigh shuddering through me. This

couldn't be real. It *couldn't*. If I let it be real for even a second, I knew I would fall apart.

"You okay?" Jack asked.

I cracked an eyelid and forced a smile onto my lips. "Yeah. Wondering whether Netflix delivers to Siberia."

He didn't smile. His eyes seemed to hold all the sadness I couldn't articulate, all the loss I couldn't let myself feel. "We'll figure it out. I promise."

His warm fingers wrapped around mine, that same strange light glimmering in tightly linked strands. But for the first time, his touch didn't make me feel better. I knew what it had cost him to help me. I hated myself for letting him pay that price.

Jack made the cab driver take the most circuitous route in the world to the motel. We stopped at least ten times so I could set up exit portals around the city. Parking lots, restaurants, back alleys, a used-car dealership. Jack said once the Otrava fully left my system I'd have a lot more capabilities with channeling. No more nausea, no more convulsions. I'd probably still need a Watcher to dump the Crossworld residue on, but that would be it.

By the time we pulled away from the Commercial Street wharf, my knowledge of significant Latin phrases had been stretched so thin it was practically translucent. Our final portal exit I named *denique caelum*, heaven at last. It may have been nothing but a grubby Tremé boarding house with moth-eaten carpet and threadbare drapes, but to me, it was heaven. Clouds had already started to gather for an afternoon storm when I collapsed on the bed in our motel room, exhausted and near tears.

The place Jack had chosen was far from nice. Faint light shone through the sheer lace curtains, casting a yellowish glow across the room. The floor was littered with mismatched oriental carpets that let off spits of dust wherever our feet landed. Besides the bed and dresser, the only piece of furniture was a faded green easy chair that looked like it had been swallowed by a Morgra demon and barfed up whole.

True to her word, Lisa had stashed a wad of cash inside the backpack, along with the pair of jeans I'd left at her house for emergencies, a few shirts, and three matching underwear sets (tags still on) that were way nicer than anything I owned. I couldn't wait to change. After scrounging around behind Dumpsters all morning, my clothes and hair had absorbed the signature scents of the French Quarter—urine, vomit, and alcohol.

"I need a bath," I grumbled from my spot on the bed. "Followed by a serious de-lousing. Then maybe a nice herbal massage."

Jack fastened the deadbolt and wrestled the rickety dresser in front of the door. He looked tired. "We should be safe here, at least long enough to rest."

"Awesome. I love rest."

He winced as he tugged off his jacket and sank into the chair, head lolling back against the cushions. The smudges beneath his eyes were more pronounced than they'd been at breakfast and, despite the tan, his skin held a gray pallor. One arm was wrapped around his torso in a tight half-hug, the other lay limp against the armrest. If his breath hadn't been so ragged and uneven, I might have thought he'd fallen asleep.

Ever since I'd met Jack, the one constant about him was that he always looked like a warrior. Whether he was eating lunch or tying his shoe, there was always a part of him that could snap into action at any moment and save the world. I'd never seen him look vulnerable before.

"Hey," I said, sitting up. "Are you sick, or something?"

Jack's eyes popped open, then fluttered a few times as he blinked himself back to awareness. "No, I'm fine. Go take your shower. I'll stand guard 'til you get out."

I gave him a skeptical look. He barely looked like he could *stand*, let alone stand guard against the nightmare hunting us. "No offense, but when was the last time you slept?"

"I don't need to sleep."

"Everyone needs to sleep. What about food? You should have eaten—"

"I'm not hungry." He sounded annoyed. "Look, we have to be somewhere at nightfall. If you want to take a shower I suggest you do it now. The Elders have limitless resources and we need to be ready for anything. That doesn't include stopping off for another leisurely meal."

I pushed myself to stand and tugged off my shoes. "Didn't anybody ever tell you breakfast is the most important meal of the day? When I don't eat, I get moody and short-tempered."

"Is that different from when you *do* eat?"

I smiled despite myself. It reassured me to hear him make snarky comments. If things were really as bad as they seemed, he wouldn't joke so easily, right?

"All right, comedian, at least lay down while I shower. You're already a superhero. You don't need to die from exhaustion to prove it." I grabbed a pillow off the bed and chucked it at his face. By reflex, he reached up to grab it, a cry of pain escaping at the sudden movement.

"Oh, my gosh, Jack. Are you hurt?"

"No." His breath came in hard puffs, both arms clamped around his torso. "Leave me alone."

I didn't say anything for a few seconds. I'd been a Channeler all my life. I'd healed skinned knees and fixed up the neighbor's poodle after Lisa's cat attacked it. And that was all before age ten. Did he seriously expect me to shower while he suffered alone out here?

"Don't be ridiculous. Let me heal you."

"No way." He pressed himself to the other side of the chair, as far away as he could get without actually falling on the floor. "You've done enough."

"Come on. You're obviously injured—"

"I don't want you to heal me."

"Don't be such a baby," I said. "Can I at least look? I won't do anything 'til you say it's okay."

Jack sank back into the chair, both arms still tight around his midsection. "You're just going to look?"

"Yes."

"Promise?"

"Oh, for goodness sake." I lifted my little finger and crossed it over my chest. "Pinkie swear."

He grudgingly let me slide his brown leather shoulder holster over one arm then the other. I tried to ignore the warm electric current that zipped through me when the back of my hand brushed his skin. The sparks didn't startle me anymore, but I still had trouble not staring at them.

Weapons safely set to the side, I lifted up his shirt carefully, then helped him work the stretchy white cotton over his head. The guy had given up everything for me; the last thing I wanted was to hurt him. When his shirt finally fell to the ground, my breath caught in my throat. A swollen bluish-purple splotch ran lengthwise along the left side of his abdomen and little lines of red stood out where blood vessels had broken. I sank to my knees in front of him.

"Oh, Jack," I whispered, gingerly touching the swollen skin over his ribs.

It had been years since I'd taken first aid, but I had yet to forget what internal bleeding looked like. The whole left side of his abdomen was swollen with blood, leaving angry red and black streaks down his body almost as dark as the tattooed glyphs on his arms. "You have to let me heal you."

"No."

"It's not a suggestion. Whatever Hansen did to you, you're still bleeding inside. I have to fix it or you're going to die."

He was silent. We both knew it didn't matter what he said. Worst case scenario, he'd spend the next few hours suffering, then once he passed out from internal bleeding or agony I would heal him anyway. Of course, I didn't say that out loud. Most guys prefer you at least *pretend* their opinion matters.

"Think of it as a public service," I reasoned. "If you die, whoever killed all those people will go free. I'll be a fugitive for the rest of my life. Then I'll perish, old and miserable and alone, all because you were too stubborn to let me help you. Is that what you want?"

Jack narrowed his gaze. "You give frequent flyer miles with that guilt trip?"

"Absolutely," I said. "You in?"

He drew what should have been a slow breath, but ended up as a wet, hacking cough. Tiny specks of blood stained the back of his hand as he swiped it across his mouth.

"Jack, come on. I can't do this without you." My voice quieted, all hint of humor stripped away. My fingers itched to touch his face, to smooth the lines of fatigue and stress from his forehead. "I need you."

After a brief hesitation, he nodded. "Okay. But not like in assembly," he cautioned. "If there's a tracker nearby, he'll sense the channel. Besides, I'm worried what effect all this is having on you."

I shook my head. "What's that supposed to mean?"

Jack's lips tightened, belying his reluctance to answer. "Remember before your test you asked me why I wasn't wearing my glasses?"

"Yeah."

"Well, at first I thought you just screwed up my prescription," he said. "It took a few hours to realize that when you healed those scratches on my face, you healed my vision, too. You healed *everything*. Do you have any idea how much power that takes?"

My eyebrows arched in surprise. All Channelers were trained in acute injuries, but existing deficits weren't something we could do normally. Not unless there was some intense anomaly or special ritual with it. I couldn't help feeling a tiny flicker of pride.

"Cool. I'm like a paranormal Dr. House."

"Dr. Frankenstein, maybe." He smiled, slower this time. "All right, but be careful. And just the internal stuff. I don't want you to hurt yourself."

It was actually a huge compliment that Jack believed I *could* control my powers enough to stop. And I really tried. When my fingers came to rest against his stomach, I didn't think about kissing him. I didn't think about how my heart pounded in perfect time with his. I ignored the velvet warmth of his skin, his breath ruffling my hair, the impossible tingles shooting down every inch of me. I didn't wonder how his body would feel, tight and warm, intertwined with mine —

"Enough."

Jack's voice was husky in my ear as he encircled my wrists with his hands and gently pushed me away. Soft and reluctant, the threads of light dissipated. I sat back, dizzy.

"Are you okay?"

"I think so," I said, half-knowing it was a lie. "Give me a minute."

I stumbled to the bathroom, willing my heart to slow. The tile wall felt cool against my forehead, but my thoughts still raced. Maybe Jack was right. Maybe I really was dangerous. At the very least it made me wonder if I shouldn't be more careful sharing power with him.

By the time I returned with Lisa's first aid kit, Jack was upright on the edge of the bed, poking a tentative finger at the area that used to be black and blue. I could still see a faint outline of the bruise, but it had faded to the greenish brown of an old wound rather than the vicious hue of a mortal injury. Color had returned to his face as well. As I knelt next to him again, a silent wave of gratitude washed through me.

"Does this hurt?" I pressed the tips of my fingers to his abdomen where the bruise had been.

"A little tender, but it's okay."

"How about your face? Looks like it stings."

Jack shrugged. "I don't get paid for being pretty."

"As of this morning, I doubt you get paid at all." I dabbed at his forehead with an alcohol swab. "I could just heal you without permission."

"You could try."

I frowned at him. "Does the word 'stubborn' mean anything to you?"

He grinned.

"Quit smiling. You'll split your lip again." Jack sat still while I smeared a glob of antibiotic ointment on his eyebrow then started on the cut at his lip. "Seriously, why didn't you bond at graduation?" I asked, mostly to break the tension. "I get it if your first assignment was a flop, but what about other Channelers? Hansen, for example? She was totally into you. Before she tried to kill you, I mean."

Jack made a pained face. "Yeah, Lori and I have an unusual relationship."

"Why's that?"

"For starters, she was in my graduating class at Monroe. She kind of mentored me through some hard times," he admitted. "Plus, she was my flop of a bond assignment. Ow!"

"Sorry." I put the alcohol swab away, trying not to hyperventilate. "So, why'd you refuse her?"

He lifted one eyebrow. "Do the words 'none of your business' mean anything to you?"

"Touché. But she can't have been the only one."

Jack shrugged again, his eyes flitting to the window. "There was someone else, but it was a long time ago. I doubt she remembers me."

"You're not exactly forgettable. Hold still." With a Q-tip, I dabbed some antibiotic on his lip, then wiped off the excess with the back of a knuckle. As soon as I touched him, my body vibrated with his power, like an itch aching to be scratched. "Did you ever tell her how you felt?"

"Who?"

"The girl. Duh."

He laughed. "It didn't exactly happen like that. I barely knew her, just from the playground in elementary school. Then, one night at a PTA event, we got caught in the crossfire of a battle. I don't even know what happened. One second, we were all playing hide-and-seek, then the next thing I knew the air was on fire and people were dying. I hid behind a couch with the other kids and watched our parents get ripped to shreds by a demon lord. There was nothing any of us could do. I remember how fragile she felt huddled next to me, but all I could think was that we were going to die. *I* was going to die." Jack stopped, examining me. I waited a few seconds for him to continue, but he didn't.

"Well, what did you do?" I asked.

"I didn't do anything," he said. "Most of the kids started running. I tried to run, too, but she wouldn't let me. She grabbed a piece of broken glass and stabbed me in the hand." He smiled as if the memory was a fond one. "I never saw it coming. She did the same thing to herself, then she wrapped her snotty little kid fingers around mine and opened a channel so powerful it took out the demon lord, his minions, and an entire city block of lesser fiends. I've never been so terrified in my life."

Jack brought his right hand out from behind him and held it open. In the middle of his palm was a small, C-shaped scar curving through the center of his lifeline. It reminded me of the one I'd gotten when I fell off the monkey bars at Lisa's house in second grade, only mine was more jagged.

I ran my thumb over the scar as I processed what Jack had said, a sharp wave of envy rising in my throat. If he and this girl had exchanged blood *and* shared that level of power, then according to what I'd overheard in the locker room they were two-thirds of the way done with the Guardian bonding ritual. All they had to do was say the right words to each other and they would be bonded. Forever.

"So, what happened?"

He shrugged. "Nothing. When I woke up she was gone, my folks were dead, and the Elders had reassigned me to residential in Monroe. They said we were too young. It was deemed an illegal bonding and I never saw her again."

His words hung in the air, hollow and sad. The sounds of distant traffic snaked in through cracks around the windowpanes, and I expelled a soft breath. Chills ran up my arms, an odd contrast to the warm slant of afternoon light through the transom windows.

"That's the saddest thing I've ever heard."

Jack gave a tight, humorless smile and rose from the bed. "Miss Bennett, I don't mean to be rude, but I also need to wash up before we leave. If you don't mind…"

I rocked back on my heels, trying to pretend he hadn't just driven an icicle into my heart. Not like I was expecting him to kiss me again, but I at least hoped to graduate to a first name basis. I sat perfectly still, studying him carefully.

"Jack, what about me?" I asked.

He gave me a strange look. "You can shower on your own. I may be stuck with you, but I'm not your nanny."

"No." I shook my head. "I mean, what if I wasn't a student? What if you'd met me next year and there wasn't all this stuff with murderers and demons and people dying? And don't say you're too old for me," I warned, before he could start in with excuses. "There are only three years between us. By the time I graduate, three years won't mean squat. I'm just asking, if things were different, would you consider…Would you ever, you know, think of me? That way?"

I could tell my face was red. It burned like someone had lit a fire under my chin. Jack stood motionless, brilliant light streaming behind him like something out of the Sistine Chapel. Sunbeams curved around his body, carving out the peaks and valleys of each chiseled muscle. Jeez, this would be so much easier if he wasn't so beautiful.

After the longest, most painful five seconds in the world, Jack let out a slow exhale. "Miss Bennett—"

"Never mind."

It was all I needed to hear. Nothing that started with my surname was going to end in a passionate declaration of desire. And given how today had gone, I didn't think I could take another rejection.

"It's okay. Forget I asked."

I rose in humiliated silence and hurried into the bathroom before the tears could fall. What an idiot I'd been, mooning over him at school, making an ass of myself at assembly. Everything I'd felt—the *déja vu*, the visions, the weird feeling like we'd known each other forever—it was all just a stupid, hormonal response to my unrequited crush.

The door securely locked, I huddled in the corner, porcelain wall tiles cold against my shoulder blades. A thin sheen of mildew covered the lower half of the shower curtain, its nastiness surpassed only by a few furry lines of black mold around the base of the tub. I spun the knob above the faucet until steam billowed out from behind the curtain.

"Miss Bennett." Jack rapped hard on the wooden surface. "Please, open the door."

I didn't answer. What could I say? I'd had my share of humiliating moments, most of them witnessed by members of the school administration. But I'd always managed to escape with some shred of dignity. This time, not so much.

"I know we've had some mixed signals," Jack said through the door, "but the situation is complicated. There are things you're not mature enough to understand."

"By all means, then," I called through the door, "keep lying to me. It's worked brilliantly so far."

"Miss Bennett—"

Overcome with impatience, I stormed to the door, twisted the lock, and yanked it open. "Look, I'm having kind of a rough day, okay? Don't get me wrong, I appreciate the rescue and all, but in the past twelve hours I've been starved, drugged, tortured, chased, shot at, ripped from my family and friends, and forced to watch helplessly while the only guy I've ever—" I stopped, uncertain. "While my substitute teacher nearly had his brain melted by a psychotic former cheerleader. All in all, not one of my top ten Wednesdays."

Jack scrubbed a weary hand down his face. "Lori was never a cheerleader."

"I. Don't. Care." I started to close the door again but changed my mind. "And my name is Amelie. *Ah-muh-lee.* If we're going to be stuck with each other the least you can do is quit acting so pompous and treat me like an equal." I gave him my sternest look, then slammed the door as hard as I dared, lest it fall off its termite-riddled hinges. Little flecks of paint chipped off at the impact.

Angry and embarrassed, I stripped off Lyle's shirt and stepped out of my underpants, balling it all into a tight missile. They made a satisfying *thunk* against the door, right where Jack's stupid face had been a moment ago.

I didn't know why I was so angry. This wasn't his fault. With the way he looked, girls probably threw themselves at him all the time. So his big crime had been what? That he kissed me? What was he supposed to do, beat me away with a stick?

More than anything, I was upset with myself. I'd long held the credo that the best way to be disappointed was to set high expectations. So, what did I think was going to come out of a crush on the most unattainable person in the galaxy?

The water felt amazing against my shoulders, as if it could burn off all the sweat and horror of the day. I spent nearly an hour in the shower with the secret hope that I might use up all the hot water before Jack got in. Unfortunately, my hands and feet started to prune long before it showed any signs of cooling. My clothes were still in Lisa's backpack, so I settled for one of the oversized white bath towels. For all the economy of our accommodations, the motel certainly spared no expense on towels. They were thick and heavy, like angel clouds you could disappear into. I wrapped one around my head and tucked the other like a strapless gown under my armpits, leaving Jack nothing but a hand towel. Petty, yes, but it made me feel better.

When I emerged, he was waiting silently by the door, hands jammed in his pockets.

"Your turn," I said coolly as I brushed past him.

Lisa had forgotten to pack a hairbrush, so I did what I could with my fingers and a tube of de-frizzer while Jack showered. I'd just slipped into a lace-edged black tank-top and jeans when the bathroom door squeaked open.

Jack slouched against the doorframe, steam pouring out behind him. He was barefoot and shirtless, frayed jeans riding low on the deep grooves of his hipbones. Water dripped off his hair, tracing thin lines all the way down to his belly button. Even the tattooed glyphs on his arms seemed to stand out more than usual, slick and dark against his tanned skin.

"You're dressed," he said.

"Yup," I confirmed. "More than I can say for you."

He paused toweling off to scan me from head to toe, just as he'd done the first day I met him. Of course, this time I knew it wasn't romantic interest motivating the scope-out. He was probably looking for places to conceal a weapon.

"Get your shoes on," he said. "We leave in ten minutes."

"I thought you said we didn't have to be anywhere 'til nightfall."

"We don't." He finished drying his hair and chucked the hand towel at me. "But if you want to be treated like a 'grown-up,' then there are a few things you need to know, *Amelie*."

The last word he said with a dry smile. It crinkled the corners of his mouth but didn't reach his eyes.

"Where are we going?"

"I need to show you something. Something you should have seen a long time ago." Jack padded across the room to Lisa's backpack and emptied all but the most essential things: money, keys, weapons…a flashlight?

"We," he said, "are going sightseeing."

Chapter Thirteen:
Impossible Things

It would have been easier to hate Jack if he weren't so nice. The way he kept his hand securely entwined with mine as we crossed into the French Quarter reminded me of those old movies where the dashing hero is charged with protecting the entitled-yet-important heroine. That's how I felt with him — important.

Creole townhouses rose up on either side of us, cast-iron galleries crawling up the brick walls like vines. Antique shops and art stores huddled at every corner with tourists spilling out of them. For a city that had been burned and rebuilt as many times as this one, New Orleans had an amazing sense of flow. Even the people seemed to float down the street, their pace leisurely and calm. It was the kind of place you could get lost in.

It was perfect.

Jack took care not to hurry. The cut on his lip had already started to heal and his sunglasses covered the scratch on his eyebrow. I guess we looked normal. Or tried to, anyway. I stopped for pralines once so he could scan the street behind us to see if we were being followed. We weren't. A few blocks later, he thought he recognized someone on the street, so he pulled me into a gift shop and made me try on silly hats until the guy had passed. It was hard not to get sucked into the illusion that we were just two regular people on a date—a little hand-holding, a little conversation. Of course, instead of sweet nothings whispered in my ear, I got brief lectures on evasive techniques.

Stay out of alleys, unless you can identify at least three viable exit routes.

Don't be afraid to use humans as a shield. A Guardian won't attack if there's a human around.

Guardian trackers can only sense you when you channel. Stay dormant, and you'll be no more visible than a human.

And my favorite, *They have orders to execute us on sight. If anything happens to me, run fast and don't look back.*

Not exactly words designed to make a girl feel cozy.

By the time we reached St. Mary's Church at the old Ursuline Convent, my last nerve was shot. Jack crossed himself out of habit then held open the heavy gray door for me, his hand never leaving the small of my back.

"The Great Books used to be housed in the convent itself," he said as we traversed the atrium. "When St. Mary's was added in 1845, the Elders moved them here."

"The Great Books?"

"Guardian holy writ. The *Book of Life*. The *Book of Blood*. The *Book of Days*. The *Book of Omens*."

"So, Guardian beach reading?"

"If you're into apocalyptic prognostications and genealogical charts."

I wasn't sure if he was making a joke. All he got was a blank stare. "I don't know what you just said."

"That's because you never listen in class. Follow me."

As soon as we stepped into the church, the smell of candle wax and incense wrapped around me in a tight hug. Apart from the hush of air-conditioning vents, the church was silent and nearly empty. Rows of wooden pews filled the sanctuary, their smooth, oiled surfaces reflecting the warm glow of crystal chandeliers above. Flecked rainbows shimmered through stained glass windows, casting pink, gold, and blue beams across Jack's face as he strode through the center aisle of the church. He reached back and caught my hand.

"Be ready to run. If anyone attacks, I'll take care of it. You get back to the safe house and stay there."

"In your dreams," I whispered back. "And seriously, 'safe house'? I prefer to think of it as the 'flophouse,' since it's really only safe for cockroaches."

An elderly Hispanic woman in the front row turned her head at our voices, but Jack pretended not to see her. Without pausing at the front, he vaulted the low gate to where the altar stood. Two wide columns rose on either side to form an arch across the coved ceiling and a series of ornate gold spires rose like stalagmites at the back of the sanctuary.

"Are you sure we're allowed back here? It feels kind of sneaky," I said. Granted, I hadn't been to church in years, probably not since Mom's funeral, but I was pretty sure God frowned upon people sticking their fingers in the Eucharist.

"This from the girl who arranged for six tons of personal lubricant to magically appear on the volleyball court during gym class last year? Since when is 'sneaky' a problem for you?"

I grimaced. "I'm going to hell, aren't I?"

"Hopefully not for a few more years."

Jack smiled as I raked a stray lock of red hair into my stupid bun. He'd made an offhand comment earlier about what a pity it was that my hair was so "conspicuous." Much as I wanted that to be a compliment, it didn't quite feel like one.

He knelt on the marble floor and lifted the cream-colored linen at the back altar. His fingers groped under the ledge, finally lodging in a groove in the bas-relief carvings. As if on a spring, something clicked and the rectangular panel slid backward, revealing a narrow entrance to what looked like a tunnel that descended straight down. My imagination conjured random scenes from Dante's *Inferno*: baleful screams of the tortured souls, gruesome sounds of joints breaking and limbs being ripped apart. Needless to say, it wasn't what I'd envisioned when he said we'd be "sightseeing."

Before I could caution him, Jack had swung his feet into the opening and dropped out of sight. I felt a wave of panic roll through my belly.

"Jack?" I whispered into the void. "Where'd you go?"

"The bowels of hell," his voice echoed back. "I thought we could go apartment hunting for you…since you'll be moving here, and all."

"I think I liked you better when you were laconic."

"Laconic, huh?" His head popped back into view. "That's a pretty big word for someone who bombed her verbal SATs. Are you coming?"

I nervously scanned the sanctuary, my eyes meeting the

Hispanic woman's suspicious glare. In a swish of black fabric, she stood and hurried toward the rectory, her knuckles white over the wooden beads of her rosary. Heart pounding, I muttered a quick prayer of my own, then followed Jack into the abyss.

Once I'd gotten a foothold on the metal ladder, Jack inched back up alongside me to pull the linen cloth down and close the panel. It clicked shut, and we were plunged into a darkness so complete it pretty much rendered my eyelids useless. The air smelled dank, like dirt and river water, and far away I could hear the thick sounds of sewage from the Quarter—exactly the kind of place where rats might live.

"Dude, you seriously need to pick up a copy of *Where Not to Take Your Date*," I whispered as Jack's arm looped around my waist. Instantly, my heart rate spiked. "So, what is this place?"

"It's called the catacombs. This was an old escape route the sisters used during the Civil War to hide mistreated slaves. After the war, the tunnels started to collapse, so rather than lose the church to a sinkhole, they gave the space to us. Our wards maintain the structure and keep anyone but angelbloods from finding it. Fascinating, don't you think?"

"Thrilling," I said in the most lackluster voice possible. "I'll be sure to write an extra credit essay when I get back to school."

"That's the spirit." He chuckled. "The ladder runs out in a few feet. Can you hold onto me?"

Sigh. "I think so."

Jack shifted Lisa's backpack to his chest, and then helped me get positioned between his shoulder blades. I hooked one arm over his shoulder, the other around his ribcage so as not to choke him, and tried to ignore the small cache of weapons tucked inside his waistband. The timing could not have been worse, but even with the mold and the germs and the threat of impending death, I couldn't quite quash that little thrill at being close to him. I wrapped my legs around his waist and inhaled deeply. As usual, he smelled amazing.

"Are you sniffing me?"

"No," I lied. "That would be weird."

As soon as he started moving, my fingers tightened into his skin. It's not that I was afraid of the dark, per se. It was more the creepy things shrouded by the dark that I feared. Zombies and demons and other beasties hell-bent on gnawing off my pinkie toes.

Jack's chest puffed with laughter beneath my iron grip. "Relax. This isn't the scary part yet."

"Mmm, not helpful."

"Try to think about puppies," he suggested. "No wait, not puppies. Think about kittens. Demons don't eat kittens. Too many hairballs."

"Hey, maybe we could try not talking for a while."

Jack was still laughing at me as he lowered himself slowly, hand over hand, until it seemed like we must've been well below sea level. I knew the French Quarter was situated at one of the highest points in the city, but that doesn't mean much in a town built on swampland. Finally, his feet touched something solid, and he lowered me onto the ground. I don't know what I was expecting. Water, I guess. Concrete. The brittle bones of my dearly departed Aunt Verna. It took me a second to find my balance on the surface of uneven cobbles. The air was like ice, but still humid enough to leave a cool sheen of sweat along my neck.

"Gosh, this place is darling." I sniffed. "And what a lovely stench. Do they have timeshares?"

There was a soft rustle as he fished around in the backpack. After a few seconds, a flashlight switched on, the beam flaring like a torch in his hand.

Smooth gray walls extended up as far as I could see, as if we had dropped into the bottom of a mile-deep, cylindrical missile silo. Five tunnels radiated off the main room, each with a rotted wooden door and a unique carving etched into the stone arch above: a shield, a chalice, an hourglass, and a half-risen sun. The fifth door was smaller, its carving less ornate. It was a serpent, tightly coiled, eyes slit shut, and the end of its tail tucked snugly between its teeth. A smattering of odd glyphs was etched across the backdrop in the same pattern as the creature's scales.

"Okay, what am I looking at?" I asked.

"These are the chambers of the Great Books." He approached the first door, the shield, and touched a hand to it. "This tunnel holds the *Book of Life*. It records all the births of Guardians since the beginning of time. You're listed in there, so are your parents, and your grandparents. Like a massive family tree."

"Sounds fun," I commented. "Next."

Jack continued to the next carving, the chalice. "This holds the *Book of Blood*. Each Guardian was formed from the flesh of one of the seven archangels, right?"

I nodded.

"Well, this tells the story of our bloodlines. Who your ancestors are, which bloodline is dominant in you. Because the bloodlines don't follow familial patterns, this is the only way we can keep track of them. We mostly use it to watch out for Lucifer's resurfacing, but it's important for bonding as well," he explained, in answer to my questioning look. "That's why the Elders always have to approve bond agreements. Some of the bloodlines don't mix well."

"For example?"

"Well, Gabriel and Michael. Too much of a power clash. Same with Michael and Raphael, and Raphael and Gabriel." He grinned. "The biggest issues are with Lucifer's offspring. Serious problems with authority. And they can't follow a rule to save their lives."

A sick feeling settled in the pit of my stomach, shrinking it to the rough size and hardness of a walnut. "I hate you a little, you know that?"

Jack's dark eyes shone with reflected light. "I wish that were true."

In silence he moved to the door with the hourglass above it. His fingertips traced the grooves of the carved stone. "This is the *Book of Days*. It's the story of our war against demonkind. Every battle since our genesis is recorded here."

"Wouldn't a military record be better kept in, I don't know, a *military* outpost, or something? This seems awfully inconvenient for the scribe." *Not to mention bloody creepy*, I added silently.

Jack frowned. "No, you misunderstand. Every battle is recorded here, with complete accuracy, *as it occurs*. There is no scribe."

"No scribe, huh?" I tried not to look impatient. "You know that's impossible."

"Lots of things are impossible. Doesn't mean they don't happen every day."

"Actually, that *is* what 'impossible' means. You should Google it," I suggested. "Wait, does Google qualify as an impossible thing?"

He muttered something under his breath. I couldn't quite hear him, but I did catch the words "faithless" and "insufferable." I paid him no mind. As my lawyering father often says, "You can't reason with crazy people, no matter how sane they look in a suit."

After another moment, Jack came to a stop in front of the fourth door, the one with the rising sun. He lifted a fist and gave the door a good, hard rap. "This is what I wanted to show you: the *Book of Omens*. It's where we keep the Guardian prophecies, oracles, et cetera."

"And by et cetera, you mean...?"

"Anything foretelling the end of the world."

"Ah." I nodded. "So, the usual bedtime stories."

"Pretty much." He knelt in front of the sun carving, his fingers probing at the edges just as they had the altar in St. Mary's. Impatient, I walked toward the fifth door and lay my hand against the glyphs behind the serpent. Despite the cool air, the stone felt warm under my fingers, as if it were alive.

"What's this one? The *Book of Missed Dental Appointments*?"

Jack glanced up, his face graying in the pale light. "Amelie, you shouldn't touch that."

"Why not? It's just a piece of rock." I looked back at the stone carving to find the serpent staring at me, two glassy black beads where its eyes should have been. Odd. I'd swear its eyes were closed before.

"It's not just a piece of rock, it's—" His voice caught. "That's the chamber to the *Book of Lies*. The symbol you're touching is called an ourbouros," he explained. "In some traditions, it symbolizes the cyclical nature of the universe—death and rebirth.

In others, it's the self-defeating nature of humanity. It's not evil…
exactly. But you, of all people, shouldn't touch it."

I sank to my knees by the edge of the door, my hands stroking
into the wood. Although the planks looked worn and splintered,
they felt smooth under my fingers. The serpent seemed to be
smiling at me.

I couldn't explain why, but there was something powerful
about that door. Even as I crouched in front of it, the darkness
around me changed, shifting into something familiar and malleable.
Whatever was locked behind that door wanted me to open it. It
wanted me to read it. As if hypnotized, I lifted my finger to the
door, the beginnings of an opening glyph forming in my mind.

"Amelie, no!" Jack's hand caught mine against the serpent just
as a cloudy haze congealed at the edges of my vision.

It was as if someone had flipped a switch inside my head. The
shutter between past and present and future began to flicker, all
mixed up and jumbled, color and shape blending kaleidoscopically.
The shock was so intense, I felt as if I'd been ripped out of reality
and tossed down a vortex. Unlike the visions I'd had before, this
one held dimension—sound and smell and touch and taste.

I saw myself with Jack again, only this time we were alone in
a sunlit room, our legs tangled up in each other like knotted rope,
the ceiling fan turning dizzy circles above us. I didn't recognize
the place, but it reminded me of him. Clean and orderly, with an
undercurrent of chaos. His hair had gotten longer and curled in
loose ringlets over his ears. I liked the way it felt between my
fingers, silky and fine.

"You know we can't stay here forever, Ami." He smiled, a lazy
fingertip tracing the line of my collarbone. "Break is almost over.

We have to get back to work."

"Mmm, not yet." I pulled him down on top of me, languishing in the hard press of his body against mine. After wanting him for so long, I could hardly believe he finally belonged to me. I slid my fingers down his well muscled back, every touch sending up golden sparks of light. "We only get to honeymoon once. Does it have to be so short?"

"Well, if you'd invited the demon hordes to the wedding like I suggested, they might have cut us more down time." He brushed a sweaty curl off my forehead, his lips soft and sweet on mine, like fresh strawberries. "Bud's making lasagna this week. He'll kill me if I let you miss family dinner again."

"Jack, don't talk about my dad," I said. "It kills the mood."

He arched an eyebrow. "There's a mood?"

"Yeah." I kissed him again, letting my hands slip lower. "*Total* mood."

"Mmm," he mumbled. "Well, in that case…"

My body melted as he took possession of me, at once nervous and excited. It was perfect. *He* was perfect. I squeezed my eyes shut, listening to the soft murmur of my name on his lips as we pressed into each other, searching for ways to be closer. My heart had never felt so full. So full, it hurt—

"*Amelie, stop!*" Jack's voice cut through the haze like a knife, ripping my vision away in a single, cruel stroke.

My eyes flew open and I blinked a few times, the heat in my brain slowing to a simmer. There was something fierce and solid about his voice that dripped like a potion over my nerves. I held his eyes while the choke of power receded.

"I'm sorry." I slid my hand out of his grip, suddenly ashamed.

"I don't know what happened."

"It's not your fault," he said. "I should have warned you."

"Warned me?"

The angles of his face were sharper in the dim light, the shadows of his eyes more pronounced. He looked as shaken as I felt. "The *Book of Lies* was written by Lucifer for his children. It finds the thing you want most in the world and tells you exactly how to get it. But it's full of tricks. What you give up is never worth the prize at the end, no matter how desperately you want it." He swallowed hard, his forehead creased in pain. "Amelie, you can't read that book. The things you want—they're not right. Whatever you think it's worth, you're wrong. You and I—"

"Stop, please," I cut him off. I didn't want to hear any more.

The dank air pressed down on me, making the back of my neck run cold with sweat. It was too much to process. Not after everything else. I brushed the dirt off my jeans and stood up. The carved serpent's eyes were closed again, but I swear the thing was smiling. It made my skin crawl.

"Just show me whatever it is I need to see and let's get out of here," I said. "This place is giving me a massive case of the willies."

Jack kept his hands pocketed as he led me back to the Omens chamber. There may have been only a few feet between it and the serpent, but each step felt like another layer of fog lifting. By the time he laid his hand on the door and said a few words in Latin, my heart had slowed its patter and my knees were almost steady.

The door swung backward with a soft squeak, its hinges shedding dust as they ground together. Inside the door lay another tunnel, even less inviting than the first. Moss grew in uneven clumps along the top of the narrow corridor and I could see nothing but shadows at the end. I followed Jack as he ducked low through the doorway and dropped to all fours. Apparently, *omens* were meant to be read exclusively by short people.

We were halfway down the tunnel when my head smacked against a rocky outcropping.

"Ow! Dammit!"

"Watch your language. This is a holy place."

"Hah!" I grumbled. "If it's so holy, why don't they have a holy elevator? Or a holy librarian who can go fetch the blasted book for us?"

I was still complaining when a soft yellow light began to filter around the edges of Jack's body. He wrestled himself out of the tunnel, then reached a hand back to help me out.

At first, I thought we were outside. High above us, pinpricks of light shimmered with a fiery intensity like stars in a nighttime sky. Jack shut off his flashlight and I blinked, waiting for my eyes to adjust to the new light source.

"Oh, wow." I took a step closer to Jack.

The room wasn't as cold as the tunnels had been, but I shivered. All around us were endless shelves of books. Some were bound in leather, others with an odd metal sheeting that looked as if it had been hammered into existence. Some had rough leather straps and metal locks around the binding. The volumes were shoved into the crevices between rocks, hollow spaces that had been formed by centuries of erosion rather than man-made tools. It was a neat effect, but not the kind of showcasing that gets one on the *New York Times* bestseller list.

"Wow," I whispered again.

"Yeah, I know what you mean. I was ten when my dad

first brought me here. He let me run around for hours reading prophecies, climbing rocks. I think he was trying to wear me out so I'd be able to focus when he finally showed me the one prophecy that mattered. That was only a few weeks before he died. I never came back. Thought it would hurt too much."

"Does it?"

"Not as much as other things."

I looked down at my hand. Traitor that it was, it had laced itself back into his grip and glowed a soft shade of gold. I mentally ordered it to stop trembling, but to no avail.

Jack led the way as I picked my path gingerly over the boulders, careful not to step on anything slick or evil-looking. I was already covered in dust, so the last thing I needed was a giant moss stain on my jeans. He held tight to my hand as we went, which made it harder to balance but also ensured that if I fell, at least I wouldn't fall far.

We came to a stop at a steep, rocky slope. My eyes had grown used to the dimness and I could tell that the lights above us weren't stars at all. They were insects—beetles, fireflies, June bugs. All the creepy crawlies you'd never want in a library. I was stunned the Great Books hadn't been picked clean by hungry swarms of silverfish.

I stood there gaping while Jack dislodged a book from behind a rock. It had a dark maroon cover and a thick lock that fell open when he touched it. He didn't even need a key.

"Don't look so surprised," he said. "Books aren't as dumb as you think. You should try reading one now and then." He settled himself on a narrow boulder and patted the space beside him.

"I read." I dusted off the rock and climbed up. "I've read all the Harry Potters, three of the Twilights, and every issue of *Cosmo* ever published. I'm a reading prodigy. Like Stephen Hawking."

"Yeah, Stephen Hawking," he muttered. "That's who you remind me of."

"Nobody likes a smarty pants, Jackson."

"Lucky for you, that isn't true. Now sit, zip it, and listen." With a hard glare in my direction, Jack opened the volume, took my hand, and started reading.

"In the days of the Judgment, one shall rise: a Son of Gabriel, a child of doom. And he shall be marked with the sign of the angel, but he is no angel. He shall possess the frailty of man, but he is no man. He alone is the sacrifice, the innocent, the last of his bloodline, who, under angels' gaze, shall be given up to the fury of the avenger. With blood of taint and hair of fire, the beast will fall upon him and his soul will be reaped, as the souls of his brothers. Before the dawn of his twenty-first year, Judgment shall be rendered, and the Angel of Death shall claim him. Only by sacrifice of blood may the Guardians' burden be lifted."

Jack brushed his palm across the page as if he could wipe away the words he'd just read. It wasn't until he fell silent that I realized I must have completely cut off the circulation in his hand.

"Blood and judgment, huh?" I said, unsteady. "Isn't that the plot of every decent action movie ever made?"

Jack's eyes found mine in the half-darkness. They glowed like the dying embers of a campfire.

"Amelie," he said, "this prophecy is why I can't bond with you. I can't bond with anyone. *I'm* the last of Gabriel's line." He flipped the volume closed with a final sounding thump. "I'm supposed to die. And you're supposed to kill me."

Chapter Fourteen:
The Value of Defiance

I felt like he'd stuck a hot poker through my small intestine, all charred and hollow inside. Something had changed in Jack's eyes, too, though I couldn't say what. He looked older, broken somehow.

"That's completely screwed up." My fingers screamed in revolt as I unwound them from his. "I'm not killing you. I'm not killing anyone."

"You may not have a choice." He gave a wry smile. "I don't know if you've noticed lately, but the war isn't going well. Demon attacks are getting more organized. We barely have enough Channelers to cover the major human cities, let alone Convergence outposts. If this keeps up, in a few years there won't be any Guardians left. Not to trample your illusions, kiddo, but the Elders have known for decades about this prophecy. They know Gabriel's bloodline is dying and they've kept it quiet."

"You're lying," I said. "And don't call me kiddo."

"Ami, think about it. Why did those victims give up so easily? Why did Lutz and Templeman die so quietly?" The cool reason in his voice struck at my chest like a knife. "You have no idea how bad it is out there. The stuff you see at St. Michael's is *nothing* compared to what we get in Enforcement. Half of the Channelers I graduated with are dead and more are defecting every day. Put yourself in the Elders' shoes. If you knew you were fighting a lost battle against an endless enemy, wouldn't you look for a way out? Wouldn't you be willing to make a few sacrifices?"

I shook my head. "Not if it meant killing a whole bloodline."

"Better one bloodline than an entire species."

Jack moved to rest a hand on my shoulder but I jerked away. I didn't want to be comforted. It wasn't like I hadn't read the news stories, or heard all the gory details of Katie's true crime dramas. Humans had done far worse for less honorable reasons. But we were *Guardians*. We were better than that. Weren't we?

"No," I said. "There are others. There have to be."

"Amelie." Jack's voice was soft, patient. "Templeman and D'Arcy were the last Gabrielite Watchers. Lutz was my great uncle. When Smalley called me back to St. Michael's, it wasn't because she thought I could prevent the prophecy. It was because she knew as soon as I died they would kill you. Maybe she thought I could help you, I don't know." He shook his head. "The Elders have known since your birth what you were destined for. This prophecy is the only reason they let someone so dangerous live."

A chill rippled down my spine. I didn't feel dangerous. I felt like a part of me had shriveled and died.

My arms wrapped in a tight hug around my torso, as if by sheer determination I could keep my heart from spilling onto the dirt. They'd planned to execute me. Even though I hadn't done anything wrong.

"That's why you came back?"

He nodded. "All my life, I've been told you'd kill me, rip the soul right out of me. The first day of school, when I realized who you were, I was terrified. But you seemed so clueless and so…not at all scary." He smiled ruefully. "I told myself it was okay to talk to you. It was research. If I had to fight you, I needed to know what you were, right? Then, when I realized you had no idea—" He broke off.

"What?" I asked.

Jack tugged the neck of his long sleeved T-shirt over his collarbone. I could see a small line of what looked like pink scar tissue. It formed an oval about the size of a robin's egg etched at the top of his left shoulder. The mark of Gabriel.

The end of his bloodline.

"I've always been treated differently. Teachers were more careful with me, my parents never let me have friends over. No attachments," he said. "Nothing I couldn't walk away from. When my dad showed me the prophecy, it was almost a relief. At least I knew what I needed to do."

"What, turn to drugs?" I blurted out. "Your childhood sounds dismal."

He laughed, halfway between sadness and amusement. "When the Elders found you guilty at trial, it was a split vote. Chancellor Thibault argued that, if they executed you, it could alter the prophecy. Akira finally decided if my death was truly meant to end the war, then nothing we did could change it. That's why I tried so hard to keep you away from this, away from me. Prophecy is law for us, Amelie," he explained. "I have to die, and you have to kill me."

A huge part of me wanted to smack him. In one day, I had lost everything—everything but him. How dare he sit there, so mature and calm, telling me now I would lose him, too?

With shaky hands, I yanked the book from his lap and hurled it across the room like a shot put. It slowed in midair and fluttered to rest against a rock unharmed. It seemed to sigh in dismay, like a small house-pet denied access to its master. We both watched as it tucked the strap indignantly around itself, and then fastened the metal lock over the binding. Evidently, some books *are* smarter than I thought.

I looked at Jack, but all he did was shrug.

"When?" I demanded.

"Saturday. My twenty-first birthday. If it's a literal reading, I'll be dead by dawn."

All at once, Bud's words came back to me, a key unlocking a door. *Stay away from him until next week.* He must have known about the prophecy. But how? And why would he keep it from me?

"You told Hansen there might be more Gray Ones," I said. "Someone besides me. Do you really believe that?"

"Maybe. I'm not sure it matters." He ran a frustrated hand across his head. "If you *are* killing Gabriel's bloodline, if you *did* rig your test, then you're obviously unaware of it. Which means you're being controlled by someone else." He paused to let that horrid little notion sink in. "And if it's *not* you, then you're being set up. Either way, you're as much a victim as anyone else."

"And yet everyone's trying to kill me."

"Absurd, isn't it?"

I was still shivering when the sound of shifting rocks drew my attention back to the corridor where we'd entered. It sounded too intentional to be a rat, more like steel-toed boots than tiny paws. Both of us slowly turned our heads toward the sound.

"Jack?"

"Run," he whispered.

His hand felt warm around mine as he pulled me through the chamber in the opposite direction. Breath tore at my chest, pushing me harder and faster than I thought possible over rocks and wet moss patches. As much as I'd hated inching through that first tunnel, right now, I couldn't be more grateful for it. The longer it took for them to get in, the more time Jack and I had to get out. Somewhere behind us, a clamor of voices rose up, but we kept going.

I barely noticed when the cavern began to narrow. Jack had turned off his flashlight but he didn't slow, not even as we hurtled toward a pitch-black crevice in the wall. At least the tunnel had the decency to slant upward, so I didn't feel like I was going deeper into the circles of hell. After twenty yards or so, it narrowed, and we were again forced to our knees.

"Are you sure this is an exit?"

"I thought so," he said, uncertain, "but it's been ten years since I was down here. There could have been a cave-in." His hands dug at the narrow space in front of us, dislodging small rocks. "Give me a second, I think there's an opening up ahead."

I waited for a moment as he dug at the earth, sending rock after rock clattering past. My mind whirled and desperation churned in my chest. "Jack, wait! What if I give up?" I asked. "Will they let you go?"

"What are you talking about?" He slowed his digging.

"I mean, if I tell them I killed you and dumped your body in the river, or something… If I turn myself in, will that be enough to end it?"

He froze for a second, and then slowly inched backward until he was next to me again. In the crowded space, our bodies nearly touched. I couldn't see his face, but I knew it was scrunched into that adorable "you're nuts" expression he wore so often.

"Amelie." I felt his breath, soft and sweet on my face. "If you're saying this out of some misguided loyalty because of what happened at your test, then please…don't. When I kissed you, it was the most cowardly, dishonorable thing I've done in my life. Just because I thought I was going to die doesn't excuse it. I made a mistake, but it was *my* mistake. Please, don't let it mess with your head. You're too smart for that."

My skin prickled, and not from the temperature. A *mistake*. That's what he thought of me. It didn't matter that he'd also said I was smart. All I heard was what a colossal mistake it had been to kiss me.

Tears tightened the back of my throat, but I swallowed them away. "You're right, I'm being ridiculous."

"Yeah, you are."

"It was just a stupid kiss, right? It's not like we're bonded."

He hesitated. "Of course not."

I rolled back onto my stomach and started wiggling up the steep path through the hole he'd made in the rockslide. Seriously, how many times did I need to be rejected before I'd finally believe him? A hundred? A thousand?

It may have been my imagination, but I could've sworn the air was getting warmer. Its scent had shifted from cool and dank to warm and pungent, the way Bourbon Street smells after Mardi Gras. Even the rocks beneath me seemed slick with heat.

"Personally," I whispered over my shoulder, "I think you're the most idiotic, pain-loving individual on the planet. You must thrive on suffering."

"I try."

"I mean, who else would spend their whole life getting ready to die just because some thousand-year-old prophetic nitwit said so—"

"I can name at least five," he grunted behind me.

"And then promptly run away with the person he thinks is going to murder him?" I purposefully scraped a few stones loose with my shoe, listening with satisfaction as they bounced off his head. "You must be a complete moron."

"Uh-huh. You mentioned."

"Seemed worth repeating." I edged forward on my elbows. "Still, masochistic as you are, and moronic as it was of you to kiss me, I should warn you that if anyone so much as lays a hand on you, I'll rip off their fingernails one by one and feed them to Lisa's cat—Oh crap!"

I stopped talking, not because I was done, but because the ground that had felt so solid just a moment ago gave a sudden lurch. A slow crack echoed through the tunnel. Then, without warning, I was falling. Sliding, really. Rocky dirt crumbled around me like sugar cubes dissolving in hot coffee, and I gave a muffled scream. Head first, my body plummeted into darkness and was swept away into the most putrid smelling tunnel of moving water I had ever experienced…including the time Smalley made me clean the school septic system.

Rocks dragged at my arms, scraping red streaks down to my elbows. I was vaguely aware of Jack yelling at me to turn around but, of course, I couldn't because of the stupid torrent of silt and sewage. Never before had I been so stuck between a desire to scream and a need to keep my mouth shut so I didn't swallow half the New Orleans Sanitation Department.

A few seconds later, the waterslide of yuck dumped me into a revolting pond o' sludge. I surfaced, too shocked to cry, too grossed-out to speak. The smell invaded my nostrils—a mixture of rotted papaya and one of those campground public toilets no one ever cleans.

"Ugh! Yuck!" I shrieked.

"Woohoo!" Jack landed behind me with an enthusiastic battle cry. His impact sent a spatter of something that smelled like decomposed burger across my face and I found myself hating him again. When he surfaced, he shook out his hair like a wet dog, eyes glittering. "Awesome! I knew that was an exit."

"Oh, you think this is fun, Prophecy Boy?" I yelled, furious. "You think it's cool that we're swimming in other people's feces?"

Brown water dripped down his smiling face as his gaze danced over me. I couldn't put my finger on his expression. Bemusement. Possibly insanity.

"*What* are you grinning at?" I splashed a floating chunk of molded apple core at his head.

He dodged the chunk but kept smiling. "Nothing. It's just… no girl has ever offered to feed my enemies' fingernails to her cat before."

"Lisa's cat. And don't flatter yourself. At the moment, I'm tempted to feed him *your* fingernails."

I glanced at the high, circular opening we'd passed through. For some reason, it left me with the uncomfortable sensation that I'd been digested by the city. Directly above us, a series of large rectangular grates ran along the length of the drainage ditch where we'd landed. Moonlight flooded through them into the small enclosure, making Jack's eyes glow silver. I held my breath as he waded toward me and lifted a hand to my cheek.

"You've got spaghetti on your face," he said. "At least, I hope it's spaghetti."

I frowned, desperate not to think about it. "Yeah, well, you've got toilet paper on your chin. *And* you're doomed. Pot." I pointed at him, then back at myself. "Kettle. Can we move it along, please? I think I'm contracting hepatitis."

He gave me that look again, the cocky half-smile. "Sure. We're almost there."

I followed him through the tunnel obediently, ducking my head every few seconds to avoid the concrete arches that supported the drainage structure. I didn't bother asking where "there" was. Jack was about as forthcoming as a park bench and, frankly, I didn't feel like wasting my breath.

True to his word, it only took another few minutes before we came to a metal ladder with rungs embedded in the concrete. When Jack finally helped me out of the sewer, I almost cried with relief. Never had the beer/fish/vomit scents of the French Quarter smelled so fragrantly sweet. Somewhere in the distance, the sound of rushing water and steamboat horns rang out. Yup. Not Hell. Definitely still home.

My knees ground against the hard cobbles as I crawled to the side of the road, fully prepared to kiss the ground. The concrete was still warm from the heat of the day, so I flopped onto my back and gave a long sigh. Through my eyelids, I could see the full moon above.

"Jack, seriously," I muttered. "No more surprises. No more prophetic caves, or haunted Graymason nests, or body-surfing sewage. If you want to commit suicide, let's just go hunt some werewolves and be done with it, okay?"

I lay still as a dark silhouette came to hover over me, blocking out the brightness of the moon.

"Well, love, if you're set on suicide, I daresay there's something more dangerous than a werewolf."

Every inch of me tensed. Not only was that not Jack's voice, I could tell by the flawless musical quality and perfect British accent it wasn't human, either.

My eyes scanned over him, taking in the cliché. Tall, dark, and psychotically beautiful, with elegant cheekbones and the most arresting violet eyes I'd ever seen on a man. The perfect echo of every romantic hero I'd conjured in my head.

"Oh, hell," I mumbled. "Who ordered a vampire?"

Chapter Fifteen:
Postcards from Hell

I hate vampires.

I know, I know...civil rights. The value of cultural difference. It's a disease, not a choice, blah, blah, blah. I'd heard it a million times in Lutz's diversity seminar. Heck, I'd even defended their bloodsucking butts from demon attacks. Still, if half the stuff in the tabloids was true, then the whole species deserved to be taken out to the park for a sunny Sunday picnic.

Poof! Problem solved.

My fist cracked through the air toward the vamp's face... just as it disappeared from view. I scrambled to my feet, scanning frantically. By the time I found him, he was standing with his back against a rough stone fence about twenty feet away. Jeez, I'd never seen a vamp move that fast.

"Convergence Peace Tenets forbid unprovoked attacks against Inferni, you know," he said indignantly. "Have you heard of them?"

"She doesn't read," Jack called from the street as he calmly pushed the maintenance hole cover back into place. "Besides, that statute only refers to superhuman force. She knows better than to channel. Right, Amelie?"

I did know that, but did he have to *ention-may* it to the *ampire-vay*? I turned back to the wall where the vamp used to be. He was gone.

"You were right, Jackson. She *is* charming…in a brutish kind of way."

The British guy's voice came from directly behind me this time, all smooth and warm like sexy butter. Not that butter's sexy. Anyway, I remembered reading somewhere that vampire pheromones could act as a natural aphrodisiac on anything they consider prey. Personally, I wasn't feeling it.

I whipped an elbow over my shoulder, throwing all my weight toward the spot where his voice came from. By the time my elbow got there, of course, he was gone. Again.

"Arrgh! Would you please quit that!" I growled, landing hard on my butt.

The vamp grinned down at me. "Graceful, too. Tell me, love, do you dance?"

"Stand still for a sec. I'll dance on your face."

"Hmm," he frowned, thoughtful. "Not much incentive, is that?"

"Amelie," Jack interrupted, "I'd like you to meet my cousin, Luc Montaigne. Luc, this is Amelie Bennett, my—" He broke off, uncertain. "Amelie."

"*Your* Amelie, eh?" Luc flashed him a mischievous smile. "Something you want to tell me, cousin?"

Jack's hand found the small of my back as he helped me up.

Instinct screamed at me to grab him and run, but I held it in check.

"Relax, he won't hurt you," Jack murmured.

"You sure about that?" I asked.

"He's already eaten tonight. Right, Luc?"

Vamp-Boy shot Jack a smug wink, then said in his polite English clip, "I've always got room for dessert."

Under the sewage, Jack registered annoyance. "Great to see you again, Luc. Remind me why we don't hang out more often?"

As we trailed the evil undead down Governor Nicholls Street, I registered mild amazement at the range of swearwords Jack managed without unclenching his teeth. He must have realized I could hear, because by the time we crossed onto lower Bourbon the swearing stopped. Thank heavens. I'd gotten used to Jack being the calm one and, at present, *I* was about four seconds away from diving back into the sewer to escape the psycho vampire. The only thing that kept me grounded was Jack's hand on mine and the (albeit, tentative) assurance that El Vampo wasn't planning to chomp me.

"So…your *cousin*, huh?" I asked, once we'd settled into a modest, six-bedroom townhouse away from the bustle of the Quarter.

"Unfortunately." Jack shrugged. "Don't be too intimidated. He's never killed anything bigger than a badger and never in the house. Blood stains the upholstery."

"Well, sure. There's that."

As soon as we'd entered the apartment, Luc had shuffled Jack and me into the laundry room to change—something about not tracking sewage on his Persian rugs. I couldn't really blame him, but still…strutting around in front of those two in a bathrobe? *So* awkward.

Admittedly, the vampire's lair was pretty swanky. Far more posh than I would expect of a secret bloodletting hideout. No manacles. No severed limbs. A little disillusioning, actually. The place was a *mélange* of cream-colored decorative molding, Edwardian tapestries, textured silk wallpaper, and what appeared to be a series of original Renoirs lining the hall. I couldn't help thinking how crazy my mom would have gone over the pair of antique elephant chairs in the parlor. *What self-respecting male vampire collects elephant chairs, anyway?*

"Sorry about this." Jack fingered the downy fluff of my bathrobe. "Luc doesn't have relationships, so he gets a little anal-retentive about his stuff."

"Yeah, he's a peach," I agreed. "Tell me again how you're related?"

"Technically, we're not. His grandfather is the sovereign ruler of the Immortal community, so he and my gramps got to be friends during the founding of Paranormal Convergence. Then, after Gramps died, Luc's great-grandfather took his widow as the first angelblood vampire familiar."

"Wow, that's…" Hmm, what was the word I wanted? "Nauseating."

"It was the seventies."

"Uh-huh." I cleared my throat, trying to push the image out of my head. "So, you're related by rumor and bloodlust?"

"Pretty much. Since we all signed the Peace Tenets, Luc's been like family. Not always in a good way, but at least he shows up for holidays and birthday parties," Jack said, then added, "whether I invite him or not."

Oddly enough, I could see that. As soon as we'd stepped into the apartment, Luc started bustling around like a concerned mother hen—fetching towels, drawing the curtains. By the time Jack and I emerged from the laundry room, he had copies of the files I'd seen at school spread across a worktable and a pot of coffee brewing in the kitchen for us. Say what you like about vampires—this one didn't lack attention to detail.

Jack and I took turns showering. After twenty minutes of scrubbing, I still didn't feel precisely clean, but at least my hair didn't smell like rotten Chinese food anymore. None of Luc's normal clothes fit me, so I ended up in a pair of black silk Armani pajamas with a drawstring waist. It could have been worse. They could have been poly-blend.

Luc looked up when I entered the parlor still toweling off my hair. "Black suits you," he commented.

"Don't get any ideas, Romeo."

His frown curled into a slow grin, at once mocking and devastatingly handsome. "Ah, Shakespeare. 'How silver sweet sound lovers' tongues by night, like softest music to attending ears.'" He laughed. "Saw the movie, did you?"

"I also saw *Buffy the Vampire Slayer*," I said. "Guess which one I liked better."

Luc gestured to the kitchen. "Have a coffee. I need to show you something."

I gave the dark Columbian brew a careful sniff before fixing myself a café au lait. It looked okay, but with the quasi-evil undead you never know. "If this is rufied, I'll flush your eyeballs with holy water."

"I look forward to it. Please, sit."

Still with the insouciant grin, Luc directed me toward the worktable he'd set up. Although I'd seen the case files we had at school, the pictures Luc spread out were completely unfamiliar. There were dozens of people I didn't recognize—old and young, women and men. About half looked like Graymason deaths, with the pale eyes and vacant, calm expression I'd seen on Lutz. The other half were brutal. Bloody.

"They were all Gabrielites?" I asked.

He shook his head. "Not all. Some were their bondmates, some innocent bystanders. Do any of them look familiar?"

"No. Why would they?"

Luc's gaze flickered to me, his forehead creased with suspicion and something I couldn't quite identify. *He thinks you killed them, genius*, my ever-present, annoyingly accurate inner voice informed me. How nice, right? The bloodsucker thought *I* was a monster.

"If you're fishing around to see if I'm the murderer, you can stop," I said. "I'm not."

"Your blood begs to differ, love."

The look I shot him was pure poison. "Look, Vlad, maybe I am Lucifer's bloodline, although I don't completely buy that either. But the prophecy said I would kill Jack in vengeance. I barely know the guy. What could I possibly have to avenge on him?"

Luc sighed, his arms laced across his chest in a kind of philosophical arrogance. "'Tis a better thing to rage against truth than go gently into falsehood."

"What's that supposed to mean?"

"It means, love, that your lips twitch when you lie." He dropped a sugar cube into his cocktail glass. "You've no idea if you're innocent in this, have you? It's entirely possible your memory has been altered. There's no denying your people are capable of it. Think," he urged. "These deaths have been happening for nearly half a decade. In the past five years, has there ever been a time when you couldn't remember where you'd gone, what you'd done? Anything unusual?"

I closed my eyes, raking my mind over lost memories, the missing chunks of time I always associated with Mom. Had anything like that happened in recent years? Luc was right that the Elders wiped human memories all the time. They had to, to protect us. I'd just never thought of them using that skill on Guardians.

"You're bent. I wouldn't kill anyone," I said. "No way."

But my gaze drifted back to the photos, searching each victim's face. Not that I wanted them to ring any bells but if they had, at least it would offer an explanation. The more I learned about all this, the more I wondered about my role in it. Had the Elders known something, seen something at the trial? Were they right to convict me?

My vision blurred as I continued to stare at the files. Between the brutality I saw there and the heady scent of Luc's aftershave, a headache took hold. Honestly, it was difficult being so close to him—to any bloodsucker, I guess. My survival instincts screamed in revolt, though my conscience urged me not to condemn him before I knew he'd done something condemnable.

I lifted the heels of my hands to my eyes. The day could *not* end soon enough.

"It's all right," Luc said with a pitying sigh. "It is a lot to manage for a female. You've had a rough night."

"Try a rough decade," I muttered, ignoring the misogyny. "At least things can't get worse, right?"

"I wouldn't go that far."

Luc shifted in the chair beside me, his slender fingers gathering the photos. This close, his eyes seemed to hold a glow of their own, like the flickering torch lights we'd passed along the street. "D'you want to talk about it?"

"With you? No, thanks."

"You sure? Immortality breeds good listeners and great lovers. We're very patient," he explained.

I fought back the gag reflex.

With deft movements, he finished collecting the file and put it away. I heard him walk into the kitchen, then the trickle of him refilling my coffee cup and pouring himself another drink.

"So," Luc said, as he took his seat again, "does he know?"

"Does who know what?"

"Jackson. Does he know you're in love with him?"

I choked on my coffee.

In love? Was I in love with him? More importantly, was it that obvious? I opened my mouth to argue, then shut it. What was the point? If a socially stunted bloodsucker could spot my affection, then did I really need to bother with denial?

"No," I sighed. "Maybe. He's impossible to read. One second he hates me, then the next he kisses me like I'm the last sip of water in the Sahara. I asked him if he'd consider bonding but—"

"Did you?" Luc cupped a hand around his jaw, entirely too amused. "And what did he say?"

"He said he can't bond because he's supposed to die. Then he threw me down a sewer."

The sound of the vampire laughing was almost enough to

make me smile. I watched while he took another sip of his gloppy red cocktail and sank onto a chair beside me.

"Well, love, I can't help you with the sewer, but to be fair, he *is* going to die. So are you, for that matter."

"It's not the same."

"No? You think because you love him, he should be allowed to live?" He absently straightened my bathrobe collar, as if he wasn't even aware of doing it. "Silly girl, think of all the Inferni, all the *Guardians* dying at the hands of demonkind—children losing their parents, husbands losing their wives. Your people believe this prophecy—Jack's death—will end the war. Would you truly sacrifice that chance for your own selfish desires?"

I didn't know how to answer. *Yes,* was what I wanted to say, but that sounded so infantile and self-centered. Especially when he phrased it like that.

Luc shook his head. "If being loved could keep someone alive, your people would be immortal. And if a lack of love were the thing that killed us, my species would be extinct. Sometimes, I think the best we can do is to find that one thing we cannot live without and cling to it for as long as we can. If your 'one thing' happens to be my cousin, then more's the pity for you."

I slumped back against the rails of Luc's breakfast room chair, mentally and physically wrought. Much as I hated to admit it, the vampire had a point. If Jack was meant to die, there wasn't much I could do about it. Maybe everybody thought I was some all-powerful Graymason, but I knew the truth. I couldn't even defeat my Wards teacher. How was I supposed to save Jack?

I decided to make myself scarce in the kitchen while the boys finished up their business. Luc had put together a satchel of documents for both of us: IDs, passports, Cayman Island and Swiss bank accounts. He'd also gotten a bunch of disposable phones, though none of them were as cute as the one Lisa picked out. When we finally made it down to the garage (in our own freshly laundered clothes, thank God), I couldn't help pausing at the door to Luc's car...Luc's sleek, black, European vampmobile.

"Nice wheels," I commented. "Stalk the suburbs much?"

"Talk to your boyfriend." Luc popped open the door and ushered me into the practically nonexistent backseat.

"Yeah, sorry about that," Jack apologized. "I wasn't one hundred percent sure you weren't slaughtering the innocent, so I figured someone should watch you. Couldn't very well do it myself."

"And the werewolf?"

"Werewolf?" Jack threw an inquisitive look at Luc.

"I had things to do." Luc shrugged. "Dane said he'd take over for a few hours. No blood, no foul, right?"

Jack gave him a disapproving look, but said nothing.

As we pulled out of Luc's parking garage, I settled into the leather, flooded by a mixture of relief and disappointment. Much as hanging with the bloodsucker upset my survival instinct, it had been nice to feel safe. Odd how the ability to drink coffee in peace can define your sense of humanity.

"Cozy?" Luc called into the backseat.

"Perfect," I grumbled. Whoever invented foreign sports cars must've had small friends.

"You two are welcome to stay at the flat. It's not much, I know, but Arianna and her boyfriends won't be in town until Saturday morning for the Peace Tenets induction. Until then, it's yours."

"Arianna?"

"His mom. Don't ask," Jack muttered and turned to Luc. "I appreciate the offer, but sooner or later the Elders are going to figure out someone's helping us. Your name is bound to come up. And if Aunt Arianna finds out you've ditched your bodyguard detail again—"

"Loathsome creatures." Luc pulled to a stop a few blocks from our boarding house and shut off the engine. "Just remember, by week's end the city will be flooded with Immortals and were-beasts for the Induction. If you're still in town, we could use you at the signing."

Jack half-grinned. "If I'm still alive, you mean?"

Luc didn't return the smile. I had to respect him for that.

"Oh, relax, cousin." Jack slapped him on the shoulder. "There are dozens to sign for the Tenets. You won't need me. Just don't forget what you promised, okay?"

It might have been my imagination, but I swear Luc flicked a glance my way.

Before I could give it much thought, Jack hefted Luc's satchel over his shoulder and pulled me out of the car. Weird how that tiny bag represented my whole future. I'd overheard enough of their conversation to realize that as soon as this was over, I'd have to run. If Jack lived through it, he would come with me. If not... Well, I couldn't think about that.

With a few words of farewell, Jack clasped Luc's hand and pulled the vamp to him for a hug. I think Luc managed to eke out a little pat on Jack's back.

"All right, enough theatrics." Luc disentangled himself. "I'm not convinced you won't be at the signing, so let's save our goodbyes, shall we?"

Jack smiled. "I love you, man."

"Sod off." Luc blushed.

As soon as we'd stepped to the curb, the vampire's car squealed away, leaving two lines of black rubber against the pavement. As first introductions to a species went, it wasn't as bad as I'd feared. Sure, he was arrogant and stunning and rude, but so are male models…and they pass for human *all* the time.

Tiredness washed over me as I laced my fingers through Jack's, pulling him in the direction of our boarding house. "Home, sweet hovel?"

"Actually, we have one more stop. It's a little one. Five minutes."

"Oh, come on!" I begged. "I'm clean. I smell nice. I want to eat a granola bar and go to bed. Whatever it is, we'll do it in the morning. Please?" I tugged on his arm again, but it was like tugging on a stalled Mack truck.

"Five minutes. You'll hardly notice."

I sighed. "Two."

"Four. Please?"

• • •

Ten centuries later, we trudged to a stop at our destination, the House That Time Forgot. Out of a mess of brambles rose a clapboard cottage that was not only smaller but decidedly shabbier than its neighbors. Bright pink paint flaked off it in sheets, and a mass of yellow weeds crawled in fingers up the dingy white porch trellis. Whatever had happened to it during the last hurricane obviously hadn't been fixed, because the poor structure listed so far to one side I actually worried it might collapse onto the house next door.

"Do you gravitate toward crappy places?" I asked as I stared up at it. "Maybe it's something in your genetic make-up. Where do you live, anyway? In a roach-filled shack?"

He gave me an odd look out of the corner of his eye. "You've seen where I live."

"No, I haven't," I argued. "How would I? Do you think I stalk you in my spare time?"

"Well, no, but in the caves..." He swallowed, clearly uncomfortable. "Never mind, it's not important."

Okay, to be fair, I *had* tried to Google-stalk him. But Google-stalking is a far cry from having your demonblood best friend park his vampmobile across the street and use his x-ray vamp-vision to spy into someone's house. That's just rude.

Eager to get the errand over with, I stomped up the rickety steps to the front door. On one side of the porch, a rocking chair had been chained to the railing, though both looked so termite-infested I couldn't imagine anyone would be interested.

Jack slunk up the stairs behind me with his mouth clamped shut and his hands pocketed. *Flustered* was such an uncommon look for him I had to double check to make sure I was seeing it right.

"What's wrong with you?" I demanded, impatient. "Do you miss Luc already? Or are you miffed I called you a shack-dweller?"

The words were barely out of my mouth when a soft creak sounded from the doorway and a familiar voice spilled out. "I 'spect he's insulted 'cause you done forgot somethin' that was s'posed to be unforgettable. Ain't that right, baby?"

I whirled, half-expecting to find another Crossworlder, or

maybe a nice, rabid werecat to round out the evening. What I got was far, far stranger.

In the doorway, looking shockingly normal in a printed T-shirt and jeans, stood Benita Bertle, resident cafeteria lady at St. Michael's. She'd tucked her hair into a bright purple headscarf and skull-shaped earrings dangled from both earlobes. Other than that, she looked like a regular person. No apron. No hairnet. No spatula.

"*Bertle*?" I sputtered, before I could stop myself. "But—"

"Hi, Benita. Sorry we're late." Jack brushed past me to give the woman a bear hug that nearly lifted her feet off the ground. "It's good to see you."

"Good to see you, too, baby. Real good. And you—" Bertle wagged a finger at me. "You ought mind yo manners, missy. T'aint right for a woman to sass her Watcher. Not in public, anyhow."

A little girl in a white eyelet nightgown poked her head around the lunch lady's girth to stare at me. "Uncle Jack, is that her?" she asked, wide-eyed.

Jack sank to his knees, one hand coming up to muss the girl's hair. "Delia, what are you doing up so late, young lady? Don't you have school tomorrow?"

"Mama said I could stay up to see y'all." The little girl grinned, flashing a row of perfect white teeth. "That's her, ain't it? She don't look like no angel killer. A prossitute, maybe, but not no angel killer."

Jack let out a snort and I felt my patience begin to thin.

"For your information, you little punk, I am neither a prostitute nor an angel killer," I told her. "How old are you, anyway?"

"Ten, last July."

"Hmph!" I frowned. "Ten is old enough to know better."

Bertle chuckled again, more heartily this time. "C'aint argue that now, can I? Come on in, y'all. Delia, why don't you head on up to bed, baby? I'll be along to tuck you in."

The little girl blushed as Jack grabbed her for a quick kiss on the cheek. "G'night, Uncle Jack."

"'Night, beautiful," he said with a wink.

I listened to her feet patter up the stairs as he led me into a narrow foyer that could only be described as eclectic. Like my house, only way, *way* worse. Every surface seemed to be covered with broken antiques, battered turntables, strange religious art, and more than a few coconuts carved into the shapes of monkey-skulls. Even the faded plaster walls were layered with wooden masks and gilt-framed portraits of slaves. It reminded me of one of those Pakistani flea markets that can fold itself up and disappear in five seconds. I gave the coconut skulls a wide berth as we passed into the kitchen.

"Why did she call you my Watcher? Is she crazy?" I whispered to Jack.

"She's a seer," he said, as if that explained everything.

Honestly, the whole situation threw me a little off balance. I'd been sifting through Jack's "caves" comment earlier and the only explanation I could come up with was that he must have seen my vision in the catacombs. Which I'd kind of suspected. So, okay. I'd been caught having sex fantasies about my crush. I mean, sure there was a part of me that wanted to curl into a ball and die of mortification (omigod-omigod-omigod), but rationally I recognized this was survivable. Like Dad said, the occasional fantasy is perfectly normal teenage behavior, right? *Right?* The problem was, if that *really* was his apartment and he'd seen the whole thing, did that mean the vision wasn't just a random, hormonal figment of my imagination? What about every other thing I'd seen when I'd touched him? Our wedding, for example. Had he seen that, too?

Good grief! Could I still call myself a virgin?

"Y'all grab yourself a seat and we'll get started." Bertle pushed me into one of four ripped green kitchen chairs. She poured some tea into a cracked porcelain mug and shoved it toward me, then sank into the chair opposite. "Baby, you ever had your aura read?"

"No, ma'am."

"Well, then," she grinned a gold-smattered, toothy grin, "you in for a treat."

Jack settled into the chair beside me. He gave my hand a quick squeeze before he set it on the scuffed Formica surface. As if by instinct, his leg stretched out to rest against mine, tendrils of warmth threading into connection through our jeans.

"Close those pretty eyes and gimme yo hand, sugar," Bertle said. "Jackson, git away from her, boy. You know I c'aint see nothin' with you lightin' her up like that."

"Sorry."

I shut one eye as Jack pulled his knee away from mine. The threads dissipated.

Bertle's hands were like a midnight breeze on my palm. Her fingers stroked so lightly into each groove I could barely feel them. It was soothing, actually.

"Can you see them?" Jack asked her after a few minutes.

"Shush, you," Bertle scolded. She kept stroking my palm slowly, rhythmically. Although my brain simmered with questions,

I kept quiet. After what seemed like an eternity, she set it down on the table and gave it a pat.

"Well, okay, then," she said, and slowly rose from her seat. As if by habit, she picked up a stack of salad plates by the sink and started washing them, one at a time. Then, she started on the dinner plates.

"Benita, did you see the souls or not?" Jack pressed.

Bertle turned but didn't pause her task. "No, baby, I din't see nothin'. There ain't nothin' to see," she said. "That girl ain't no Graymason."

He sat up straight in his chair, his hand reaching for mine. "What do you mean? Are you saying the *Book of Blood* was wrong? She's not Lucifer's bloodline?"

"Oh, she Lucifer's, a'right. But she ain't no Graymason." Bertle wiped her hands on the edge of her T-shirt and spun to face us, a glimmer of amusement in her eye. "That girl's a Wraithmaker."

Chapter Sixteen:
Wraithmaker

I sat motionless at the kitchen table.

Jack and Bertle stared at me expectantly, like at any moment I might grab my chair and start smashing things. Granted, there was plenty in this house that could benefit from a close encounter with a kitchen chair, but their expressions wigged me out, nonetheless.

"Wraithmaker." I rolled the word over my tongue. It sounded vaguely familiar. "So, what is that? Like at Christmas? With fake pine cones and ribbons and stuff?"

Bertle arched an eyebrow at Jack. "Trained her well, did ya, baby?"

Jack lowered his forehead onto the table with a thud. "Amelie, I'm going to say this one last time. You. Must. Do. Your. Homework. I'm not kidding. Our world is full of dangerous things. When you neglect your studies, you deny yourself the tools to deal with them. Every assignment—"

I lifted a hand to stop him. "Allow me. Every assignment is a rare window into the ancient and noble tradition of the Guardians, a key to the mysterious power of the Crossworld, blah, blah. Don't forget the part about how I'm not living up to my potential."

He glared at me. "Benita, can we have a minute?"

"Sho 'nuff, baby. I'll just go see 'bout Delia." Smiling, she pushed herself away from the counter and sauntered toward the stairs. Jack waited until she was gone, then leaned forward.

"Ami, this is serious. I'm not always going to be around to look after you. I need to know you can take care of yourself."

"I totally can. Pinkie swear." I held up a pinkie to show my commitment.

"That's not good enough. I need you to promise me, no more shortcuts. No more screwing around in your lessons, no more pranks. You're off the Otrava now. There's no telling what you can do once you're properly trained and bonded—"

He stopped, probably hearing how ridiculous his words were.

Properly trained and bonded? We both knew I wasn't getting bonded. Even if I did prove my innocence, no one would bond with Lucifer's bloodline. I'd be lucky if they let me live.

"Amelie, I—"

"Save it," I said, my voice quiet. "I know you're right. If the Elders let me back into school, I'll work harder, okay?"

He paused, thoughtful, and then stood. I watched him pluck a thick, leather-wrapped Bible from a bookshelf and open it on the kitchen table.

"Okay," he said, "History 101. Wraithmakers are like the Guardian version of a necromancer, only less creepy. In Deuteronomy, they're called bone-conjurers…ones who can bring back the dead. But it doesn't work the same way with us as it does with humans. A human necromancer raises spirits by letting them feed off his or her energy. So the spirit can stay active only while the necromancer is nearby. They have no form, no soul. It isn't like the thing is alive, do you understand?"

"Yeah. Sort of," I said. "Not really."

"Okay, Wraithmakers aren't like that," he continued. "They're the flip side of a Graymason. Graymasons can take souls out of a body and funnel them into the spirit plane, right? Well, Wraithmakers can bring them back."

I stared at him, pensive. It wasn't that his words didn't make sense—they did. I just had a hard time believing something so bizarre could be true. Especially about me. "So, you're saying *I* can raise the dead? Like, I could bring back Elvis? Or my mom?"

"Elvis, probably not. Your mom? If you could find her, yeah," he said. "But Charlotte's been dead for ten years. The longer a spirit's gone, the further away it gets. Its mortal memories, personality—all that starts to degrade. It's not like summoning a spirit from the past. Any diviner can call up a fragment of spectral energy. Wraithmakers don't deal in fragments. They give life to lost souls."

"Uh-huh. This is creeping me out. Are you saying I'm some kind of zombiemaker?"

"No, zombies are the walking dead. They're just reanimated corpses," he explained. "You actually make souls *live* again. Eat, breathe, love. All you need is an empty vessel. Do you understand?"

"Sure," I said. "How?"

He flipped the book closed with a sigh. "That, I don't know. It's been thousands of years since either Graymasons or Wraithmakers have existed. I doubt there's anyone alive who..."

I waited to see if he was going to continue. He didn't. "Who what?"

"Forget it. It's too dangerous."

"Dude, you say that a lot," I noted. "This is my *life* you're talking about. Didn't you just finish saying how I need to study more? Learn more? How am I going to find answers if you don't help me?"

"Some answers aren't worth finding."

I was getting ready to argue when the intentional *thud-thud* of footsteps sounded in the hall. Bud did the same thing whenever Matt came over to watch TV—usually during one of Lisa's break-up phases. It was a pointless gesture since Matt and I were totally platonic. Still, I recognized the *thud-thud*.

"Y'all 'bout done?" Bertle paused in the doorway.

"More or less," Jack answered. "There is one more thing."

Of course there was one more thing. Wasn't there always? I took a swig of my tea and braced myself for yet another life-destroying nugget. "Bring it," I said.

"Amelie, you're an only child, right?"

"Uh." That *so* wasn't where I thought he was going. "Yeah. Why?"

"Are you sure? I mean, *really* sure?"

I gave him a dark look. "Let me think…boring family camp-outs, dress-up tea parties for one. Unless you count my imaginary friend Lurlene, I can safely say, yes, I am an only child. I'll ask again. *Why?*"

Jack looked at Bertle.

"Lemme try somethin." She took her seat across from me and clasped my cold hands between her warm ones. "Baby, you know how sometimes the moon looks so big in the sky, you swear it could fall on top of you?"

I glared at Jack.

"And y'know how sometimes that moon done shine so bright, you think yo eyes might just burn up from it?"

"This is a metaphor, isn't it?"

"Pay attention," Jack hushed me, stern.

"Well, baby, as big and beautiful as that moon may look, you gotta know it ain't real. There ain't no such thing as moonlight. That's just sunlight reflected off a big 'ole rock in the sky," she said, with a wiggle of her fingers out the darkened window. "That's what you are. You got a light so big and beautiful inside you. But, baby, it ain't yours."

I switched my gaze back to Jack, fully confused. "I suck at metaphors. Can we maybe do this without the imagery?"

"Okay," he said, taking a deep breath. This time, it was his turn to hold my hand, which, honestly, I preferred. "Remember a few minutes ago I said that Graymasons and Wraithmakers are like flip sides of a coin?"

I nodded.

"Well, that's more true than you know," he said. "You've heard about Graymasons—the ones we were created to defeat, the ones who broke the walls to the Crossworld and let all the vamps and weres rise. They're basically soulless and evil, right?"

"That's the rumor."

"Well, it turns out we were partly wrong about that," he admitted. "They do have souls. Big, powerful, twisted souls that got so horrified by what they'd become, after a few generations they started splitting off all the good parts of themselves into separate beings. One soul, two bodies. Like twins. That's what a Wraithmaker is. Still Anakim, still Lucifer's blood…but like a shadow-self." He dropped his gaze. "If Benita's right—which she always is—that's what *you* are. Amelie, the reason your birth only showed up once in the *Book of Life* was because only one soul was born. It just got…fractured. You're not an only child. Whoever's doing this is your twin."

Silence fell over the table—the kind of silence that, in horror movies, is usually followed by a scream. Except, no scream.

"I don't have a twin," I said.

"Yes, you do."

"No, I really don't."

"Benita?" Jack glanced across the room at Bertle, his eyes pleading.

"Don't you think my parents would have mentioned if I had a twin? I'm not an idiot, Jack. Don't you think *I* would've noticed?"

"Not necessarily. Benita, a little help?"

Jack and I could have gone back and forth like that all night, and neither of us would have budged. It just seemed so ridiculous, the idea that I could have a sibling and not know about it. The only redeeming part was that Jack was still holding my hand. That felt nice, at least.

"This is ridiculous," I said, shifting gears. "Let's talk about something else. Y'all think the Saints have a shot at the Super Bowl this year?"

"Amelie." Jack's forehead creased into a disapproving frown. "In the past millennium, there is only one recorded birth to Lucifer's bloodline. Yours. So either *you are the Graymason* and you've been secretly portaling around the world killing people for the past few years. Or, as Benita says, you're a Wraithmaker—a splinter part of the Graymason's soul. It would explain how you healed me so completely at assembly. And how the real killer managed to attack us while you were standing next to me. Now, I know this is hard, but I need you to try to wrap your mind around it. Either you're a killer, or you have a twin. Are you a killer?"

Was I? I didn't know anymore.

Strange as it sounded, the Wraithmaker thing made sense. I mean, how else was I supposed to explain all this? That awful voice at my test was male, so what? I had a *brother*? Hadn't I always wanted a brother? Someone to watch *Star Trek* with. Someone to help me make fun of Dad's ghastly tie collection.

I found myself staring at the battered old tabletop, questions flooding my head. If I did have a brother, what happened to him? Was he taken? Did my parents give him away? Had they known he was evil? How could they not have mentioned it? How could I not have sensed it?

What the hell was I?

"Amelie, are you okay?" Jack asked.

"Baby, just give her a minute," Bertle said softly. "She'll be all right."

I could hear their voices, but they sounded far away—tinny and distant, like through an antique phone line.

"So, I'm...moonlight."

"Yes."

I pulled my hand from Jack's and pressed it to the hollow beneath my throat. "This soul," I said, "you think it belongs to my twin brother?"

"If he dies, you die, yes," he confirmed.

"Take me home."

"Amelie—"

"*Take me home!*"

I rose out of my chair and stumbled toward the door. Behind me, the clatter of coconut skulls hitting the ground rang out, but I didn't stop. I had to get out of there. A vague memory of telling Luc things couldn't get worse hung in my head. What a *stupid* sentiment! People who say stuff like that *deserve* to have their world fall apart. If I could just get home—back to Bud, back to my mom's antique toilet collection, back to my awesome Pepto Bismol room—things would be okay. Everything would go back to normal.

"Amelie, stop." Jack's voice called out from the porch behind me but I didn't listen. I darted across the street, desperately trying to hail a cab. The evening mist had left the asphalt slick and the reflected street lamps made it glitter like black glass. My feet sloshed through murky puddles as I went, soaking the edges of my jeans. I barely noticed. Maybe I deserved that, too.

I was halfway to the corner when a rusted yellow cab with a white-haired driver pulled up beside me. It was muddy from yesterday's storm, but to me it looked perfect. My ticket to normal.

"Where to, dawlin'?"

"Home," I said. "Old Metairie. But I don't have any money—"

"Amelie! What do you think you're doing?" Out of nowhere, Jack's hand caught my elbow, yanking me out of the street.

"Get off me, Jack. I want to go home." I tried to shove him away, but he held on tight.

"Ami, cut it out. I'm not letting you go."

"Hey, miss. You okay?" The cabbie leaned his head out the window, his brown eyes wrinkled in concern.

"She doesn't need a cab." Jack waved the taxi on as I stumbled against him.

"I think the lady can decide whether she needs a cab. Miss, you in trouble? You need some help?" The driver's hand fumbled for his radio, 911 at the ready.

I quit struggling. Confused, I looked at Jack, then back at the cab driver.

Did he really think Jack was going to hurt me? *Jack*, who had risked his life for me? Given up everything to help me? The idea was so ludicrous I couldn't help it and I started to laugh. Completely cracked up. Tears rolled down my face, my body doubled over. I laughed so hard I had to wrap my arms around my waist to keep from cramping.

"I'm sorry, sir, she's not feeling well," Jack apologized, handing the driver a rumpled twenty. "Thanks for your concern. I'll make sure she gets home safe."

The driver glanced from me to Jack, then back again. His worried expression rapidly shifted into one of disgust. "Damn drunk kids," he muttered as the cab's tires squealed off down the street.

Of course, that sent me into another wave of uncontrollable giggles, which quickly degraded into wracking sobs. Jack practically had to carry me back to the "safe house."

Pathetic.

I suppose I could have walked the last few blocks. If I'd been less of a mess, I might have tried. As it was, I didn't want to. Everywhere Jack touched me, threads of warmth appeared, like liquid fire on a winter's night. Neither of us said a word until we were inside the hovel and he'd settled me onto the bed.

"I'm sorry," I croaked. My voice was shot from the crying jag and my tongue felt like I'd been sucking on chalk.

"For what?"

"Everything," I said. "Being nasty to Bertle. Torturing Smalley when all she did was try to help. Letting you risk your life to save me when I don't even have a soul worth saving."

Jack untied my right shoe and set it under the bedside table. Then he started unknotting my left. I was grateful. My own arms were so slack with exhaustion I doubted I could have managed it myself.

"Ami, why do you do that?" he asked.

"Do what?"

"That. Refuse to look on the bright side."

I shrugged. "Not really seeing a bright side."

"Exactly my point," he said. "You're a Wraithmaker. Granted, that's not the best news, but at least it means you're not a psychopath."

"I share a soul with a psychopath."

"Again, not ideal. But your share of that soul is pretty cool. Some people don't have half the warmth and creativity you do. Just because their souls are freestanding doesn't make them better than you."

He gave up on the knotted lace and tugged the shoe off by force. Little sparks shot up my ankle and I smiled. The idea of a "freestanding" soul struck me as funny; as if a soul was something you could prop up on a stage and brag about.

"Besides," Jack continued, peeling off my socks. "I'm not convinced you don't have a soul of your own. The existentialist, Georg Hegel, had this theory that God isn't something that exists 'out there' in some abstract form. He thought divinity, what he called the 'Absolute,' could be found in the connections between every living thing; that we all share a consciousness, a little bit of God, in the space between us." He lifted his gaze to mine, the hint of a grin tugging at his mouth. "I doubt any living thing could so thoroughly get under my skin as you have, without being deeply connected to me. Which means that even though you're made of Lucifer's blood, you must have a little bit of God in you."

I slumped deeper into the bedspread. I didn't know why he was trying so hard to make me feel better. Pity, I guess. The sad thing was, it was working. "You know," I said, "for a guy who's complained almost constantly since I met him, you've turned out to be quite the little optimist."

He groaned. "Amelie, never refer to a man as 'little,' even by measure of his optimism. Didn't Miss Anselmo teach you that?"

I couldn't help giggling. It actually hurt, given my last frantic bout of laughter, but I didn't mind. Jack got me a glass of water while I changed into the tank top and boxers Lisa packed for me. It took about four seconds to down the whole glass.

"More?" he offered.

"No, thanks. I'm so tired I'll probably end up wetting the bed." I tucked my legs under the covers and pulled the sheets up to my chin. "Will you lie with me until I fall asleep?"

"Sure." Jack vaulted over me to the other side of the bed and doubled the pillow against the headboard. "But I'm not getting under the covers, so no funny business."

"Relax," I promised. "Your virtue is safe with me."

I rolled over so my head rested on his chest, then waited while he settled his arms around me. He'd insisted we sleep in shifts, allegedly so we'd be alert to intruders. I figured maybe he was afraid to share a bed with me, like I might throw myself at him during a wild REM cycle.

"Thanks, by the way," I murmured into his chest, absently sketching a protective ward there. Tiny sparks flew up at the contact. "This was possibly the worst day of my life. You made it bearable."

"At least you're safe, right?" He reached over to turn the light out. "Maybe it's true, every cloud has a—"

"If you say 'silver lining,' I *will* hurt you," I threatened, pinching him on the stomach. "Little optimist."

Laughter rumbled in his chest, deep and warm and alive. It made me want to curl into him, wrap myself around his heart and stay for a long, long time.

"Jack, can you tell me something?" I whispered after a minute.

"Sure. What?"

"I don't care. Anything. Tell me about yourself. The more sleepy-making the better."

"Sleepy-making, huh? Let's see." He made a thoughtful noise. "Well, I'm a Virgo. You know that. My favorite color is green—"

"Green. Why green?"

"I don't know. I like trees, I guess. Cedar's my favorite smell, too, especially when it snows." He clicked his tongue. "Um, I crochet sometimes, when there's nothing evil to kill."

"You crochet? Like with frilly yarn and needles?"

"They're called hooks. And if you're going to make fun…" He started to get up, but I tugged him back.

"Wait, keep going," I said. "I like hearing you talk. Tell me about your family. Focus on the boring parts."

"Well," he hesitated. "My parents died when I was eleven. Then Akira ordered me moved to residential. I don't have any other family, except for Luc—"

"Luc." I snorted, with no small measure of disdain. "What's his deal, anyway? Are all vamps so…" Plenty of adjectives sprang to mind, but I didn't know if Jack's and my relationship was at the place where I could start insulting his people. I settled for "*Human*?"

"You know, I can't really bore you to sleep if you keep asking questions."

"Right. Sorry."

His hand stroked little circles over my back. "The Montaigne clan are one of a few lines of *born* vampires—the royals. It's like a brutal, murderous aristocracy and Luc's family happens to hold power. They're very political. Very image-based. The born vamps prefer to be called Immortals, though Luc's not as picky about that as his mom. Usually, any one of them has four or five armed guards with him."

"How did you meet—"

He shushed me again. "We've known each other as long as I can remember. There were three main families who formed Paranormal Convergence: mine, Luc's, and a werewolf clan by the name of Delinsky. My friend Dane Delinsky was the one Luc sent to watch over you Monday night. He's a decent guy, mostly. Not terribly regimented, but he's got a good heart. And yes, they're both very *human*—souls of their own and everything. That's what the Peace Tenets are about. Is this boring enough?"

Jack's thumb brushed against the back of my neck in slow strokes. Mmm, best bedtime story ever.

"More," I murmured and felt him smile.

"Um, it'll be ten years on Saturday since our families first petitioned for the Peace Tenets," he continued in a whisper. "Hundreds of us showed up—vamps, werewolves, you name it. The vamps and weres had been hit pretty hard by demon attacks and with all the vampire in-fighting, Immortals were actually facing extinction. They still are. It was the Gabrielites who championed the Peace movement, but in the end, over a hundred Guardians signed the petition. Luc and Dane and I were just kids then." His chest rumbled with silent laughter. "You should have seen it. Luc pitched such a fit when they said we couldn't sign it, I thought it might become an international incident. In the end, Dad only gave in because it was my birthday. That's what Luc was talking about before, the thing his mom is coming in town for…the Induction."

"Induction. Right." I wiped a smidge of drool off the corner of my mouth. The golden threads connecting us seemed to change texture, glowing thick and pliant against my skin. I nestled into his chest.

"If you'd paid attention to your theory lectures, you know it takes ten years after a petition is filed for a Guardian law to be ratified. That's why we get so many petitioners to sign, so when the law comes up for Induction ten years later there'll still be plenty alive to ratify it. The Peace Tenets shouldn't be a problem. There's a lot of dissent about it since the war effort's failing right now, but we only need one of the original petitioners from each group to pass it. It'll be good, you'll see." He tightened his arms around me, his breath warm against my hair. "Once the law gets ratified, everyone will be treated as equals. No more bigotry, no more distrust between species. The Inferni will be our allies against demonkind. Maybe the Elders will even train them to fight alongside us, instead of treating them like some hostile protectorate."

I had to admit it sounded good. *If* they could be trusted.

The tricky thing about Inferni was that even though they lived in our world, ate our food, and drove our cars, they all still carried demon blood. Maybe it wasn't as thick or toxic as true subterraneans—but could we really trust creatures who, for centuries, hunted humans as if they were no better than animals? Liberals like Jack would tell you Crossworlders must have souls because their origins were human. But I wasn't so sure.

Heck, what did I know? I barely had a soul myself.

Right?

Chapter Seventeen:
Under Pressure

Jack woke me before dawn. Thursday morning. Only two days left until the prophecy.

It took me a few minutes to register where I was. The whole room looked dim and swimmy, and I couldn't figure out why there were no Beanie Babies on my dresser. Or why my dresser had been painted puke green and hauled in front of the door.

"Hey." Jack's husky voice brought everything back in a flood. "You okay to keep watch for awhile?"

I blinked up at him. "How long have I been asleep?"

"Seven hours. You need more?"

I shook my head. "You should have woken me sooner."

"I tried," he said with a smile, "about three hours ago. You flicked me in the face and told me to piss off."

"Oh. Well, I'm sure you deserved it, then." I tried to sit up, but the sudden movement left me light-headed. "Do we have any granola bars left?"

"I think you ate the last one at Luc's. Along with all my breath mints and a half-eaten box of Red Hots you found in the seat cushions."

"I don't remember that."

He grinned as he unstuck a clump of hair from my face. "I can't believe I ever thought you were dangerous."

I had to stifle a yawn as I stood, so I leaned against him while the head-rush subsided. It was nice, like leaning against a good-smelling brick wall. My pride might not have let me say it, but I owed him *so* much. And not just one night's sleep, either. I owed him my life. It wasn't a debt I could ever repay, and honestly, I didn't know how to try. In a weird fit of gratitude, I wound my arms around his waist for a hug.

"What's that for?" he asked, confused.

But I buried my face in his chest and kept hugging. It took him a second to relax, but eventually he sighed and his arms looped around me too. If it had been up to me, we would have stayed like that for another seven hours.

He didn't speak after we parted. Just slipped into the warm spot I'd vacated and fell asleep.

My body made creaky sounds as I settled in for my turn on watch. I hated all the carefulness and sitting around. We needed a plan. Preferably one that didn't involve psychic lunch ladies, pompous vampires, and flea-bag motels. Don't get me wrong, I was as thrilled as the next girl about hiding out with the world's most unattainable bachelor. But there had to be something else we could do. Something useful.

I slumped back on the dust-covered cushions and stared up at the stained ceiling. Yeesh. Was it even possible my biggest drama used to be figuring out who I should invite to the school gala? Had

I really been that shallow?

Small beams of gray light slanted through the windows, casting flickery shadows across the bedspread. Jack looked so peaceful, fist curled around the hilt of his short sword like a little boy with a teddy bear. He probably loved that thing as much as most kids love their teddy bears. *Strange what this world does to us.*

After what seemed like hours—and probably was—I tugged back my moth-eaten flannel throw and padded toward the bathroom. The mirror over the sink was so old and tarnished it even made the smattering of freckles across my nose look colorless. I tried to splash some water on my face.

"Great," I muttered as chilled water dribbled under the collar of my tank top. "It's gonna be one of those days, isn't it?"

My clothes were still in Lisa's backpack, so I dragged it into the bathroom and started unpacking. T-shirts, jeans, super-cute silk halter top. With my luck, Jack would probably have us scaling a skyscraper before noon. The silk top went back into the pack. I'd just decided on a sports bra and T-shirt over some jeans when the bag began to vibrate. It startled me at first, until I realized what it was.

Lisa's phone.

I dug through the pack until I found it, yellow and flowery, at the bottom. "Hello?"

"Ami!" Lisa's voice squeaked over the line like a manic frog. "Omigosh, I've been so worried. Did the jump go okay? Of course it did. You're alive, right? Oh, we were so worried! I *said* you'd get in trouble. But did you listen to me? No, you didn't. Because you never listen!"

Despite myself, I smiled. No matter what the tragedy, trust

Lisa to fit a lecture in. "Hi, Lis."

"Don't 'Hi, Lis' me. Where are you? No, wait! Don't tell me. If they torture me, I don't want to have to give you up."

"Relax, I don't even know. It doesn't matter, we won't be here long. Jack's like a psycho-nomad with a taste for one-star lodging."

"Is he still with you?"

"Yeah, he's asleep. Kind of a weird night. I'm in the bathroom right now."

"Omigosh, y'all didn't—"

"No!" I said, too loudly. "No, of course not. It's not like that."

It took about ten minutes to brief her on everything— the prophecy, my alleged twin brother, my dubious status as a Wraithmaker. The one thing I skimmed over was Jack. I had yet to sort through the kissing parts. And my feelings for him were *waaaay* too intense to put into words. Still, the omission left me with a guilty knot in my belly. I'd spent the better part of twelve years letting Lisa manage the details of my life. It felt weird to hide stuff from her now.

"Hey, how's Bud?" I asked, deliberately changing the subject. "Still in Baton Rouge?"

"No, he came home yesterday, as soon as he got my message telling him not to come home."

"Typical."

"Tell me about it. Elder Akira finished interrogating us last night, but Bud and Henry are both still in lock-up at school. The Elders aren't technically allowed to hold Bud since he hasn't done anything wrong. But—"

"But they know he'd help me if he could."

"Yeah. Katie thinks they'll probably wipe his memory. And

Henry—" She groaned. "Wow, I wish I'd seen it. According to Alec's dad, Henry grabbed a broadsword at the interrogation and started screaming that *he* was the one who helped Jack break you out. Said if they wanted to stop him, they'd have to kill him. It took like four tranquilizers and a stunner charm to bring him down."

"Sounds major." I paused to crack open the bathroom window as a stereo blared to life behind Lisa. "Where are you?"

"At Alec's house. His dad's got a secret phone line."

"Tell her I got detention for defending her honor," Alec shouted in the distance.

"Did he really?"

"Well, he got detention, but mostly for calling Akira a closed-minded troglodyte," she said. "Chancellor Thibault made them drop the rest of the charges against us. They didn't even freak about the arsenal break-in since it was allegedly an attempt to stop Henry. Pretty gullible, right?"

"That's grown-ups for you." Much as it killed me to think of poor, sweet Henry in lock-up, at least I knew my friends were okay. That was something. And who knew, maybe Jack had a back up plan to break Bud and Henry out. I wasn't putting anything past him.

"Lis, ask Alec if his dad can do anything for Bud. And Henry, too. Losing Smalley is going to be hard enough. He doesn't deserve to rot in prison for the rest of his life."

"I will," she promised.

We fell into a semi-awkward silence. In the background, I could hear Matt and Alec sparring while Katie urged them to take it easy. It was hard knowing how little they could do for me...and how little I could do for them. I think Lisa felt it, too. Neither of us wanted to admit that, overnight, my friends had morphed from a vibrant part of my life into a useless piece of history—like turning the page of a book to find the rest of it suddenly blank.

"I should probably go," I said.

"Yeah, I know." She was quiet for another moment, though the line stayed open. "Look, the Chancellor's trying to work out a deal. Immunity for Mr. Smith-Hailey and a stay of execution for you, in exchange for your surrender. It's not ideal, obviously, but we can always break you out later."

"Thanks, I'll keep it in mind," I said. I was about to hang up when another thought occurred to me. "Hey, Lis, if you needed to get a copy of your birth certificate, what would you do?"

"I'd ask my mom. Why?"

I stared at the phone. How can some people be so smart and so dense at the same time? "Let me rephrase." I tried again. "If you were a seventeen-year-old fugitive with no access to your parents and you needed to see your birth records—"

"Ahh," she said, "that's harder. Guardians don't keep records about stuff like that...you know, because of the Great Books and all."

"Right. Of course." Seriously, was I the only one who had no clue about the stupid Great Books?

"You could try Louisiana Vital Records," she suggested, "but they'll probably need a parent's signature. Same for hospital records. There's always the Guardian Internet Database, but that's a lot harder to pick through. Is this about your alleged twin brother? Oooh, do you think he's hot?"

"I'll pretend you didn't just say that."

She gave me her Internet passcode so I could bypass the

human lockouts without tipping off any trackers, and quickly hung up the phone. If I didn't get some coffee soon, my execution would be a non-issue since I'd perish from caffeine withdrawal. I milled around the bathroom until my stomach began to rumble, then went back into the bedroom to watch Jack sleep some more. It sounds boring, I know, but if you saw the guy, you'd understand why it wasn't.

He was amazing when he slept. His body held a faint luminescence that seemed to intensify the closer I got. I found myself playing with that glow—holding my hand over his heart until I could feel the strands of light, then tugging at them until they glowed brighter. Even his face lost its careful diffidence in slumber. He looked so much more like the relaxed future-Jack I'd seen in my visions.

So weird.

I remember reading somewhere how human beings cycle so many carbon atoms during their lifetime it was not only possible, but probable, that every human on the planet contained a carbon atom that once belonged to Jesus of Nazareth. Or Martin Luther King, Jr., or Elvis. I always thought that was cool. It gave me some bit of comfort to think of all those people, all that history, being inside of me. I tried to time my inhale with Jack's exhale, so I could take in as many of his carbon atoms as possible.

Jack had been asleep over four hours when impatience finally got the better of me. We had less than two days until he was supposed to die and our leads were nil. With Lisa's passcode, all I needed was a few minutes on a computer and I might be able to verify the story about my supposed evil twin. Even if I couldn't, at least I'd be able to hunt down some clues, right?

So far, we'd been thinking about this as a serial murder case. But the more I thought about it, the more I realized that wasn't the whole story. If what Bertle said was true, then the first crime wasn't murder at all. It was kidnapping. So, if I could find out who had access to my mom around the time of my birth, and who had opportunity to alter the birth records, then maybe I could figure out who was doing this now. It wasn't much, but it would give us a starting point.

Luc had packed us a mini computer pad with a satellite modem. It took a few minutes to activate the modem and link it to the Starbucks Wi-Fi across the street, then another minute to talk myself out of checking my email. No doubt the Elders had tagged my account. If I logged on, even for a second, they could find us. I stared at the Yahoo welcome page with the longing of a forbidden lover. It just seemed like torture, another scrap of normal I couldn't access.

Resigned, I entered the web address for the Louisiana Vital Records Registry. According to the website, I needed to be eighteen, not a criminal, and willing to wait eight to ten business days for them to process my request. Or I needed my dad.

So much for bureaucracies.

I tabled that quandary for the moment and, using Lisa's passcode, logged on to the Guardian search engine. If the Elders were tracking Lisa's code, too, then they'd be able to see whatever I searched for. I knew I might only have a few minutes before they locked onto the transmission signal.

I typed in "Charlotte Lane Birth" and hit the search icon.

The hit came up instantly, though it wasn't exactly what I wanted. "*Charlotte Lane Heralds the Birth of a New Guardian*

Dream Team."

It was an old *Guardian Times* article celebrating St. Michael's "latest crop" of outstanding warriors. I watched carefully as a photo of my mom with a group of young Guardians digitized on the screen. Dad looked awesome with his battle garb and broadsword. He had one arm slung over her shoulder and an easy smile at his lips. Super badass. They wore the old Guardian uniform, before we moved to lightweight Kevlar gear. Black leather armor was stitched over every inch of the stretchy material, with panels of hard carbon along the forearms. Like Batman, minus the cape. It worked great if you were fending off an airborne demon attack, but the limitations in a sword fight were far from ideal.

The resolution on the photo was grainy, though I could still recognize a few of the others with them. Gunderman in the back row, with his floppy hair and lanky body. D'Arcy up front, caught mid-blink. Even Lisa's parents grinned gleefully from the rear of the pack. My mother couldn't have been more than eighteen or nineteen in the picture, her face a bit leaner than I remembered. She smiled proudly at the camera, one hand intertwined with my dad's, the other clasped firmly on the arm of the man beside her. He was tall and handsome, with wavy brown hair and a nice profile.

Mom's Watcher.

Everyone liked to gossip about what happened between them—how Charlotte had betrayed him. As far as I could tell, none of it was her fault. She'd done nothing any other pregnant mom-to-be wouldn't have done. Obviously, I didn't know the details. Nobody knew the details.

My mom and dad were a couple all through high school. They'd gotten engaged, set a date for the wedding, hired a band, the whole nine yards. When bond assignments came up and Charlotte was given to a recent grad she'd never met, they were horrified. They postponed the wedding. They talked about leaving the Guardians, defecting to the human sector. But Mom couldn't do it. As a child of Raphael, she had the mission in her blood. So Dad defected, and Mom bonded with Bobby.

Everyone expected Charlotte to leave Bud. I think even Bud expected her to leave. But she never did. They got married a year later, and she was pregnant in no time.

I wouldn't have known anything about the accident if I hadn't overheard them talking one night. My dad kept saying how it was the right decision to save the baby. How even though it crippled her bondmate, a child's soul, no matter who the child was, was worth the sacrifice. I figured, for whatever reason, it must have come to a choice between risking the life of her unborn child or letting Bobby get brutalized by demons during a jump. She'd obviously picked me.

I had to wonder, did Mom ever regret it? If she'd known what bloodline she carried in her belly, would she still have sacrificed him—sacrificed her career—to save me? To save *us*?

According to my dad, Bobby moved away after I was born. He never said why, but it didn't take a genius to figure it out. He came back to the house once, I remember, years later. Dad tried to usher me off to bed, but I'd clung to the staircase railing, mesmerized. Before that night, it never occurred to me my mother was broken. I figured all moms had those bouts of silence, those days where their eyes stayed glazed and they couldn't force themselves to eat. I had no clue, until I saw her with him.

She didn't speak for weeks when he left again.

The words on the article scrolled down Luc's computer pad, unread. It was the photo I wanted. If those people were my mom's closest friends in high school, maybe one of them knew something about the kidnapping. Assuming that's what it was. Try as I might, I couldn't imagine my parents willingly giving up their child…even if someone told them it was pure evil.

I tapped the download icon and waited while the image saved. Then I shut it down. About two minutes too late.

By the time I glanced out the window again, Starbucks was crawling with Guardians. Creepy Daniel stood with his back to the entrance, a dark gray duster thrown over his uniform. In his hand, he held a newspaper, rolled into a loose tube. No telling what was under it. A knife? A gun? Whatever it was, it didn't look promising. Marcus stood beside him, blond hair whipping in the breeze like Fabio on a cover shoot. The rest of them scurried around, well-trained lemmings in trench coats, their own rolled-up newspapers clutched in hand.

So much for not striking around humankind.

Annoyed at myself, I stuffed the computer pad back into Luc's satchel and started sketching out the containment wards to set up a portal. Jack was going to kill me when I told him I'd blown our safe house. Oh, well. At least we had plenty of time to get out before the cavalry figured out my Wi-Fi piggyback.

"Hey, Jack." I gently touched his forehead, and he jerked awake. Probably not the best idea to startle a sleeping man with a deadly weapon in his hand.

"Easy," I said. "Just a friendly wake-up call."

Jack rolled over, his eyes squinting at the light streaming in behind me. He leaned back and stretched his arms overhead.

"What time is it?"

"Almost ten." I settled onto the bed beside him, cross-legged. As adorable as he'd been a few minutes ago, it was nothing compared to the sweet, bleary-eyed look of amusement in his eyes now. "What are you smiling about?"

He shrugged, his hands laced into a cradle behind his head. "You're still here."

"Where else would I be?"

"I don't know. The mall? Eating omelets somewhere?" He tugged at my tangled red ponytail. "Hey, that's a good nickname for you. *Omelet*."

"Very funny." I gave him a nasty look. "The good news is, despite my near starvation I *didn't* abandon you to go on a breakfast run. And as you know, I consider that a rather large sacrifice."

"I appreciate it. Thanks."

"You're welcome."

"So, what's the bad news?"

Faint clanging noises rose up from across the street. "Bad news?"

"Yeah, you said that was the good news. When someone points out the good news, they usually follow with the bad."

"Right. Well, there are two things," I admitted. "The first is I've been thinking—"

"God, help us."

"About my dad. Lisa told me they're holding him at the school," I said. "So I had an idea about what we have to do next."

He sat up and quit smiling. "The answer's no. No way."

"But it's our best shot. We have questions. He knows the answers," I said. "What are we supposed to do? Wait until the

Elders wipe his memory? We'll never find out who my brother is."

"Ami." Jack leveled me with a glare. "You're talking about breaking into a warded, maximum security facility to rescue a guy who hasn't picked up a weapon in decades. It's suicide."

"Not necessarily. We'll have the element of surprise," I countered. "They think I'm guilty. Guilty people run away. They'll never expect us to come to them."

"Because only an insane person would do that."

"Look, if you've got a better idea, let's hear it. I'm all ears." I paused, arms laced across my chest. "Come on, Jack, you know I'm right."

There was turmoil behind his eyes. "But he's a civilian."

"Not entirely. He's trained. Out of practice, sure, but trained. And without the Otrava, I'm sure I can shield him in a portal jump. If you get me in, I'll get us out. Please?" I gave him the puppy-dog eyes with just a hint of tearfulness. It worked on teachers all the time, though usually my goals had more to do with late homework than felony jailbreaks. "Jack, I'm begging you."

"Ami, he's a defector."

"He's my dad."

Jack opened his mouth to argue, then shut it. He knew I had a point. Or maybe he was just a sucker for tears. I didn't care. I'd lost nearly everything that mattered in my life. It was time to reclaim my dad and my past and start solving the mystery.

After the world's longest pause, he finally nodded. "Fine."

"Fine? Really?"

"Yeah." He threw off the covers and stood, grabbing his weapons belt off the bedside table. He looked grumpy yet determined, a sexy combination if ever I'd seen one. I was on the brink of launching myself at him for another hug when he asked, "So, what's the other thing?"

"The other thing?"

"With the bad news," he said, impatient. "There were two—"

"Right," I said. "About that. We should probably get moving soon. There may have been a tiny security breach while you were sleeping. Not a breach, really. More of a hiccup."

On the street below, the noises picked up. I could already make out the vague sound of Marcus shouting and Creepy Daniel swearing at no one in particular. Apparently, Jack heard it, too.

"Omelet," he growled.

"Sorry." I smiled apologetically. "But the good news is, I know a great place to grab some breakfast."

Chapter Eighteen:
Undone

We waited until full dark to move on St. Michael's. Totally *James Bond*, right?

As soon as Luc pulled onto Prytania Street, I could tell things had changed at the school. Deep green palm tendrils draped over the wrought iron fence, their edges fizzing on contact with the warded metal tines. The usual faint glow around the perimeter was amped up and shimmering, a sign that the wards had been fortified recently. Most humans would assume the glow came from the twinkle lights strung in anticipation of tomorrow night's commencement formal, but I knew better. Maybe the Elders wouldn't be expecting us, but we were idiots to think they wouldn't be prepared.

Luc turned his Porsche down a side street and pulled to the curb as Dane's pick-up screeched to a halt behind us. I wasn't quite sure what to make of Dane yet. He seemed nice enough when we met, in a friendly puppy sort of way. He had a full head of shaggy brown hair and a round face that lit up when he smiled. Which he did a lot. I think we might have been friends if we'd met under different circumstances. Not so possible with the mega-weird vibe between him and Jack.

Jack tried to be casual about it but I didn't miss how diligently he positioned himself between Dane and me. Every time I moved, even to gesture to a new target on the campus map, Jack reoriented himself so he filled the space between us. I tried to ask what was up, but he just muttered something about lunar cycles and violent werewolf mating patterns.

Violent werewolf mating patterns? Um, yeah. After that, I didn't mind so much.

"So, cousin," Luc said, cutting the engine. "This is how you want to spend your last night on earth? Really?"

"Luc, we've been over this. Bud has information—"

"Which you desperately need. Yes, it's not for me to judge. Lord knows I've had my share of evenings crouched in the bushes with a woman. I'm merely wondering if you've considered the alternatives."

"Alternatives?" Jack caught my eye in the rearview mirror. "I'm listening."

"Well, Brazil is lovely this time of year. As is Mexico. I could charter a jet for you. Champagne, caviar, a well-trained companion of the finest breeding," he offered. "You'd leave Saturday, after the Induction—"

"Very subtle, vampire." I kicked the back of his seat. "If bribery doesn't work, just call your bodyguards and have them tie him up for you. I'll bet you've spent your fair share of evenings in *that* situation too, huh?"

Luc met my glare in the rearview mirror. "Must you speak?"

"Bite me."

He sneered. "I don't fancy your type."

"Why, too sober? Too much self-esteem?"

Jack frowned at us across the blue light of the console. "Can you two at least pretend to cooperate? We're on the same team here."

"Yeah, Dracu-Luc," I said. "Play nice or I'll ride with the werewolf."

"I'll give you fifty quid if you do," Luc offered.

"Both of you, cut it out!" Jack said, irate. "Luc, quit goading her. She's unstable enough as it is. And Ami, Luc has put himself at risk, both physically and politically, to help us. He deserves your gratitude, not your contempt."

"Oh, please! He's a sneaky, self-serving man-whore who doesn't know the first thing about—" I stopped. "Hold up, did you call me unstable?"

"He was being kind," Luc said.

"*Luc!*"

To be fair, Luc was far from the Mother Teresa of vampires. When we'd first approached him with the rescue plan, his immediate response had been to offer us vodka martinis, probably spiked with Ambien. I suspect it was some lame plot to knock Jack unconscious so he could drag him to the Peace Tenets signing on Saturday.

Evidently Luc's mom, a vampire aristocrat named Arianna Fassnight (no Montaigne, interestingly), had threatened to cut Luc off financially unless he hunted down at least three of the original peace petitioners from each group. And since he'd dismissed his minions, the poor bloodsucker had been forced to actually *do* the legwork himself. So far he had vamps and werecreatures accounted for, but he hadn't found a single Guardian signatory. I couldn't decide which would be more tragic—losing the Peace Tenets or denying Luc a chance to cope with poverty.

"Tell you what," I suggested diplomatically. "Let's get my dad, then Saturday afternoon we can take one of Luc's vamptastic cars and drive to Tijuana. You don't mind, right vampire?"

"Not a bit," he said generously. "Anything but the Ferrari."

"What's wrong with the Ferrari?"

"I lost my virginity in it," he said, as casually as if he'd been describing a business meeting.

I flashed a quick look at Jack. There were a few mental images I never thought I'd have to deal with, and chief among them was the crazy-hot vampire being deflowered in the backseat of an Italian sports car.

"He's kidding," Jack assured me. "You're kidding, right?"

"The night of my fifteenth birthday party," Luc mused fondly. "It was Beatrice Boudreaux, Mum's yoga instructor. Honestly, if not for that woman's flexibility and the Rachmaninoff on the stereo, it might have been a complete disaster."

"I'm going to be ill," I said.

Unwilling to stomach the details, I let myself out of the car and headed for the azalea bushes lining the street across from St. Michael's. Normally, a mud-strewn canopy of pink, semi-poisonous plants wouldn't hold such appeal. But when the alternative was a blow by blow of—

Never mind. My brain felt dirty thinking about it.

A few minutes and several troubling images later, Jack crawled into the bushes behind me carrying a backpack full of C4 and a few remote detonators. He handed me one of the heavy gray bricks, stuck something metal between his teeth, and started pulling a tangle of black wires out of the pack. I couldn't help but be slightly turned on by how focused he looked as he labored over the wires. It almost silenced the Rachmaninoff in my head.

"There," he said, when they were finally loose. "I have to go set the charges with Dane. Will you be okay for a minute?"

"Do I need a babysitter?"

"I think we've established that you do." He pulled a baseball cap low over his golden curls. "Try meditating. Maybe it'll keep you out of trouble."

"Yeah, that'll work, for sure."

He kept to the shadows along the gray stone wall and disappeared around a corner before I had a chance to get irritated. The meditation thing went poorly, as expected. After a few failed attempts, I dug out the computer pad Luc gave us and turned it on. In all the hubbub of planning Dad's jailbreak, I'd completely forgotten to show Jack the photo I'd found.

It only took me a few seconds to boot up the screen, a soft glimmer illuminating the leafy darkness. If Jack had been there, he would have scolded me for risking the light, but I knew the danger was minimal. One of the benefits of being an aspiring career criminal throughout my prep school years—I had the guard rotations memorized. They never came outside the gates so late.

I'd just gotten the photo loaded when Jack returned, covered in a thin sheen of sweat. He dropped to his belly and scooted under the bushes beside me.

"Charges are set." He glanced at the computer pad, then back at me, suspicious. "Tell me you didn't just log on to an unprotected local wireless network again."

I gave him my dirtiest look. Pointless in the dark. "I wanted to show you this. I figured it'd be a good place to start for a suspect list." I tipped the screen so he could see.

"Class photo, huh?" he muttered, distracted by the detonators in his hand. "Is that Chancellor Thibault?"

"Thibault?" I scooted the computer back and scanned the blurred back rows. No Thibault. "Uh, you may want to reconsider giving up those glasses, dude."

Jack shot me a sharp glare, then pushed the detonators into my hands, a light tingle reverberating at his touch. It took a few strokes but soon the photo zoomed in over Mom's bondmate's face.

"There," he said. "Thibault."

I could see what he meant. The two men had the same wavy hair, the same squared jaw. I squinted at the photo, trying to imagine Bobby-the-bondmate with twenty years and a lot of politics on him.

"Jack, you don't think…"

We both stared at the photo for another few seconds then at each other. Before I could say a word, Jack grabbed the computer pad and scrolled to the text beneath the photo. We both saw it at the same time. Robert Martin Thibault, assigned as Watcher to Charlotte Lane the year of their graduation.

"Holy crow," I said. "I didn't even know they were in the same class. How did we miss this?"

"It's Alec Charbonnet," he muttered.

I glanced up. "Alec?"

"Your brother," Jack said. "If Thibault figured out what

bloodline she carried, he may have decided to take Alec from her out of revenge. Or maybe he thought he was doing her a favor. Who knows?"

The evening song of cicadas seemed to quicken along with my heart. In my mind's eye, I saw Thibault's gnarled legs, all bent and twisted like melted candles. Those injuries could easily have happened during the botched jump with Mom. And Alec certainly fit the bill as my twin brother. My age. Tall like me, with green eyes. His hair was darker, but it *could* have auburn highlights. Would that satisfy the "hair of fire" line in the prophecy?

"Didn't he leave class right before your test on Tuesday?" Jack asked. "Thibault approved the testing schedule and site assignments. He could have told Alec where to go. They would have had plenty of time to set up the wards at your test site. Hell, they could have done it the night before."

"God, I'm so stupid," I whispered, panicked. "We have to call Lisa. And Katie! She's practically dating him. We have to warn them—"

Jack shook his head. "You can't. Think about it. If he suspects they're onto him, he's got a reason to hurt them."

"Jack, I have to do something."

"They're safer not knowing," he insisted. "And I hate to say it, but we don't have time for this. Dane's holding live explosive charges, Luc's waiting for the go signal, and we've got less than thirty minutes before shift change. It's now or never for your dad."

With shaky hands, I shut down the computer, slid it into my pack, and followed Jack across the street to our position on the north end of campus, away from the wrought iron front gates. The smell of magic burned in the air, and moon-shadowed leaves danced across the lawn like tiny black fairies. Until that moment, I'd never noticed how much the place resembled a fortress.

Hopeful as I'd been about getting my dad back, all I could feel was dread. What if Alec decided to use Lisa and Katie as bait? Would he hurt them to draw me out? And what about Matt? He was too brave not to fight back—would Alec kill him when he did? It'd been over twelve hours since I'd talked to Lisa. *Twelve hours.* They could all be dead by now.

Jack must have noticed the vacant look on my face because as soon as we reached the wall he tugged me into the shadows. "Look, if your head's not in this we can still abort. I won't risk you getting hurt. Not even for Bud."

I blinked my eyes into focus. I could do this.

"Amelie?"

"I'm fine," I lied. "Let's go."

Jack had set explosive charges all along the south corner of the wall, each block of C4 marked with perimeter-disabling glyphs. Of course, once they went off, we'd still have another layer of wards before we broke through to the security building. That was where our handy vampire alliance came in. I was more than a little curious how Luc had managed to come up with six pounds of military-grade explosives plus a rocket launcher with just a few hours notice. Best not to dwell on it.

"As soon as the charges blow, we have to move fast," Jack warned. "We'll only have a few minutes before reinforcements arrive. Assuming our diversion works and we can get a clear path in, we're still cutting it close. Are you sure you're up for this?"

"Just get me in."

Jack gave a quick nod. "Plug your ears."

I did, but it didn't help much. When Jack pressed that button, it sounded like the entire city block had exploded. It didn't even matter that it was on the opposite side of campus. The ground shuddered, car alarms screamed and, most importantly, the dome of shimmering light around St. Michael's flickered.

And went dark.

"Ladies first." Jack made a cradle with his hands and boosted me over the wall. I landed hard on my butt amidst a pile of deceptively fluffy-looking bushes. Like a hawk in flight, Jack leaped over the stone wall and landed beside me. On his feet.

"Show off," I said.

Jack stayed by my side as we sprinted across campus toward our target. We were still about forty feet from the security building when I heard Dane and Luc start their assault. It began with a crack, followed by a slow hiss like the bottle rockets Dad and I used to set off on the Fourth of July. I barely had time to register what it was before another explosion rang out, along with the soul-crunching sound of my beloved school's walls crumbling.

At least it was just the janitorial wing. We'd chosen that as the target because it shared a ward blanket with the security building and would be empty after hours. I didn't think I could bear it if the main campus got hurt.

The acrid smell of diesel and gunpowder rolled off the target as the next two rockets hit, their glow lighting up the sky in a sick flash of orange. For a moment, it looked like the warded perimeter would fail. Its brightness flickered like a summer brown-out. Then the glow stabilized.

"Dang it," Jack muttered. "Stay close."

Ducking low, he ran toward the security building. We didn't

have enough time to mess around setting off multiple charges and Luc and Dane didn't dare linger with the rockets. Guards already poured out of the buildings toward the south campus. If anyone recognized Luc, there'd be hell to pay at the Peace Tenets. We couldn't risk it.

Dane's tires screeched down the street in the distance and my stomach gave a little dip. Whatever fortifications the Guardians had put on the interior wards, there was no guarantee Jack and I could get through them.

"Jack, what are you doing?"

He'd extracted a metal-encased device and was attaching it to the wall of the security building. It looked like a small, black cake pan with a tiny red dome. He flipped a switch on the side and it started beeping. "Plug your ears again."

Before I could breathe, he'd scooped me up and tossed me into a dark green Dumpster a few yards away. Yeah, you heard me. A *Dumpster*. Filled with *garbage*. The muted aroma of ink toner and day-old mac-and-cheese seeped into my clothing.

"You've got to be kidding me," I muttered.

He pulled the heavy lid closed and lowered himself on top of me only seconds before the world exploded.

Heat flared against the metal walls as the Dumpster lurched across the pavement, slamming into the west wall with a hard clang. Shrieks and wails rose up like demon cries as metal buckled under the heat. The only thing that kept me from completely wigging out was the feel of Jack all tingly against me.

"You okay?" he asked when the pops and bangs had settled into a low crackle of fire.

I didn't know how to answer, so I contented myself with

flicking a handful of cheese sauce at his face. Chuckling, he pried himself off me and used his shirtsleeve to open the scalding metal lid. Billows of black smoke thickened the air, blocking out the light of the full moon.

"The coast is clear," he said, peering out the top.

"You think?" I choked on the smoke.

The breeze had picked up again, and although the temperature was probably only in the sixties, it felt like a sauna. Pieces of flaming paper swirled in the air and bits of charred furniture smoldered in bright orange piles on the ground. Without a word, Jack vaulted easily over the lip of the Dumpster and hauled me out, careful not to let me hit the scorched edge.

In the security office, the remains of a desk huddled against one wall, while a splintered ceiling fan turned lazy circles from the force of the fire. Dented metal filing cabinets lined the far edge, alongside a few overturned chairs in what used to be a makeshift waiting area. Everywhere I looked, piles of rubble and scorched drywall littered the room. Through the blown-out door, I could see vertical lines of iron bars illuminated by a few residual patches of fire.

"Daddy?"

I pushed past Jack toward the cell block. It didn't matter that the hallway was still dark and filled with smoke, or that I hadn't checked for guards. All I could think about was getting to my dad.

"Ami? Is that you?"

I hurried toward my father's incredulous voice, so focused I didn't even notice the flurry of movement to my left.

Jack's body slammed into the guard with a cringe-worthy thud and they both hit the ground rolling. I couldn't see because of all the smoke, but it didn't take a military expert to know Jack was in trouble. I scrambled to my knees, desperate to make sense of the fight. Every so often they moved into a patch of firelight, but before I could see where Jack ended and the guard began, they shifted again.

"*Lucé*," I shouted, and a flash of light zipped through the air in a jagged streak.

The room was still clouded with smoke but at least now I could tell which man wore the guard uniform. He was standing over Jack with his sword raised, about to plunge the tip of it into Jack's belly.

"*Desisté!*" I screamed, my hand outstretched. "Lay off my boyfriend, you twerp."

The man's body froze at the command. Jack didn't hesitate. As soon as he realized what I'd done, he rolled out from under the guard's sword strike, grabbed the weapon from him, and cracked the hilt of it into his skull.

"Thanks," he said, breathing hard. "*Twerp*?"

"I'm trying to swear less," I explained.

"Good for you. *Boyfriend*?"

"We should probably hurry, don't you think?"

Jack drained energy off me while I unmade the cell's wards. If the heat of the flames wasn't enough to make me sweat, the fury in Bud's glare would have been. It wasn't until the lock clicked open that I realized his anger wasn't directed toward me at all.

"You!" Bud's fist flew at Jack, slamming him into the wall with the force of a small truck. "What have you done?"

"Sir," Jack held up his hands in surrender, "I know how this looks. You have every right to be upset."

"Upset?" he fumed. "Do I look *upset* to you?"

"You look upset to me," I noted.

"Mr. Bennett," Jack said, "if you'll just let me explain—"

My dad drew back his fist again.

"Hold it." I attempted to wedge myself between them. "If you could both maybe dial back the testosterone for a second, I'd love to hear what the hell's going on."

Dad's eyes went back to Jack. "You didn't tell her?"

"Of course not," Jack snapped. "How dumb do you think I am?"

"Tell me what?" I piped in.

Neither of them answered.

"Seriously, tell me what?"

Behind us, Henry shuffled to the edge of the cell. His face was bruised and puffy, and a thick band of white fabric held one arm in a sling. "I think they're referring to the fact that Jackson is your bondmate."

"Excuse me?"

"*Henry—*"

"She deserves to know, doesn't she?" The Archivist shrugged his narrow shoulders and shifted his gaze to me. "The Elders thought it was too dangerous to tell you. A child of Lucifer was bad enough, but a bonded one? And with Gabriel's son? There's no way they could control that kind of power."

I glanced back at Jack. "Tell him it's not true."

But Jack stayed suspiciously silent. So did Bud, which worried me even more than the pitying look on Henry's face.

"You don't remember, do you?" Henry sighed. "The Elders thought if you knew your power, you would turn on them. They couldn't risk it, so they took your memories. I doubt they ever meant to let you live past the prophecy."

I tried to filter Henry's words through the rush in my brain, but my thoughts kept getting jumbled. Me and Jack? *Bonded*? Was that even possible? I remembered the bizarro need to protect Jack at assembly, the strange visions, the wicked amounts of power we'd generated together. Even how Hansen had laid into him while we were escaping. If we were bonded, then that meant...

"Wait a second. *I* was the girl you told me about?" I looked at Jack. "The one who'd stabbed you in the hand and forced you to bond? The one who ruined your life? That was *me*?"

Jack stared at the ground, silent.

It was the silence that bothered me. If he'd denied it or called me an idiot I probably could have handled that. But to just sit there like a lump? A giant part of me wanted to hit him, or kick him, or poke him with something sharp. *Anything* that would get a response.

"Jack?"

He looked at me helplessly. "What do you want me to say?"

"Tell them you're not my bondmate," I said, frantic. "Tell them it's a mistake."

But he didn't. He just kept staring at his shoes, his eyes all dark and intense. And all I could think was how perfect he'd felt snuggled next to me last night, and the way my skin vibrated when we touched. And suddenly I knew why he couldn't tell them it was a mistake.

"Oh, my God," I breathed, finally. "Oh, my God, I'm such an idiot. *That's* why Smalley gave me the portal locus code. She knew we were bonded. She knew we could survive the jump."

"Ami, don't be mad," Jack begged, but I wasn't listening.

Bit by bit, pieces of the puzzle took shape in my head. Everything fit. Our matching scars. The way I healed him. The freaky *déjà vu* and weird glowy stuff.

But…*why*? Why had he lied to me? Was I really that repulsive? Was the thought of being bonded to me so awful he had to lie about it for *ten years*?

"I never meant for you to find out like this." Jack took a step toward me, but I dodged out of reach.

"Stay away from her. Can't you see she wants nothing to do with you?" Bud hurried to block his path.

"Sir, this is between me and your daughter."

"There's *nothing* between you and my daughter."

"Is that your decision? Or is it the Elders'? I forget," Jack said, voice thick with sarcasm, "who's running her life this week?"

While they argued, I slumped against the wall. My body felt like one of those wind-up dolls whose spinner had run down, and all I could do was sag lifelessly.

Jack was my bondmate.

If that was true, then why all the subterfuge? Why did he leave? I didn't care who'd ordered him away. If it had been me, nothing would have kept me from him. Not age differences, or lost memories, or angry parents. *Nothing!*

In robotic silence, I worked Henry's locks, then sketched out the portal containment wards for our escape. Distant shrieks of armed guards rang out down the hall, but Dad and Jack kept arguing. I don't even think they noticed I'd left the conversation.

I lit up the wards with the usual incantation, and by the time I turned back, Jack had his sword out and Bud looked like he was ready to start swinging.

"Enough," I said, quietly at first, then louder. "*Enough*!"

They both looked up, shamefaced.

"Jack, if you didn't want to be my bondmate, fine. I'm not such a pathetic lump that I'll disintegrate without you. I just wish you hadn't lied to me."

His sword dropped by his side. "I *had* to lie. To protect you. *Everything* I did was to protect you."

Dad snorted. "So you dragged her in front of a firing squad?"

"Bud, I'm warning you—"

A clatter from the hallway interrupted whatever Jack was about to say, and we all froze, eyes fixed on the door. I wasn't sure if it was the smear of blood along his cheek or the crossbow he leveled at Jack's chest, but when Alec Charbonnet entered the cell block, his smile didn't seem as charming as before.

"Have I come at a bad time?" he asked.

Before I could breathe, Jack raised his sword and started backing toward me until his body pressed tightly into mine.

"Lay one hand on her," he threatened, "and I'll kill you."

"*Lay one hand on her—*" Alec mimicked, laughing. "If you'd shown half that courage last Monday, we wouldn't be in this pickle. Do you have any idea how much trouble you've caused us? We were trying to make her look innocent. Then you muck it up by letting her channel with you?" He made a disapproving sound. "Shame on you, Smith-Hailey. Ami, come here."

"She's not going anywhere." My dad stepped up next to Jack, one hand gripping my elbow. Like I might actually *go* with the crazy crossbow guy. "Who are you?" he demanded.

"Alexander Charbonnet, at your service." Alec bowed politely. "Don't worry, Mr. Bennett, I won't let anything happen to your daughter. I'm afraid I will have to kill her Watcher, however. Deepest apologies." The last words were said to Jack, along with a contrite nod.

"Mighty well-mannered for a serial killer," Henry noted.

Jack still had one arm pressed protectively across my torso. His gaze bounced between Alec, my dad, and the mouth of the portal I'd left dormant at the far corner of the room.

"Alec, quit being an idiot." I elbowed my way around Jack. "It's over. I know who you are."

Alec frowned. "What's she talking about?"

"Sweetie, what *are* you talking about?" Bud asked.

"You don't have to lie anymore. I know I have a twin," I said. "Chancellor Thibault is Mom's old Watcher. He must have kidnapped Alec when—"

"I know who Bobby Thibault is," Bud broke in, "but why would you think—"

"I get why you didn't tell me," I insisted. "But you can't deny this anymore. Alec is my twin brother. He's the Graymason who's been killing all those Guardians."

Alec lowered his crossbow, his eyes gleaming wickedly. I noticed his hands were coated with blood, too, as was the sword at his belt. Admittedly confusing, since Graymasons didn't need to draw blood to kill.

"You think I'm your brother?" he asked, skeptical.

"Well, yeah. I mean, it makes perfect sense. Thibault must have discovered what you were and he somehow managed to sneak you out—"

"Amelie, listen to me," Bud broke in. "I don't know who that boy is, but he's not your brother. You don't have a brother."

I stared at my dad. Was he lying to me again?

With a grin, Alec shut the outer door, dimming the sound of the alarm. "Fun as this is, we really must be going. I took out as many guards as I could, but more are coming. So unless you want to watch the rest of your little party die as well, I suggest we take that portal." He nodded to the silver puddle of light on the wall. "Your sister will be upset if I let you get injured."

My sister? I stared at him, trying to find evidence of the obvious rip-roaring insanity infecting his brain. But there was nothing. His hair was neatly combed and he looked me straight in the eyes when he spoke. Totally normal.

Jack was the one who broke the silence. "Amelie has a twin sister?"

"No," Bud answered, confusion plain on his face. "I mean, she *did*…for about three minutes. But the baby died."

"Are you sure?" Jack frowned at my dad.

"Of course, I saw it myself. I was there when we buried her."

Alec steadied the crossbow. "Yes, it's stunning what memory modification can do. Very useful. Ami, say goodbye now."

"But I don't underst—"

It's odd how you never know when your whole life is going to get thrown to the dogs. One minute you're orchestrating a jailbreak with your high school crush. Then you blink and everything's in raw, bloody pieces on the floor.

With eerie calm, I watched Alec's finger squeeze the crossbow trigger. My first instinct was to duck. Not that ducking would have helped. The bolt wasn't aimed at me. It whistled past my shoulder and landed with a thud in its target—the center of Jack's chest.

Chapter Nineteen:
Tin Man

I watched as blood spread across Jack's chest in a wet, crimson stain.

This couldn't be happening. It couldn't.

In a few seconds, he'd get up and yell at me to hurry with the portal so we could go snorkel in a cesspool, or something. And I'd grumble but I'd do it. Because whatever else happened, we stuck with each other. Maybe that's why I got so angry when he sank to his knees on the cold white tile.

"Jack, get up," I snapped at him.

He toppled sideways, his eyes searching the room in soundless panic. Blood dribbled onto the floor in tiny, dark rivers.

"Get up!" I repeated louder. "We have to go."

Confusion clouded his gaze but he kept breathing, little air bubbles forming around the shaft of the metal bolt.

I sank to my knees beside him. With every passing second, it felt more real. More solid. More horrible. His eyes were glazed, his hand shaky as it patted the air in search of mine.

"Amelie," Bud said from a few inches away. "Get back."

But I couldn't move. Jack's lips moved in meaningless twitches. Inside me, something cracked and broke, a torrent of emotions flooding forward. Heat ripped through my brain, white-hot and strange like the chemical fires Gunderman made in the school lab. Green. Sharp-smelling.

The first flash of memory exploded in my head like a fireball.

It was kindergarten, my first week at St. Michael's. The merry-go-round zipped in dizzy circles, Ty Webster pushing it harder and harder. I screamed at him to stop, that I was going to fall, but he wouldn't. When I hit the ground, sharp rocks dug into my palms, embedded so deep I couldn't tell what color they were.

A line of kids gathered to laugh at me. I remember thinking if I were tough like my mom I'd get up and shove Ty Webster. Maybe kick him, or call up a channel and turn his hair blue. Dad had warned me not to channel at school, since most kids didn't get their powers until puberty. He didn't want anyone asking questions. So I stayed put, curled in a ball, my head buried at my knees.

I cried that way until an older boy with blond hair and glasses pushed his way to the front and picked me up. He didn't say anything, just carried me to the healer and stayed in the waiting room while she dug the pebbles out of my palms.

He was waiting for me when I came out. He asked if I was okay and walked me back to class. The next day, I gave him some animal crackers out of my lunch to say thank you. He smiled this awesome, crooked smile, then bit the head off each animal cracker, one by one. That's how he gave them back to me, slobbery and decapitated.

There were a few more lightning flashes of memory, somewhat less intense. Lisa and me crouched behind the sandbox in first grade, spying on that same boy. His third grade piano recital when he screwed up his solo but I gave him flowers anyway. Pink tulips. He snapped the heads off those, too, and gave the stems back to me.

The memories unfolded like road maps of my life. Strange and complicated. But nothing prepared me for the searing hot needles that scraped across my mind at the next one.

It didn't surface naturally like Dr. Evans promised. It felt more like someone had heated up a scalpel, then excavated the memory from my brain with sharp jabs.

I was in a sage-colored room with a carved white mantle and crown molding that descended nearly a foot from the ceiling. Rich tapestries hung on the walls, pictures of angels spun with deep reds and gold. Gilded wall-sconces shimmered unevenly, casting flickers of light across the polished hardwood floors. It was almost time to leave the PTA meeting, but all the kids had hidden for one last round of hide-and-go-seek. I'd chosen a spot behind the Christmas tree so I could look out the window.

I thought they were shadows at first. Black clouds billowed out of nowhere, thin seams of gray light staining the air. The sky was practically flooded before I realized they were demons.

Things happened fast after that. I stayed hidden. I heard my mother's voice in the hallway, calling to me, but I was too scared to answer. By that time, the room was on fire. Tapestries flapped in the heat; oil paintings melted into the walls. Even the Christmas tree was in flames. More screams came from the hall, a few tearing sounds, and a crunch like chicken bones in the garbage disposal at home. I clamped my hands over my ears to shut it out, but I couldn't. It was like a recording in my head. My mother's screams. The chicken bones.

When the blond boy grabbed my sleeve and dragged me from the burning tree to behind a couch, I didn't fight. He put his hand over my eyes, and tried to push me out the door. "*Run!*" he yelled, over and over again. "*Run!*"

But I couldn't.

I couldn't do anything.

My mind clawed at comprehension like fingernails through a sandcastle. Demons were close. My mother was dead. I would die soon, too.

Oddly, what troubled me most was the heat. Not the heat from the room, but from the black fire growing inside of me. Power burned at my skin, staining my thoughts. The fear, the rage. I had to get it out. My eyes were cemented shut, but somehow my hand managed to find a shard of broken glass.

The boy didn't yell when I stabbed him, or when I stabbed myself. Even when the Crossworld energy brought him to his knees and shudders of agony ripped through him, he didn't let go of my hand. That boy.

Jackson Smith-Hailey.

Through my pain, I saw the room flood with pink light, a seashell glow we could feel as much as see. A burst of power hurtled out of us. I'd never felt anything so violent. It burned through the walls, tore up the ceilings. In the back of my mind, a thousand anguished cries echoed—souls of the damned as they scurried back to hell.

That's all I remembered of the fight.

Jack held me after, for hours it seemed. The rescue crew tried to pry me out of his arms, but he kept screaming at them to leave us alone. I think they must have drugged him, because he was unconscious when they finally hauled him away.

And me?

I let him go.

I sat there like a useless lump and let them take him. Just like I let my mother get ripped to pieces while I hid.

Disgust pulsed through my body as the momentary flash faded back to reality—to Jack, bloody and limp in my arms. I wouldn't let him go this time.

"*Inergio*," I yelled at the portal.

Jack's head lolled against my chest as I hooked both arms under his shoulders, careful not to disturb the wound.

"Amelie, don't make a fool of yourself," Alec said from across the room. "I won't let you escape again. Jackson's death isn't the end, it's the beginning. Your sister needs you. The Guardians need you."

I glared at him. "What you need is an attitude check. *Doloré*."

Instantly, Alec crumpled to the floor. I didn't entirely know what the curse would do to him, since it wasn't in any of our books. But it'd been effective enough when Ms. Hansen used it on Jack. And if *she* hadn't been damned to prison for throwing an illegal curse at a Watcher, then I probably wouldn't be, either.

"*Inergio*." I tried the portal again.

In a wash of power, it flared to life, casting flickering shadows across Bud's stunned face. Jack's feet trailed dark smears across the tile as I dragged him toward the portal. I'd made it halfway there when I felt the burden lighten.

"I've got him," Henry said. "Amelie, I've got him."

He had to say it a few times before I understood. Together, we hefted Jack to the mouth of the portal, then Henry grabbed my dad by the shirt. Alec would be released from the curse the instant we left. If he had a death wish, he might even try to follow us. But what else could I do? Even if I had enough power to channel a killing curse *and* make the jump, I didn't know if I'd want to. Despite what everyone thought, I wasn't a killer.

"Ready?" Henry tightened his grip on my dad.

"The shields will be weak," I warned. "Don't let go of me."

Henry nodded. "Do it."

"*Familia fides.*"

Every atom in my body stretched and squeezed like Silly Putty as the portal activated, sucking us in. Demons thrashed at my shields, but I clung to Jack. He was my source. As long as he lived, I could use his power as an amplifier.

After what seemed like an eternity, a tiny speck of light appeared in the distance. I fumbled toward it, my grip tight around Jack. It was like being stuck at the bottom of a lake. For the first few seconds it isn't bad—kind of dark, heavy. Then your oxygen gives out and you know you need to breathe, but the surface is still twenty feet above you. So you kick and thrash, and your lungs keep getting tighter and tighter 'til you can't feel anything but dizzy.

In short, it sucked.

I was barely conscious when my body slammed into something soft and a cloud of Strawberry Shortcake perfume erupted around me.

Jack had fallen silent. He lay beneath me on his side, the wet stain of blood from his chest leaking onto my bedspread.

"*Exitus!*" I closed the portal with a wave of my hand, and glanced around to make sure I hadn't lost anyone. Bud lay in a crumpled ball at the foot of my bed. Poor Henry half-dangled off my dresser, covered with the shattered remnants of a vanilla body glitter jar.

"That went surprisingly well," said Henry, sliding off the dresser with a *thunk*.

I rolled Jack onto his back, trying to keep the crossbow bolt steady. The blood flow had slowed, but I could still feel his pulse.

"Dad, show Henry where the linen closet is. I need clean towels. Lots of them. Then go downstairs and make me some coffee. Extra caffeine."

My voice must have sounded authoritative, because the men scrambled to their feet and scurried away without question. By the time Henry returned with the towels, I'd ripped off Jack's shirt and started mopping up the blood with a Beanie Baby. It's a real testament to how freaked out I must have been, because the whole shirtlessness thing didn't even distract me.

"Don't you die," I ordered as I tugged the bolt out.

My dad hadn't returned with the coffee yet, thank God. Don't get me wrong, I really did need a boost, but the thought of having Dad around while I did it made me uncomfortable on levels I wasn't ready to visit. Healing Jack touched me in ways I couldn't describe. Ways I couldn't control. Ways I didn't want to share with anyone.

Carefully, I laid my hands over his bare chest and pulled open the Crossworld channel.

"*Salve pacem.*"

Every ounce of strength I possessed poured into the charm—every bit of love, every memory I had of him. Light welled inside me and hovered for a moment, tentative. The portal had drained my Crossworld energy horribly and for an awful moment I wondered, will there be enough? Will *I* be enough? Tears of frustration formed in my eyes as I squeezed them tighter.

Finally, painfully, it gushed at Jack.

"Yes." I breathed a sigh of relief. Shadows from the channel slithered ugly pathways over my skin, but I kept going. Healing. Pulling. Forcing life into his body.

"What's she doing?" Dad demanded from the doorway.

Henry smiled sadly. "What she has to."

Under my hand, the vibrant hum of electricity pulsed, hot and vicious. It knitted his flesh together—first the deepest wounds, then the tissue surrounding, then, finally, his skin.

The whole room smelled like burned leaves and vanilla body spray; the air practically crackled with magic.

After what seemed like forever, Jack's breathing stabilized and I collapsed beside him, the channel still lingering. Blood coated my bedspread in thick puddles, its sweet, coppery smell stinging my nose. I hated that smell. It was death. Death and magic.

I must have dozed off because I didn't even struggle when Bud finally dragged me off Jack and wrapped a Hello Kitty blanket around me.

"Hey," I said, drowsy. "Guess I should have stayed home from school, huh?"

"You think?" He sank onto the edge of the bed and combed the hair out of my eyes, like he used to when I was little. "You remembered it, didn't you? The attack?"

I nodded.

"I was afraid of that." He looked at the ground. "Are you okay?"

"No," I said honestly. The truth was, I didn't want to think about it. If I thought too hard about it, I'd have to admit it was my fault. It was *all* my fault. Mom's death. Jack's bonding. If I had just answered Mom, none of it would have happened.

"I could have saved her," I whispered. "If I'd been braver—"

"Baby, no," Bud said, his lips warm against my forehead. "Don't do that to yourself. You were seven years old. A lot of people would have died that night if not for you."

"But she called to me. I was too scared," I said. "God, Jack was right not to want me. I'm nothing but a coward."

"Oh, Ami." Bud sighed. "There are a lot of names I want to call you right now, but 'coward' isn't one of them. You think a coward could have done this? You think a coward could love that boy as much as you do, even knowing you'll lose him? Love takes courage, sweetheart, maybe more than most people know. That's not something a coward can handle."

Tears pricked behind my eyes, blurring Jack's outline into a mush of white and red. How had everything gotten so screwed-up?

Bud held me as I cried—deep wracking sobs that cut through ten years. It took what felt like hours to cry it out. When he finally scooped me into his arms, all I wanted was an endless stack of pancakes and maybe a *Star Wars* marathon followed by a year of sleep.

The worst part was, we weren't even safe yet. Jack still had the stupid prophecy on his head and aside from knowing the

Graymason was female, we weren't any closer to figuring out her identity.

Dad lugged me to the bathroom and sat on the toilet while I showered. I mean, he had the seat down and everything. I guess he just wanted to make sure I didn't pass out and crack my skull open. On any other day, it would have been mortifying. Okay, scratch that. It was pretty mortifying. Not scar-my-psyche, white-padded-walls, long-term-therapy *awful,* but still nothing I cared to tell Lisa about.

I waited until he left before I pulled on my tank top and pajama pants, then I sat at the edge of the bathtub for a minute so I didn't fall over. Or throw up. Henry had stripped the bed while I showered and replaced my Strawberry Shortcake bedding with Smurfs sheets.

Smurfs.

Which meant Henry was either in cahoots with Bud on the whole Sabotage-Amelie's-Love-Life agenda, or it was time to visit Bed Bath & Beyond.

Jack lay between the sheets looking pale, yet alive. The only reminder of the gaping wound in his chest was a patch of dimpled red skin. I sat cross-legged next to him, tracing my fingers over the scar. It looked like a lily—the trademark flower of funerals. Because *that's* what we needed—*more* foreboding.

"Hey." I nudged his sleepy form.

No response. Good.

"We need to talk," I said, weirdly nervous. "Since you're kind of in my bed, and the couch sucks rocks, I'm thinking I'll just crash here next to you, if that's okay. I mean, I know I bug you and it wouldn't be okay normally, but I'm hoping you'll cut me some slack since I kinda saved your life. What do you say? Truce?"

He lay perfectly still, shadows coloring the half-moon hollows under his eyes. It was eerie how connected I still felt to him. I wasn't ready to be apart from him yet. Oddly, the thought of saying that out loud scared me almost as much as the actual being apart from him.

I'd just curled onto the pillow when a muffled knock sounded at the door. Henry stuck his head in.

"Is this a bad time?"

I glared at him.

"Right. I just wanted you to know, I tried to call Miss Anselmo on the cell phone in your bag. No answer. Same with Miss Shaw and Mr. Marino." He gave a deep sigh. "They could be sleeping. It's too soon to panic."

My heart gave a lurch at their names. *Crap, Alec might already have them.* They could already be dead.

Henry must have read the panic in my eyes. "Try not to worry. They're resourceful and he's got no reason to hurt them yet."

Yet.

No, he might not hurt them *yet*, but he would soon. Another reason to feel guilty…like I needed one.

"Thanks, Henry."

"Sleep tight." He smiled. "If you don't mind, your father instructed me to leave the door open."

Yeah, that figured. The fate of the world hangs in the balance and Dad's worried about my virtue.

Achy and tired, I slid between the cool sheets next to Jack and lifted his arm into a cradle under my head. His body hummed against my skin, warming me from the inside out. Even now, strands of golden light glimmered wherever I touched, the same glow I'd marveled at in the motel. How had I not recognized the bond? Was I a total idiot, or just tragically oblivious to all things romantic?

My fingertip sketched out a weak protection ward along the curve of his chest, but it sputtered and died.

Super.

The real Graymason could show up any minute and I was totally spent. I didn't even know if Jack wanted me to fight. He'd been stalking death since the day I met him. What guarantee did I have that, come Saturday at dawn, he wouldn't just walk off a cliff, eager to become victim number three hundred and twelve?

"You're such a jerk." I let my hand settle over his heart. "How am I supposed to save you when you won't save yourself?"

The answer came as soon as my eyes fell shut.

. . .

I stood in a dark cavern, smooth rock walls rising up on all sides as if they'd been carved out by water. It took me less than a second to recognize it as the antechamber of the Great Books. Five doors arched before me, the familiar lines of their carvings barely visible in the sleepy light. Only the door with the ourbouros glowed. The *Book of Lies*. Brilliant white light poured out through the cracks around the door's edge, and just as before, something old and powerful urged me toward it.

With each step, the light intensified, painfully hot, until the outline of a person came into focus. I don't know what I expected. Whatever I thought I would see, it wasn't this.

My mother.

At least, it looked like my mother. Chestnut curls spilled down her back, her eyes bright blue. She held her arms out, shimmery white fabric flowing around her like it was no more substantial than air. Then it hit me. It wasn't. And neither was she.

As much as I longed to run into her arms, to hear her tell me everything would be fine, I couldn't. She was a lie.

It finds the thing you want most in the world. Wasn't that what Jack had said?

"My mom is dead," I told the woman. "You're not real."

Her eyes grew sad and she lowered her arms. "I'm as real as you want me to be."

I watched in awe as she changed, shifting forms through every person I'd ever cared about—Bud, Lisa, Katie, Matt…even Lyle. She finally settled on Jack. Not the half-dead version I'd left beside me at home, but the Jack from my visions—beautiful and strong. My breath caught in my throat.

"This one? This is what you want?" the thing asked in Jack's voice.

I shook my head, fighting back tears. "It doesn't matter what I want. It's impossible."

But even as I said it, I remembered Jack's words—that impossible things happen every day. And I couldn't help wondering if, maybe, it was too soon to give up.

The Jack-thing smiled his adorable crooked smile. With that long, loping stride, he took three steps toward me and caught me in his arms. "Omelet," he sighed. "Anything's possible."

Then he bent his head to my ear, and started whispering.

Ancient words.

Chapter Twenty:
Little Lies

The sound of demon hooves awakened me—a herd of hell-beasts storming the suburbs. Or possibly construction equipment from Mrs. Peabody's renovation next door. My eyes fluttered open, scanning the room. Hello Kitty curtains, Pepto pink walls, rainbow stickers. Yup, still my room. No hell-beasts, thank God.

I stretched out on the bed, only to find empty space. Where was Jack? How long had I been asleep?

My hand slapped around in search of the alarm clock. Six p.m. Probably Friday. I tried to sit up, and immediately felt like yarking.

"I wouldn't move too fast, if I were you." Dane's eternally amused voice came from the rocking chair in the corner. I turned—slower this time.

"Hey, wolf-boy. Does Jack know you're in here?"

He gave an impish grin. "It's a full moon tonight. What do you think?"

I'd take that as a *no*. Frankly, I wasn't too worried. In my current state, no sane being would want to mate with me—even a hormonal werewolf on a lunar high. My head throbbed from dehydration and hunger. I couldn't see my face, but dollars to donuts it resembled the hairball Lisa's cat barfed up last week. I sniffed the air.

"Did y'all clean up, or something? It smells like ammonia in here."

"Henry did it," Dane explained. "Luc threatened to hire a maid service if we didn't get rid of the blood stench. Dragging humans in at this point seemed like a bad idea."

"Agreed." Never underestimate a werewolf's grasp on the obvious. "Where is Dracu-Luc, anyway? Getting cozy with the neighbors' daughters?"

"Good guess, but no. Your house has some nasty anti-vampire wards on it. Luc was stuck outside most of the night. I think he's back to Arianna's errand list now," he said. "You hungry?"

As if on cue, my stomach gave a loud rumble.

Dane chuckled. "Come on, let's get you fed."

It took all my resources to swing my legs out from under the covers and hobble down the wide stairs. Dane let me keep a hand on his shoulder in case I fell, and stayed close until we got to the kitchen. Judging from the rich, syrupy aromas drifting out of it, breakfast had been on for a while.

"They're waiting for you," he whispered. "Don't be scared."

"I'm not."

"Really?" Dane gave me a nudge through the entry. "In that case, maybe you should be a little scared."

Indeed, Bud and Jack sat, staring across the kitchen table at each other in complete and terrifying silence. They looked like some creepy reenactment of a western stand-off at high noon—

except the streets had been replaced by a breakfast table, and the guns were swapped for waffles. As soon as I entered, Henry set down his spatula, switched off the stove, and hurried out. Clever guy.

"So," I said, "howzitgoin'?"

More silence.

O-kay. Judging from the glare, Bud obviously knew I'd slept with Jack. Jack didn't look too pleased, either.

My hands shook as I poured myself a cup of coffee and grabbed a plate, heaping it with waffles from the platter Henry set out. The coffee was tepid—like I cared.

Jack waited until I'd downed two giant plates of food and a quart of orange juice, then wadded up his napkin and tossed it on the table. "Bud, would you give us some privacy?"

I nearly spewed my coffee.

There is nothing—*nothing*—my father hates more than being dismissed in his own house. I remember one time, Elder Horowitz came over and suggested Bud "go for a walk" so he could speak to Mom in private. Dad went ballistic. His face turned purple. That little vein in his forehead started throbbing.

Hiroshima–Part Deux.

This time, astonishingly, Dad's head did not explode. He froze for a moment and his fingers quit drumming. Finally, he stood, shooting off just the tiniest hint of a homicidal glare. "Thirty minutes," he said. "Not one second more."

The whole house rattled under his footsteps. After a minute, the door to his office slammed, and I swallowed my last bite of pecan danish.

"Well, that was interesting," I said. "Blackmail? Or did you spike his herbal tea with Valium?"

Jack pushed his coffee mug away. "We need to talk."

"You think?" Apparently, everyone had a handle on the obvious today.

Light filtered over Jack's skin as he led me up the stairs, a low-level glow shimmering through him. I wanted to take it as a good sign—maybe he'd decided to spare my heart and not shred it into itty-bitty pieces.

"Sit down!" he ordered, when we reached my room.

Or not.

I obediently plopped on the edge of my bed and stared at the carpet. "Look, I know what you're going to say. And before you get all pissy, you should know that I remember."

He narrowed his gaze. "You *remember*?"

"Yes," I said. "I mean, not everything, obviously, but enough to get why you hate me. What I did—bonding you like that—it wasn't fair."

He hiked one eyebrow, but didn't speak.

"I mean, we were just kids. It's ridiculous to hold you to something that happened so long ago, which you never agreed to in the first place." My voice sounded more certain than I felt, thank goodness...almost like I believed the trash coming out of my mouth. "So, since you didn't choose this, and since there's no one trying to kill us at the moment, I want to tell you that I absolve you."

Jack's evil eye intensified. "You *absolve* me?"

"Sure. It was only a partial bond, right? And no one expects you to honor it. So...you're off the hook. You know, *free*." I fluttered my hand in a stupid little motion, then stuck it out in front of me. "Can we still be friends?"

Okay, wow. *Friends?* Did that sound as lame as I think it did?

I sat there like an idiot with my hand dangling in the air while he stared at it. Of course, I wanted him to argue, to tell me I was wrong. Screw the Elders and screw the prophecy. We could run away and live in a ramshackle cabin somewhere with a weapons arsenal of our own and a two-headed guard dog, or whatever. Happily ever after, right?

"I called Chancellor Thibault," he said, his eyes still glued to my hand. "If I surrender, Alec will let your friends go. If I don't, he'll kill them."

I dropped my hand. "You did what?"

"I called Chancellor—"

"Yeah, I heard you," I said acidly. "That was obviously a rhetorical expression meaning, *'How could anyone so smart do something so stupid?'* When is this supposed to happen?"

"Midnight," he said, "at the gala."

My nose wrinkled. "They're still having that thing?"

Just goes to show what hubris the Elders are capable of. With all the diplomats and financial benefactors attending, they'd have to take the wards down. Jack and I could probably get on campus easily enough, but the place would be crawling with guards.

I folded my arms across my chest, trying not to convey how boneheaded I thought the whole idea was. "So, what's the plan? Weapons? Explosives? Horde of flesh-eating zombies? How do we go in?"

For the briefest second, Jack's eyes warmed. Then his game face was back. "There's no plan, Ami. *We* don't go in. *I* do."

I frowned. "When I said I absolve you, that wasn't meant as a suicide suggestion. For the moment, we're still bonded."

"Only partially."

"Great, then I can partially kick your ass." I prodded him with my toe. "Dude, you're not going in without me. We'll wait until Lisa and Katie are safe, then I'll take out Alec. I can totally do it," I insisted. "You saw what happened last night."

"I didn't, actually," he said, "but Bud mentioned you were badass."

"Bud said 'badass'?" I asked, doubtful.

"I'm paraphrasing. What he actually said was that you make him want to start drinking again."

Outside my window, the sky had blended to a mélange of taffy and cotton candy. It made the pink of my walls practically vibrate with color. With an almost imperceptible sigh, Jack lowered himself beside me. His skin felt warm through the thin fabric of his T-shirt, and I tried not to shiver. Already, threads of bond-light swirled between us.

"I screwed this up, didn't I?" he asked softly. "Us, I mean."

I didn't know what to say. Was there still an *us*? That seemed to be the million dollar question…not that he'd helped clarify things.

"It wasn't your fault," I replied. "It was mine. I needed someone to open the channel and you were there. Wrong place at the wrong time, I guess."

"Amelie."

"I mean, it could have been anyone," I prattled on. "Matt, Kel…even Lyle, I guess. It's not your fault I had a crush on you." My cheeks flushed with heat. I hadn't meant to say that.

He squinted. "Crush?"

"It was stupid, I know," I admitted. "The flowers, the cookies.

I probably drove you up a wall. You were just too nice to tell me to buzz off."

"I *did* tell you to buzz off," he pointed out. "Several times."

"I'm not the best with feedback."

He took a deep breath and let it out slowly. "If you want to know the truth, I didn't mind that much. Actually, I kind of liked it."

Okay, either my hearing was shot or I was hallucinating. Or he was trying to make me feel like less of a ginormous loser. "Jack, you don't have to say that. I already told you, you're off the hook."

"I heard. Thanks."

Jack lifted a hand to push the bright tangles back from my face, his eyes searching mine. I'd gotten so used to seeing that guarded look of his, the one that kept the world at bay. But when I stared up at him now, it was gone.

"You know, Omelet, I could have taken a bolt to the heart. I would have happily given up my soul. But this?" His fingers trailed down my wrist, sending off yellow sparks of power. "Do you have any idea how awful this week has been? Not the beatings and impending death—that wasn't your fault," he cut me off before I could get defensive. "I'm talking about everything else. The sightseeing and the hand-holding and—oh yeah—the singing in the shower? What was that, anyway? Justin Bieber?"

"Don't even start." In a fit of drama, I grabbed the cell phone off my bedside table. The call log told me Luc had been trying to get me, but I hit the icon to ignore his messages. Whatever the vampire wanted, it could be dealt with later.

"Here." I handed the phone to Jack. "Why don't you record your complaints, then whenever the lecture-urge arises, just hit play. Save your breath."

"Great idea." He took the phone and held it to his mouth. "Amelie Bennett, you're the most annoying girl on the planet. You make me want to throw myself off a bridge. And, unfortunately, I am one hundred percent, head-over-heels, crazy in love with you. There. Satisfied?" He hit the stop icon and tossed it back in my lap.

I stared at the fallen rectangle like it might bite me. Okay, hallucination check. Did he just say what I thought he said? I hit the play icon and listened carefully.

Yup, there it was. *One hundred percent, head-over-heels, crazy in love.* I did it again, just to be sure.

"Jackson," I asked carefully, "are you on any illegal substances I should know about?"

"Nope."

"Eaten any strange looking mushrooms?"

"Not lately."

"Any near brushes with eternal damnation that might be affecting your judgment?"

He grinned. "That hard to believe, huh?"

I hit the play icon again.

You know those moments where something amazing happens and you swear you're going to remember it forever? Like the first time you see a rainbow for real, after years of staring at rainclouds, thinking there's color hidden there when really it's just pollution? It wasn't like that.

I didn't *think* I would remember this forever. I *knew* I would.

After the fourth or fifth replay, he pried the phone out of my hands and tossed it on the bed. Then he sank to his knees in front of me.

"You're such an idiot. I've loved you since the day you showed up at my stupid piano recital with flowers you picked out of Smalley's private garden. Or maybe it was the animal crackers, I don't even know." He ran a hand through his hair. "That night at the PTA meeting, you didn't *force* me to bond. I could have run away like the other kids. I came back because I was looking for you. Amelie, I'm crazy about you. I always have been. I'm pretty sure I always will be."

Then he kissed me.

Which is a bit like saying, "Then the sun exploded and the walls started melting."

As intense as our kisses were before, they always had a sense of desperation attached to them, like everything could fall apart in an instant. This was different; there was no anger, no secret. He was oxygen after being underwater for years. All coherent thought exited my head as I melted into him.

There was nothing hurried this time. His lips pressed, cool and sweet, against mine, with just a hint of salt from a cut at the corner of his lip. One of his hands slid up my spine to circle the back of my neck, guiding me closer, fitting my body to his. And it did fit, perfectly, like we'd been molded out of the same clay. With every touch, I felt something I'd lost being given back to me, some piece of me that I hadn't known was missing.

His fingers wound into my tank top as I scooted backward on the bed, pulling his weight down on top of me. He couldn't seem to stop touching me and I didn't want him to. The feel of his fingers skating over my ribs, under my shirt, lighting up my skin like a bonfire—it hurt, but not in a bad way. I felt my heart expanding, making room for him to move in permanently.

"Jack." I touched his broken lip with my finger. "Do you want me to heal you?"

He shook his head. "No more healing, I promised your dad."

"You care what my dad thinks?"

"Well," Jack frowned, his eyes troubled, "he's kind of my father-in-law. Granted, I'll be dead soon, but for the moment, it seems wrong to disrespect him."

I tried to nod, but it was more of a Bobblehead move. Maybe it was a mistake to bring up my dad...or anything about the future, really. Jack hadn't given up the notion that he would die, yet here he was, with me. Strange as it was, it didn't exactly feel like an ending.

"You know I won't let you die," I said.

"It's not your choice."

"I'm your Channeler, Jack. 'Wither thou goest—'"

He shut me up with another kiss that sent explosions to my toes and made me forget my middle name. Every nerve in my body lit up like a power station. My legs twined through his, my hands pulling his shirt up over his head, but it wasn't enough. I couldn't get close enough to him. In all the times I'd watched him fight, it never occurred to me how that physical power might translate to...other stuff. Now all I could think was that I couldn't wait to find out. The problem was, I didn't just want him for one night. I wanted him forever.

We kissed until my lips felt frosted and worn and my hair was damp with sweat. It was like every dream I'd had about him, only this time I knew I wouldn't wake up. His hands stroked my back with urgent tenderness as I trailed my fingers over the scar on his chest. Scary how close I'd come to losing him.

"What are you thinking?" I whispered.

"About weapons," he admitted, sheepish. "Whether you have any here."

"Well, the toilet brush is probably the most lethal thing we own. You can call Luc. I'm sure he has a spare surface-to-air missile you could borrow."

Jack grinned. "Thanks, but it's not for me. I meant for you. They'll come soon, once I'm gone. Luc will help you if he can but, Ami, they won't give up. You're too dangerous."

"I still seem dangerous to you?"

"Well, maybe not *now*, while you're all warm and…" He made a vague gesture at my body, pajamas clinging in rumpled disarray. "*This* version of you is terrifying in a completely different way."

I pinched him hard on the belly. "Watch it, buddy. I *am* dangerous, and don't you forget it. Now hold still."

My intent was just to heal him, maybe patch up the rough spots before we headed off to face the enemy…again. No way could I have known what would happen when I opened the healing channel.

Or tried to.

It was like pulling on a tug-of-war rope, only there was no one on the other side of the ditch and the ground behind me was an endless pit of ice cold fire. I felt my grip slide off the power strands, vertigo slamming into me. The first thing to hit was confusion. It made no sense why such a small healing channel should make me so sick. Every muscle went rigid. Blackness ripped through my head like gunfire.

"Amelie, no! Shut it off! Close the channel!"

I heard him in the back of my head, yelling for help, but I couldn't stop it. My head flopped backward, a cacophony of shouts rising as people hurtled into the room. The air oozed fire, hot and musty at the same time, with a metallic tinge that turned my stomach. I could smell it, like wet, burning leaves. It stung my senses.

I tried to give the darkness to Jack, the same way I had at assembly, but for every rohm of power he drained off me, five more flowed in. I couldn't shut the channel.

"Henry! Bud!" Jack shouted. "I need help!"

There was a clatter in the hallway, then my father's voice erupted. "What the–? What in God's name did you do to her?"

"I didn't do anything," Jack insisted. "We were just kissing—"

"You bastard, get your hands off my daughter!"

"Bud!" Henry cried.

All at once, Jack lurched away from me and a popping sound like broken glass exploded against the wall. I tried to reach out for him but my arms were lead.

"You were supposed to keep her from channeling. That was the deal," Bud yelled.

"Sir, I didn't—" Jack was silenced by another crash.

My body convulsed on the bed, and coppery blood pooled inside my mouth. I wanted to ask what "deal" they were talking about but nothing would respond. My brain had short-circuited.

Jack scurried back to my side, his fingers trailing over my hair. "Ami, you have to close the channel. Now!"

"She can't," Henry interrupted. "Jackson, you're her conduit. She can't close it with you here. Not with that much Otrava in her."

Jack's fingers froze on my forehead, terror seeping into me through the bond. "I can't leave her. Not like this."

"If you stay, she'll die."

"But—"

"Boy, you have five seconds to get out of my house." Dad raised a fist, ready to knock Jack out the window.

"Jackson, I'm sorry," Henry concurred, "but you need to go. Now."

Jack hesitated only a moment. I could feel the conflict in him, his desperate desire to stay with me sandwiched between waves of wordless terror. I flinched as his fingertips left my forehead in a velvet sweep of pain.

No! I wanted to shout. *Come back!*

Before I could pry my mouth open, a new presence emerged beside me. It wasn't so bright or warm as Jack, but it pulled on the darkness in steady, even tugs.

Slowly, the pain receded and my room came back into focus. It looked like a smashed antique toy store. My Hello Kitty lamp lay in pieces on the ground; the mosquito netting over the bed had been ripped down in wide strips. My pillow lay in a blood-covered heap beside the bed.

"Henry?" I croaked.

"Shh." He put a wrinkled hand over my forehead to draw out the last of the dark energy. "You have a huge dose of Otrava in your system. It'll fade in a few days, but for the moment, you're grounded."

I sat up, immediately wishing I hadn't. "J–Jack needs me. The Graymason—"

"Amelie, Jack was the one who gave you the Otrava," Henry said quietly. "He didn't want you following him tonight. He wanted you safe."

I stared at him, struggling to make sense of his words. No matter how hard I tried, they wouldn't fit together. "That's ridiculous. Jack would never do that."

"People do ridiculous things for love," Henry sighed. "I'm beginning to think Judy was right with all her talk of destiny. There may be only one way this can end."

Before I could comment, one of the cell phones Luc gave us started ringing. Not a big deal, since he was the only one who had that number. Honestly, my heart was already shredded. Did I really need to add to the trauma by interacting with the undead?

I powered it off.

A perfect orange moon cast odd patterns through the lace curtains, like a haunted doily on the carpet. Eleven eleven p.m.

So that was it, then? In forty-nine minutes, Jack would be dead? He'd be *dead*, I would be digesting poison, and there was *nothing* I could do about any of it?

"You'll be okay," Henry assured me. "You two were only partway bonded—"

"You were only partway bonded with Smalley," I said. "Are *you* okay?"

He didn't bother answering—just sat on the edge of the bed, holding my hand while I sent hate vibes into the world. This sucked…more than *anything* had ever sucked in the history of the whole sucky universe. I might have cried myself to sleep like that, too, if things hadn't gotten so loud downstairs. Footsteps crashed, furniture cracked. My father boomed expletives.

"Stay away from her. She's done enough for you people!"

I sat up straight as the door to my room exploded inward. Dane stood behind it—but not any version of Dane I'd seen before. Moonlight shimmered under his skin in a thousand glittery shards, as if he held the moon inside him. His face was mid-transformation from human to pure nightmare, teeth bared and fingers extended into knife-like claws.

"Amelie." My name emerged as a growl, like the things you hear on Animal Planet that make your skin crawl. If it hadn't been Dane I might have freaked out completely. Henry and I watched as his body convulsed like a wild dog being electrocuted, and the transformation dissolved.

"Dane, what's going on?" I demanded.

He shook himself once more until his face came back into focus. "The phone," he said. "Luc called. He says it's not the prophecy they're after. It never was."

"What are you talking about?"

"The Peace Tenets," Dane said, still a growl, but slightly less terrifying. "Jack's the last living petitioner. If he dies, it's all over."

I looked at Henry, waiting for translation. He looked like he'd been kicked in the stomach. "Mr. Delinsky, are you sure?"

Dane nodded. "This is what they wanted all along. If Jack doesn't sign, the truce ends. It'll be Guardians against Inferni all over again."

"But, Mr. Smith-Hailey is gone," Henry said. "What choice do we have—"

Dane shuddered again, obviously struggling to keep his form. "There's no ch–ch–choice. Unless you want us all to die…you h–h–have to save Jack."

My gaze flitted from Dane to Henry, then to the window where Luc's car had just screeched to a halt on the front lawn.

"Well," I stood, ignoring the newly furry Dane-creature clawing my carpet, "it's about freaking time."

Chapter Twenty one:
End Game

Luc hit the accelerator as we flew through another red light. Cars fishtailed behind us, swerving into each other to avoid his meteor-like path.

"Luc, two-thirds of the people in this car are not immortal," I yelled. "Slow the hell down before I kick your ass sideways!"

"Silence!" he commanded. "Your blather distracts me."

"Don't distract him, child," Henry muttered from the backseat.

Ever since we left the house, Luc had alternated pretty steadily between bouts of stony silence and spurts of wild complaint—with most of the complainy bits centered around what a pathetic excuse for a Guardian I was. Likewise, I alternated between guilt for not taking his call sooner and a burning desire to slap him silly.

We bounced onto the sidewalk, skirting around a four-way stop sign. I screamed.

"Newsflash, Luc! For some people, life consists of more than just your little problems, you know?"

"*Little* problems?" he sputtered. "My people are facing

extinction!"

"Well, maybe you should have planned better."

"Maybe you should answer the blasted *phone*," he yelled back, his fist slamming into the steering wheel.

"Mr. Montaigne," Henry broke in with a nervous glance at the fractured steering wheel. "If you could calm down for a moment, I think it might behoove us to discuss our strategy—"

"That's 'Lord Montaigne' to you, *peon*," Luc fairly spat. "Do you even know who I am?"

If I had to guess, I'd say yes, Henry knew, since Luc had been throwing titles around since he arrived.

"Royal dauphin."

"Heir to the Immortal throne."

"Future Sovereign of the Southern District."

It sounded impressive…until the image of him and Beatrice Boudreaux squeaking around in the backseat of a Ferrari popped into my head.

I shut my eyes as the last of Dad's emergency Queller dose worked its detoxifying magic on my body. It wasn't as excruciating as the first time at school. Maybe the Otrava dose wasn't as high, or maybe I just knew what to expect. Either way, my pain had a purpose. My bondmate—the guy I would swim naked through jellyfish for—was scheduled to die in twenty-three minutes. If I wasn't in perfect channeling shape by the time the clock struck midnight, I could lose him forever.

Luc careened onto the I-10, nearly crashing into a concrete pillar. Not that mere concrete could have stopped him. He probably would have ordered it out of the way and kept driving.

"This is more than a mere tragedy! This could mean death to

my people, not to mention the end of our Crossworld brethren. Dane's pack will be hunted like dogs! My people slaughtered at the hands of madmen! Do you wankers have any idea of the gravity of this situation?"

"No. And don't bother explaining again," I snapped. "We're far too feeble-minded to get it."

At this point, we'd have to be blind, deaf, and completely moronic *not* to get the "gravity of the situation." Under threat of his mother's wrath, Luc and his royal guard had managed to track down the last remaining Guardian petitioner for the Peace Tenets, one Vincent Fiori, former trainer at St. Michael's.

Luc was ecstatic (read: less annoyed) to find Fiori—a bona fide Guardian of a respectable bloodline, former Enforcer—recently retired from his academic post. Unfortunately, he was also dead.

His soul had been taken.

Since Fiori's bloodline was Remiel, not Gabriel, Luc concluded there must be more to the case than just a prophecy. So he combed through all the deaths we'd originally classified as "collateral damage," only to discover that every single victim had been on the Convergence peace petition. Including Headmistress Smalley.

"This is preposterous." Luc swerved around a corner, narrowly missing a lamp post. "If you'd heeded my call in the first place, we wouldn't be in this predicament."

"If you'd put it together sooner, you could have avoided the whole thing."

"If you hadn't dragged all your bloody drama into my home—"

"Could we, perhaps, keep our focus on the task ahead?" Henry begged. "Or at least on not dying before we arrive?"

Luc's foot hit the accelerator so hard I thought the needle

might pop off the odometer. It was a miracle we hadn't picked up a police tail yet. Maybe they couldn't see us since the car was traveling faster than the freaking speed of light.

By the time we screeched to a halt on Prytania, the commencement gala was in full swing. The whole main building seemed to dance with light. Paper-bag luminaries lined the front walkway, casting haunted, quivering shadows over the wide front porch. Beams of muted gold coursed out of the vaulted front windows. Even the thick vines twined around the oak trees seemed to writhe like restless snakes.

A chill crept down my arms as Luc, Henry, and I approached the front gate. If the wards were up, Henry and I could probably still get through, but for Luc it'd be like walking into an electric fence. *Not that I'd mind seeing him nose-dive into one.*

Before he'd had to shift again, Dane suggested we dress to blend, so Henry grabbed Dad's funeral suit and I snagged one of my mom's old formal dresses that I kept in the back of my closet. Black, stretchy, slit up the side for fighting…with a couple of rhinestones thrown in for effect. Sexy, yet functional.

Luc, on the other hand, looked like a Calvin Klein ad come to life. Pale light gleamed off his violet eyes, casting shadows along the elegant hollows of his cheekbones. Every silky dark hair in place, every line of his tux flawless. He wasn't especially tall— maybe six-feet on a good day—but he had a presence that would fill up a banquet hall. I could see why people might want to follow him…when he wasn't acting like a complete ass, that is.

"I thought you said this was a huge event. Why are the wards down? And where are the guards?" Luc sniffed the air. "And why do I smell blood?"

"Blood?"

I took a deep whiff. Maybe a nice magnolia scent underlying the familiar burn of magic, but certainly no blood. I was about to diagnose him officially psycho when I saw it—the heel of a black leather Guardian boot sticking out from under a bush near the side gate. My elbow dug into Luc's ribs.

"Look," I said, pointing. "I bet they're down all over the place."

Luc frowned and closed his eyes. "I hear their heartbeats," he said. "Four weak ones along the front, three on each side, and two in the back. There are too many to count inside."

"Mr. Smith-Hailey must be here," Henry observed.

"How do you figure?"

"Well," Henry reasoned, "if it was the Graymason who took them out, you wouldn't hear heartbeats, would you?"

"How much time do we have?" I asked.

"Thirteen minutes," Luc replied, "give or take. What's the plan?"

A sick feeling slid through my stomach. Crap, we needed a plan. "Let's split up. We can cover more territory, maybe find Jack a little faster."

"Splendid idea," Luc said. "If we hurry, we might be in time to collect his body."

I sneered at him. "Not helpful. What about my classmates? They could look for him—"

"Or they'll start screaming and the guards will kill you on sight. Lovely plan."

Did I mention how much I hate stupid, know-it-all vampires? "I see, and what do you propose, exactly?"

"I'm not a strategist. My objective was to get us here quickly.

I accomplished that."

"You," I pointed out, "are precisely why politicians should not be allowed to run empires."

Henry ignored us completely as he slid through the gate and stalked up the main path. The weapons belt under his coat was loaded with throwing knives, glyph-carved grenades, a few canisters of tear gas, and Jack's curved short sword. I recognized it immediately by the marks etched into the blade.

"Henry?" I called out.

He stopped barely long enough to tug Jack's sword out of his belt and hurl it into the ground at my feet. It stuck in the mortar between two cobbles, wagging back and forth.

"Give that to Jackson when you see him," he called.

"Where are you going?" Luc asked.

"To pull the fire alarm," Henry hollered.

I exchanged a sheepish glance with Luc. The fire alarm. Why hadn't we thought of that?

With a look of exasperation, Luc snatched up the sword and shoved me into the bushes. In the distance, the main door cracked under Henry's boot, followed by the soft hiss of tear gas and a banshee-yowl that could only be the fire alarm.

"So it begins," Luc said.

Students flooded out of the main building. Veronica Manning hurtled past in a frothy pink dress, Keller Eastman at her side. Skye Benedict and Ty Webster followed with panicked expressions, alongside a handful of visiting dignitaries from the European consulate. But no sign of Matt, Lisa, or Katie. And no Jack.

"This isn't working." I shoved Luc to the side and yanked the sword from his hand. "I'm going to find him."

"Amelie, wait—"

Without a backward glance, I bolted for the stairs. I had no idea when I'd be able to channel, or if I could channel at all. I had about eleven minutes to figure it out. Light and warmth ignited in my chest as I pushed my way through the flood of terrified younglings. Jack was in there. Somewhere.

My mind was so focused on the path in front of me I barely noticed Creepy Daniel until he was on top of me. Literally.

A flash of light burst out of my periphery as something flat and hard cracked against my temple. Bright pain bloomed above my left eye and I stumbled to my knees, Jack's sword suddenly huge and unwieldy.

"Welcome back, Guardian Bennett. I worried someone else might kill you first." With a few quick jabs, Daniel flicked the sword from my grip and brought the tip of his blade to my throat. "I've been looking forward to this."

That earned him my best *go-screw-yourself* look. "Really? That's what you fantasize about in your personal therapy? I'm flattered."

"Insolent child," he said in a low voice. "Thibault was wrong to let you live."

I tried to wipe the blood from my eye, but only succeeded in smearing it across my cheek. So, Daniel knew about Thibault, which meant he must be part of it, too. "Yeah, well, maybe y'all can discuss it from your adjoining cells at the mental hospital."

Daniel laughed crazily.

The lights from the trees twinkled in his sword's smooth surface as he drew it back. I leaped sideways, avoiding the strike by mere inches.

"*Desarmé*," I screamed, flinging out a hand. The air buzzed a little and Daniel's sword leaped, but he kept its hold.

"You can't even channel, can you?" Daniel's lip tugged into a sneer. "A pitiful excuse for a warrior."

I frowned. "As pitiful as you letting your bondmate get killed?"

Daniel's laughter evaporated instantly. He strode forward and with a snarling grunt, planted his foot so far up my ribcage, I swear I heard something crack. I fell backward onto the hard dirt, unable to breathe. I'd just begun to wonder if I could manage a scream sans oxygen when a tuxedo-clad blur knocked Daniel sideways into a concrete garden bench.

At first, I assumed it was Luc. But as I peered more carefully at the two tussling figures, I could tell the newcomer wasn't quite graceful enough—or pretty enough—to be the vampire.

The bench overturned and the two men hit the ground, rolling across the lawn in a melee of dirt and flying fists, each trying to get a stranglehold on the other's neck. It was artful—like a synchronized swimming demonstration, except with rampant bloodshed instead of Speedos. Both wore tuxes, both had brown hair, both about the same size. And I had no idea who the other guy was.

I scampered to where Daniel's sword had fallen, intent on helping, but in the dim moonlight it was impossible to tell the men apart. So that's how I stood, Jack's sword in one hand, Daniel's in the other.

Finally, one of the men got the other in a chokehold, ready to snap his opponent's neck. Suddenly, I smelled it. It was faint, barely enough to detect under all the smoke and magic searing the air. *Drakkar Noir*. Dripping off the boy who was about to die.

"Lyle!"

I lifted both swords and ran at Creepy Daniel. The first sword came down in a diagonal slash, cutting through his hamstrings. The second, Jack's sword, I used as a club against the back of his skull, the way I'd seen Jack do before. Daniel gave a gurgle and fell to the ground, unconscious.

"Thanks," Lyle rasped and collapsed on the ground.

I dropped to my knees beside him. "Hey, Lyle. Next time you want to impress a girl, try a box of candy, okay? It's better for your health."

He croaked back laughter, his windpipe still half-crushed from Daniel's grip. Whatever he might have said next was lost under a symphony of coughs. His cheek was already turning purple from the fight, and one eye had begun to swell shut.

He spat out a mouthful of blood. "Ami, I'm so sorry. I never should have—"

"Save it." I handed him Daniel's sword. "If we're both alive at sunrise, we'll discuss it over breakfast. My treat."

"So, we're dating?" he asked, hopeful.

"Better."

His eyes widened. "Bondmates?"

"No, dorkus," I said, smiling. "Friends."

My blood-covered fingers curled around his lapel as I bent to kiss his bruised cheek, trying not to inhale. If he and I were going to hang out, we'd need to have a serious talk about aroma moderation.

I moved quickly as I scouted around the main hall, scanning the faces of the fallen guards. Henry wasn't among them, thank goodness. I wasn't sure why, but something warm and magnetic pulled me toward the Hall of Angels. That *had* to be the place, right? It even fit with the line from the prophecy, "under angels' gaze."

Normally, I preferred to have someone watching my back. But since Luc was MIA and Henry was probably dead, it looked like I'd have to do without. Most of the office doors had been left open because of the alarm, which just upped my paranoia that I might get jumped at any moment. So basically, until I had my full powers back, I was no safer than a clay pigeon waiting to be launched.

Strands of Crossworld power slipped through my fingers… still not enough to channel. If the Queller worked the same as before, my power would strengthen in a few minutes. I just wasn't sure I had a few minutes.

By the time I got to the Hall of Angels, the bond-warmth inside me flared like a Halloween bonfire. Jack was definitely close. And in trouble. I did another quick scan of the surroundings, then sidled up to the door and gave a firm tug.

Nothing happened.

"*Abertura*," I whispered, and pulled again, harder. Still nothing.

Okay, whatever wards held this door shut had been charged with a level of power I couldn't touch yet. Which meant the Graygirl, if she wasn't already in there, had to be nearby. I'd just begun to entertain the possibility of hacking my way through with Jack's weapon when I felt an icy hand on my shoulder. I swiveled, blade at the ready.

"Brilliant. Abandon me to a beating on the front lawn, then threaten to chop my head off?" Luc griped. "Bloody Americans."

I lowered the sword. "Luc, you scared the crap out of me. Where were you?"

"Got tossed by one of your trainers. Blond gentleman. Bit like a Viking. He kept trying to interrogate me."

"That's Marcus. You didn't kill him, did you?"

He arched an eyebrow. "Do I look like a murderer?"

"Frankly, yes," I admitted, "but Marcus is a good guy. He just follows orders a little too mindlessly. He's actually kind of funny once you get him talking. There was this one time—"

"Much as I'd love to hear it," Luc said, with no small measure of sarcasm, "there remains the tiny matter of saving my species."

"Right, sorry."

Luc led me down the corridor lining the main offices until we reached the door marked *Faculty Lounge*. He shoved it open.

I'd expected something grand and elegant, with wooden beams and vaulted ceilings. But the room was nothing like that. The walls were gray and rough, à la industrial sandpaper, and the floor hard and slick. At the back corner, a narrow metal staircase wound upward, spiraling in tighter and tighter circles. A dank smell, like wet sheep's wool, teased my nose and I pinched it, determined not to sneeze. The last thing I needed was my allergies causing some unexpected demon rift.

"Let's go." Luc pressed a hand to the small of my back, pushing me toward the stairs.

"Quit groping me."

The smell grew stronger as we neared the top, and the mildew took on a chalky flavor, like the air of a stonecutter's quarry.

"Do you even know where you're going?" I snapped.

"Stunningly, yes. Some of us actually studied the school's blueprints." Luc yanked the face off an intricate grate set low in the wall and crawled through it, disappearing into the darkness.

Okay, call me paranoid, but I was beginning to think there

might be something about me that made men want to crawl
into dark holes. Maybe Lisa was right that I should rethink my
feminine mojo.

Inside the heating duct, pale dust bunnies lined the vent walls
like permanent tenants. Luc wriggled around on his elbows until
we reached the right opening—the one that led to the Hall of
Angels—then backed up beside me.

"You go in first," he said. "Once you get a handle on the
situation, signal me."

Below us, black smoke billowed into the hall, the chandeliers
and torchieres dark and bent. Chunks of plaster were scattered
across the floor and teardrop-shaped scorch marks stained the
walls above the sculpture alcoves. I had to swallow another sneeze
as the smell of fuel pushed its way through the mold.

I wrestled out the grate and leaned my head through. Thirteen
feet up.

Around the edges of the room, a series of gray blocks was
cemented to the walls, each one stuck with a metal pin and draped
in black and red wires, not unlike the wires Jack had untangled last
night. My stomach plummeted. I'd prepared for a personal threat,
for my friends in danger, for Jack at death's door. But this? What
kind of maniac takes a whole building hostage?

A smart one, my unhelpful inner voice muttered.

"Shut up," I said.

"Excuse me?" Luc asked from behind me.

"Nothing."

I muttered a quick prayer of gratitude for Henry. If he hadn't
pulled that alarm, there'd be more than just a building at stake.

There already was.

About halfway down the hall, Jack knelt in the center of a charcoal circle, his hands black with blood and limp by his sides. A ripple, like waves of heat, blurred the air around him, but I could tell he was in bad shape. His body sat, hunched, crimson whip-marks staining his shoulder blades, and forearms shredded. It looked like someone had tried to carve the tattooed glyphs out of his skin with a knife.

"Holy crap!" I breathed. "Luc, help me down."

Luc clasped both my hands in his and swung me down from the vent. I hit the ground hard and fell, only vaguely aware of the bloody smears my hands and feet left across the smooth marble floors. The blood didn't worry me nearly as much as the crackle over my skin at the grate's threshold—like a wall of electricity being breached. It couldn't be an accident the room was warded so heavily when the rest of the building wasn't; and not just the doors, either. Whoever did this was serious. But what were the wards for? Anti-demon? Containment?

I only wasted a second thinking about it. Wards weren't my priority. My priority knelt on the floor about twenty feet away. And if I didn't get him out safely, our whole world would be plunged into war.

I snatched the sword from where it had fallen, pulled myself to my feet, and hurried toward Jack. Whatever charm held him in place would probably affect me, too, so I'd have to be careful. Tightness gripped my foot as I lifted it across the circle's smudged boundary, and a numb sensation skittered across it.

"I wouldn't do that if I were you."

A deep, cigarette-tinged voice spilled from the edge of the room and I froze. The last time I'd heard that voice, it had been offering me a future, wishing me luck with my post-graduation goals. Lying to me.

"If I were *you*," I retorted, "I'd throw myself into a lion pit at lunchtime. But I guess we can't always get what we want."

The Chancellor laughed. "So much like your father. Pity Alec neglected to finish him yesterday. The boy's always been too soft."

He hobbled forward, his legs weak and buckled. Any sympathy I'd felt for him before had evaporated. His cane flicked in a quick gesture toward the circle, spatters of blood flying off it. Probably Jack's blood. Sick bastard.

"What did you do to my bondmate?"

He smiled. "It's not as bad as it looks. Our perceptual vortex worked so well at your test, I thought it might make a nice prison for your boyfriend. Excuse me, your *bondmate*," he corrected with a condescending nod. "It's a mercy, I think. Dulls the pain."

The suction slipped over me again as I pulled my foot out of Jack's vortex. Through the layers of smoke, I could just discern the outline of three figures standing behind Chancellor Thibault. Their faces were obscured, but I knew who they were. My best friends—the people I'd grown up with.

They stood in a row, their hands bound behind their backs, blindfolds cloaking their eyes and gags over their mouths. Katie's body quaked with sobs, the bodice of her ice blue halter constricting. Behind them, Alec stood with his double-bolted crossbow. He'd obviously come as Katie's date. The blue of his cummerbund coordinated with her dress, just as Matt's vibrant red matched the glittery orange and crimson stones sewn into Lisa's dress. The two girls had even styled their hair with similar clips, clusters of gemstones that reflected the orb-light like crystals of ice in Katie's blond twist and licks of fire through Lisa's brown curls. My friends looked amazing. I could only imagine the jealous snit Veronica must've had when they arrived.

"Glad you decided to join us," Thibault said with a smug grin. "Alec assured me you would. Your sister very much wants to meet you."

"I don't have a sister," I told him. "If your soul-sucking lap-dog wants to meet me, she can 'friend' me on Facebook like everyone else."

I felt myself backing up, eager to put as much space as possible between me and the raving lunatic. My fingers spread open as I pulled at another channel. This time there was nothing—no answering crackle or buzz like there'd been before. Just a fizzle of darkness. I shook my hand and tried again. No luck.

Suddenly, I understood what the wards around the room had meant. "Blocking spell, huh? Lucky I brought my sword."

"Amelie, dear, don't be so dramatic. We're all family here." Thibault's thumb whispered absently over a small metal box in his hand. Good grief, was that a detonator?

"Family?" I said, trying to sound calm. "You've killed hundreds of people."

"Out of necessity," he pooh-poohed. "Do you have any idea what will happen if Guardians join with Inferni? If we train them? Let them fight with us?"

"Um, world peace?"

"*Armageddon!*" In an instant, his pleasant expression dissolved into rage. "Heaven will stand open and the armies of God will come; the angels will rise and all shall be judged. I, for one, refuse to stand beside those murderous infidels, proclaiming their innocence as if they were still besouled, singing their virtue as if they carry God's blessing. They disgust me!"

"That's a nice speech," I interrupted, "though I don't think 'besouled' is a word."

He stamped his bloody cane on the ground. "Any Guardians who support the Tenets have already denied their makers and turned their backs on the angels. Charlotte would have been among them had she stayed with the Guardians. It is by my mercy that they died."

I felt something cold go through me. "Leave my mom out of this."

"Child, I can't leave your mother out of this. She's the one who started it." His eyes gleamed dark in the fiery light, like black flames. "Sacrificing her Watcher to save an Immortal child? That's just the kind of gesture Guardian liberals needed to fuel this—*insanity*. It was disgraceful."

My eyes narrowed. "My mother sacrificed you to save *me*. There's nothing disgraceful about that."

With unsteady strides, the Chancellor limped toward me, broken glass crunching beneath his boots. Before I could react, he lifted his cane and whipped it across my face. I was able to get a hand up in time to deflect most of the bone-crushing blow, but it still left bright spots across my vision.

"Liar," he roared. "Who told you that? Your father?"

"No, I—"

"*Who?*"

"No one," I yelled back. "I overheard Mom and Dad talking about it a few weeks after you visited the house. She was upset. Dad said something about how it was the right decision, to save a child's soul. I thought they were talking about me."

Behind me, the air carried screams and shouts through the walls and I could hear the distant sounds of slamming doors and running feet. It made me nervous to think that people would be coming back into the building so soon. Thibault was clearly several cans shy of a six-pack and, for the first time, I realized he just might be nuts enough to blow up the whole school.

As if on cue, he turned to Alec and said, "Kill them."

Alec didn't move. His gaze danced between Katie and Lisa then slid back to me. "That may not be necessary, sir. Katherine supports our cause. When the time comes, she'll fight with us. The other two aren't as committed, but they *will* defend our people if there's an uprising. I think we should let them go."

I stared at him, trying to read his intent. Alec knew perfectly well Matt would never fight against the Inferni. His politics were so far left, he made Jack look well-balanced. Alec could have mentioned that, and it would have been Matt's death sentence. But he didn't.

Why?

"He's right, you *should* let them go," I said. "Unless you're a coward who hides behind children."

Thibault laughed again, his thumb tapping the detonator harder this time. "Child, you have no idea what you're dealing with." He swept an arm to where Alec stood. "Very well, Alexander. Keep the traitor, but let the rest go. Their souls will be devoured by worms come judgment day."

Uh-huh. Because *that* didn't sound nuts at all.

Alec lowered the crossbow and, with one hand, cut Katie's flexicuffs and gag. For a moment she seemed paralyzed. Then he whispered something to her and she sprinted—smart girl—out the door. Next, he untied Lisa, and retreated a few steps as Lisa untied Matt. Matt's hands were dark, knuckles stained with dried blood, his face bruised and puffy. It made me wonder what kind of fight he'd put up when they tried to take him. As soon as Lisa was done with his bindings, she ran straight for me.

"Omigosh, Ami. Are you okay?"

"I'm fine." I hadn't realized how scared I was until her arms encircled me, firm and familiar. After so many days thinking I'd never see her again, it was like a brief reprieve from hell.

"We'll get help," Matt promised from behind Lisa's shoulder. "Don't worry, we'll find help and we'll come back."

"Don't," I told them, hushed. "The doors are warded from the outside. Besides, y'all are the only Guardians who know the truth. If I can't fix this, it's going to be up to you to tell the Elders. We already have a war with demonkind. The last thing we need is more killing."

"Ami, I'm not leaving you," Lisa said.

"Neither am I," Matt insisted. "Come on, they don't want you. If Smith-Hailey's dead, that's it. No more Peace Tenets. That's all they want. We'll find another way to save the Inferni."

"He's right." Lisa touched my cheek like a worried mother. "Sweetie, you're a mess. Just come with us. No guy is worth your life."

All I could do was stare at her. Jack's sword felt so heavy in my hand—so heavy, I thought I might drop it. My shoulders slumped as I glanced at him, still hunched in the center of his perceptual prison, knowing he was about to die. Alone.

"Lis," I said softly. "He *is* my life."

It took her a moment as the gravity of what I'd said washed over her. I watched her face harden from hope to annoyance, then finally to resignation. She nodded. "Then I'm staying with you."

"Lisa—" Matt began.

"No, Mattie, she's right. You need to go. Who knows what Alec's been telling Katie. You have to set it straight. Besides," Lisa looped her free hand through mine, "Ami and I have been on missions tougher than this. If I stay, we have twice the chance of getting out. That's what we want, right? A happy ending?"

Matt looked stricken. I could see the conflict inside him—his affection for me, his political loyalties, his love for Lisa. We all knew he would have died for her in an instant, but *leaving* her? I didn't know if he could.

She must have seen the same conflict, because she smiled, tiptoed up to him, and kissed him tenderly on the mouth. "Pookie, trust me," she murmured, her cheek against his. "Have I ever steered you wrong?"

I decided it was a bad time to bring up the mullet she made him get in fifth grade, during her "Gone Country" phase.

"Can't you talk her out of this?" Matt asked me over her shoulder.

I shrugged. "Doubtful."

The truth was, I didn't want her here any more than he did. But I also knew the more time we wasted arguing, the more time Thibault had to change his mind, and the more likely both of them would end up dead. Besides, I'd never been able to talk Lisa out of anything before. *Why should now be any different?*

Matt was close to tears as he kissed Lisa on the forehead and whispered a soft, "I'll be back. I love you," and hurried out. The door gave a final-sounding thud behind him.

Silence settled through the air and I tightened my hand around Lisa's. In all the times I'd imagined us fighting together, I'd never really thought of us dying together. It seemed unreal.

"Okay, here's the plan," I whispered, trying to keep the emotion out of my voice. "In a few seconds, we're going to meet someone. She's a Graymason...don't ask. Once she lowers the perceptual vortex around Jack, I'll distract her. You open a portal, grab Jack, and jump him to someplace safe. I'll shield you from here as best I can. Then I'll do the closure and see you back home, okay?"

It was a lie. I knew I wouldn't see her back home. I also had no idea if I could shield her and fight off my sister at the same time, but it seemed like the only chance we had. Luc's hands would be full with Alec, and I still had no clue what to do about the explosives. If Lisa could just get out safe with Jack—

"I'm sorry, sweetie," she said, her eyes sad. "I can't do that."

"Yes, you can. You've always been stronger than me—"

"No, you don't understand. I can't leave you." Her small hand plucked Jack's sword out of mine and let it fall to the ground with a clang. She kicked it toward the middle of the room. "I've told you a thousand times, Ami, you're my sister. I'll always take care of you. That's what we do, right? We look out for each other."

For the first time since Matt left, I let my gaze wander around the room. Alec had lowered his crossbow. Thibault stood against the wall, a look of infuriating triumph on his face. Lisa hovered by my side, her hand interlaced with mine, a soft smile at her lips. Small shifts of orb-light leaped at the stones of her dress, reflecting the clips in her hair—like a thousand tiny flames come to life.

And my heart dropped.

Because I knew who she was. The person standing next to me, the girl who had been with me through every anguished moment of childhood, every horror of adolescence, every heartbreaking loss I'd suffered. My best friend. My sister.

With hair of fire.

Chapter Twenty two:
Dead Man s Party

I squinted into her baby blue eyes. It reminded me of one of those weird 3-D art prints where you have to wait for the art to pop out at you. Only, I didn't know what I was waiting for. Maybe for something dark and ruthless to climb out of her mouth and rip the silicone mask off, revealing her true identity—like a macabre *Scooby Doo* episode. At least that'd make sense. Because this sure as heck didn't.

How could Lisa be the killer? Wasn't she the one who told me about this whole Graymason business in the first place?

Because she wanted you to stay out of it, my inner voice reminded me.

But she'd helped me escape, hadn't she?

After she got you convicted.

Well, what about the phone call? When she lent me her password and told me how to do that info search on Mom? *So you'd come after Bud, nitwit. How else would Alec have known where to find you?*

I never saw it coming. Not one iota. I trusted her completely. She'd been able to orchestrate everything because I, genius girl-detective, had *told* her everything. Because betrayal was not covered in any of my *Nancy Drew* books.

"But you don't even look like me," I argued. "You're way—"

"Prettier, I know."

"I was going to say shorter."

"I take after Mom." Lisa scrunched up her nose. "I'm so sorry I couldn't tell you. I almost did the first day of school. But then at assembly, with *him* there," she gestured to Jack, "and that stupid bond. I figured the best thing would just be to kill him ASAP, so I opened the rift. It was a long shot but, well…nothing ventured, nothing gained, right?"

I couldn't speak. Words flooded my brain, but there seemed to be some communication breakdown between my head and my mouth.

God must hate me. It was the only explanation.

Seriously. All I'd ever wanted was to be a Guardian. I wanted to kill demons, protect humankind, do all the things I was made to do. But, in the space of a week, I'd been reduced to a blood-tainted, broken-souled, half-bonded, fully-doomed fashion victim with a ruthless serial killer for a sister.

What was next, a plague of frogs?

"Oh, Ami, don't look at me like that. If you'd taken my advice and stayed away from him, we wouldn't be in this mess. And we've still got to find you a proper Watcher before the real fighting starts. That'll be fun, right?" Lisa gave my hand another squeeze, then trotted across the hall to Alec.

She didn't even get within twenty feet of him when I saw it.

Silvery strands of light stretched between them, calling out to each other. Holy cow, *that* was how she'd known what my bond with Jack was—because she had one herself. With *Alec*. That must have been what I saw the first day. The silver glow that had bugged me so much.

"Ew." I muffled a groan as she flung herself into his arms, their heat flaring like gunpowder. I swear, watching her kiss him would have made my stomach turn anyway. But the rest of it—how their bodies seemed to melt together, how breath flowed into her more freely. It was worse than watching *The Notebook* for the fiftieth time. How had I never noticed that sap-fest before?

"What about Matt?" I sputtered.

Lisa frowned. "Ami, I love Matt. I always will. But it's not enough." She shook her head, "He could train for a thousand years and he'd never be strong enough. I tried to tell him that. Alec and I are a better match."

"I...but...you... How long? How did you hide it?" I pointed at the swirly silver threads, unable to think straight.

"Five spectacular years. And, trust me, hiding our bond was the hardest thing I've ever done. Of course, Mattie was a useful distraction, but do you have any idea how difficult it was *not* to think about Alec? *Not* to let myself want him, even when he was right there next to me. Impossible!" She proudly tiptoed up to give Alec a peck on the cheek. He blushed.

Ugh, vomit! *That* was how the bond glow got triggered? By *hormones*? Jeez, no wonder Lisa kept trying to hook me up with other guys. "This is twisted. You know that, right?"

"Amelie, you mustn't blame your sister." Chancellor Thibault had kept mostly quiet, but now he hobbled forward, the remote detonator (thankfully) forgotten on Uriel's statue alcove. "Once Charlotte made her allegiance to the Inferni publicly known, there was no going back. It was traitorous what she did, saving an Immortal child over her own bondmate—even the Elders knew it. Child or no, it shouldn't have happened. I'd have been a fool not to see the writing on the wall."

"What are you talking about? What wall?"

Lisa rolled her eyes. "It's a metaphor, Amelie."

"You see, dear, Paranormal Convergence had already been formed. It was just a matter of time before the Peace Tenets were proposed." Thibault slid a gloved hand along the shaft of his cane, fingers coming away red. "I was with Charlotte when she learned the news of your bloodline, even before your father did. That's when my plan began to take shape. Of course, I had no idea you were to be twins. It was lucky I got the right one."

"Well, I *was* the firstborn," Lisa added indignantly.

"True enough, darling." Thibault patted her hand. "Jonathan and Carol Anselmo had agreed to hide the child. After all, it wouldn't do for me to show up with a daughter the same month Bud and Charlotte lost one," he reasoned. "I should have killed your mother then, but Bud was paranoid. He had that bastard Horowitz watching us."

Paranoid with good reason, you freak, I couldn't help thinking. "What about Alec?"

"What about me?" Alec cast a fond look at Lisa, his heart encircled with wisps of silver light. As long as they didn't start kissing again, I could probably hang onto my dinner.

"I knew Lisa would need a Watcher someday," Thibault explained, "so when Alec's parents were killed in battle, I adopted him and started administering greater demon blood infusions. His body acclimated brilliantly."

Oh, snap! Greater demon blood. Like Meeks's stupid potted plant! "*That's* how you followed Jack and me through the portal at my test!"

Alec smiled.

"It was perfect," Lisa noted happily. "By the time the Peace Tenets got signed into probationary law, I had my full powers and Alec was strong enough to bond. We had a list of the Guardians who needed to die and half a decade to get the job done."

"But y'all were like twelve years old! That's—"

"Efficient?" Lisa asked.

"Repugnant!" I shouted.

My eyes drifted back to Jack, still imprisoned in his cozy, silent nightmare. I envied him. As horrid as it must've been, locked in a sensory prison, at least he didn't have to deal with *this*. It was... sickening. Horrifying. They were like some twisted little Stepford family. The whole thing made me want to throw myself in the vortex with Jack.

"Well, it's almost over," Lisa said with a disapproving glare. "Seriously, how many times did I warn you not to get involved with him? I should just kill him now."

As soon as she said it, my heart stopped. She was my *best friend*! I'd spent my whole life next to her, letting her tell me what to wear, how to act, who to date. I trusted her. And now she was going to rip my heart out like it was nothing?

"However," she continued, "because I love you, I'm willing to be nice."

"You'll let him go?" Hope crept into my voice.

She laughed, a sweet tinkling sound that should have belonged to a woodland fairy. "Don't be an idiot. If I let him go, it's the end of the Guardians. No, he has to die. But I'll let you say goodbye to him. Think of it as my partial-bonding gift to you two." Her finger leveled at the vortex, she added, "And if I catch you trying to open a portal, he's a dead man. *Dilué!*"

It shimmered for an instant under the command, then dissolved in splintered lines of light. At the same time, I felt the wards around the room weaken, tiny quakes of power coursing into me.

The moment the force field fell, Jack's head jerked up. He looked stunned and groggy, like a prince awakened from an enchanted sleep.

"Jack!" As fast as my feet would carry me, I hurled myself at him.

"Ow," Jack muttered around my kisses. "I thought being dead's not supposed to hurt."

"You're such a moron," I breathed. "I told you I wouldn't let you die without me."

"Amelie." He groaned, but he didn't stop kissing me. "You can't be here. It's too dangerous."

"Oh, you have no idea what danger is, mister!" I pulled back just enough to frown at him. "I'm so mad at you right now. You *drugged* me?"

"I-I had to," he stammered. "I couldn't let you die."

"Dumbass," I breathed. "You think I want to live without you?"

Jack nudged his nose against mine as I tightened my grip on him.

We held each other for a few more seconds before Jack struggled to his feet, his eyes focused on Lisa. He knew what she was, I could tell. He'd probably known since the moment Bud said the word "sister." Not that he would tell *me*. Noooo. Heaven forbid anyone actually *share* such useful info.

"You swore you wouldn't let anyone hurt her," Jack said to Lisa.

"And I won't," she promised. "She'll come with us. Matt and Katie are our witnesses. They'll spread the word we've been taken prisoner. In a few years, when the Inferni have been depleted, we'll be back as heroes to lead the Guardian resistance as it *should* be led—without stupid Crossworld politics. Trust me, demonkind won't stand a chance."

I couldn't hold back the scowl. The heroes-to-the-resistance thing sounded like a huge hassle. I'd far prefer to sit on a beach with Jack until it was over.

"And you'll keep her safe?" he persisted.

Lisa smiled. "Haven't I always?"

Thibault let out a deep sigh from the edge of the room. "Your family loyalty is touching, dear, but can we please get on with this? Mercy is not what I trained you for." He gestured to Jack. "That boy is a traitor, and it's time for him to die."

Lisa caught my gaze. "Ami, I'm sorry about this. We should have finished it years ago. If I'd known how complicated things would turn out—"

"Each prophecy in its own time, dear," Thibault lectured.

I'm not sure, but I think she rolled her eyes. "You ready, Jackson?"

Jack's eyes filled with sadness as he turned to me. "Ami, I'm sorry."

"You can't be serious." I looked at him, panicked. "You're just going to go with her?"

"I have to. I'm the last Gabrielite. It's prophesied."

"No!" I shook my head. "What about the Peace Tenets? The Crossworld will go to war! Luc says the Immortals—"

"Will have to find another way to survive," Jack finished. "Omelet, I don't like this any more than you do, but your sister's right. Too many Guardians have died already."

"So, you're going to let her start a *war*?"

"The war is already started. We're just choosing sides," Lisa said. "Don't you get it? Katie was right! We've crippled ourselves trying to uphold the Peace Tenets. If they pass, we'll all die."

"So, make Jack promise not to sign," I suggested, desperate. "Hold him prisoner."

She looked at me like I was an idiot. "If he refuses to sign, prisoner or not, it'll be seen as an act of aggression. The Inferni will turn on us and—stop me if you've heard this before—*we'll all die*. The only way out is if all the signatories are dead. It's prophesied. There's no way they can blame us."

"But there has to be another way—"

"What do you suggest? Should we put everyone to sleep for a hundred years?" Lisa sounded annoyed. "Amelie, this isn't a school prank. You can't just magic it away with fairy dust and wishes."

"Nobody said fairy dust."

"Yeah, well nobody promised you a happy ending, either!"

"Amelie, please," Jack begged. "You know I love you. I'd do anything for you. But you can't keep looking for a solution that doesn't exist. Maybe this is how it's supposed to end. Maybe we're not supposed to be together."

I stared at him, horrified. "Excuse me?"

He let go of my hand and turned to Lisa. "Do it. I'm ready."

Okay, I was getting pretty pissed myself at this point. *Not supposed to be together?* Seriously, if we got out of this alive, I was going to kill him!

Subtle as a breeze, I tested another shred of power between my fingers. Yup, all systems go. I hadn't forgotten about Luc, still waiting for my signal in the ceiling vent. If we were going to do this, it had to be now.

"Stop!" I shouted as her hand touched his chest.

"What now?" Lisa demanded.

My eyes darted to the grate. Luc and I hadn't agreed on a specific signal, but if it was too subtle for him, then his species probably deserved to die. "I just wonder what the vampires have to say about all this."

"Huh?" Lisa asked.

Jack frowned in confusion. "Ami, what are you talking about?"

"I said," my voice rose, "what would the *vampires*—"

All at once, Luc swung out of the metal grate, his body catapulting toward Alec as if shot from a string. He hit Alec in the chest with his feet, knocking the crossbow in a spiral toward the wall. I barely processed the scuffle before Thibault was in it. He limped out of the smoke, a deformed nightmare. With an ugly sneer at his lips, he twisted the top of his cane and detached it, revealing a long, slim blade that could have run through any demon.

"Behind you!" I screamed.

In a movement too fast to track, Luc turned, scooped up a chunk of plaster, and hurled it at Thibault's head. The Chancellor crumpled, a thin trickle of blood at his temple. Luc dove for the crossbow at the same time as Alec, their bodies colliding with a hellish crack.

"Luc!" I'd just taken a step to help him when I felt it.

Lisa's channel.

It burned through the air in searing waves. The kind of Arctic wind that strips the skin right off your face. Jack must have had the same idea as I did—to help Luc—because he'd scooped his sword off the ground and readied it for a strike. He was in motion when she grabbed him.

"No!" My hands flew out in a defensive splay and I screamed, "*Redivivus!*"

Instantly, the flow reversed itself, Jack's life force funneling back into him. I held the channel as Lisa's face twisted with fury.

"*Silencio!*" she screamed, at the same time I yelled, "*Desisté.*"

I felt her silencing command hit me and dissipate like steam. It was much the same effect as when Channelers tried to heal themselves—which is to say, useless. My freezing spell vanished in a similar puff and I realized we couldn't curse our own souls any better than we could heal them.

Lisa must have understood about the same time because, quick as a bunny, she flattened her hands back on Jack. "*Doloré,*" she said.

"*Salvé pacem*, you evil cow!" I responded, before the pain curse could rip into him. Her upper lip curled into a snarl.

"*Maledictus!*" she cursed him. "*Tenebrae!*"

"*Immunis!*" I deflected. "*Concordia!*"

It was pathetic. We couldn't fire on each other, so in the art of war, Jack became our canvas. She threw weirder and weirder spells at him, and I kept returning to the basics—curing, calming, deflecting. Thank the gods of irony Lisa made me pay attention to that lecture in Hansen's class last year.

I was vaguely aware of Luc and Alec moving like ghosts in my periphery. Every so often, they would slow and I'd think it was over, then they'd be off in another blur of dark hair and expensive clothing.

"Stop it!" Lisa finally ordered me. She sounded furious. "This is ridiculous. You know he has to die. It's *prophesied*, for heaven's sake!"

"Prophecies were made to be broken."

"That's *rules*, moron! *Rules* are made to be broken. *Prophecy* is law!"

I shrugged. My relationship with the law was patchy, at best.

It was probably a good thing we'd stopped, because Jack looked like he was about to keel over. Though none of the spells took hold, each carried its own brand of Crossworld poison. It billowed into him like black ink through water.

"Dang it, Amelie. I don't like killing innocents any more than you would, but if it's a choice between a few petitioners and the end of our species, then I'm willing to sacrifice."

"Yeah, *other* people. What kind of lame-ass sacrifice is that?"

"Oh, grow up. It's us or the Inferni. Either he dies now, or we all die slowly. So go away, and let me kill him!"

"Never!"

Lisa narrowed her eyes to slits. "You can't beat me. I am you!"

"And I am you," I retorted. "Which puts me in the perfect position to make your life a living hell."

I was spared elaborating on the nature of that hell by a gut-wrenching crunch, followed by a shriek of agony. All three of us turned to see Alec, huddled on the floor with his arm at an odd angle, a metal crossbow bolt lodged in his thigh.

Lisa's hands flew to her mouth, silver sparks at her fingertips. "Alec!"

Sick as it was, I couldn't help feeling sorry for her. Over the past week, I'd seen Jack beaten to a pulp more times than I cared to count, and it never got any easier. Maybe I *did* want to rip out her eyeballs at the moment, but the kind of pain that came with seeing your Watcher get hurt wasn't something I'd wish on my worst enemy.

Luc's face was bruised and bloodied as he turned, the crossbow leveled at Lisa's heart.

"Luc! Stop!" Jack yelled.

But Luc didn't stop. He was vengeance personified. Like every nightmare I'd ever had come to life. His eyes seemed to burn with hellfire and his face had morphed into something inhumanly, brilliantly monstrous. Make no mistake, it was still Luc haughty and beautiful—but it was a version of Luc that didn't belong on this plane.

It was demon.

I wish I knew what happened next, but the truth is, I don't. My eyes fell shut to the chink of the crossbow launching. A blink, that's all it was. In that instant, a soft swish of air brushed my skin like the whisper of dragonfly wings, and a rustle of fabric sounded. When I opened my eyes, it was over.

Jack stood between Lisa and Luc, clutching her small body to his torso like a baby kangaroo. Her hands were flat against his chest, and a red stain had begun to spread along his spine where the crossbow bolt protruded. But the bleeding didn't come in fierce pulses as it had last night. It barely trickled at all.

The first thing to hit was relief. If he wasn't bleeding, then it couldn't be that bad, right? I would heal him, just like before. We'd be together.

That's when I saw his eyes.

Empty.

Nothing but frozen lakes of ice, all the way to the pupil.

Jack hit the ground with an awful thud, his skin dull and papery. For a long time, nobody moved. No screams, no shouts of triumph. Just silence. I thought of the times I'd watched him sleep, his body limp and warm, his breath so sweet on my face as I matched my exhale to his. He looked as if he could be sleeping now. Except he wasn't.

I couldn't remember anything; not where I was or why I'd come here. I couldn't scream. I couldn't move. All I could do was stare at him.

His body was sprawled in a sort of half-collapsed languor that I didn't think a living person could manage. My brain couldn't process it. It wasn't Jack. It couldn't be.

Chancellor Thibault scrambled to sitting and re-sheathed his cane with a soft *shink*. Then came the maniacal laughter.

"At last! Gabriel's blood is dead!" His joyful burbles filled the room, shallow and shrill.

Luc's crossbow clattered to the ground and he whirled, puking blood onto the floor behind him. My body ached, my limbs like lead pipes. I expected Lisa would celebrate, too. This was what she'd wanted, wasn't it? No Peace Tenets. No Jack. Her bondmate safe. She was free to do whatever she liked, go wherever she wanted. I couldn't stop her.

With painful slowness she stepped away from Jack's body, her eyes fixed on him. The air seemed to grow quiet and still around her.

"Ami, I'm so sorry," she whispered. "I never meant…at least, not like this."

I slowly sank to my knees in the ash, unable to speak. It was a lie. This was exactly how she'd meant it to end, how Jack had planned it. What kind of idiot was I to think it could be any different?

"Just go," I whispered.

"But I can't leave you. Ami, please."

She reached out a hand but I flinched away. I didn't want to touch her. I didn't want to hear how she'd done this for me, or how it would be okay, how we would always have each other, blah, blah. I couldn't take it. Not anymore.

Lisa's eyes met mine in a brief, tearful flicker as she paused in front of me, but she said nothing else. There was nothing to say. She wasn't sorry. She *had* meant to kill him and that's what she'd done. After more than a hundred deaths—some bloodless surrenders like Lutz, some hard won by Alec's sword, like D'Arcy—the enemy, my sister, had won.

Her victory rang like a hollow slap between us. Then she was gone.

I don't know where she and Alec portaled, but wherever it was, they didn't bother taking Thibault. They didn't need him, and I guess he didn't need them anymore, either. He sat in the rubble of the fallen statues, happy, like a child in a sandbox.

It's weird how death doesn't come all at once. It doesn't ride in on a stallion, swinging a scythe and yelling about the apocalypse. Real death teases. It prods. It inches up behind you with its claws out, and laughs while you bleed.

I cradled Jack in my lap as his soul unwound itself from mine in soft twitches. The space it left behind felt cold and damp, how a cloud might feel before a snowfall.

"You couldn't have stopped it, Amelie," Thibault said. "He had to die. They all did. The prophecy says it's the only way to end the war." His words grew quieter in my head until they dissolved.

It wasn't fair, not one bit of it. For five days, Jack and I had been chased through hell and told to be heavenly. We'd been buried alive and ordered not to scream. And for what? A stupid prophecy?

I was *done*.

Done with prophecies. Done with demons. Done with stupid politics and holy wars. It wasn't my war anymore. These weren't my rules. And nothing that had cost me this much deserved to be written in stone.

My lips brushed Jack's face where my tears had fallen— his beautiful face, with its hard curves and tiny imperfections. I smoothed back his golden hair and stroked each of the little lines around his eyes where they crinkled when he laughed.

It couldn't end like this.

With a violent tremor, my fingers coaxed the sword out of his lifeless grip. If there was one thing I'd learned in the past week, it was that death, like everything else, is negotiable. The world doesn't shut off when you close your eyes. Things aren't true because someone wrote them down. And, most importantly, Lisa wasn't the only one with power.

"*Redivivus,*" I whispered.

A violent wind sprang to life, whipping my hair. Out of the corner of my eye, I saw Luc sit up, the demon rage on his face having faded to pain.

I turned to Luc as Thibault eyed us suspiciously from across the room.

"Good luck at the signing. Tell Jack I'm sorry. And Luc—" I struggled to think of something profound for my final words, something that would stick with him for eternity. Nada. "Just try not to be such an asshole, okay?"

Luc scrambled to his knees, struggling to rise. He was still bleeding from a cut on his forehead and several of his fingers looked broken. Maybe some ribs, too.

Yeah, Jack was going to hate me for this, but what choice did I have? I was a Wraithmaker. This is what I was born for, right? I shut my eyes and let the world go silent inside my head.

Things were about to get ugly.

"*Ex dona spiritus. Bis vivit qui bene vivit.*" With hard cracks and shrill screams, the world splintered into jagged pieces around me.

"Amelie, no!" Luc yelled, but it was too late.

I've read about humans who try to stab themselves. They hesitate. There's always a part of them that doesn't want to die, so no matter how committed they think they are, they still hesitate in the end.

I didn't.

A kick of adrenaline pumped through my veins and I lifted the blade high. It barely made a sound as it descended into my heart.

Chapter Twenty three:
Just Like Heaven

That was the *plan*, anyway. Unfortunately, plans and vampires go together about as well as Kleenex and hot tubs.

"No!" Luc launched himself at me. The tip of the blade had barely broken the skin when I felt it being knocked out of my hands. Before I knew it, my fingers were empty and I was pinned to the ground by a hundred and eighty pounds of vampire. "What do you think you're doing?"

"Get off me, you stupid…*Crossworlder*! This is none of your business."

"None of my business?" he yelled, about four inches from my face. "I swore an oath to protect you! You think I'd let you kill yourself now?"

"I'm not killing myself!" I hollered back, narrowing the gap to two inches.

"You had a blade to your bloody chest! How is that not suicide?"

"Because you're a blind moron." I snake-wiggled out of his

iron grip. "Now get off me so I can finish!"

Poor Luc looked so confused. His face was pale and blood trickled from a gash at the side of his cheek. Above our heads, light and wind swirled, the channel I'd called still pulsing with power.

"But what—"

"She's trying to save him." Thibault's amused baritone broke in from the edge of the room. "A life for a life. Isn't that right, child?"

I glared at him evilly.

He sneered. "Your sister warned me you'd try, though I admit I didn't think you had the nerve. Perhaps you take after your mother more than I realized. Pity you have to die."

That was when I noticed what he had in his hand. The little silver box with the red button—the remote detonator we'd all conveniently forgotten. In a flash, my fingers unwrapped themselves from Luc's throat and extended toward Thibault.

"*Desisté*," I shouted, throwing all my remaining power at him. Which wasn't much given the lack of a Watcher, the semi-mortal wounds, and the channel I was still trying to maintain for soul transfer. Nonetheless, that command should have done something—other than make him chuckle.

"My dear, naïve girl," he tsk-tsked. "I admire your tenacity, but I'm afraid your sister thought of that already." His hand dipped into the collar of his shirt and he pulled out a circular, glyph-carved silver pendant. The protective charm swung like a pendulum between his fingers. "Think of it as diplomatic immunity…for me, at least."

Call me jaded, but if he thought a little chunk of metal, no matter how charmed it was, would protect him from a field of explosives, I wasn't the only one with naiveté issues. "Wow, you really are insane, aren't you?" With a small nod at Luc, I curved my fingers toward Thibault again. "*Doloré! Desarmé! Incendia!*"

The volley of curses bounced off him like a rubber ball off concrete, each one pushing his cackles to a more ghastly pitch. Tears of laughter streamed down his face, but for once, I didn't care if my attack failed. It wasn't meant to succeed—not in the traditional sense, anyhow.

In a blur of arms and legs, Luc flew at Thibault. His momentum was so great I swear I heard Thibault's bones crack as the two collided. They skidded over the rubble, the detonator hitting the ground hard. Despite his crippled appearance, the old man was still quick. He rolled to his knees and drew his sword.

"Luc, be careful!"

"Get the detonator," he shouted back.

Right, the detonator. On hands and knees, I scrambled across the floor, my eyes never leaving the metal box. Every muscle in my body was on fire, my bones fusing to each other from the residual Crossworld burn. I could practically feel my skin melting into the floor.

Don't give up, a voice whispered in my head. *Jack wouldn't give up.*

I pushed harder.

Unfortunately, Thibault also heard Luc's directive about the detonator. He jabbed his sword into Luc's belly and thrust upward toward the heart, at the same time rolling his own body toward the silver box. It was a brilliant move, tactically. A blow to the heart was one of about three things that could kill an Immortal. If Luc hadn't twisted out of the strike so quickly, well, I think we can all say "vampire kebob."

With bare hands, Luc gripped the sword and shoved it at Thibault, using it as a lever to force him backward. He also managed to slice up his palms worse than any slasher movie I'd seen, and re-situate the fight right over the detonator.

Fan-freaking-tastic.

"Go to Plan B," Luc yelled, though I wasn't entirely sure what Plan A had been.

Around the room, eight gray blocks of explosives still clung to the walls. Okay, new agenda. *Plan B: Don't Die.* If I couldn't get to the detonator, maybe I could disable the explosives.

I concentrated on not hurling as I dragged myself to the first block. A silver cap slid out of the gray putty-mound with a harmless *splooch* then dropped to the floor. *Thunk.* Not exactly James Bond, but effective enough.

There was no point in standing up. My brain had already gone fuzzy from the Crossworld draw, and the outer edge of my vision was tinged with black. At least that meant my channel might still be active. I caught glimpses of Luc and Thibault still duking it out, hand to sword, though I had no idea if I was seeing accurately. Luc was so hacked up and dripping blood it was a miracle he hadn't passed out. At a glacial pace, I made my way around the room on hands and knees. *Splooch, thunk. Splooch, thunk.* Eight times. I counted.

Across the room, Thibault's sword slammed into Luc's stomach again and Luc fell. This time, he didn't get up.

"Ah-ha!" Thibault snatched up the detonator. "Victory!"

Like King Arthur wielding Excalibur, he raised his hand and brought it down hard on the button. All around me little pops went off—eight of them—each with its own terrifying puff of smoke. Then the room was silent.

Dust and ash still danced through the air, the marble floor littered with debris. Thibault's face slowly registered confusion, followed by annoyance. He jabbed at the detonator again, his knees jack-knifing to the floor.

"No!" he growled. "No, you've ruined everything!"

"Not quite," I mumbled, still dizzy from the lingering channel. "*Ex dona spiritus. Bis vivit qui bene vivit.*"

I'd long since given up hope of finding another sword to finish myself off. Jack's blade was buried somewhere under the rubble. My vision had tanked so badly all I could see was pinpricks of light, and the channel's power made my brain lobes feel like they'd been fused together with a soldering iron. I reached blindly around Jack's body and grappled for the crossbow bolt still stuck in his back. With a hard yank, I tugged it out, lifted it high, and jabbed it toward my chest.

Again.

This time, I hit the mark.

It was as if a cold hand had wrapped around my heart and given it a squeeze. I yanked the bolt out and let it fall. Blood poured out of me in thick, uneven spurts that spattered onto Jack's skin.

"There," I gasped. "*Now* I've ruined everything."

Then I died.

· · ·

It wasn't as bad as I'd thought—the dying part. It kind of felt like the time I fell into the deep end of Lisa's pool in first grade, with my clothes all soggy and my tennis shoes like bricks. Water had flooded my lungs and the need for oxygen had felt like a hole in my chest. Same deal—only it was blood choking me, and there was an *actual* hole in my chest. Go figure.

I pressed my ear against the rumpled folds of Jack's shirt, listening for his heart—that melodic rhythm that had lulled me to sleep last night. No dice.

"But—but, the prophecy! The angels!" Thibault sputtered, unaware of Luc behind him, slowly working the sword out of his stomach.

I shut my eyes as Luc lifted Thibault's blade and brought it down in a final, slashing arc. I couldn't be too sad. Not that I reveled in anyone's death, but that man had been such a heaping jug of crazy, I couldn't imagine the "angels" being anything but relieved to have him off the planet.

Jack's body stayed alarmingly silent beneath me.

Come on, I pleaded silently. *Breathe.*

I squeezed my eyes tighter until an image of Jack's face surfaced in my mind. The hard line of his jaw when he got angry, the crooked curve of his lips when he smiled. Even when he tried *not* to smile. God, he was beautiful.

The wind seemed to sigh as a sharp electric current pulsed between us in deep, kaleidoscopic colors. Images drifted in my head, then I felt his heart sputter.

And begin to beat.

Maybe being a child of Lucifer had its perks after all.

By the gift of my spirit, he who lived once shall live again. Simple words, even in Latin. The price for them hadn't been specified, but I couldn't imagine it would cost more than my life.

With every breath, his heart got stronger. Sure, mine was

weakening, but I didn't care. It didn't matter what happened to me. I could die knowing that things were as they should be. Jack would live, the Tenets would pass, Matt and Katie would be safe, and Thibault wouldn't hurt anyone again.

Jack would live.

In groggy lurches, Jack's arms tightened around me, his chest filling with air. One hand smoothed away my blood-spattered hair as he tipped my face to his.

"Omelet?" he said softly.

I opened my mouth to answer him, but nothing came out. Well, that's not true. A lot of stuff came out. Blood mostly, and some spittle. He handled it well, I'd say. A scream ripped through his throat and he sat up like he'd been stuck with a branding iron.

"I tried to stop her," Luc gasped from across the room.

Jack's face twisted from confusion into horror as he registered the blood covering Luc's shirt, Thibault's dead body, the crossbow bolt beside me. Denial and rage and horror flashed through his eyes in quick succession, probably just how I'd looked before when I'd watched him die. Only it was worse. Because he knew I had done this for him.

"No, no. God, no." He slid one arm under my head, his fingertips trembling as they stroked my face. "Amelie, what did you do?"

I opened my mouth again. I wanted to let him know it was all good, that I totally had this under control. But all that came out was a wet gurgle.

"Don't talk," he begged. "Just breathe. You're going to be okay."

I knew he was lying but I tried to nod anyway. There was

something so…fragmenting about being stuck between worlds. Part of my consciousness was lodged in my body, viewing it all through blurry eyes and clogged ears. Another part of me seemed suspended in limbo. Clear-headed. No pain.

At some point, Matt hacked through the doors with a glyph-carved battle axe, Lyle at his heels with a mace in one hand and a knife in the other. They'd obviously raided the arsenal again. As soon as he saw me, Matt halted, and Lyle stumbled over him like some *Three Stooges* episode. It might have been funny under other circumstances. At the moment, not so much.

"Holy crap." Matt made the sign of the cross over his chest.

Lyle paused for a second, then dropped his weapons and skidded to stop at my side. "Matt, get a Channeler. Now!"

"We sent them all away." My friend hung back, confused. "Where's Lisa? Is she okay?"

"Who cares? Find Hansen! Find anyone!"

Matt stared around the room, dazed, for another moment. Then he left.

With a strangled sound, Jack laid me on the ground like a broken doll. His hands came down over my ribs, where the narrow hole still gaped, black and runny. Maybe he thought he could fix it, or something. I knew he couldn't. Our bond had begun to loosen again. Everything buzzed and hummed in my head, at once quiet and deafening—ironically like a perceptual vortex. I wondered if that was what death was. Just a great, black, empty nothing.

"She's going to die," Lyle said.

"She's not going to die," Jack hissed.

"She will if we don't find a healer." Lyle stripped off his tuxedo shirt and tore it into long strips, wrapping them around my torso like one of Gunderman's pressure bandages. "Ami, I'm so sorry," he whispered. "I never should have left you alone. I should have protected you."

As soon as he said that, a knife of fury zipped through the bond, cold and sharp, like lightning bolts over my skin. With the back of his hand, Jack shoved Lyle aside so hard he flew across the room and slammed into Remiel's statue. I flinched as Lyle slid down the wall, Remiel's staff cracking over his head with a hard shudder.

"She's not yours to protect," Jack snapped. "Luc, I need you!"

"Me?" Luc paled.

"Your blood," he said. "I need your blood."

Cold air clung to my skin, odd smells of chemical ash crowding me. I watched Luc's throat move as he swallowed nervously. "You can't be serious."

"The hell, I can't."

The vampire's injuries had already started healing themselves, so although he was dripping scarlet, he didn't flinch too badly when Jack grabbed him by the collar and lifted him off the ground.

"I asked you for one thing, Luc. Keep her safe. You swore an oath, do you remember?"

The vampire glanced around the room like a trapped animal. "Cousin, please. Ask for something else. Money. Status. Anything you want."

"*She's* what I want."

"Anything but that."

In a flash, the first impression I'd had of Jack returned—fierce and dangerous. Cold chills slid down my skin as I felt his fury sear through the bond.

"You brought her here, Luc. She's the only thing I've ever cared about, and you took her from me." Jack met his cousin's eyes with the coldest, most unforgiving glare I've ever seen. "Now heal her," he demanded, "or I'll see that your entire species burns in hell."

Then, without another word, Jack released him.

Lyle had quietly picked his way back through the rubble to keep administering first aid, but the wound at my chest continued to gush. My whole body felt cold.

From the place where I hovered, half-spirit, I could see everything. Even things I shouldn't have been able to see. Jack bent over me, surrounded by a dark ring of rage and lingering death. Wild pulses of colored light zipped through his body, like fits of love and pain, fighting for dominance. Lyle looked like he wanted nothing more than to run away. But he stayed at my side, whispering empty words of reassurance.

And Luc.

I've always made decisions based on whatever seemed most fun, or most intuitively *right* in the moment. Luc's life, by contrast, held an endless gravity. His guidepost was obligation, first to his people, and second to his family. Every other thing—the cars, the women, the excess—was nothing more than a distraction.

In that instant, I understood. When Luc had taken aim at Lisa, it was with the full knowledge that her soul was connected to mine, that her death would mean the end of me, too. But he'd done it anyway. Because he needed Jack alive to save his people. To him, that was worth any price. Even betraying a friend.

Luc shut his eyes and drew a breath. "She has to consent. It won't work if she doesn't."

"She will," Jack assured him. "Ask her."

I wanted to protest that I was too beat to consent to anything except a pillow, but before I could say a word, Luc shoved his bloody knuckle in my mouth. Reality blurred.

. . .

In the dream, I was dressed in silk robes, with long white swathes of fabric pooling against the floor. My feet were laced with leather sandals, and my hair draped in uncharacteristically perfect waves over my shoulders. Around me, there was nothing but light— pure white light, like being immersed in a liquid moonbeam. Despite the *Twilight Zone*–esque quality, I felt weirdly calm.

"Hallooo? Where am I?" I called into the blinding brightness.

"You're in the Immortal plane. This is where our souls go when they're preparing to cross over." Luc's voice floated up behind me and I turned. It was too bright to see him clearly, but he seemed to be sitting in an antique elephant chair like the ones I'd seen at his apartment. Strange, since I could swear he hadn't been there a moment ago. Neither had the chair.

"O-kay. Why am *I* here? And why do I look like Aphrodite on her wedding day?"

"Because you're dying," he said, as if he were talking to a four-year-old. "Whether you continue to die is negotiable, if you accept my offer."

"What offer? Where's Jack?" I looked around, growing more uncomfortable by the second. "I want to go home."

A soft pop sounded in the back of my head and suddenly I was back in my room, sitting cross-legged on my bed with twenty Beanie Babies tucked in my lap. The silk gown had melted into my favorite jeans topped off with a ratty old T-shirt that read *My Karma Ran Over Your Dogma.*

"Better?" Luc asked casually from the corner rocking chair.

I frowned. "I thought you couldn't come in here."

"That's true," he said patiently. "But we're not really here, remember? We're—"

"In Immortal pre-hell. Yeah, I got that." I chucked a Beanie Baby at his obnoxious Immortal head. "What I don't get is why."

"I've already told you," he said. "Your heart is dying. Soon, your soul will depart. For a few moments, at least, you're between worlds. I've given you enough of my blood to allow me to bring you here, but I can't change you unless you accept my offer."

Again with the offer. *Freak.*

"I'm not accepting anything until I see Jack." I kicked the rest of my stuffed animals onto the floor and pushed my way out the bedroom door.

Into an overgrown English garden.

It was nighttime. The sky blazed with stars. All around me, tall grass and weeds lined a high stone wall, the scents of a hundred different flowers making my head spin. My feet caught on brambles as I turned back the way I'd come, but the door was gone. Instead, there was a pond teeming with goldfish and vibrant green lily pads that looked like they'd been lit with nuclear waste. On a bench beside it sat Luc, absently twirling a silver chain with a carved locket between his fingers. He had on the same dashing tuxedo he'd worn at the Hall of Angels. Minus the stab wounds, of course.

"Jeez, can't you take a hint?" I grumbled. "If you want to be useful, go get my boyfriend."

Luc sighed. "Amelie, Jack can't save you now. He may care for you, but he's only mortal."

"Mortal or not, he can kick your ass."

In the dim starlight, I was stunned how well I could see Luc roll his eyes. "This isn't working."

"Figured that out by yourself, genius?"

Luc held up a hand and shut his eyes in a rock star diva moment. Who knows, maybe he was consulting an oracle. When he tuned back in, the carved locket had begun to glow green, and from his pocket he drew out a small vial of red liquid.

"Jackson says if you're to understand, I need to do this properly."

"Do what?"

I tried not to hurl as he took my hand and pressed the locket and vial into it. "Amelie Lane Bennett, Daughter of Lucifer, angelblood Guardian...will you do me the honor of joining my clan?"

I paused, waiting for the punchline. "This is a joke."

"I assure you, it is not. As a royal Immortal, I am authorized to sire one fledgling into the Montaigne bloodline. If you are willing, I invite you to be my chosen."

I stifled a snort. Make that two snorts. As if the guy didn't have enough odious features. The very notion of Luc—pompous, materialistic, vampire Luc—inviting me to join his bourgeois family was so comical, I thought I might bust a gut laughing.

"Yeah," I finally said. "I want to be related to *you*."

"So that's a yes?"

"Oh, please. Bite me, loser."

I snatched the locket out of his fingers and tossed both it

and the vial into the pond. He looked momentarily puzzled as he watched them sink. "Just a moment," he said, and repeated the thing with the eyes closed and the hand up. This time, when his eyes opened, the puzzled expression had vanished and he had a grim smile on his face.

"Jack says that counts," Luc declared. "Welcome to the family."

Then, the bastard bit me.

The next images flickered in my head as I was transported back to the Hall of Angels, my consciousness floating about four feet above my body.

I saw Luc pull his mouth off my throat and chomp deep into his forearm, tearing through muscle and vein. Fresh blood poured out of him, but not onto the floor like before. This time it poured into *me*—onto the scratches at my arms, the bite mark at my neck, the wound at my chest. Like an animal, it burrowed through every inch of me. My body lurched under the force of Lyle's CPR, and Jack bent over me, frantically breathing air into my lungs. It was ghastly. I'd never seen so much blood in my life. I looked like a disgusting version of the Lady of the Lake, my skin spattered red and white, hair and arms splayed as if floating in a pond of crimson sludge.

I knew the instant my heart took over on its own.

Fiery pain seared through me and I screamed. My eyes flew open. The look on Jack's face was terrifying. Not panic, not rage. Just dread. I barely had time to wonder why, when Luc quit with the slasher-fest and lifted his wrist to my lips.

"*Drink,*" he commanded.

And suddenly, I got it. Everything Luc said in the dream, the reason he'd balked at saving me… I understood it all. My lips latched onto his wrist and I sucked, eager and impatient, like a hungry infant. So vomitrocious!

"You're going to be okay, Omelet." Jack pressed one last kiss to my head, then he grabbed Lyle's arm and drew him backward until Luc and I were alone.

"My blood is my covenant, given only to you," Luc murmured. "May nothing in heaven or hell challenge it. By Immortal law, I accept you as my fledgling and vow to foster and guide you 'til the end of days—I, as your master, and you, my Immortal charge."

It might have been my imagination, but I thought he choked a little on the last few words. I was too gone to notice.

The clouds of power had quit swirling above me, though the air still felt heavy enough to swim in. It wasn't until my body began to heal itself that I noticed Katie lurking behind Matt at the edge of the doorway, an expression of disgust on her face.

All in all, the vibe in the room seemed to be one of relief. Thanks to Jack, the Peace Tenets would pass—that was really all Luc wanted. And thanks to Luc, I would live, which was what Jack wanted.

Great, right? Everybody was happy.

So why did I still feel like punching someone?

Chapter Twenty four:
Cocktail Party of the Damned

Life sucks sometimes, but we all muddle through.

That's what my mom used to say. Only she neglected to mention that some days we wished we hadn't muddled through. Some days, we woke up, pretty sure we'd be better off as a bowl of demon chowder. Take today, for example.

"There must be some mistake. *This* is the new charge?" A British girl's nasal voice crawled through my ears like a whiny child at the end of a storm drain. "Isn't she a bit *clunky*?"

"No mistake. Tyrannus said she was half-dead when he brought her in," another voice said. Older. Still British. Slightly less irritating.

"Perhaps Tyrannus collected the wrong corpse."

"Don't be rude, Annabelle. I'll admit, she's not his Highness's usual taste, but no woman looks her best after two days in a coma. It's extraordinary she survived the change at all."

"She could still die," the first girl commented, hopeful.

"Not likely. She's Lucifer's."

"Hmm. Grigorem?"

"The lesser half." The older woman's voice radiated disappointment. "Pity, that. She might have been useful at the Sovereign Trials."

The first girl—Annabelle—snorted. "You can't honestly believe Lady Arianna will allow an *angelblood* to stand with the dauphin?"

"If he insists—"

"Spare me, Marguerite. Master Luc has yet to blow his nose without seeking his mum's counsel. Can you imagine him presenting this pitiful mutt as his chosen? What will the populace say?"

"Manners, Annabelle," the older woman—Marguerite—scolded. "The populace will be pleased to have the dauphin represented at all. Parliament's nearly given up on the Montaigne line, what with Lord Dominic's disappearance and Master Luc knocking about like a drunken sailor. Although, if he's settled enough to foster a fledgling, then perhaps—" A pause. "Did she just move?"

Annabelle let out a beleaguered sigh. "I'll fetch the Master."

• • •

It goes without saying, I despise British accents. Especially on vampires. How they all manage to sound like announcers for *Masterpiece Theatre*, I'll never know.

My skin felt tight and dry. I imagined it flaking into powder as my body shifted for the first time in two days. Flashes of awareness drifted through my head—kaleidoscopic colors, the sensation of falling, the memory of screams. It was all muted by a dreamy fog of anesthetic and painkiller.

Clearly not enough painkiller.

"Monkeycrud." Swear on my soul, it was the only word that sprang to mind. "Monkeycrud, monkeycrud."

Never in my life had I experienced anything so uniquely painful. Not even the Queller compared. I was grappling for new swearwords when the most obnoxious voice on the planet interrupted.

"'But soft! What light through yonder window breaks. It is the east, and Juliet is the sun.'"

Yeah, Shakespeare. That'd help, for sure.

I pried open one crusty eye to see Luc at the edge of my bed, his cheeks sunken and skin paler than usual. Faded jeans hung loose on his hips and a black, long-sleeved T-shirt hugged the lean curves of his shoulders. He looked stunning, as usual, only the arrogance was tempered by…good grief, was that compassion? Whatever it was, it freaked me out.

"Morning sunshine. Did you sleep well?"

"Ugh," I groaned. "Kill me now."

"Too late for that, love." He pressed a cool hand to my forehead. "Sad to say, you may be *unkillable* for quite some time."

The amusement in his voice flooded every corner of my mind, like a breeze through an empty house. I ignored the way my body creaked as I pushed myself up on one elbow. My eyes felt like they'd been glued shut. I could almost hear the skin tear as I pried my eyelids fully open.

I was lying in a narrow bed with beige sateen sheets and a fluffy beige blanket draped over my favorite flannel jammies. Someone had taken great care to line up my collection of stuffed animals along the dresser—a good thing, since, apart from my hair and Luc's eyes, they provided the only color in the whole monochromatic room. Light beige wallpaper and beige-painted trim wrapped around me, broken only by a few dull seascape watercolors. It looked like every other hospital room I'd ever seen, each detail designed to foster feelings of…beige-ness, I guess.

A huge machine beeped reports of my vital statistics with glacial slowness, and an IV bag hung above me, dumping fluids into my bloodstream.

I sat up carefully and waited for the room to quit spinning. What a freaky dream—with Jack dying and me dying, and all that blood-drinking. And then the whole bit with Luc vampifying me. Yeesh. What would Freud say about *that*?

An IV lock stuck out of my arm, so I tugged it loose. Seriously, if I never saw another syringe, sword, dagger, halberd, or pollaxe in my life, it would be too soon. As the needle exited, a trickle of blood pulsed down my unusually pale forearm. I licked it off.

Yeah, that's right. *I. LICKED. IT. OFF.*

"Ack!" I screamed, realizing what I'd done. The fact that it tasted like salted honey did nothing to calm me. "Ew, ew, ew!"

"Relax," Luc said. "That impulse is normal. You'll probably need a good pint or two before the cravings settle."

I stared at Luc, my face curdled into an expression of pure disgust. *Normal?* He thought this was *normal*?

All at once, I was flooded with images—visions that sliced through my mind like frozen razorblades. I saw myself crying blood, my skin parched and cracked like faded newspaper. I saw Jack bruised and beaten with his eyes whited-out and Lisa perched on a pile of dead people. The images vibrated with terror, like someone had taken all the worst parts from a Grimm fairy tale and spliced them together into a twisted slide-show montage. Horrifyingly enough, it ended with me curled in Luc's lap, sucking blood out of his arm like juice from a fresh orange. Three awful words echoed in my brain.

My Immortal charge.

Oh, hell no! With a determined swoop, I shoved back the covers and launched myself at Luc's throat in a flying tackle. We crashed sideways and landed on the ground with a thud.

"A vampire? You made me a *vampire*?" The chill of the tile radiated up my knees like cracks through a frozen pond.

"Immortal fledgling," he choked out. "Watch the hair."

Before I could slam his head against the floor again, he flipped me over as effortlessly as one might toss a bag of feathers. His eyes held an odd mixture of annoyance and curiosity as he arranged himself on top of me in a way that left me completely immobilized. "Look, this isn't how I envisioned eternity, either. But we're stuck with each other, so I suggest you get used to taking orders."

"Get off me, you freak."

"Not until you calm down." He squeezed his knees together until I thought my ribs would crack. "Unsavory as the situation is, I'm afraid it's not negotiable. Jack and I need you on board and cooperating by winter solstice."

"Why?" I jerked around under him, trying to get free. As wiry as he was, the guy sure had a grip like a python.

"Because that is when Arianna returns, and that is when you declare fealty to me before the Immortal populace."

I quit struggling. "*Fealty*?"

"Yes, and try not to scowl when you say it," he advised. "My publicist insists you meet with the event planners as soon as possible. Although, obviously, no one's letting you out of the house until our wardrobe people have a go at you."

It occurred to me I could probably break his nose with a quick head-butt to the face. If not for the prospect of getting bled on again, I might have done it.

"My attendants are handling music and venue, but you'll want to give suggestions on the guest list. Then there's the small matter of your training."

"My *training*?"

"You know," he explained, "how to address a dignitary, which fork to use at dinner, how to eviscerate a foe without getting sinew stuck in your teeth…that sort of thing. Mum's already taking applications for who gets to work with you, but she wants your input."

As a demonstration of my *input*, I hiked a knee into the back of his head and used the momentum from the blow to roll him off me. My hand clutched at the…beige…furniture as I pushed myself upright and stumbled toward the door.

"Wait!" Luc practically teleported to a spot four inches in front of me and took a defensive stance.

"Really? We're doing this now?"

"Amelie, you've been in a coma all weekend, you've lost ungodly amounts of blood, and you're on enough painkillers to subdue a rabid hippo. I realize it'll take you a while to feel comfortable here, but this is your home now. I suggest you accept that."

My eyes swept the room again, looking for anything homey.

Thick drapes had been drawn across the window, and for the

first time since waking, I noticed how dim it was inside the room. Shadows seemed to coat the walls and ceiling in gray strips. The only light was a pale line of orange around the curtains which, peculiarly, made my eyes water. I could tell my dad had been to visit, since no one else would have known to set out my collection of Beanie Babies in perfect rainbow-colored order. And there were no flowers. Bud knows I hate flowers, partly because of my allergies and partly because they always die a horrid, wilting death.

Luc's efforts notwithstanding, I felt about as comfortable here as a speech-writer at a mime convention.

"One more time," I grumbled ungratefully. "Where's Jack?"

An exasperated sigh gusted out of Luc's chest. "Must you be so contentious?" he asked, which proves he'd never read my disciplinary file.

"You should have considered that before you turned me into a vampire."

"It wasn't by choice and you're not a vampire."

With hands like ice, I lifted two fingers to my neck and waited. And waited. Finally it came. *Bah-bum.* It was so soft I almost missed it.

Yup. Definitely a vampire.

I didn't know what to feel. Angry? Confused? Homicidal? My life had been wrecked and re-made so many times in the past week, I needed a freaking flow chart to keep track of it. And what had it gotten me? Jack was alive, at least. My friends were safe. My dad was free. But I was…what? A monster? A demon?

"You're an Immortal fledgling," Luc said, quasi-sympathetically. "You don't need to drink blood, though I can't imagine why you wouldn't. And while you're not mortally vulnerable to sunlight, you may want to wear sunscreen."

"And if someone drives a stake through my heart?"

"Then I wager you'll die. Though that's rather similar to being a Guardian, isn't it?"

I desperately wanted him to be lying, for it to be some elaborate joke. And yet, the world looked too different, the details too vivid for it to be normal. Even Luc's eyes held a full pallet of color I'd never noticed before—flecks of silver shot through brilliant blues and purples. Like staring at a dusk sky reflected in the Caribbean. It was kind of...mesmerizing.

Jeez, I had to get out of there. Whatever freaky ritual he'd done, I was still *me*, right? No amount of vamp-infected blood would change that. And if I was still me, then I was still bonded to Jack. So wherever Jack was, that's where I needed to be.

My fingertips charged with Crossworld power as I cocked them at Luc's face like a gun. "You know I can hurt you."

"But you won't."

"Keep getting in my way and we'll find out."

With a hard shove against him, I propelled myself through the doorway where the hall stretched out in both directions. Circular, glass-blown lamps cast quivery shadows on the walls, and identical doors seemed to go on endlessly.

I shivered. Everything felt cold. Cold and damp. And dead.

By the time I found the staircase, I was ready to cry. My sluggish heartbeat left a hollow space inside me. All I wanted was for Jack to fill it.

Voices rose from below and I hurried toward them. With each step I could sense more—the crackle of fire and human heartbeats, bitter-tinged fumes of sweat and aftershave, the sickly sweetness of shampoo and laundry detergent. Beneath it all, Jack's scent wrapped around me. Toasted marshmallows and sunshine.

"Amelie." Luc's voice rang from the top of the stairs. I slowed my pace, but didn't turn. "Our laws are not negotiable," he said. "You have until sunrise to say your goodbyes, then you belong to us. You are my fledgling, do you understand?"

I could feel his gaze boring holes into my back. What was I supposed to say? *Yes, sir, whatever you say, sir?*

"Dream on, vampire."

Harsh beams of light spilled through the giant picture windows on the first floor. It didn't matter that the panes were tinted, or that it wasn't a midday sun as I'd first thought. Even the dim pink brilliance of dusk was blinding.

The staircase opened onto a huge foyer—a cavernous space with high, carved arches and coved ceilings painted with the rococo-like frescos we'd studied in Art History. Only in these, instead of heavenly clouds, blue skies, and angels, the heavens were dark and stormy, the angel wings ran black with blood, and the humans cowered and shrieked below. Sheesh. Vamp or not, whoever had chosen *that* for their home décor needed a serious therapy intervention.

I pushed my way across the polished marble floor through a set of double doors. Instantly, I could breathe. The biological *need* wasn't as pressing as, say, a few days ago, but it felt good nonetheless. Like wandering out of hell and into…home.

My dad reclined on an overstuffed chair looking tired but tense. Henry sat on the couch, beaten but alive. His face bulged in uneven hues of purple and blue, his nose a misshapen lump.

In the center of it all, Jack paced a nervous line in front of the fireplace. His eyes were fixed on the floor, hands locked in a white-knuckled grip. I could hear his heartbeat, strong and familiar, floating above the other sounds in the room.

"Jackson," I said, and he stopped pacing.

In fact, everything froze. Even the last muted beams of sunlight seemed to halt in their path. The only movement was the fire dancing across the walls like fairy-wing shadows.

After a second, his eyes flickered up, but he still didn't move.

"Jack?" I said again, more softly.

That's when I saw it. It crept through him—a golden pulse in his chest, radiating outward in impossibly beautiful waves. Before I could say another word he closed the distance between us.

"Omelet." His voice was thick as he traced an outline along my face, my cheeks, my jaw. "I'm not dreaming? You're real, right?"

"Yeah."

"And I'm not dead?"

I smiled. "Not that I know of."

Jack swooped me into his arms and swung me around. "Don't ever do that to me again, okay? Never."

My face was so smushed into his neck I could barely speak. "*Mmkay.*"

With astounding vigor, he sprinkled kisses across my forehead, over both eyelids, then down to my mouth. Brilliant golden warmth surged between us and I melted with relief. I didn't realize until that moment how much I'd been relying on our bond for confirmation—of myself, of my soul. It was like at the field test, when he first kissed me. I knew everything would be okay if I just held onto him. Maybe my soul wasn't mine, and maybe my blood was demon, but if God was willing to let me keep *him*, then there had to be some good left in me. Right?

"I love you," Jack whispered, his forehead pressed to mine. "I don't want to live without you."

"So don't." I tiptoed up to kiss him again.

It wasn't nearly long enough before my dad started clearing his throat. Not like Jack and I were doing anything gross—just a little kissing and some PG-13 groping. I'm surprised he let us get *that* far.

With great effort, Jack put me down, a faint flush crawling up his cheeks.

"Later," he whispered.

We spent the next few hours in a strange combination of family reunion and top-of-the-hour newsbrief. Henry's heroics had gotten him promoted to Headmaster. And while that was a bittersweet triumph, he took it well. His first act was to order renovations on St. Michael's, including UV tinted windows and silver-plated cells for the newly matriculated vampires and werecreatures. He'd also ordered a whole bunch of books on necromancy and death magic for the library. I think Henry hoped once I sorted out the whole Wraithmaker thing I might be able to find Smalley. I had my doubts but, hey, everyone needs to dream, right?

Jack got promoted, too. Sort of. The Elders decided to make him permanent lead trainer for St. Michael's, an honor he'd accepted on the sole condition that he'd have no direct authority over me. Translation: While at school, I was someone else's problem.

I couldn't feel too upset about it. Dane had volunteered to fill in when necessary and Marcus, while not as smokin' as Jack, would make a decent substitute trainer. Marcus had suspected something was amiss when Daniel turned up injured the day after D'Arcy was killed. He couldn't prove anything at the time, but it all made sense now. Daniel's bondmate died guarding a family of vampires and (surprise, surprise) Daniel blamed the Peace Tenets. It was an easy sell for Thibault to recruit him as Lisa's local muscle.

As far as Henry knew, my creepy former trainer would spend the next few decades tucked away in a psychiatric care facility making friendship bracelets and working through his loss issues. I almost felt sorry for him. Scratch that, I *did* feel sorry for him. Grief may pretend it's a quiet emotion but it's not. It'll eat you from the inside then spit you out in little pulpy chunks. No one deserves that kind of loss, not even Daniel.

Dad assured me Lyle was doing well and currently being courted by every office from the DWC (Demon Waste Containment) to the Enforcement Guild. My heroic ex-boyfriend had come out pretty firmly in support of me, even threatening to launch a protest unless I was granted immediate re-admission to St. Michael's. Apparently, those boyish charms could be used for more than just schmoozing girls on his rec room couch.

Matt and Katie, unfortunately, had a rougher time.

Katie was cleared of suspicion (mostly) and sent home under heavy guard. Bud said she'd refused to take his calls. Her mom wasn't clear why, only that she wanted nothing to do with me.

Matt was held for interrogation for almost fifteen hours, way longer than anyone else. No one believed he didn't know anything about Lisa. Given how tight they were, the Elders didn't see how she could have kept it from him. I guess *he* had trouble understanding that, too. He'd bowed out of the Induction ceremony as well as the celebration that followed, claiming illness. But we knew better. Last Bud heard, Matt's parents had announced he'd be taking some time off from school.

I didn't blame him.

Nobody mentioned Lisa.

I don't think anyone knew what to say. You don't stop loving someone just because you start hating them. Lisa had been my best friend for so long, the idea of going through life without her seemed foreign and impossible. It must have been equally strange for Bud. I thought of all the times she'd slept over, how he'd joked about giving her a room of her own and called her his second daughter. I couldn't imagine what it was like for him to learn that's exactly what she was.

Confusingly enough, Bud didn't even suggest I come home with him. Seriously, the man didn't think I could go to the grocery store without ending up on the back of a milk carton, yet he'd suddenly decided it was okay to start shacking up with my new vampire family?

Maybe Armageddon really *was* upon us.

Bud seemed subdued as I walked him to the door. "Ami, I'm not sure what to say about all this. About him." He gestured to Jack, who watched us from the pocket doors of the parlor.

"You don't have to say anything," I told him.

"I just always thought if you had enough time, enough distance to figure out what you really wanted…" The frown lines in Bud's forehead deepened. It was weird to see him fumble. I mean, the man made speeches in front of juries, for crying out loud. You'd think he could manage a father-daughter moment without turning into Elmer Fudd.

"Kiddo," he tried again, "God's greatest gift to us was free will, the freedom to choose our own path. It's what differentiates us from the angels. It's what makes us special. I don't want anyone to take that freedom from you like they did your mother. Not the Elders, not the Guardians. And certainly not *him*—"

I silenced him with a big bear hug. "Daddy, I'm not Mom. I *chose* Jack."

"No, you chose survival," he insisted. "It's not the same. Do you think you two would have bonded if demons hadn't attacked that night? Do you think anyone believes you're a vampire fledgling because you chose it?"

I didn't answer, largely because we'd agreed not to talk about my dating life, but also because it seemed wrong to start a verbal assault on Luc who, despite being a sociopath, *did* bring me back from the dead.

"I'll figure it out, Dad. I'm not a little girl anymore."

His face was tight but he nodded like he understood. "I guess not."

We hugged for a long time before he left. I think we both knew things would be different. He wouldn't be making me breakfast tomorrow morning. I wouldn't be stocking the fridge next weekend. Heaven only knew what would happen to the laundry. Maybe it was for the best. Parents need to grow up sometime too, right?

As soon as Annabelle handed Bud and Henry their coats and shut the door, Jack slid into place behind me, until his lips brushed against my hair. "You okay?"

I didn't answer at first.

I wasn't okay. Not yet. My mind kept racing with worries about what would come next, whether my friends would forgive me, how far Luc would take the whole fledgling thing. Whether Jack and I

would ever complete our bond. I guess worrying was normal…as
far as any of this was normal.

"I'm still pissed at you," I said finally.

"I know."

"You should have trusted me. We take care of each other,
Jackson. That's what being bonded means. You can't make
decisions like this without me anymore."

"*I know.*"

He threaded his arms around my waist and guided me onto
the wide leather couch. My body was heavy with exhaustion, my
face achy from smiling. Don't get me wrong, it was good to see my
dad. And I wouldn't have missed the debrief for the world. But
there was something draining about my new vampire senses. It's
hard to listen to someone when you keep getting distracted by the
microscopic speck of dust at the edge of their eyelash. I tried to
focus on staying pissed.

"If we're going to be partners I get a vote in what happens.
You can't treat me like a little kid anymore."

"That's true. I can't." He kissed my neck.

"And no way am I staying here with Luc."

Another kiss. "Mmmhmm."

I nuzzled closer, resting my head against his heart. *Bah-bum,
bah-bum, bah-bum.* So strong and lyrical. What I wouldn't give to
hear mine match his rhythm the way it used to. Embers glowed
black and gold in the fireplace, like living jewels, and the chill
threatened to return.

"I think my heart's dying," I whispered. "Am I going to be
heartless someday?"

"You'll be fine." His arms tightened around me. "Angel blood and demon blood aren't meant to go together. They're at war right now, inside you. But once your body works through the change, you'll be okay."

The change.

That was the same word those women had said in my room. The way everybody said it, it seemed like it deserved a capital letter.

"The Change," I repeated, trying out the new spelling. Totally worked, by the way. "What is that, anyway?"

"Luc didn't tell you?"

"No, he quoted *Romeo and Juliet*, then I tried to strangle him."

"Understandable," Jack said. "Did you at least say thank you?"

"For bleeding on me?"

"For saving you."

I shrugged. "Same difference."

"Still, it might be polite to—"

"Hey, you know what'd be super cool?" I said, delicately. "*Not* getting lectured by my boyfriend about how to behave with my vampire sire."

He stared at the ceiling, fingers rubbing the back of my neck.

For the next few minutes I let myself sink into his kisses. I loved the feel of his body next to me, the rise and fall of his chest against mine. He was all the best parts of humanity—warmth and love and self-sacrifice. I knew I'd never be as good as him, but he made me want to try.

"Do you think someday we'll understand this?" I asked once he'd finished nibbling on my collarbone.

"What?"

"The prophecy? Luc? Lisa?"

Jack frowned. "I've been thinking about that. The 'sacrifice of blood' must have been yours, not mine. I mean, technically I *did* die before dawn so that part was satisfied, but you and Luc did most of the bleeding. And the 'fury of the avenger' must have been about Luc, too, not Lisa. She didn't seem especially vengeful. Misguided, but not vengeful."

"So, it's true, then." Luc's pompous tenor snaked in from the edge of the room. "I keep telling you, 'It's all about me.' But do you listen?"

Jack gave a low groan. "Speak of the devil."

"Hello, cousin. Having a nice evening?"

Seriously, who did a girl have to exsanguinate to get a little privacy? "Lovely to see you again, Luc," I called, super-politely. "Thanks for stopping by. Take care, now."

Jack gave me a warning look. "Amelie, it *is* his house."

"Yes, it's my house," Luc concurred, "and that blood in your veins is mine, too."

I gave an involuntary shudder. Seriously, if I was going to go along with this farce, we'd need to have a major talk about boundaries. If that failed, we could always talk about baseball bats and chloroform.

Jack didn't say anything for a long time, but he also didn't move his hands from my waist. Eventually, Luc muttered, "Until sunrise," and stalked out of the room.

"*Until sunrise*," I mimicked. "Who does he think he is, anyway? Emperor of the universe?"

"No, just the Southern District." Jack's scarred fingers tucked a lock of hair behind my ear. His eyes had gone all soft again and I felt the bond squirm between us, restless and hungry. "Luc could make things very difficult for us. You have to be nicer to him."

"Why?" I argued. "He owes you. You single-handedly saved his species, right? He should give you anything you want. His house. His vamp fledgling. A new car."

"A new car?" Jack cocked an eyebrow.

"It doesn't have to be fancy," I said. "Maybe an Audi, or a small BMW. Something from this century."

"Hmm," he considered, "I wouldn't mind an El Camino."

"Is that like a convertible?"

"Sort of."

With a delicious stretch, he reached over his head to shut off the lamp so we could see better out the huge picture windows. I'm not sure how much he saw, but with my new vamp-vision it was clear as daylight.

Fireflies danced across a low field of bluebonnets, their progress broken only by the massive oaks that curled in gnarled clumps over the earth. In the distance, a waning gibbous moon shimmered above a silver mirror of lake. As I focused my hearing around the crickets and household sounds, I could just make out a trickle of water—a natural spring beneath the lake—that sent gentle ripples through the moon's reflection. It made me wonder where Lisa was. Whether she was looking at the same moon—if she was okay.

"So, what happens next?" I asked, eager not to think about her.

"That's up to you."

"Cool. I was going to suggest Jamaica for our honeymoon, but with the whole sun-sensitivity thing, Antarctica might be more appropriate."

"Ami, I'm serious."

"So am I," I insisted. "There's a penguin-watching expedition somewhere with our names on it. Cozy fires. Darkness twenty-four/seven. We could take one of Luc's jets…only not the one he joined the mile-high club in. Too sentimental."

Jack groaned. "Show some respect. That *is* your Immortal master you're talking about."

Ah, yes. *Master Luc*. Like I wouldn't think of *Star Wars* every time I uttered that one.

There was something careful about the way Jack trailed his fingers through my hair, like he wanted to say something but couldn't figure out how. I snuggled in deeper and stared at the endless night sky. I'd seen it a thousand times before, but never like this. Stars and planets filled the heavens, some glittering like brilliant sparks of scattered gunpowder, some duller—oranges and reds. I could have stared at it for hours and not gotten bored.

"Amelie, I have to ask you a question. It's important, so I want you to think carefully before you answer." His fingers moved nervously over the bare skin at my neck. "Are you sure about all this? About me?"

"Yes. Absolutely."

He frowned. "No, I need you to think first. I mean, you have a lot to lose now and I have practically nothing to offer. Crappy car, low-paying job, studio apartment. That's all. Your dad hates me. And if people at school find out we're together, there'll be no end of crap from the student body."

"I can handle crap from the student body."

"Not to mention the Immortal community," he continued. "Do you understand that Luc is the only male descendant of the current sovereign? Which means, as far as his people are concerned, you're not just his fledgling. You're royalty."

He let that carrot dangle as visions of corsets, uncomfortable shoes, and guillotines filled my mind. "That sounds like a huge pain in the ass."

Jack nodded absently. "People are being nice about this now, but once they have time to think about it…I mean, how long do you expect Luc to tolerate his Immortal charge playing house with his angelblood best friend?"

"Describe 'playing house.'"

"Amelie, this is serious," Jack grumbled. "If the Immortals catch even one whiff we're involved they could question your loyalty. They could call for your death."

While he talked, I'd rolled over so my belly pressed against his, my face nuzzled his neck, the threads of our bond knitting together like a luminescent sweater-vest. Man, he felt good.

"The smart thing would be to pledge fealty to Luc and defect from the Guardians. You'll be eighteen in a few months. Aunt Arianna's already started the media circus. Luc's not bad once you get to know him. And you'd have eternity to acquaint yourselves. He'll give you everything you want, Ami." Jack's eyes filled with sadness as he dropped his gaze to the ground. "You'd be safe with him."

"I would, huh?"

"Completely."

I pretended to consider. "And I could have anything? Cars? Beach house? Apartment in Paris?"

"Anything," he promised. "For the rest of your life."

The rest of my life.

Did he have any idea what a long, dull road that would be

without him? With a sigh, I pulled my lips off his neck, fingers lightly stroking the purple hickey I'd just made. "You're right."

"At least think about it before—" He froze. "What did you say?"

"I said, you're right. It's the obvious choice, isn't it?"

The fire had gone out in the hearth; only moonlight and the flickering glow of our bond remained. I dropped a gentle kiss on his lips. "You should get an El Camino, no question."

Relief flowed through his exhale and he smiled. "You're twisted, you know that?"

"I never denied it."

"We'll have to pretend we're not together," he warned. "We'll have to hide the bond until we can get away—find an Elder to finish the ceremony. And they'll come after us. It won't be easy."

"Nothing worth having is."

I sealed my body against his and let the warmth seep into me. Raised lines of skin pressed through his thin cotton shirt—shiny, dimpled scars where Thibault had cut him. My heart ached at the memory.

"So, you're sure about this?" Jack asked. "Because if you say yes, then we have to do it right. There can't be any mistakes." The light was back in his eyes, an edge of anticipation at the corners. "No more sneaking off together. No more breaking protocol—"

"Ah, protocol, my old nemesis."

"I'm serious. Starting tomorrow, you and I are on hold. Henry talked to Akira, and she's willing to keep quiet about the bond. As far as anyone at school knows, you're with the Immortals and we're just acquaintances."

I sighed. *Acquaintances.* Possibly the ugliest word in existence.

"This is going to blow major chunks."

"It's only a few months."

"That's supposed to make me hate it less?" With a long sigh, I snuggled deeper into his arms. "Well, we have until sunrise together, right? I mean, as long as it's dark, we're in the clear?"

He arched an eyebrow. "What did you have in mind?"

Between us, the bond simmered in tiny spasms of light. Only this time, when I pulled my lips away, the glow didn't fade.

"Jack," I said, "how do you feel about Antarctica?"

Acknowledgments

"Once upon a time, in a town far muggier than this one…"

That was how the Angel Academy trilogy started a handful of years ago. Which was appropriate at the time, since I didn't plan to write a book, let alone a trilogy. Really, I was just making stuff up to get my sweet, gorgeous daughter to go to sleep already.

And she did. But not before listening carefully, commenting on the plot, asking questions about the characters, giving suggestions on how various conflicts should resolve and, after an hour of procrastination on the sleep issue, finally noting, "Mommy, you should really write this down."

So that's what I did.

Hence, I owe the first debt of gratitude to my kiddos: Avery, for challenging me to be better than I thought I could, and Evan, for showing me there's nothing in the world that makes a soul shimmer like unconditional love. You two turkeys are my North Star—my heart—and I will love you forever, around the universe and back again.

That said, I have to admit this book would still be sitting at the bottom of a virtual scrap pile without a few key people. Leigh

Michaels, without you, I never would have believed I could be a writer. You're an inspiration and a guidepost. C.J. Redwine, if you hadn't harassed me to query, I'd still be sitting at my computer hopelessly web-stalking agents but not sending anything out. You are, in a word, awesome! Barb, Diana, and Kaye—my Tuesday Writers—you took my excess adverbs and gave me love and skills in return. I can't thank you enough. Stephanie and Noelle—my saviors—you guys keep me sane. Seriously! Don't ever stop! Michele and Lynda Gail, thank you both for making me look organized (yes, it could be much, *much* worse). And Jen, Sam, Sara, Emery, Angie, Tara, Sharon, and my sweet DoomsDaisies, thanks for keeping me connected. To everyone at Ozarks Romance Authors, MORWA, and Sleuths Ink, y'all are the most amazing, nurturing, and talented group of writers I've ever met. When I sit amongst you, I am humbled.

The core of my inspiration, as always, comes from my family: Roger and Allison, you drove me crazy throughout childhood. Thank you, because without y'all, I might have been really bored. (P.S. Robert and Jonathan, try not to kill each other and be nice to your mother.) Carolyn and Russell Cornelius, y'all are not only the bomb-diggity of parents, you are also ridiculously cool people. I'll be forever in awe of your endurance and compassion, no matter what life throws at you. (And it's thrown a lot!) So Mom, thanks for keeping my heart linked to New Orleans, and for sending me newspaper clippings and magazine articles over the years so I never forget where I'm from. And Dad, thanks for showing me what real heroes are made of. I love you madly. Snaps also go to my high school alma mater, Louise S. McGehee, where I learned how to question everything, laugh at adversity, and kill demons while wearing a school uniform. *Noblesse Oblige*, y'all!

Predictably, there are a whole lot of folks who worked their fingers to the bone (um, not literally…I hope) to make this book come alive. My fabulous agenting duo, Pam Van Hylckama Vlieg and Laurie McLean—there are no words for how grateful I am to you. Y'all believed in me and you made me believe in myself. (And Pam, for putting up with my mood swings, I owe you more chocolate than Belgium produces in a year.) Likewise, I must thank the awesomtastic, fabuloriffic people at Entangled Publishing. Heather, I don't care what my mother says, I'm convinced we're sisters. Jaime, you simply rock! And Liz… Holy crud, Liz! I think you might be the single most capable, dynamic, visionary, talented, beautiful, inspiring person I've ever met. I will never stop having a girl-crush on you. Thanks for the edits, the late night phone therapy, the awesome cover design, and for the million-bazillion other things you've done to make this project and this publishing house a success.

Everyone involved in this deserves an all-expenses paid trip to the Bahamas. Not that I'm in a position to offer such a thing… but just so *you* know, *I* know you deserve it!

Buckets of love and gratitude!

-Cecily White